ALSO BY ARTHUR PHILLIPS

Angelica

The Egyptologist

Prague

THE SONG IS YOU

Duckworth Overlook

THE SONG IS YOU

a novel

ARTHUR PHILLIPS

First published in the UK in 2009 by
Duckworth Overlook
90-93 Cowcross Street
London EC1M 6BF
Tel: 020 7490 7300
Fax: 020 7490 0080
info@duckworth-publishers.co.uk
www.ducknet.co.uk

First published in the USA in 2009 by
Random House, an imprint of
The Random House Publishing Group,
a division of Random House, Inc., New York.

A catalogue record for this book is available
from the British Library

ISBN 978 0 7156 3873 6

Book design by Simon M. Sullivan
Printed in the UK by
J F Print Ltd, Yeovil, Somerset

FOR JAN, OF COURSE

The Muses are virgins. . . . Cupid, when sometimes asked by his mother Venus why he did not attack the Muses, used to reply that he found them so beautiful, so pure, so modest, bashful, and continually occupied . . . in the arrangement of music, that when he drew near them he unstrung his bow, closed his quiver, and put out his torch, since they made him shy and afraid of injuring them.

—FRANÇOIS RABELAIS,
Gargantua and Pantagruel, 3:31

THE SONG IS YOU

JULIAN DONAHUE'S FATHER was on a Billie Holiday record.

He loved her music, back when it was hip, not fashionable (a fan's distinction). April of 1953, on leave from the Army, four days prior to his deployment to Korea, where—who knows?—his eighteen-pound contribution to that eternal stalemate may have been the final increment of military sacrifice necessary to balance the scales, prevent defeat, and fix the parallel, he took the train from Virginia up to New York, and he saw his idol perform at the Galaxy Theater, which is now—if you are the sort to track down historic sites—a three-story Banana Republic with a framed photo of Holiday on the butter-yellow wall of the dressing room all the way to the left.

He spent more than he should have for a third-row seat in the center, arrived early, and lived ninety of the best minutes of his life, shaking his head and sighing, smiling with half his mouth until, without thinking or hesitating, surprised by the strength of his desire, he shouted, " 'Waterfront'!" during a bustling near silence after the applause for "My Man" had receded and Billie was consulting with her band, her back to the audience, her golden calves completing the electrical circuit between the hem of her silver skirt and the straps of her black shoes. " 'I Cover the Waterfront'!"

She peered over her shoulder. "Somebody say something?" she purred, sly and sidelong, and laughter speckled the hall. She turned, stepped forward, shaded her eyes against the spotlights, and squinted down into the front rows. "Was that you?" She had addressed him directly.

"Yes, ma'am."

"Polite, too." The audience cheered. "Handsome white soldier," she mused, and in his retellings for years after, she now levitated slightly, and every other noise faded away as his goddess coolly examined him groveling down in the pit, eye level with her feet, less than a child—a worshipper. "Did you have a request, honey?"

"Miss Holiday, I sure would love to hear 'I Cover the Waterfront.' "

"Would you now?" She kept her eyes on him as she turned her head, only a little, and called to her band: "Well, boys, the pretty gray GI wants 'Waterfront,' so let's do that for him. Don't want him to put us on report, now, do we?"

He later wondered, often, whether she, way up there, could feel the empress's power she held over him. "Literally anything," he would tell his second son (named for an alto man whose first album came out a decade before the boy's birth, and after his wife had—for the second time, in some cases—rejected Miles, Charlie, Harry, Dizzy, Percy, Woody, Herbie, Teddy, Jimmy, Lionel, Dexter, Lester, Wynton, Wardell, Hampton, Duke, Count, Chet, Nat, Hank, Thad, Mal, Art, Max, Milt, Bix, João, and Illinois), "I would have done anything for her, Julian."

Billie counted off the tune and started the pre-refrain verse, with only the piano accompanying: "*Away from the city . . . ,*" something extra, that expendable introductory piece—most singers didn't know it, and most instrumentalists never played it—and the soldier hoped that Holiday, having sensed that he was different from all the others, was perhaps granting him more than she allowed lesser supplicants. She hit the chorus, sang the title, and the bass and drums entered, and minor fans applauded, having only then recognized the song, and the thought intruded: he would gladly have killed for her. In the lyrics, she was waiting by the water, longing for her lover's ship to return. She was singing the music he had ached to hear, was singing it *to* him, as if he, soon to head off by sea to war, was that lover for whom she pined, and this thought vibrated in him like a recently arrived arrow: he would murder the officer to his left for her, or the young woman to his right. He knew this was strange. He was not a violent man, but this was, as he later said, how love felt just then. Having been lofted up to this pinnacle of musical rapture, he looked down at the world of men and considered erasing it.

And the urge passed. By the second eight bars he could examine this gift and the real woman offering it to him. She sang with her eyes closed. He watched the swaying hibiscus in her sparkling hair, could almost smell it. He imagined finding a role to play somewhere in her life, the ease he would feel among her Negro friends, how effortlessly he would adapt to the role of efficient business manager and then earn the right to long and glorious nights drinking with the band, friendship with Lester Young or Jimmy Rowles, and then he and she might walk into the empty street, and he would drape her fur stole around her neck. They would lean into each other as they moved into the light of the street's single lamp . . . and he whispers a joke about one of their musician friends' resemblance to a basset hound, and her gentle laughter becomes the sound of her hands clasping around his biceps, compressing the cloth of his sleeve . . . Onstage, tonight, she sang the word *stally*, as if she had forgotten if it was *starlit* or *starry* and forged a hybrid instead. The soldier told himself he had flustered her.

She hit the bridge, and he wondered if he could still learn an instrument and then be able to travel with her, worried whether the rumors of her continued use of narcotics were true, and he knew, too, that the song—his song—was more than half-sung already. It was not that he hadn't heard it—he had heard every breath, every sneeze of the hi-hat cymbal, the brushed snare, each profound thump and wood rattle as the bassist's left hand crept up and down his instrument's black neck like half of a hesitantly aggressive spider—but the song had not cast him into thoughtless ecstasy, only inspired all this mad musing. He imagined this song playing during a party or a wedding, thought of children and vast front yards, imagined "boys not unlike *you*," he told Julian. He thought of growing old in New York or dying young in Korea, of learning to play jazz or distinguishing himself in battle, rescuing his platoon. She finished her chorus.

The tenor-sax man stepped forward to take sixteen bars. It was not Lester Young, "the President," at whose side Billie had made so many classic recordings, or Paul Quinichette, his replacement in the old Basie band, called "the Vice President" for how closely he duplicated Young's sound, but an imitator of Quinichette's. This tenor, derivative of a derivative, had been dubbed "the Speaker of the House" by one of the jazz magazines, prompting dissenting correspondence from Julian's father, who, rating men like Getz, Cohn, and Sims ahead of this guy, insisted he was, at best, "Secretary of Agriculture."

Billie strode back in at the bridge and sang out the chorus, and when she finished, she opened her eyes and smiled toward the third row, winked and blew a kiss at where she recalled her fan having been, but the descending head-on spotlights blinded her, and the kiss drifted off target a little to the left.

The woman to his right turned to him—while he was still as dazzled by Holiday as Holiday was by the lights—and, as if stunned herself by the reflection of the singer off his face, she felt herself become light-headed, too. She fell the first distance into love with the man so in love with the singer. "You had," she later told him in French-accented English, "a face of such perfect happiness, but only for an instant, and then you were so terribly sad again." ("The sad face, oh yeah, they love the sad face," he used to joke whenever Julian caught him sitting alone, believing himself unobserved, buckling under pain or memory.)

He spent that night with her, and the next, and the next. He gnawed on the idea of going AWOL for a week or forever but instead stepped timely onto his train, off to his war, which ended a month or so after his arrival and only a few weeks after his injury. He underwent several surgeries, first to save the leg, then to limit the amount lost to infection, then to maintain a viable remnant to support a prosthetic, and finally, necessarily, to save his life, at the definitive cost of the limb. "They took it in slices, like salami," he liked to say. "Actually, Sam," he'd imitate an indecisive housewife at the butcher's, "make it a full pound. I've company coming."

At the end of that final surgery, in an Army hospital in Japan, with the threat of more operations still hovering, he awoke, in early evening, to a gift. The nurses installed a record player in his room, set it to 33⅓, and propped an LP's sleeve against the wall behind it: a photo of Billie Holiday in close profile—her hand held up in a grace-ful gesture illustrative of some lyric, eyes closed, mouth open, head tipped back—and in gray lowercase: *lady day at the galaxy.*

He was in deafening pain (as he was, on and off, throughout the rest of his life) and sometimes, for a moment or two, did not hear peo-ple speaking to him because of the concentration required to contain his own sounds of suffering. In this case, he only caught one of the nurses saying, "—from Paris." The Frenchwoman had sent the LP to Korea, Julian's father never having had the chance to inform her of his wound or transport, and the gift (which she had spotted in a record-shop window near her parents' apartment on the rue des Bons En-fants, listened to once in amazement, and then wrapped in yellow paper and actual *straw* for protection) had followed the soldier around Asia as he shed bits of his leg on his travels, in a tent near the line, in Seoul, in Tokyo, in this snowy suburb.

He couldn't stand, couldn't yet move, so the nurses started side A: "Violets for Your Furs," "Glad to Be Unhappy," "Them There Eyes," "My Man." "My Man" had been the song just before Billie took his request, and he lay in bed, sweating in December, his hair stuck to his head like a newborn's, his dressing wet and yellow, his lips writhing against each other as another fever was wringing him out. " . . . *For whatever my man is, I'm his, forevermore . . .* Well, that is nice. Thank *you.*" The applause roared, and he had the urge, despite his pain, to shout out " 'Waterfront'!" as it faded. The applause ebbed away, into foam and then nothing. The tone arm bobbed over the deep black space as it skated toward the label with the two blackbirds perched on telephone lines that become a musical staff. The whispering ended, the tone arm flew home, the LP stopped turning, and he wept like a child.

He fell asleep calling desperately for the nurses to come and turn the record, more desperately than he'd called for the medic when he reclined on the soft earth with his splintered bones clawing up at him. When he woke, in morning light, from a morphine- and fever-swirled dream of the Frenchwoman, it was to "Billie's Blues," the number she had done after "I Cover the Waterfront." "Good morning, soldier," said a new nurse. "I thought you'd like some music. And, natch, it's *always* a good time for a little happy hour," she added as she screwed in a new bag of morphine. "Stormy Weather," "Willow Weep for Me," and "Autumn in New York" finished side B. They had amputated his past, not just his voice, but even her singing his song. He refused to let the nurses play the record again, and he threw away the enclosed letter, with its gentle mention of "an unforgettable concert." One nurse took the rejected vinyl home, happy to have some new music in godforsaken Japan, and she spun it enough that it eventually caught in her ear. She would hum it, now and again.

A week or two later she was on duty, he was awake, and she whistled "I Cover the Waterfront" in his room. "That's my favorite song," he said glumly, and the nurse shifted from whistling to singing, in mid-word, "-*terfront*." She sang a little more, off-pitch, imitating Holiday's inimitable warble, and he felt a flutter of something—not love, just something warm, not for her, but released by her.

She brought his record back the next day. He was awake, though facing the window, turned on his side by the nurses on a blood-circulating schedule. Unseen, she placed the tone arm at the start of side B. It hissed, and then applause coalesced, and behind him he heard his own voice: " 'Waterfront'! 'I Cover the Waterfront'!" A spliced moment later, Holiday cleared her throat ferociously, and the piano sang its first chord. "Play it from the beginning again," he said into the pillow and his wet arm. "It hasn't hardly started, hon," said the nurse. "Please," he said. Again he heard his voice, resonant from a full body to echo through, every limb, the voice he once had. They had kept it for the record. His voice had mattered, been necessary to reproduce the experience—never to be repeated, even if minor—of sitting in the Galaxy Theater one specific April night, twenty months before, amidst men and women of that period (he explained years later to Julian, conjuring 1953 for the boy's astigmatic 1973 imagination), and falling in love with Billie Holiday (a historical, vaguely operatic or George Washingtonian figure to the child), and, also, of standing next to your future wife without knowing it yet, three minutes and nineteen seconds (plus the time for that exchange with the singer) before you met her, before you had to part from her, before your leg was shattered and taken from you in regular slices, and your belief in joy with it, until the day you heard your voice again, in a hospital room with a view, through a dirty window and chicken wire, of dun snow and dun sky and clouds of smoke from neighboring factories.

He collected copies of the LP for years. Friends gave it to him at times of celebration and sorrow. His wife gave him two more copies. He gave extras to worthy friends, sent them to Army buddies. He played it often, on anniversaries (of the April concert, of their June wedding, of his wife's premature death). And then it was out of print for years when jazz devolved from being pop itself into a genre for connoisseurs, and his supply of the album dwindled to two.

In later years, Julian couldn't remember what his father had done that so angered him, couldn't recall what lesson he thought he was teaching the old man. It had surely been for his father's own good— Julian could remember that barbarian chant rattling his adolescent heart. He could have simply hidden the discs, or sold them to some store from which he could have—in later, wise remorse—ransomed them back. But no, it had been—for reasons he could no longer summon—crucial that his father see, from his upstairs wheelchair by the high window, both albums hit the bonfire, see the flames melt the vinyl and burst through the sleeve until, on the cover, Billie Holiday, in close profile, with head tipped back, spewed fire.

It would be too melodramatic to say that Julian destroyed him, but too kind to say his father ever looked at him again as if Julian had never done it. In the years between the crime and the renaissance of classic jazz on compact disc, penitent Julian hunted for the vinyl LP but failed to find it, and he and his father did reach a point where discussing Julian's late mother did not automatically result—verbally or tacitly—in references to the desecration of his father's most cherished relics of her.

When the label that bought the Bird on a Wire catalog reissued two Billie Holiday concerts as the CD *Summer Holiday,* Julian had already pursued several false leads over the years, bringing home the wrong concerts, studio versions of "Waterfront," even a drag queen doing a Holiday impression (*I Am Billie!,* Stonewall Records, 1979). He kept his quest to replace the LP secret from his father, listening to the records alone to protect him from disappointments, but the old man had discovered this last disc in Julian's room, and Julian came home to find him listening to it, clearly believing it had been left lying out for him as a cruel joke. Julian showed him the collection of failed purchases, and his father, now laughing, extracted a filial promise that they would open and listen to records together from then on.

Thus *Summer Holiday.* In 1985 Julian, visiting from film school, carried with him the sealed CD and a CD player to suture onto his father's old stereo. He presented his latest discovery in its long, slim box. "Seems *possible,*" Julian said. His father studied the liner notes: Recorded live in concert at the State Theater, Minneapolis, 1952, and the Galaxy Theater, New York City, 1953. Track fourteen: "I Cover the Waterfront."

Conversationless, bumbling, Julian sweated to connect the CD player to the rest of the elderly hi-fi and produce anything besides robotic clicking. A trip into town was necessary for a requisite cable, and a second trip to two different stores for a golden and rare umbilical adapter. When Julian returned, both times, his father hadn't moved, sat with the unopened CD in his lap. He silently looked at his hands while Julian swore unimaginatively every time he misattached the cords or pricked his finger on a lurking staple.

He wouldn't let Julian skip ahead to track fourteen, or even to ten, the first song at the Galaxy. First they had to travel to Minneapolis thirty-three years earlier and take in the entire show where some man had shouted, "'God Bless the Child'!" and Billie replied, "All right, honey, that's a fine idea." Julian watched his father's face for a concert and a half. What could he still hope to feel? If the headphoned engineers had restored the whole exchange, dusted off a crumbling reel in the Bird on a Wire archives, would his father enjoy the fleeting sensation of a wife, a leg, a future before him? Julian watched him: his eyes were closed, but he was surely awake, for he rubbed his hip, the geographic end of his right side ("the Cape of No Hope," he called it), a nervous gesture but palliative of some eternal ache. He didn't seem any more agitated when the applause followed track thirteen, "My Man," nor when a blue 14 formed on the CD player's screen, and the applause rolled over seamlessly, the applause that nestled within it the sound of his own hands, his excitement, his capacity to love the singer soon to be diverted and channeled toward his future wife.

In Julian's childhood living room, his past actions and his father's history awaited the next sounds from two black boxes on the floor, waited to receive their newest meaning, perhaps their final meaning. If Julian's behavior was ever forgivable, not irrevocably cruel, then this moment would determine it. If music can ever restore a lost past, then this was the moment. Redemption! We do crave it. But music is different: we tolerate songs without redemption. *Will the one I love be coming back to me?*

Ground control to Major Tom:
Commencing countdown, engines on.
— Lincoln-Mercury ad

1

JULIAN DONAHUE'S GENERATION were the pioneers of portable headphone music, and he began carrying with him everywhere the soundtrack to his days when he was fifteen. When he was twenty-three and new to the city, he roamed the Brooklyn Heights Promenade, claimed it as his discovery, colonized it with his hours and his Walkman. He fell in love with Manhattan's skyline, like a first-time brothel guest falling for a seasoned professional. He mused over her reflections in the black East River at dusk, dawn, or darkest night, and each haloed light—in a tower or strung along the jeweled and sprawling spider legs of the Brooklyn Bridge's spans—hinted at some meaning, which could be understood only when made audible by music and encoded in lyrics. *Play on, Walkman, on, rewind and give me excess of it.*

Late in the evening of the day he completed his first job directing a television commercial, Julian sat in the fall air and listened to Dean Villerman on his Walkman, stared at Manhattan, and inhaled as if he'd just surfaced from a deep dive, and he had the sensation that he might never be so happy again as long as he lived. This quake of joy, inspiring and crippling, was *longing*, but longing for what? True love? A wife? Wealth? Music was not so specific as that. "Love" was in most of these potent songs, of course, but they—the music, the light, the season—implied more than this, because, treacherously, Julian was swelling only with longing for *longing*. He felt his nerves open and turn to the world like sunflowers on the beat, but this desire could not achieve release; his body strained forward, but independent of any goal, though he did not know it for many years to come, until he proved it.

Because years later, when he had captured all that—love, wife, home, success, child—*still* he longed, just the same, when he listened to those same songs, now on a portable CD player, easily repeated without the moodicidal interruption of rewinding (turning spindles wheezing as batteries failed). He felt it all again. He pressed Play and longed *still*.

When he was first married, Julian worried how he would feel about particular songs if his marriage should expire prematurely, in Rachel's death or her infidelity (yes, he had imagined it before he knew it, perhaps imagined it so vividly that he caused it). And he prepared himself to lose music for Rachel, as the price of love, the ticket torn at admission: he assumed that, whether the marriage worked or not, he would never really find his way back to the music, that old songs would be sucked dry of promise or too clogged with memory.

But no, music lasted longer than anything it inspired. After LPs, cassettes, and CDs, when matrimony was about to decay into its component elements—alimony and acrimony—the songs startled him and regained all their previous, pre-Rachel meanings, as if they had not only conjured her but then dismissed her, as if she had been entirely their illusion. He listened to the old songs again, years later on that same dark promenade, when every CD he had ever owned sat nestled in that greatest of all human inventions, the iPod, dialed up and yielding to his fingertip's tap. The songs now offered him, in exchange for all he had lost, the sensation that there was something still to long for, still, something still approaching, and all that had gone before was merely prologue to an unimaginably profound love yet to seize him. If there was any difference now, it was only that his hunger for music had become more urgent, less a daily pleasure than a daily craving.

Julian Donahue married in optimistic confusion, separated in pessimistic confusion, and now was wandering toward a mistrustful divorcistan, a coolly celibate land. He understood little of what had transpired between the day he said he could not live without this woman and the day when the last of her belongings (and many of his) left their home. If he forced himself to recall, he would revisit particular arguments, understand they were scaffolded by interlocking causes and built upon the unstable ruins of previous arguments. He saw that old arguments had been only partially dismantled either to mutual satisfaction or to no one's, or to her satisfaction (perhaps feigned) and his relief, or to his satisfaction and her mounting resentment, to which he had been blind. Perhaps all of this swayed upon some swampland of preexisting incompatibility, despite mutual feelings of affection and lust all signatories probably felt back at the start. Obviously he would not downplay the role of Carlton, though it was wiser not to think about that, and he had become skilled at cutting off those fractal thoughts before they could blossom.

The day Rachel announced her indistractible thirst for his absence, Julian was consulting his music collection, hunting for the song that would explain to him, even obliquely, the bleak atmosphere in his home, the two magnetized black boxes circling each other, attracting and repelling each other from room to room.

"I want to play you something," he said, kneeling in front of his CD shelves when Rachel entered behind him. "I was thinking about Carlton, and . . ."

He must have been present for *something*. He recognized his dumb urge never to think about her again even as he failed to stop thinking about her, perhaps because of the energy required to stop those other thoughts. Photography still in his apartment claimed there had been

Eiffel Tower kisses and golden beach sunsets; he hadn't thrown those
out yet. He had drawn her portrait a hundred times and shot eight-
millimeter video of her and sometimes still watched it when he was
home alone and in the mood to mope. When there were animal
shows on cable, he would put on the CD of *Summer Holiday* and mute
the TV, switching back and forth with the remote, hitting Video
Input over and over: Rachel sleeps on her side, her hair fanned out behind her and her arms pushing in front of her, as if she were soaring
through the sky; the polar bear rears back and with both fists double-
punches straight down through the ice to reach the seal; Rachel bats
a dream pest away from her face; the seal is consumed in eight bites;
"—*I cover the waterfront* . . ."

Lately he watched the animals more and Rachel less and sometimes felt as if all human affairs—but especially his own—could be
sufficiently explained by the wily, competing coyotes and babysitting,
gnu-gnawing lionesses and fascistic ants. After he was separated from
Rachel and returned to the wild, he watched animal channels for
hours at a time because they helped him fall asleep. Later, when he
was sandbagging the new structures of mind necessary to keep pain
from splashing over all his daily activity, when he could consider those
years and still go to work, the animals remained. When he was able to
think about his past, to consider and not just feel his pain, to calculate
how thoroughly Rachel had broken and discarded him, how compre-
hensively they had misimagined each other, the baboons and orcas offered a certain stabilizing hope for the years ahead, and soon
everything seemed explicable by animal behavior. Aggressive Team-
sters on a commercial set were expressing threatened alpha status;
gallery openings served to tighten group bonds for the protection of
like genes. One *had* to be less heartbroken, since our cousin primates
died from emotional trauma or recovered from it quickly. Litters in
the wild of almost every species included a certain number of unfeasi-
ble offspring, starved by the mother and siblings, or just eaten by
them.

Urges that had once driven Julian—to pursue and capture shampoo models, for example—were explained and defused by animal
shows. That old behavior was just what countless cheetahs did,

spreading seed. More and more of life dripped down beneath him, reduced by the immutable laws and relaxed habits of the animal kingdom. Entire species went extinct; ours would, too, someday, or evolve into something unrecognizable, a higher species that would pay no more attention to our obsessively cataloged feelings than we do to the despairs of *Australopithecus*, and all of this vain *heartbreak* that we cling to as important or tragic would one day be revealed—by TV scientists—for what it is: just behavior.

2

IT WAS SNOWING, and so Julian would have stayed in, but he needed toilet paper.

He would have hit the bodega on the corner for it, but it was snowing hard, and silence was accumulating quickly, and so he just wandered instead toward Atlantic Avenue, into the silent night, forgetting his errand. Behind the snow, the air was green, as if a cinematographer had lowered a heavy grad over a camera's lens. A locked bicycle sprouted a teetering white heart from its saddle. Thuggish street-side garbage bags dressed themselves as jolly snowmen. Two beagles, set leashless for their evening walk, called to the city like merry muezzins, plunged in and out of cresting snowbanks, closely read the road's white expanses and highlighted areas of interest.

Urgently recalled to his original mission, Julian stopped at the first opportunity, an unmarked wooden door where smooth lanes of snow collided into slush, gray with boot prints. He stepped through a hole in the night, into noise and heat and light. "Bathroom?"

The muscle-clumped bonsai barman jerked his chin toward the back of the room, where peeling blue painter's tape on the floor and an array of monitor speakers defined a trapezoidal stage, held by instruments but no humans. A woman's scream rang out, twice and then a third time until a girl opened her phone. "I'm at the Rat!" she shouted into it. "Where are you? I *know* it's snowing!" Easily the oldest in the room by a decade or two, Julian turned down the hall next to the stage. Under a single bulb and a reproduced poster for a Hendrix concert he was old enough to have attended as an infant, someone had written on the wall a long passage in Greek, and then some sharpie had added in English, "That's not funny, Stavros. I'm gonna kick your Sparta-loving ass."

Across from the phone were two doors, plainly the facilities, but the first bore the fussily hand-painted words in gold D. MELANOGASTER under a picture of some sort of fly, washing/soiling its forelegs, but offering no evidence of gender. The second door boasted the same delicate script, C. SORDELLII, and an illustration of, maybe, a nest of worms, even less gender-specific, if possible. Julian opted for the worms, only to be charged by the reflection of a young woman exiting a neon-pink stall and closing the flaps of her jeans. The sight of her hands on the silver buttons filled his vision, and then she was yelling over his downcast, retreating apology, "Can't you bloody read?"

On the wall over the urinal was posted the Rat Calendar of upcoming acts. He didn't know *any* bands anymore: 12 Angry Mental Patients, the Youthful Mouthful, the Hungarian Veterinarians, Dystothèque, Lisping Picts, Spermicidal Tendencies, Imaginary Wife, the Long Purples, Home School Class Slut, the Deranged Curates, Girl Urologist, Weepy Fag.

He paid his toiletry debt with a drink at the end of the bar farthest from the stage. He examined the home-burned demo CDs for sale in a yellow cardboard wine box: Cait O'Dwyer, *Your Very Own Blithering Idiot*. He intended to leave after the beer, anticipated taking a sentimental walk with his iPod. The club kept filling. He grew older with each arrival. He had accepted that he was older than baseball players (even knuckleballers), older than astronauts, older than *Playboy* models, older than rock stars and Oscar-winning directors, but now he was reminded that he was older than people who went to nightclubs to hear live music, as his parents used to do. He calculated to be sure: yes, he was older than his father had been in those memories of his parents going out on the town. He wrestled with his coat, and then a band was taking the stage at the far end of the room. Julian recognized her jeans from the pink stall.

The rules of this game had not changed in the years since Julian used to club. The band enacted the archetypal tuning ritual: the fuzz of a guitar plug tickling its metal hole, about to be clicked home; the drummer adjusting his snare, testing his work with iambic 1–2—pause—1–2's; the excessively hilarious in-jokes between bassist and drummer; the strained chumminess distinguishing those on one side of the tape from those on the other. But then no shadow of artificiality darkened the girl singer's face when she stepped across the boundary, the last of the four, touched with the tip of her leather boot the set list taped to the floor by a monitor speaker prostrate before her, and cooed to her guitarist, "Play well, please, you shit."

She was, that first night, still local. She led a local band in a local gig at a local bar. She was of the neighborhood, despite her obvious foreignness: in her Irish accent she made a joke about a health-code-cracking restaurant up the street. Nearly half her set was covers, but the crowd knew her originals well enough to shout along with the choruses. She sang with her eyes closed, and her dark red hair fell over her face until she pushed it away with both hands. Julian stood at the back, near the door, vaguely suspicious (at least to himself) because of his innumerable, rimy years, and she sang, a coincidence,

> *"You stood in the back*
> *You didn't know why*
> *I could have reached out*
> *I should have reached out."*

All these kids paid her a tribute in attention they would not have paid some debutante desperate for their love. They craved *her* attention; Julian could see it on the boys' faces, and the girls'. Her star was rising, and confused resentment mingled with the crowd's desire for her. There were grumblings of complaint. Two boys next to him could be heard briefly between songs: "She used to be so righteous. I saw her last year. She just *did* not care what you thought," griped one, studying her despite himself, his artisanal pilsener, ironically named, pinched between two knuckles at groin level. Julian had cast boys like this to advertise beer like that.

"She's changed?" he prodded the kids.

The boy explained before the guitar drowned his voice: "Signed."

Her implicit mercantile sluttishness: Julian heard it already, that first snowy night, autopsied by a flanneled adolescent Julian had helped create, all because this Irish girl singing to fifty people (happy to come out in the world-erasing snow for her) had been signed to make a CD that would likely sell 118 copies.

Julian Donahue was a director, and he watched, like a director, to see what people liked now and why, silently edited her performance. The outside edges of her hands were pronounced and long. They gave her gestures an extra grace and expressivity. The intricately inked forearm and the white T-shirt worn with no bra so that the occasional implication of her breasts skimming the unseen surface of the cotton (probably lit like the inside of a tent on a summer day) carried the force of a whispered obscenity. She held the mike with both hands and bent her body to the left, a rock-girl standby since Janis Joplin at least. Julian knew she meant for men to imagine she was singing to them but kept her eyes closed or stared just over their heads so she could deny responsibility.

He hadn't been to a show like this in years, but they were still the same. The Vegas lounge singer looks each supper clubber in the eye, flirts with a front-row gentleman while the rest of the audience laughs, and no one is fooled, no one is hurt, nothing is at risk behind the sequins. The rock girl, though, is at risk, and so is the flanneled fool who wishes she'd open her eyes and look at him. These boys were going to be absorbed, soon, into larger crowds of other boys harboring the same fantasies, nauseous with desires indistinguishable from their own, and they resented it.

It was nearly impossible for Julian to form a judgment of the actual music under these conditions—a first exposure to the songs, distorted through backfeeding amps, clattering glasses and bottles, people shouting at the barman for attention—and so he bought the demo CD because she was pretty and to try to keep up, a little, for work. Maybe she was someone he should have heard of. He'd ask Maile.

The singer covered the mike and yelled something at her bass player, chastising him for some musical misstep. He took a step back, looking down and off to the side. "By any chance, does anyone here know how to play the bass?" she asked the crowd after that song. "It would be a great help to us up here." Even her bassist laughed, then closed his eyes, nodding.

When she was a little out of breath, her T-shirt swelled with every inhalation. Julian wasn't immune to a beautiful young woman inflating like a bellows before an orange fire, but his reflex after attraction was to look for the biological meaning in the attraction, encoded but only temporarily mysterious. Some canny evolutionist could explain: The display of expansive lung capacity implies an ability to carry offspring to term? Expanding the chest is a sign that the female is seasonably warm? Even an actress drawing a deep breath to settle herself before a take extolling shower cleanser could have the same effect on Julian as this songstress, charging through her torn-jeans maneuvers, back-to-back with her guitarist/likely boyfriend. There had been a moment, a day or two before, when a coffee-shop counter girl suddenly jerked herself back and expanded in a prelude to an enormous yawn, and Julian had had the impulse to spread his hands over the opening accordion of her ribs, and he'd understood, a little, what promised delights those scarlet-throated frogs on TV all discerned in one another's erotic balloonery.

The singer's eyes were now half-closed, hooded with sleepy availability. He had been distracted briefly by lung capacity but soon saw the obvious: singers' breasts heave; they perspire; songbirds throw back their heads and writhe, howl, shut their eyes. Certain mystifications drift around singers, but they are merely people of a certain talent, one being the evocation of sexual desire through methods most of us cannot duplicate: crank mating calls, evolutionary teasing for the price of the cover and a two-drink minimum.

He stepped back into the silent white street, bought the toilet paper, returned home, where his brother, an uninvited guest again, was lying on his couch watching a *Jeopardy!* rerun. "I opened some wine," Aidan said, then shouted at the TV with cold disgust, "Who are the Picts?"

3

"SO OKAY. We're done, and you are coming along *great*. I want you to remember what it felt like when you played without looking at your hands. It felt great, no? Oh, I have a present for you." Cait fished a CD from her bag and gave it to the girl. "In my opinion, these are some of the best rock songs with piano. And the very best one is a girl playing, you'll notice. They all learned, just like you, scales and chords and études first. Pick your favorite of these and try to play what you hear, without reading anything, as part of your drills, okay?"

"Knock knock."

"Who's there?"

"Boo."

"Boo who?"

"Why are you crying?"

"Oh, *very* funny. *So* amusing. You could be on television. If they had a show about *stupid* jokes. Say, do you want to play me the piece you wrote?"

The girl shook her head very slightly but very fast, like a hummingbird with a bad attitude.

"Please, oh please?" Cait poked her. "Pretty please? Really? Well, okay." Cait put her own hands on the keys, played just in the range she could reach without crossing in front of her pupil. "This is a very old Irish song that my da used to play me. Do you want to hear the words? It's not a very happy song."

"The good ones never are, are they?" the little girl asked in all seriousness, and when Cait laughed, she looked hurt and asked, "What's funny?"

"You are. I know what you mean, but you're *wrong*. There's loads of great happy songs. Listen to that CD. You'll see."

"Why do you have to quit?"

"Oh, baby, now you *are* going to make me boo-hoo. I'm going to be traveling too much, that's all. Wouldn't be fair to you or my other tinklers. I'll still *see* you. And Sarah's a mate—she's a really good teacher. You'll love her."

"Will she sing with me?"

"No. In fact, that reminds me. I have to warn you. Don't, under any circumstances, let her sing. She's got a dreadful voice. But she can play like an angel any music you hope to hear. All of that, all of your Johnny Bach book, and all your precious Elton, too. But promise me something."

"I promise."

"You haven't heard it yet."

"I still promise. That's the way I am."

"Oh, good, then I won't tell you what it was, and I can always say you promised, no matter what I ask you to do."

"Who tells *you* what to do?"

"Do?"

"Who says when you're not practicing hard enough?"

"That's a good question. I suppose my bandmates."

"What if nobody buys your record?"

"Wow. Well, ah, then I'll be putting poison in Sarah's tea in a flash and coming to see if you'll have me back."

"Are you nervous? How do you know you don't need lessons anymore?"

"Quite a day for good questions. Well, I don't play piano in the band. I don't know. I suppose I probably *do* need lessons still, but a day comes when you just feel ready, you know? Oh, oh, oh, now quit that, please. If you get all teary, then I really am going to slobber on you. Here, sing this with me instead."

4

SOME WEEKS EARLIER, Julian Donahue had noticed that "What's Left"— a pop song that had used to haunt his solitude and that had been playing on his stereo the cherry-blossom morning he proposed to Rachel—was, but for one consonant, perfectly composed for an approaching job. "*You left so fast, you didn't stay to watch me cry*" required only a single alphabetical step to reach "*You left so fast, you didn't stay to watch me dry*," and then very nicely described a new oven cleaner, which toiled selflessly while its people, according to the storyboard sent over by the agency, frolicked in a park and drove along a Pacific cliff-side highway.

And so Julian spent Saturday, the day after his snowy discovery of the Rat, in a recording studio in Queens, though the rapids of melting slush delayed the engineer by two hours and the singer by three. (The band, fortunately, existed only as a computer file.) Standing in the control booth, Julian pushed a button, and his voice drifted through the glass partition into the gray, dimpled studio, carrying disembodied suggestions to an eight-hundred-dollar-an-hour vocal chameleon with the face of a zealous nun and the body of a self-indulgent monk as to how she could achieve the same tone of pained loss from the original lyric while still punching the selling word *dry*, so that any woman who purchased Spray-Go would feel the liberating pleasure of the traditionally male role, the colder heart, the one who could stalk out without regret, indifferent to the pain of whomever she left behind (her husband, her oven cleaner).

He leaned against the back wall of the booth and watched this fiendishly proficient singer twiddle the knobs of some internal control panel until she produced a perfect impression of the song's original voice, a two-hit pop star from twenty years earlier, just inside the target market's musical nostalgia range. A song could be neutered as easily as this. "What's Left," which had long exercised a matador's power in Julian's headphones, could be sung by an identical voice, over a computerized but identical band, and, with the change of a single letter, be shown up as mere spattered notes and jerky rhythm, no more hypnotic than any other one-calorie jingle. "Nice, Louise. You nailed that one."

Two weeks later, he was on set for a hair conditioner, watching the product's brand manager rise from his canvas chair and march with dainty urgency across the colored floor. "I really, I must." His accent, his unshakable formality, his resemblance to a dapper mole, and his fevered love for his product were already mimicked by laughing art guys from the agency. "You cannot, Monsieur Donahue, pardon my insistence, you cannot light the Product like that." He went down on one knee beside the dollops of hair conditioner on the glass pedestal. "You cast it in this excess of blue, and you blanch it of its essential identifying hues." He let his other knee touch the ground and cupped his hands around the conditioner to demonstrate how its color changed in shadow.

Julian, Maile (his production assistant for the last four months), and Vlada (the director of photography) consulted, stifling laughter, avoiding eye contact. The afternoon crept away as Maile, on her knees before the glass pedestal, sprayed food coloring and Vlada handed gel after gel up ladders to grips while Mr. Rousselet sat next to Julian and stared at the video feed, and the two professional beauties in bathrobes who would soon lather their manes on camera sat in the far back under a NO SMOKING sign and ignited each new slender cigarette off the orange tail of the last.

Julian plugged his iPod into the studio's sound system and felt a physical relief as the day's silliness was replaced with a sense of purpose. The soundtrack effect, as he had learned decades before: music could inject the quotidian with significance, lyricism, uniqueness. The third song, a female voice: " 'I'd sooner die,' she said, she said, and she almost believed it, her little drama." The music swept through the cubical black room: the embarrassing idea of believing too much in one's own little drama penetrated everything, here quickly like solar wind, there slowly but relentlessly as a line of ants. It affected how Mr. Rousselet leaned in to peer at the video assist, then squatted before the mauve mammarial domes of the Product and spritzed color himself. The music changed how the two models moved, surreptitiously touching each other's fingertips in their shadowed cloud, how Vlada looked sadly through his viewfinder, his Serbian manner making everything around him tragic and unimportant at once.

Julian hadn't loaded or downloaded any new pop music in months and could not at first understand the song's unfamiliarity. No, yes, he had loaded a CD, the demo from that Irish girl at the Rat, loaded it two weeks ago and never listened since. It caught him by surprise, that afternoon in the studio and then later, the gloaming settling over the Manhattan skyline like colored mist over hair conditioner, as he walked with time to kill before dinner with a film-school friend in town for the weekend, a man who had risen fast in Hollywood to second-unit director but then stopped, happy to do well-paid crowd scenes and cutaways indefinitely, when in school he'd always in-sisted—nearly shouted—that a true auteur could only work outside the studios and would write, shoot, direct, and edit everything him-self.

The demo CD had a little hiss, and the levels were too low here and there, and the bass was too hot on three tracks, buzzing his ears: the gritty authenticity of the rough-mix demo that had secured the deal that would produce a new CD with cleaner versions of these same songs. The guitar even screwed up its solo introduction on the very first track. The music stopped, and a male voice said, "Whoops." There was male and female laughter, and they started the song again; they left the mistake there, a daring way to open a disc meant to wow dim, deaf record executives, and when the musician played it right the next time, Julian felt a humming in his neck and in his kidneys.

The next day, shooting was delayed almost immediately; Maile presented him with a model, and Julian studied her face slowly, a face he'd hired from a photo, before shaking his head and her hand: "Thank you, but not today. Maile, sign her papers with my apolo-gies." This was somewhat for the client's marketing managers visiting the set—corporate sleepwalkers for whom a day amidst cameras and lights watching a director's offhand dismissal of high-rent beauties, damn the expense, was one of the job's titillating perks, a whiff of diva glamour.

But the last-minute firing of models was becoming increasingly common, and Julian was lately frustrating modeling agencies with his sharpening standards and his refusal to explain them. Early in his ca-reer, he'd realized that the final test before engaging a model had to be the search for premonitions of aging. Not symptoms: premoni-tions. Julian could—often at a glance—see how and where most women's faces were only temporary versions of their older selves. He could spot the shame even in some of the modelinas of nineteen or twenty; he could see their old-womanhood lurking, while the ideal faces (and that Irish singer's, come to think of it) gave no hint, showed no vulnerability. Others would hire those same women, obviously; he had no exclusive claim on them. But he would never book the esteemed übermodel whose dark secret he had glimpsed. Despite advances in CGI, even the best retouching guys couldn't reliably erase the truth, and so Julian maintained his standard, his trade secret, and all of his ads—from the prosaic floor cleaner sold by a magnificently beautiful "housewife" identifiable by her rolled-sleeve oxford to the exalted mascara shot close enough to show pores—produced in the client the same paradoxical sensations of danger and safety, lust and exaltation. He was, for several years running, the single most rehired director in the city, though it was a very rare marketing person who could have explained why.

The problem, however, had arisen in the last eight to ten months: there were fewer women whose future elderliness (even elderly beauty) was imperceptible. He was hiring slightly younger than he used to, but the bottom limit loomed as large as the top. He couldn't explain this to frustrated model-house reps, because he didn't want to disclose his tricks, but the truth was plain: more and more women looked merely temporarily beautiful. He knew this was likely a result of Carlton and Rachel; certain events were going to permanently affect one's vision. Still, he was saddened to see the effect, the growing endangerment of one species of beauty.

He pointed to six possible replacements in the binders, gave Maile time to call to check availability, authorized her to pay rush penalties, and left the set with an air of purpose, but only to ride the F train and listen to his iPod.

And now Julian sits on the F train in a nearly empty car. At the far end, wired to a slender iPod full of hip-hop, a young black man dressed for corporate life bobs and mutters to himself like a Talmudic scholar. Julian is slightly affected by the dismissed model's face and disappointment. She smelled of breath mints not quite eradicating the evidence of a recent noisy purge, and now from the banking train's orange plastic seat he examines the reasonably but not impossibly pretty girl across from him. Hers is a kind of prettiness he appreciates all the more, considering his daily routine shaping and, frame by frame, preserving ludicrous beauty, and in his headphones a love song plays, a different girl singing, an Irish girl, and she sings of the vast golden fields of possibility that stretch out before him, there for him to wander through, the sun will never finish setting. It is physically impossible—with the right song—for a certain sort of man not to feel (before he remembers how to think) that the girl across the subway aisle hears and feels something, too, that she will be his co-star in this romance-glazed landscape. She's looking up now, a smile approaches, but no, she's listening to her own music on her own iPod, maybe a dirge about the fate of a doomed sea voyage, and Julian closes his eyes and the lyrics to the Cait O'Dwyer song begin to lodge in his memory.

He climbed back to the surface of Manhattan at Twenty-third Street, right where he started. Something snowy was falling out of a clear blue sky. He returned to the studio, where Maile had conjured one of his requested girls. He watched the makeup artist add moisture to this Italian model's lips. Each sweep of the brush added to the girl's ripe succulence. A precise amount of visible humidity was necessary to evoke sex without bringing to mind dull biology and oral hygiene. "Wait." He stopped Makeup when she would have moved on to the Italian girl's eyes. "More to the lips. Again. More. Again. Once again. Done—thank you."

5

BACK IN 2006, Ian Richfield and Cait O'Dwyer were put in touch by a mutual friend who knew they had both recently fled crap bands. They arranged by email to meet at Ian's apartment. He offered her a beer, they exchanged war stories, tested for shared acquaintances, and then she said, "Well, let's give it a go," not very hopefully.

And up until that moment, Ian often recalled, anything was still possible. He imagined subsequently that when she said, "Well, let's give it a go," he said nothing, simply grabbed her, any part of her he could reach and hold on to, took her on the floor, ran his hands over and under her oversized sweater, seized the back of her head and pushed her face into his, fell to his knees, pressed his cheek against her crotch.

No. He had laughed and said, "Wow, listen to you. All right, chief, let's *do*, let's give it a go." And partially because it was his hands' first reflex whenever he picked up his guitar to practice alone and partially to see if the cute Irish girl knew anything about music, he started the Cure's intro of Hendrix's "Foxey Lady." She nodded like a surgeon and told him to take it up a third. He clipped his capo, and she was right there, no errors, no lost words, even quoted the ad-lib from the record—"*This is a good intro*"—but something more: she played off of him, filled in the spaces he left for her, offered him ideas. She sat on the speckled stepladder he had stolen from one of his house-painting jobs, but then stood up halfway through the song and turned up both her volume and his. "*I won't do you no harm. You've got to be all mine, all mine.*" He played this song—which he had studied from an old CD of his uncle's the very day his parents had bought him an electric guitar—with a ferocity he'd always assumed was only granted to a musician in front of an attentive crowd. He took twice the solo space, keeping the rhythm moving without bass or drums and without interrupting the flow of his ideas. As the fuzz of his last chord was still drifting down to the floor of his loft, he could *still* have changed things, and in recent self-abusive musings, he swung his guitar off his shoulder, tipped over his brown folding metal chair, attached his mouth to her ear, and his hands corrugated her breasts before the amp was done buzzing.

No. He didn't. There was this moment. This one moment had come and waited for him, and when he stood still, it had gone on its way forever. That very first song ended, and they both knew: the sound had been a multiple of them both. And they knew. They sat in a long silence as the sound they had made traveled down the street, out to sea, up to distant stars. Only the low hum of his amp persisted, and he was afraid (as she looked at him and he considered leaping at her) that the pickup from his guitar would pick up his heartbeat and play it for her. He pressed his tongue against his upper lip and rolled his black pick with its clean whorled thumbprint over and under his knuckles. She reached for the cigarettes she no longer had in her bag, having quit a week earlier, and he walked to the fridge for two more beers. They chose.

The choice was mutual but they had opposite reasons: he was a coward, she was ruthless. In his defense, he hadn't known the choice was going to be inscribed eternally as grave marble law. That was *her* will, enforced from that moment on with flinchless discipline. If he'd known, he told himself, he would have chosen her over the music, over anything. He would have.

"How about 'London Calling'?" she suggested. He played everything she asked. Their vast vocabularies and listening histories—their long educations for this moment—overlapped almost without overhang. He called more and more obscure favorites (Cramps, Creeps, Crito's Apology, Crooked Bastards, Crud), and she almost never pleaded ignorance, rarely even hesitated, just requested different keys until he started to compensate for her range automatically. He had never known anyone to keep up with him at calling tunes, let alone force an admission that he was weak in the canonical Irish bands. She couldn't really play guitar but she could sing him through his part of a Pogues song, "Na-na naa rhythm and then up to the five and back down and then break for two bars of unintelligible slurring."

He especially loved how she handled the songs originally sung by men, how she either sang the lyric straight (singer wants girl) and then gleefully, evilly put it over as a blood-red lipstick-lesbian tune, or reversed the pronouns (singer wants boy) and then she could vary it, do it as neurotic girl or raging girl or seductive girl or funny girl. The best, though, was when she kept a man's lyric the same but then somehow turned its meaning around, kept it in his words but put the whole thing in quotation marks, as if she were singing what a man had once sung to her and now she was only recalling it. Elvis Costello's "Alison," a jealous ex-lover's unhinged ballad, became in her mouth Alison's defense and grudging admission of shared guilt: "*I heard you let that little friend of mine / take off your party dress*" became as much about the girl's remorse as the man's jealousy.

"This is something I've been fooling around with, if anything comes to mind," he said and played a chord pattern, and in minutes she found some words and a melody that he desperately wished he'd written and then knew he never could have, not with infinite time or infinite musical training or infinite therapy. He suggested "Infinite Monkeys" as a title. She wisely disagreed.

Two years had puffed away since that first afternoon in Williamsburg. They wrote all the band's songs together. He contributed almost equally to all band decisions (*almost*—it was her increasingly magnetic name that drew all shiny good fortune to them). And he had adjusted his personality around the pointlessness of his feelings for her, molded himself around their absence. As if he were constantly carrying a heavy box down steep stairs, his posture had come to reflect his predicament; he curved, slouched, withdrew even when standing. He ground his teeth when he thought about it, stood naked in front of the mirror in the bathroom, looked at the pale slump and scrawn and dangle of the case he'd been issued. There was nothing to be done. A gym-designed coat of mannerist muscles would not add anything important; what he lacked was unacquirable.

When they played he stood up a little straighter, watched her for cues, for the reflection of his music on her face. Something awoke and rustled between them onstage, sometimes from the first note, and that current—even when her back was to him and he was looking down at his hands or pedals—powered part of the band's appeal. Men liked her, but women—in audiences, at the record label—saw how Cait looked at him and understood the underlying balance, and they found Ian more attractive as a result of her attention, as if she brought the best of him out to where everyone could see it. He pictured her when he slept with some of those girls after gigs. He suspected she knew that.

Offstage, she fixed him in place with compliments and ironic bossiness, and he tended not to look at her at all when they spoke. He was the only one in the band she called by name, implying a permanence to his position that was professionally reassuring but personally debilitating. When they wrote together, or when one presented the other with something prepared in private, with no audience to absorb the excess, he felt the room crowding with their other selves, lives unled and correspondences unwritten, happinesses opted against, and he could not believe she did not see it, too. He sweated to ornament her fears and tall tales and fake self-portraits, and with the remnants of his energy he hid the rest of himself from her. The best of him was a child's drawing of her on an off day.

He had no illusion that this was bittersweet or somehow necessary to make art. It just burned. Anyone who felt this would take their hand off the stove at once, but he was locked in position, inches from the source of his pain, for as far into the future as he could see, because if he was going to be a musician, if he was going to protect the one profound and real thing about himself, the one thing he loved besides her (but which only she made appear at its strongest), then he would be a fool to leave a singer who so obviously was going to go all the way.

And her? Cait didn't notice that Ian was in pain, or, if she did, the knowledge came only in flashes, which she denied at once, joked away. She reminded herself (in the voice of a childhood priest) not to have so much vanity that she cast everyone around her as extras in her drama. More determining, two years of success had led her to an impenetrable and unfalsifiable superstition that their situation—whatever it was—worked, and to change it, perhaps even to *think* about it, would put at risk all they had gained. Whatever percentage of their professional good fortune depended upon a mutually felt but unspoken tension, it was critical enough that only a psychopath would tamper with it. And so she was never so controlled and business-minded as when they were alone during their collaborative sessions in Ian's latest apartment (never in hers).

And he, as co-conspirator, would prepare the room for her arrival with the attention paid by a criminal to his fiber evidence, leaving no sign of any other person in his life, without implying there was any inviting space for her. If someone had spent the night, all trace of her was gone or closeted before Cait arrived. Photos were drawered, gifts were stowed, and his cell was off, not just muted; he didn't want to look at the screen with her watching (besides, if he took a call during their work, she would cluck like a CEO and tap an imaginary watch on her wrist). He carefully turned off the volume of his landline's antique answering machine, which might otherwise broadcast throughout the room his life's entanglements. When they were writing, she would only nod after a successful experiment, or after a misstep, she would shake her head and laugh and say in a posh English accent, "I'm afraid that's shit, that is." And he would beg in his best Dickensian moppet voice, "Please, mum, can we try again, please?"

He considered her ruthless, in his moments of pain, but also in moments of happiness, experienced mere feet from her but bound right wrist to left ankle by her rules: nothing could evolve, nothing could be consummated, nothing repressed could surface, nothing previously accepted could be ignored. One must not speak of it, in case one could no longer sing of it. Instead, she only kept directing his attention to the wondrously charged air they could tame and make dance between them.

6

THE TAIL END of a damp morning's jog, pushing through icy clouds of his own visible breath. As if to tease him in his months-old mood, like a banderillero with a worthless bull, Julian's iPod suggested his old no-fail song, and he had to laugh in the cold air: *that* song of eight thousand categorized possibilities. His own iPod felt free to mock him. When he was in high school, he had discovered the no-fail song's magnetic field only by chance: if it played unexpectedly on the radio or a mix tape, then the night ahead would provide effortless adventure, Zen promiscuity. If, however, Julian ever *intentionally* used the song to inflate sagging confidence, it had no effect; its potency was only accidentally available.

The song had once flung him from victory to coincidence to miracle across a single day. The memory of that day came back to him in pieces now, as he jogged, and the first piece to arrive was not one of the women's faces, or a perfume, not even the season or weather the day his triple crown had been awarded. No, the first recollection was the sensation against his ear of an old-model headset's padded disc. It was orange (the next memory), which meant it was connected to his silver-blue cassette Walkman, which fixed that extraordinary day prior to reliable portable CD players, so probably 1988; he had been twenty-three. And only then, after that calculation, did the whole day return, the Manhattan October. He had even—the next day, not sure he still lived on the same planet as everyone else—suggested to a bartender friend that there should be a drink called an October Manhattan, and he pledged to finance the research and patent if his friend could reproduce in a glass the experience Julian had had over the previous nineteen hours, the feeling that his well-being and the well-being of the whole world were connected through his headphones, and that the recognition of that connection would always lead inevitably to his meeting and sleeping with some stranger.

Or, on that day, three strangers in succession. If such a thing were a matter of some statistical improbability, then two-a-days should have happened 50 percent more often, but they never had. No, something impossible occurred that day, a meteor landing at his feet with a steaming whimper, a jowly basset hound wishing him a brisk "Good day," a broken bottle reconstituting itself. And any man should have looked back across those two decades, with the same song in his ears, and felt warmly nostalgic.

Except nostalgia like that requires some identification between the recalled and the recalling selves, and as Julian couldn't imagine even talking up a stranger now, could hardly remember sexual arousal, he didn't feel anything besides amusement at the boy who had done *that* so many eons ago. He remembered him but could not hear what he was thinking from this distance.

He jogged down Atlantic Avenue, past the unmarked door of the Rat, its melted snow refreezing into silver seascapes, recalled, for a moment, Cait O'Dwyer's voice and laid it over the song he was actually hearing. Two girls in their twenties were on the sidewalk, but instead of the no-fail song stoking a longing for the girls, the girls' proximity somehow damaged his iPod's electronics, and all the potency seeped out of the music, and the girls disintegrated as soon as he looked carefully, and he thought irresistibly of his estimated taxes.

"Never Gonna Love Anyone (but You)" shuffled up next, the first time in ages. He used to play it for Rachel, early in their engagement, as a promise. He'd stood on the new bed, straddling her as she awoke to him singing along with the CD, demanding she join him on the chorus. He also sang it as a reminder to himself, a little jingling spur to the heart, when he found, to his disappointment, that even an engagement had not transformed him into a monogamist.

Before and after his wedding, Julian still indulged in the perquisite struggling actresses and relaxing models his work delivered him. He sampled here and there a tasty intern. Once it had been provocative. But by the time he was engaged, it was only evocative, recalling previous negotiations and love songs. Romance and sex became not joyless—not at all—but a pleasant exercise in recalling previous joy, an infinite regression with infinitely diminishing returns. He had still laughed through drinks and kisses with all his parts alert and his sense of destiny and romance sharp, and his mind never wandered, he didn't check his watch mid-grope, he savored their bodies and the atmospheric vicinity, the ice cubes in the water resembling dental X-rays, her clear-polished nail running lightly over the pale pink grooves of her adman lips, the dual, peelable scallops of bronzed calf joining under the muscular *H* at the back of her knee as she walked from table to coat check, while a not-at-all-bad piano player laced together "All of Me," "All of You," "All the Things You Are," and "All the Way."

He'd also tasted enough by then to know that it was, at least, not what all those songs of longing had been hinting at after all. But that wisdom never prevented the next liaison.

He had always intended to be monogamous. He embraced the idea of it, in principle and for him personally, and especially with his girlfriend-become-fiancée-become-wife. But metamorphosing from polygamous to monogamous was not the simple molt that pop music had long promised him. In fact, opportunities for seducing other women only increased upon his engagement, multiplied even more fruitfully after his wedding. Propaganda songs for true love alternated with contrarian pop music that kept promising some unknown, almost unknowable blurry bliss in *that* one's eyes (no, wait, *that* one's), and both types of song seemed credible but seemed also to refer to experiences that he hadn't yet had; he was not yet living the life described by music, and (the music implied) this was *his* fault. For all that he loved his wife, adored her company, expected their union to last a lifetime, he was never for long free of the old sensation of longing, longing for something that had turned out, to his puzzlement, not to be her either.

His brother, Aidan, aware of his infidelities in those days, viewed Julian as a pig. "This carnal gluttony is beneath you," he scolded, but Julian argued that his sin wasn't quite gluttony.

"Then it's a failure of your imagination," Aidan filed new charges, and that accusation hurt, though it came from a man who had likely never touched a female. It stung Julian because he still viewed himself in those days as a man of vast imagination, an artist no matter the literally commercial nature of his work. But Aidan was inexcusably right: Julian could *not* imagine—even with Rachel—how such an arrangement would exist as they aged, how aging would affect sex and romance, what familiarity might breed (whether contempt or something less easily imaginable). And, in the light of Aidan's scorn, Julian's next few exemptions to the marital contract were spoiled, not art but failure, the gutless repetition of previously praised work.

Toward the very end of his polygamous life, he wandered (not for the first time) down a dim, fetishistic alley to see where it led him (complimenting himself for his imagination as he roamed). This last game began by him saying, "Tell me what you're doing to me," demanding from his partner a play-by-play narration. Then it became: "Tell me about a time you've done this to someone else," as it was done to him. Later: "Tell me about someone walking in on us, walking toward the building, going about her day while you do this." Later still, in its most rococo formulation, the girl he was holding, a struggling and eventually failed playwright, narrated a long history eight removes from Julian himself: (1) a woman in a restaurant sitting alone recalling a night she once spent in the arms of (2) a rough man (a kickboxing champ), who in turn had later watched in anguish through binoculars as (3) a woman in the apartment across the street from his stood naked and spoke on the phone to (4) a former lover, who, at that very moment, was doing to (5) another woman what the woman on the phone was describing to him, and then, afterward, that other woman left his apartment and told of her adventure to (6) a close girlfriend, who later indiscreetly repeated it in the steam room of a health club to several barely loinclothed women, one of whom (7) had an obsessive attraction to (8) another listener in the sauna, who was the very woman just then placing her hands on Julian.

There had to be a last one; that was the last one. And then he became different. As is often the hope but rarely the case, the stimulus to change that Julian required was his wife's pregnancy, and then the effect was photon fast, a microwave conversion from boy to man, dog to human, unimaginative to imaginative, as he knelt on the bathroom floor and pressed his ear to Rachel's belly. The change that had been promised but not produced by their courtship, engagement, wedding, honeymoon, homemaking, even by his beloved brother's disappointment in him, had occurred at last. With this new growth, Julian's fingers swelled until his wedding ring could no longer be slipped off.

As if purging old toxins, his unconscious mind then spit up acidic dreams of jealousy. He would dream Rachel was ferociously promiscuous, and he would, restrained by invisible wires, watch her betrayals, or learn of them from casual friends or passing thugs or his own snickering parents. The dreams scorched him. He writhed, bound his hands in damp sheets, stripped the covers from Rachel until she swatted him, and he would awaken, nightmare-pounding and amazed. He had never felt jealousy in waking life, at least never at these temperatures, and never once, not a pale red ember, over his wife.

Otherwise, the end of other women's appeal was neither painful nor, considering how much energy he had spent over the previous twenty years pursuing and avoiding them, particularly disturbing. Rather it was like he had finally developed antibodies strong enough to keep his system clear of infection. He had never expected to be an elderly philanderer. He had always thought loyalty would win out, and when it did, with a small black-and-silver ultrasound photo (knees hiked to the chin, the sea-horse spine, the string-of-pearls vertebrae, the tiny fist of greeting), Julian looked at passing women with a feeling of gratitude and a fond, regretless farewell. It was a feeling, he later told Aidan, much closer to love than when he had longed to buy them food, walk them through parks, touch their cheeks. He saw them and he would hurry home to his wife, so eager was he to make love or stroke her hair or simply watch her maneuver that impossible abdominal luggage around the room. Even when he discovered, to his laughing astonishment, that pushing a stroller or wearing a Baby Björn was even more appealing to single women than a wedding ring or (according to one friend) walking beagle puppies, the women held no power over him, and his laughter was colored by relief.

During Rachel's pregnancy and for two more years, he was permitted to live in a gated garden with walls of flowering vines, long promised but never accurately described by music, and he felt, these thirty-three months (sleepless nights, sexless weeks, lingering fat thighs notwithstanding), that he was earth's most fortunate man. He longed—no matter the music around him—for nothing but slower days and endless evenings.

" 'Waterfront'! 'I Cover the Waterfront'!" Julian had found Rachel pressing his headphones against the striped armor of her belly. "That's your grandpa on lead vocals," she said, her chin on her chest, and Julian choked with love for her.

The question had occurred to him, then and later: If there had been no child, could he ever have become a real husband? He wondered if Rachel asked herself the same thing, though he believed back then that she never knew of his delayed arrival in the marriage. Either way, he did become a real husband. He loved how she was pregnant, then loved how she was as a mother, but he loved, too, how she was when they were alone, as if he were seeing her clearly only then, whether the child had clarified her or cleared up his blurry vision, sharpened his hearing to the tones of her voice. "What are you looking at?" she had asked, turning away from the enormous movie screen propped against the foot of the Brooklyn Bridge, to face him, floating on their blanket in the sea of people in the August dusk, lit in occasional flashes by the fires of the Civil War rolling toward Tara. He was staring at her, at this face he suddenly realized he'd never seen in detail before. "You are so . . ." He shook his head and took her hand. "True enough," she said.

"Never Gonna Love Anyone (but You)" ended, and his iPod offered a Liverpudlian pop star's country-western spoof, "No Inhibition," the chorus being, "*All my serotonin's done gone been reuptook.*" Julian began to sprint.

He had held hands and exchanged vows under flowering magnolia branches and supportive stars to the applause of friends and family. He had been present when a head crowned through the blood-red dawn of his wife's vulva. And he had sat immobile, thumbtacks piercing his throat and eyes, ready to tear the skin from his face, as that same little head was covered again by moss and blood-rich dirt. And he had come back from that day. One can. He could. Not all the way back, but far enough to realize that it was not the only thing that had ever happened or ever would happen to him, although there were days still, despite his efforts, when he could barely manage to hope that anything would ever happen again, and he would quote animal television or songs to himself and get in the shower, just get in the shower and get out of the shower.

Running from the shower to play her the song in his head, the last time he tried, overexcitedly bounding from a weeping shower to play her the song that would fix it all: What was the song? What song could have explained anything at all? That mix-tape urge, the well-plucked quote, the song that would hit the right note and express what he could not; it was a romantic-comedy myth and, like all of them, useless once you'd hurt each other badly enough. (Of course, his job was to fill the airwaves with even less plausible myths, that joy and love were found in yogurt containers and hair fixative, for example, though, to be fair, he'd once believed that even this was sort of true, once.)

Rachel coming to a set in the middle of shooting, presenting him with a gift: a canvas director's chair with GENIUS stitched across its back strap. It was a bite-and-smile ad, early in his career, and contrary to the seat, he was failing at it, and beginning to panic slightly, when Rachel arrived. There was chip dust and nausea in the air, take 44 or 444 or 4,444, the poor actor visibly sickened now at the sight of the approaching chip—what had the the line been? *That's more crunch than a man can stand.* "Seriously? Oh, my God, Jules, you can't make him do that again," Rachel insisted. "He'll have grounds to sue you, and I'll represent him." And what had she done exactly? Somehow lightened the mood, relaxed the product manager, brought the actor a drink, and whispered something to him, touched him on the shoulder, somehow achieved what Julian couldn't.

Julian reached his front door, and the iPod offered some modal monks, a craze of twenty years before for Gregorian chant, reminding even the savviest ad guy that you can just never, ever know what might hit. He stood on his stoop in the icy rain and spun the dial looking for that Irish singer.

7

"BABY BOY," said his brother, looking up from Julian's couch where he hovered over pens, maps, and forms like a vulture over carrion. "You run in this weather? Self-hatred."

Julian battled his slurping shoes. "I feel like we said twelve o'clock. And I feel like I never gave you a new key."

"A man of deep feeling, but clumsy with facts."

Aidan, older than Julian by almost a decade, had for many years won what passed for a living from his arsenal of facts. Wielding five jagged, unfinished master's degrees—paleontology, criminology, Russian literature, social work, and Ottoman history; his business card read "Aidan F. Donahue, A.B.D. (mult.)"—he wrote crossword puzzles and entries for encyclopedias of various arcana, as well as friction fiction for gentlemen's magazines (under the name Anna Karenin, as whom he also answered lifestyle and intimate grooming questions). He competed in drawings, radio call-ins, magazine sweepstakes, trivia nights in bars (where he hustled by playing drunk and dim in early rounds to juice the betting, answering "Henry the ninth" or "You know, that king who looks like a playing card"). He had contracted by age fifty-four a chronic inability to wed or cook, though he had a useful case of obsessive-compulsive disorder, and his miniature, rent-controlled apartment—closing in from all sides with books and games—was, where possible, alphabetical.

Tuesday nights, having elided certain facts, he was slightly paid by an understaffed community mental-health center to lead a support group for divorced fathers. His near degree in paleontology served just as well as one in psychology would have, and Aidan was legitimately therapeutic for the distraught dads who had bonded with young sons over the study of dinosaurs and now, with limited custody, were burdened with highly emotional expertise in a field their supersonically aging children had tired of under their pooh-poohing mothers' roofs. Group therapy scored rapid successes as all thwarted solid paternal emotion was sublimated into gassy arguments over whether T. rex had feathers. "That's okay," Aidan consoled. "You have a right to feel that."

Outsiders who knew both brothers were rare, but they could reasonably have expected Aidan to grimace from envy of his younger brother's wealth, glamour, suavity. Aidan was the taller, but beyond the long nose over the puppety overbite and the lower lip buried under a miswoven shag rug of black beard, he lacked Julian's symmetries and modern packaging. And yet, despite his high-top sneakers and pill-dispensing cardigans, his sea serpent's breath and perennially pollinating dandruff, he viewed Julian with a steady and loving condescension, equal but opposite to the fond condescension the younger man felt for him. Aidan said pityingly more than once to his own laughter, "Peewee, you grew up so much in the old man's shadow, you should really only have one good leg: the one that got some sun."

"I've advanced to the third round," he said today, drumming his palms arrhythmically on the papers coating Julian's square table of green-edged glass. "And I could use your help. They want to know what color Jaguar I want if I win. I'll never drive the death trap, but for resale value, what do you advise?"

Aidan journeyed into the thickets of his world for weeks and months, answering his phone or not, based on nothing Julian could ever identify (except around the time of the Incident), then returned to Julian's civilization without fanfare, as if he'd seen his brother only yesterday. His life struck outsiders, sometimes even Julian, as relentlessly depressing and claustrophobic, scraped together from the slightest opportunities, led in crooked spaces, under low, flaking ceilings, constrained by unforgivingly binding finances. But Aidan was an optimist, and from these unpromising materials he lathed a life of romance, provoking and then tilting against his enemies—game-show producers, patent-office clerks, rival domain-name claim jumpers—with a zest for combat.

"You're looking spry, Cannonball," Aidan said to his brother, who was basketing sweats and slush-spattered socks. He looked Julian over just once before returning to the precision work of adhering a Racing Green sticker to a black spot on the sweepstakes form. "A new Boleyn on your arm?" Aidan appointed himself the keeper of all personalities he came to love, most especially Julian's, and he viewed them as objective and immutable, to be rigorously preserved in their original state. His common criticisms, "That's not like you" and "That's beneath you" and in Julian's case "You're so like Dad, J, it kills me," reflected his belief in his loved ones' factual better natures. He strove to rinse his brother of the corrosions of cynicism, self-admiration, and philandering, for all of which corruption he blamed their father. "She won't bring you any joy, you know."

Among Aidan's most remarkable views—held either out of sincere belief or merely for the delight of proving them to lesser minds who had the audacity to debate him, and then immediately disproving them once the lesser minds capitulated—views as varied as "Shakespeare produced nothing but meretricious pap" and "Slavery is by no means obviously evil"—most confounding to Julian was Aidan's dislike of music. Not indifference, but active dislike. "There's one Bach sonata that I can just about bear," Aidan would cede, implying an extensive effort to give music a fair chance. "But music is, at the very minimum, inflammatory, exclusionary, divisive, encouraging of snobbery and solipsism."

"Can you make this stop?" Aidan now asked vaguely, waving at the air as if bees were approaching his ragged beard with colonial intent. "I tried to turn on your television, but your vast array of remote controls stymied me. You obviously buy the same brand for each device to make it impossible for visitors to control your environment, and then you take narcissistic pleasure in being called to rescue them, infantilizing them and making of yourself a heroic figure."

Julian walked to the stereo, passing the bookshelf and rubbing the balding spine of a red velour photo album for luck, then turned off the quiet voice and guitar of João Gilberto. "You entered on your own and picked up a remote control in my absence, and that was due to my narcissistic tendencies?"

"A red herring, sir. You could have invited me in, told me to make myself at home, summoned the vicious squawking music all by yourself, and I would have been powerless to squelch it, even with all these glittering black simulacra of deistic control laid out before me like so many thunderbolts. But you will tolerate no Zeus but yourself." Aidan spoke without looking up, intent as he was upon sketching on one of his contest forms, smiling behind his mustache at the geometric perfections and pretzel logic of his psychological profiling. "The administrators require," he said of his drawing resembling a maze, "a map to get to my apartment to deliver the prize."

There was no point mocking Aidan's credulity by asking why the sweepstakes prize van would have any trouble negotiating Manhattan's numbered streets. Julian couldn't guess what the answer would be, but he knew it already existed, and he didn't ask. Aidan told him nevertheless, having sensed that someone could suspect him of foolishness or credulity: it was *not* because the prize committee actually needed a map but rather that they had "no corporate interest in engaging in an enterprise with a partner in whom cynicism is so dominant that he cannot even agree to play a simple game. If I laughed at the map, as *you* do, they would know that I would laugh at them when accepting their money. They don't want Bobby Fischer holding up the giant check with a sneer . . ." He trailed off, looked down. Bobby Fischer was an unfortunately apt example, Aidan's whirring gears stamping the analogous coin before he could stop himself. "Rachel sends her love," he concluded, clumsily collaring a new subject and prematurely mumbling the message he'd meant to lay out later, with more finesse and alcohol.

Aidan had come for lunch with Julian as a tentative ambassador, empowered to discuss semi-reconciliation by the sister-in-law whom he had loved since she nursed him after the Incident. But the inadvertent Bobby Fischer reference brought to his mind the Incident brought to mind the woman he credited with saving his life afterward brought to mind that she had asked him to test the waters in Julian's home, and then the words were out—"Rachel sends her love"—self-revelatory in a hundred ways, the embarrassing autonomy of his intricate and rigidly trained mind.

"You see her much, do you?" Julian changed direction, flopped in a towel onto the chair across from Aidan, feeling almost equal to the task of mapping his brother's patterns of thought.

The pejorative "know-it-all" is no more fair than any other applied to some poor outcast who did not choose and cannot control an unpopular trait. Aidan had liked producing the answers since as early as he could recall; he couldn't help it. A rare question he could not answer: When did you first feel that perfect inner completeness that comes from answering a question posed by a teacher, a parent, another child, a TV-cartoon professor?

Aidan could not relax in the presence of unanswered trivia, and to be cut off mid-answer was *physically* uncomfortable, a sour taste in the throat and an ache in the rectum. (Julian, age six: "How do you spell *parrot*?" Aidan, age sixteen: "P-A-R–" Julian: "Wait, no, I know it, R-O-T, right?" Aidan: "Please don't do that. Please don't ask me if you know the answer.")

Considering some people's negative reaction at being shown up by a child, Aidan could never be certain of receiving praise for being right. The only unwavering approval came from his mother and, later, from Julian, but only when Julian was between four and thirteen years old and saw in the giant genius an almost unearthly being. (Julian, age twelve, puzzling over a biology textbook: "How do we know Lamarck is wrong and Darwin is right?" Aidan, age twenty-two: "Cannonball, if Lamarck was right, we'd both have one leg.") So, in an environment usually annoyed by him, it must have been genetic, this pleasure in knowing something about everything. If, by the way, Lamarck is wrong and the other fellow right, then Aidan's genetic mutation might have shown some usefulness, either for earning or for mating. It didn't. His dominant personality trait was therefore dismissable by evolutionary biology as irrelevant (one of the reasons that for many years Aidan tried to defend intelligent-design theory; it would have been nice to feel he existed for a good reason).

By the time he was fifteen, having the facts at his fingertips was so essential and habitual to him that he defined himself as that—knowledge itself, a superhero or Greek god of data. And with that conscious self-identification, a loop began to carve itself in his mind. As with dance students who feel, as they improve, that the music they have long practiced to must be slowing down, so Aidan's speed of recall and reply had always to accelerate or he felt not just his quirky powers failing but he himself, his soul, melting away from inside him, as if he were being deboned, leaving only a heap of flabby skin and spotty beard to be stomped on and torn by all the world's passing cleats and high heels. When he moved to New York in his early twenties, when speed was still paramount to him, he was answering all questions—even from strangers asking directions in the subway—as if he not only had the answer but had even known that *that* question was going to be asked. His reply would begin most pleasurably before the question finished.

And so, the Incident. Aidan was fifty-three when, in peak mental condition, he scaled to the apex of the television game-show mountain and in that thin and pure air was accepted to compete on *Jeopardy!*, a trivia contest whose gimmick was the reversal of questions and answers (Quizmaster: "Its capital is Paris." Contestant: "What is the capital of France?"). This show had long loomed as Aidan's destiny, watched obsessively, statistically analyzed, trained for, auditioned for again and again, meditated over, contemplated with teachers and trivia-bar comrades and the two sufficiently drunk girls in college whom he once convinced to play strip Trivial Pursuit with him, but whom he then released, with his apologies, before things went too far.

The day came. He performed well, unseating a champion and then holding that title himself for two more days, winning more cash than he had earned in the previous three years, before his ghastly end.

The fourth day, endowed with purpose, as if fulfilling an ancient prophecy, he opened the game by quickly clearing two categories: "Space Travel" and "The Underworld." With only a few seconds before a commercial break, Aidan selected "Whose Fault?" for $1,000. The host read out the question beaming white-on-blue from millions of screens across the country:

> THE 1347 BLACK DEATH WAS
> CAUSED BY YERSINIA PESTIS,
> CARRIED TO EUROPE BY THESE
> UNWELCOME INTERLOPERS.

Aidan clicked his signal button, the podium lights circling his name illuminated, the host called Aidan's name, and Aidan, with the same look of stern satisfaction he had worn for three days, replied: "Who are the Jews?"

Fans of the show, and Aidan's brother and friends, long debated whether the episode should have been broadcast at all, or whether this single moment could have been edited out. But if it had, how would anyone have understood Aidan's cement silence for the remaining twenty-two minutes or his refusal even to make a guess for the game's final, written question?

"Ohhh, nnnnnnoooo," came the host's pained reply. "Saul?"

"What are rats?" the furious competitor to Aidan's left nearly shouted, though the director perversely (or in paralyzed wonder) kept the camera on Aidan, whose face now displayed an amazing array of legible thought, projected with clarity even through his beard and mustache and glasses. He had known the answer was "Rats"—it was a gimme. They would have accepted "fleas" as well. He did not believe, had never believed, that Jews carried the plague. He had never held an anti-Semitic belief in his life. He didn't hate any group, except idiots, defined as anyone less intelligent than Aidan but who believed himself to be more intelligent. He had Jewish friends (though not for much longer in most cases). These thoughts visibly pass first.

Then comes the pain of having been not just wrong (a clenching around the nose and upper lip that his friends and family knew well) but having appeared insane, even evil, on national television. Then, as Aidan's eyes narrow and slowly move to his left in an unfortunate expression that TV translates as suspicion, the canny viewer will see that

Aidan is noticing only now that Saul Fish of Saint Louis Park, Minnesota, is definitely Jewish. Saul went on to answer nearly all the remaining questions, winning the game by a wide margin as Aidan simply stopped trying, his signal button dangling untouched at his side.

Aidan was not much comforted telling himself that the speed of synaptic connections required for high-stakes competitive trivia will cause the best players' brains to bypass, simply for convenience, certain neural gateways (such as self-censorship), and in the case of a brain like Aidan's, the risk of affectless information hitching a ride from one memory bank ("Carriers of Bacilli") to another ("Famous Racist Slurs," over the bridge word *interlopers*) was unavoidable.

Aidan, in the months between the recording and the broadcast, nearly convinced himself that the producers would avoid airing his disgrace to the nation. He even returned to trivia nights in bars from Harlem down through Brooklyn and onto Staten Island, where one Saturday he hustled well enough to finish four hundred dollars up and still leave the local quizzicists believing he'd just been lucky. That night, feeling almost himself again, he came home, turned on the television, and saw the ad he'd recorded months before, in the studio before taping his first game, "Hi, I'm Aidan Donahue of New York City. Watch me this Monday on *Jeopardy!* right here on WABC." His victorious debut was forty-eight hours away; his foregone conclusion would follow seventy-two hours later.

Julian saw the same ten-second spot, surprised his brother hadn't mentioned being on the show, and assumed Aidan had suffered an early defeat and so kept a minor embarrassment to himself. He was therefore puzzled to watch Aidan's easy victory on Monday evening and yet be unable to contact his brother, leaving a congratulatory voice mail that Aidan listened to in tears. Tuesday's still more impressive victory, Wednesday's thoroughgoing destruction of his opponents, reminiscent of a Viking pillage of an undefended Kentish town, and Thursday's Incident were watched by Aidan's brother, his editors at various magazines and websites, the patrons at a dozen bars of his trivia-night circuit, the Jewish woman he had taken out twice in the interval, none of whom he had told, none of whom could reach him as he sat on the floor of his apartment, rocking, as the unmistakable theme music began.

Aidan's Thursday afternoon had passed in rising hopes and ebbing confidence, flash sweats sweeping the pencil from his fingers as he tried to compose a crossword. It was coming, tonight, in an hour, in minutes—maybe they just skipped this episode and blamed a spoiled tape—no, there he was, "Space Travel," "The Underworld," any moment now, and now: "Who are the Jews?," and then all of time screeched to a halt, and Aidan's flesh burst into flame, and then the universe, having shrunken to a single dimensionless dot, exploded outward in poisonous ripples and scalding dust. The empirical fact ("no longer a matter of scholared disgreement") of Jewish responsibility for the bubonic plague seeped onto Islamo-fascist and Holocaust-denial websites with intellectual pretensions, footnoting the scientifically unimpeachable work of biohistorian Dr. Aden Donald Hughes, Ph.D. Aidan's income dried up for months, requiring a careful budgeting of the *Jeopardy!* winnings. He was blackballed from trivia bars and denied writing assignments, even those related to pubic grooming. He watched (as did millions of others) the late-night sketch-comedy routine in which an actor with a motorized, knee-length black beard and magnifying-lens spectacles plays *Jeopardy!* against a hooded Klansman and Elie Wiesel with the categories "Slurs," "Jew Evil," "Those Troublesome Darkies," "Subhuman Races," and "Justifiable Child Murder." (Wiesel pulls off a stunning upset.) He duly and hourly Googled himself (an exercise that had previously returned very few and very accurate hits) and read the dozens of editorials from publications around the nation that shredded him to make a potpourri of points: "The Underwiring of the Freudian Slip" (*Psychology Today*), "Burned in the Melting Pot" (*The New York Times*), "Jews in Jeopardy" (*Commentary*), "Good Question, That: Who, Indeed, *Are* the Jews?" (*American Jewish World*), "Mistakes in Knowledge vs. Mistakes in Taste: Editing the High-Speed Trivia Show" (Gameshows.com), "Saul Fish: Our Prince" (*Temple Beth Israel Newsletter*), and "The Year's 10 Most Grotesque TV Moments" (*Entertainment Weekly*—Aidan's grainy face, with his eyes malignantly shifted all the way to the right, filling the magazine's cover). He received a single job offer during this time, a superficially

THE SONG IS YOU | 49

plausible request to submit work for a projected *Golden Treasury of Improving Children's Verse*, a helpful sample of which was enclosed for guidance with the offer:

> *A mathematician of Jewish descent*
> *For Christ our Lord's murder refused to repent.*
> *With wily logic algebraic*
> *He remained staunchly Hebraic,*
> *And so to eternal impalement was sent.*

He noticed with pained shock and then weepy horror and then muttered grumbling the sudden apparition of stickers and stenciled graffiti all over New York bearing the image of his own mournful, disoriented face at the very instant after his infamous reply. Dozens and then hundreds of him gazed, befuddled and shameful, from subway-car doors and stop signs and traffic-light control vaults and newspaper boxes and car bumpers and the sides of delivery trucks and, huge, on bedsheets suspended from the overpasses of expressways. He received scolding and congratulatory letters, even wedding proposals, though he was by then fully committed to his stumbling steps toward a deep breakdown, at the bottom of which the only voice that caught him and slowly and unsteadily hoisted him back to the surface was that of his nearly-ex sister-in-law, Rachel.

She reached him not through overt pity—when Aidan was no longer returning Julian's calls or opening up for the Chinese-food guy, only slipping money under the door—but simply by leaving a message saying she had done some research and learned that Aidan's ubiquitous face was the work of an art student who had created the black-and-white schematic image to fulfill an assignment for a class on Viral Marketing. And Aidan, at last, returned someone's call.

He came to her apartment, and she welcomed him with an expression of such open love and kindness that he felt tricked and was about to turn back and scurry home. At the last moment she corrected her face and said, as coldly as she could, "I've learned something that may interest you, a strange fact or two." That brought him into the apartment, bare-walled and oddly furnished, as she'd only recently left Ju-

lian's. She spoke carefully of the facts: the art student had begun selling the stickers and stencils from a website to map how quickly an
image could disseminate through a community's consciousness, but
now he was making real money, thanks to the dazzling speed of
Aidan's face's proliferation. With Rachel's pro bono legal assistance,
Aidan negotiated a percentage of the site's revenues, and a fair
restoration of his income resulted. After that he found himself at her
door every evening and sometimes more often, waiting on her step
when she was out, finally accepting a key and a dedicated couch.

And so today the premature revelation leapt out: "Rachel sends
her love."

"You see her much, do you?" Julian asked, tightening his towel.

"Did you hear about the surgical procedure they approved?"
Aidan recovered. "It was in the paper today. A new technique reduces
the number of open-heart surgeries, turns them into just lasery, scopy
things, out of the hospital in a day." He sucked his teeth. "And then
all the incivility to follow."

The Aidan non sequitur challenge. After their regular Wednesday
dinners with him, Rachel and Julian used to debate whether Aidan
truly thought his listeners made such conversational leaps with him or
whether he intentionally gutted all the connective tissue so that the
listener would beg Aidan for enlightenment. You were certainly not
allowed to blithely agree, not just inattentively say, "Absolutely right,
Aid." He would see at once you were humoring him.

Rachel always insisted that either possibility was the behavior of a
sweetly childlike mind, a prodigal boy's brain, enjoying its own
strength or showing it off, and that if Aidan had a weakness, it was
only his inability to see that most people simply did not care. "Which
is really a most enviable strength," she'd once said. Julian, who would
normally have defended Aidan against anyone (reserving for himself
the right to mock him), would take the role of attacker after these
Wednesday dinners, simply to enjoy watching how easily and gladly
Rachel would leap to the barricade. "He's his own species," Julian
complained, and she corrected him: "He's his own man." Rachel's
easy love for Aidan reminded Julian of their mother, Pamela, the last
woman who had been Aidan's defender, thirty years before.

"You don't know what I mean, do you?" Aidan asked, shaking his head at Julian. "Why don't you just say so if you're lost?"

"All right, I'll bite. What incivility follows from less open-heart surgery?"

"Don't patronize me," Aidan fired back. "It's beneath you. Where are you taking me for lunch?"

8

A PIECE OF MUSIC'S CONQUEST of you is not likely to occur the first time you hear it, though it is possible that the aptly named "hook" might barb your ear on its first pass. More commonly, the assailant is slightly familiar and has leveraged that familiarity to gain access to the crisscrossed wiring of your interior life. And then there is a possession, a mutual possession, for just as you take the song as part of you and your history, it is claiming dominion for itself, planting fluttering eighth notes in your heart.

The exact moment of infection: Julian Donahue is standing on the F-train platform at York Street, in front of a peeling poster decorated with a supine rat with its tongue lolling from under Xed-out eyes, cheerfully advising that rodenticide has recently fumed the area. On the floor, near his foot, as ready proof, there is a tightly wound golden-red coil of rodential innard. On closer inspection, it is a shiny, springy clip-on tornado of exotic hair extension, a follicular concoction molted from a Brooklyn head of arabica-latina-afra-italian curls, and the sight of bunched hair (even fake hair) against the dirt of the floor reminds Julian of Rachel's incurable phobic refusal to remove the gritty, soapy hair-jellyfish from the shower drain: "Just step up, mister," she had told her new fiancé, "because I never, ever do it." The Irish girl is on Julian's iPod, and this time—why *this* time?—this time, the hi-hat figure at the opening of "Coward, Coward" prophesies the hissing arrival of the F train, and the man next to Julian is drenched through with sweat. Sweat streams off him in rivers onto his workout clothes and his blue gym bag held in a brown hand with knuckles gray and cracked. Carlton used to ride in a pack of the same blue material on Julian's back, and on trains he would "hoo-hoo-hoo!" a whispered shout of delight into Julian's neck, and the bass line weaves in and out of the hi-hat—Julian hasn't noticed it before, this jigsawed interplay of the rhythm, propulsive, urging something up and on, and the sigh of the train's opening doors encourages the bass and drums in turn.

Julian steps aside to let off a well-dressed, blond-braided Scandinavian giantess who silently bumps her fist against the sweaty fist of the black man entering, and the Irish girl sings, "*'Will you leave no trace at all?' she asked him. / 'Will you leave no trace at all?'*" Rachel in a fight once: "Is this all there is of you? You're barely here. I can put my hand right through you," her fists thudding against his back in no way disproving her point. The Irish girl sings, over a low guitar and that braided bass and hi-hat, "*She wasn't asking him for a favor.*" This time Julian can't see the singer, doesn't bring her physical body to mind, so there are no bellows, no heaving breasts or writhing. This is only sound, how the blind hear music. The experience is detached not only from any rational cause—Swedish fist? Curled rodent extension? Hoo-hoo-hoo?—but from the source of the music as well: the Irish girl's body is nowhere accounted for in this blackboard-blanching equation. The disembodied voice filters all feeling and also causes it. The dense terrine of feeling in Julian—regret, hope, sorrow, faltering ambition, longing—startles him. It could not be produced in such concentration and quantity without the voice, and so, after this moment on the train platform, he comes to crave the voice because it reveals the feelings he could not find in silence.

And after that first shock of love comes trepidation. A younger Julian would have reset the needle, rewound the tape, replayed the track again and again, sucked the song down to its marrow until it held nothing but thick nostalgia, accessible only years later. But, older now, aware of how rare this experience was, he rationed "Coward, Coward." If it showed any signs of weakening, of becoming merely catchy, he skipped it, set his iPod back to shuffle and hoped the song would recharge, surprise him.

And the singer did. She wielded that bodyless, faceless, lipless, lungless, breastless voice, animating a different cluster of meaningless material each time. Two weeks later, in the silence after a Beethoven sonata finishes: the ornate pediment of a high-story window he'd never noticed before on a block he daily walked; a homeless man licking the inside of a jam jar with a thin and pointed tongue; Aidan's old story about how the sound of an unnecessary MRI reminded him of their late mother, Pamela (the machine's relentless magnetic-robotic chant of *pam!pam!pam!pam!pam!pam!*), as he lay in the heavenly white training coffin; the mist from a sidewalk fruit vendor's hose sprayed through his berries, sprinkling Julian's face, carrying their scent (triggering in turn the recollected aroma of a strawberry tea Julian had years ago been offered by a potential client in an interview for a Czech beer commercial), mixing with a sourceless breeze of free-range New York City garbage; and the silence after Beethoven ends, and the Irish girl sings, *"When it's all just flavor, and you've got none left to try."* She was telling him that she *knew*, she actually *understood* and could explain all of that—window, jam, *pam*, mother, fear, death, garbage, tea, work—could fit it all together in a pattern he didn't even know he'd been seeking.

He was not insane. He did not think it was anything but coincidence and crackling brain function. He did not believe she literally understood or wished to help *him*, but when the song was working—collecting and filtering and compressing sensation and offering it back to him—there was a wondrous bonus notion that the headphones were a unique two-way connection between his mind and that voice, which must therefore be aware of him.

9

THE IRISH GIRL performed that night. The crowd was larger, challenging the bar's legal capacity, and Julian thought she had changed in the last weeks, maybe even developed. She was slightly more coherent as a performer, as a projector of an idea and an image. The previous gig, something had distracted and dislocated her, as when color newsprint is misaligned and an unholy yellow aura floats a fractioned inch above the bright red body of a funny-pages dog. It had been perhaps the bass player's mistakes or, if the hipster snob was to be credited, the seductively whispering approach of success. No matter: she was clearer tonight, even if he could still see her strive, from one song to the next, for an array of effects: the casually ironic urban girl, the junkie on the make, the desperate Irish lass whose love was lost to the Troubles, the degenerate schoolgirl, the lover by the fire with skin as velvet succulent as rose-petal flesh. These shifting roles hung unevenly on her, a matter of youth, nervousness, or, most fatally, inauthenticity (whatever *that* is, which makes one hundred singers merely entertainers while the next is a transmitter of truth).

He tried to reconcile what he saw onstage with the effect her music had on him when she was not there. The gap was not unbridgeable, but it was an engineering problem, and he was disappointed with her for not living up to his headphone experiences, and disappointed with himself for having let music again lead him into fantasy when he certainly should have known better by now. Still, his professional reflexes set to work: if he'd been directing her in a music video, for example, he would have told her to let all her old ideas of singers go, all the women she'd wished to become when she was a girl, to forget all the voices she'd imitated and all the praise lavished on her, and simply to think instead about the lyrics, to imagine no one was listening or ever would, to sing despite herself, as if she meant to keep quiet but the songs kept breaking through. "Don't even think about whether *I* like it," he imagined himself having to remind her.

"Let's all have a drink then, all right?" she said, willing to cut short her whistles and applause. "And then we'll play more music. And then have another drink. And so forth." Even this implication of a churning Celtic thirst for booze seemed a put-on, though the younger men, hunched in troops or paired with briefly outshined dates, found the notion aromatic. He watched her move off the stage.

The band had not yet risen to the altitude of dressing rooms and backstage demands, so they occupied the end of the bar near the stage, far from Julian's shadowed post by the door. Some flannel yielded space to her. The rest of the band barricaded her, sliding stools across the floor. The bassist she'd scolded was pale and spotty, his thick, wavy hair gelled toward a central ridge, likely in the second month of filling in the flanks of a misguided mohawk. He wore a black velvet blazer built up at the shoulders: Bowie '83, Ferry '85. On her other side swayed the guitarist: gas-station shirt, truck-company cap, pale hiking boots: pure, uncompromising Seattle '92. The drummer: a Goliath with a shiny tan head and a neatly shaped soul patch, a statement that he could also play jazz or batter the fans of an enemy soccer team.

She dealt some card game Julian didn't recognize, and soon the four of them were slapping the bar and dropping coins and accusing one another of cheating. She had many roles to play, offstage but still swept by the public eye. She had to be one of the guys, albeit the one who was a girl. She had to be their boss and their foil, and she had to listen to their boasting and evasions, and to their thousand deniable kisses blown under their breath, for with a label in the future, the drummer and the bassist especially must have known how fungible they were. Rhythm sections must ingratiate on a steady beat, unless they are brilliant musicians (which these two were not), or her songwriting partner (the guitarist comfortably carried that aura), or her lover, which, Julian would now have bet, watching her offstage, none of them was. "That's *so* unfortunate, lads," she clucked, dragging the pot to her.

The crowd was almost entirely what Julian's world called "self-denying consumers," who vainly believe themselves unaffected by advertising. They weren't the sort to ask her to sign a napkin or pose for a phone photo, which left the young men milling about with no excuse to approach her. Still they milled. Even those with dates kept an eye on her at the bar, and she tolerated the cacophony of those buzzing male gazes with ivory nerves while Julian watched the calculations and consequences skim over the boys' faces: her time sitting semi-accessibly, unescorted, at any bar these fellows could afford was now countable in months if not weeks.

"Miss O'Dwyer?" opened the wisest boy, avoiding the others' informal "Cait?" "Miss O'Dwyer, may I buy you a drink, or should I just fuck off straightaway?"

There was much to be said for this line of attack, and she did reply:

"Very kind. Mine's still full, but you can top up Bass's glass, and if you don't mind losing at cards, you can pull up a chair."

The bassist glowered at the male intruder and snarled, "Yeah, top me up."

"Oh, be polite, Bass," Cait scolded. "We can't all be bassists."

At the other end, the bartender dealt Julian another round recycled-cardboard coaster off a pillar of them. "Same again? Say, you came to hear her before, right? You like?"

"It's all right."

"Come on," he said, pulling Julian's beer.

"It's all right."

"But it's not Glenn Miller, I hear you. Oh, no, wait . . ." The barman turned to the Irish beauty playing cards and back again. "You know her? Label guy? Lawyer? No? Dr. Feelgood? Oh, Captain, my Captain, are you her dad? No? The guy who checks in for the family and manages the trust fund and is desperate as donuts to bang her? No, no—*no! Ffffff*, I *knew* it: she swings gray. That hurts, won't deny it. And you can't deal with all this awful noise so you sit in the back and collect her discreetly at the end and squire her back to your mansion where you have sad sex in front of a dying fireplace while your butler watches through a hole in the wall. Awful. Oh, man, cut her loose. Ehhhh, but wait, you dress kind of gay. All right, I'm stumped." His biceps strained against the sleeves of his T-shirt, and his pectorals distorted its image of two suggestive Dominican monks kissing their fingertips under the calligraphic words: THE LAY BROTHERS. "You're not going to tell me, fair enough. But you really don't think she's flawless? And you're not gay or stupid? Must be generational."

"Even by your standards," Julian answered, "I can prove she's not flawless. I can think of ten things she could do to make her more what she wants to be, what *you* and all these others want her to be. She's an inefficient machine."

The band retook the stage, the music started again, the barman serviced other thirsts. And Julian proved his case and amused himself by illustrating the blank backs of eleven coasters, hiding his usual storyboard J.D. signature in various details, cartoons numbered 0–10, 0 being Cait O'Dwyer as she appeared tonight (under a yawning, bored

Cupid holding a drooping banner labeled A FAIR BEGINNING), then each successive drawing, captioned with his directorial advice, showing her with augmented power and allure until number 10: a glowing and levitating archangel of destruction spewing flames from her mouth, combusting saucer-eyed young men in flannel shirts, while a fellow with a clipboard and an embroidered J.D. on his lab coat's lapel nods approvingly, though still not impressed, perhaps a little tired. Each numbered, gnomic caption encircled its illustration: #1: Indulge no one's taste but your own. #2: Never fear being loathed and broke. #3: Repeat only what is essential; discard mercilessly. #4: Sing only what you can feel, or less. #5: Hate us without trepidation. #6: All advice is wrong, even this: a little makeup would not go astray. #7: Never admit to your influences, not dear Mum or Da, nor the Virgin Mary (competition). #8: Laugh when others think you should cry—we will gladly connect the dots. #9: Even now, cooing, swooning ghouls of goodwill scheme to destroy you. #10: Oh! Bleaker and obliquer. (Julian had by then, after eleven pretty good cartoons and several drinks, earned the right to make no sense at all.) "You can keep those," he said, pushing the coasters to the barman. "I suspect they apply to the Lay Brothers as well," and the barman–Lay Brother laughed his confession.

She'd probably see them, Julian thought, before throwing them away, or the bartender might take credit for them, casting Julian in the appropriate role of Cyrano. And then the hi-hat began "Coward, Coward," and he gave her his full attention, the effect of the music nearly as strong in person as it had been on the F train.

When she finished, he left at once, before anything could spoil. He went straight home, relieved to find an Aidanless apartment. He took a beer into his living room, and with his appetite for music sharpened by what he'd heard and felt at the Rat, he was soon caroming through his CDs, engrossed in a pointless musical idyll rare since the leisure of school days. He swung through his collection with what he felt was random compulsion, one song paused and blinking its consumed time after less than a minute because a chord or a voice or the liner notes reminded him of another song. This singer had something in common with that one, this guitarist with that, and he sprinted through his library, uncovering connections and evidence of relations—a shared session player, a common lyricist—like a drunken genealogist. Julian held this CD case, and the artist who filled it with music had once held *that* case. He pushed Play to prove it.

It took some more beer and listening to the Sundays before the illusion of randomness melted away: this gundog pursuit was of the Irish girl's influences. All the beloved songs he'd been driven to sample, they led to her, the genome of her talent, the roots of that increasingly potent demo. And now he burned through his discs even faster, confirming suspicions within seconds, spotting the Irish girl lurking in the undergrowth: a chord, a vocal trick, a way of singing over or against an instrument, a breath of phrasing: Billie, Ella, Janis, Alanis, Sinéad, Patti Smith, Edie Brickell, Annie Lennox. She'd likely deny Madonna and Stevie Nicks and Belinda Carlisle, but that didn't change the facts. He paused—almost panicked—when he realized he didn't own any music made since she was ten years old, but then he calmed down, decided that, whatever he was missing, she'd studied his favorites as classic texts, and he continued to draw conclusions: Nico, the Pogues, the Pixies, the Sugarcubes, the Sundays, PJ Harvey, Siouxsie, Courtney, the Cranberries, the Jam and the Clash and the Sex Pistols, Paul Westerberg, definitely Elvis and maybe Elvis, Iggy Pop, a U2 flyby, a sliver of Bowie, and Mick and Keith, of course, and Ray and Dave, of course, less John and Paul than Shaun and Paul, Moz and Johnny, and . . . Astrud and João? No, not Astrud, someone less restrained. Juliette Gréco? No, but nearly that. He chased the Irish girl through rainforests of Brazilian music, shoving aside melancholy bossa queens and feather-headed samba heroines, dipping into French imitators, Shirley Bassey remixes, Norwegian club DJs with bossa overtones, losing sight of his prey, losing faith he'd heard what he thought he'd heard, feeling foolish, drinking too much, and building teetering towers of CDs on the rug.

And then he remembered Elis Regina laughing, almost manically, near the end of *Waters of March* in 1974. Here it was, 3:11 into the song, and he had the Irish girl's trail again: she was there in the MGM Studios, Los Angeles, thirteen years before she was born. He was right; he knew he was right. He listened to the whole song twice, imagined her doing the same. He could tell what she had listened to, what she had taken in and taken on. And when he fell asleep, on his couch, just past three in the morning, it was to Cait O'Dwyer singing.

The window was open a drafty inch, and Julian smelled an early ion of spring, so he rolled to his side to find, next to him on the park's grass, Carlton, grabbing his toes and laughing while Julian stroked his head and fell in and out of dozing, as relaxed as a yogi willing to let a fly walk across his face. He closed his eyes, opened them again, the scents of spring in his nose, Carlton's soft hair under his hand, the squirrels coming close to the diaper bag smelling of milk and nuts, the Cait O'Dwyer demo still playing—no. No, he hadn't known this music then, so this was not the park, there was no grass, no more grabbing of toes.

10

OFFERINGS MADE TO CAIT O'DWYER between January and March 2009, abridged:

Copy of Rainer Maria Rilke's *Letters to a Young Poet*, from an amorous and resistible A&R assistant at the label. Forgotten, unopened and unmourned, on the B-61 bus back from Fairway.

39 invitations for drinks during set breaks at gigs, deflected with varying degrees of charm and irritation.

Drawings, tapes of original songs, and framed photos, from piano students, as good-bye and thank-you gifts.

Homemade muffins and cookies, from three mothers of students.

Rides home ending with wishes of good luck, warm embraces, overlong handshakes, and one outright lunge lipward, from fathers of students.

Invitation, left anonymously, to Bible-study group, citing Jesus' love for Cait.

Invitation, delivered in person, to film premiere by famous English film star who lived part of the year in Brooklyn, across the street from his ex-wife. Declined, with implied willingness to hear further invitations.

Eleven coasters with cartoons and insightful advice implying someone only half impressed with her, at most, someone described by Mick the barman as "moneyed-up, oldish, dignified in his cups, arrogant." Kept and reconsidered, coming as they did soon after an email from her mother warning her again of the fate of semi-successful musicians ("loathed or broke") and an evening's insecurity thinking she was less than the sum of her too-obvious influences and had no one to tell her anymore when she sucked.

2 demos from aspiring singer-songwriters, tough-waif division.

Flowers, flowers, flowers.

Offer from Martine and Rico on the second floor to set her up with a guy, a really good guy, a Web-designer friend, a sweet, sweet guy.

Wine, from uncle who had taken it upon himself to convert her from beer.

Tea samples.

A twelfth coaster, implying, half-convincingly, an indifference to actually meeting her, maybe more than half-convincing, considering Mick's story about being bribed . . .

They played a club in Poughkeepsie, and they were granted a private space upstairs, something less than dressing rooms but more than a reserved table. On a long buffet, covered by a stained and fraying paper tablecloth, a few plastic-wrapped sandwiches and bottles of beer were laid out by an old man in a filthy Brooklyn Dodgers cap.

They played well that night, and the club was full, and the crowd responded like fans. This felt like kind of a big deal, and also an omen, a nicely legible, freshly slit goose's entrails: they had followers waiting in places they'd never toured. Cait wanted to celebrate with Ian, but when they were done, and Prince, on the stereo, rattled the wooden stairs that led up to their loft, he wasn't there. Still sweating, she lay on a stuffing-spitting green couch and clawed at the hide of a navel orange. "Where's Ian?"

Drums drew a purple velvet pouch from his jacket pocket, and Cait threw orange peel at his face. "Don't be a git. Go outside with that." Drummers were so congenitally moronic, but still she felt her anger rising at Ian.

Drums complained but repocketed his crop. "I'll smoke on the ride home."

"Genius. Where's Ian gone?" She hated how she sounded.

"He's still down at the bar," Bass answered. "He's meeting some-one."

This did not mean, Cait soon learned, that he was downstairs trolling the shoals of the bar for a perquisite due a man in his position. No, according to Bass, he had *arranged* to meet someone. Ian, at that moment when he should have been drinking with Cait upstairs or fishing for easy pleasure belowdecks, was instead intertwining clammy fingers with his "girlfriend," whose existence Bass and Drums had known of for some days, maybe weeks, while Ian had been treat-ing Cait like . . . like . . . "What's her name?" she asked, allowing the weight of her boots dropping to the floor to pull her up to sitting. Drums brought her a beer. "Cheers," she said.

"Man, tonight *blistered*," Bass tried, reading the boss's mood. "Did you see the boys' faces during 'Blithering,' Cait? I think you caused some cardiac infarctions."

"Infractions," said Drums.

"Does she have a job?" She did better that time keeping her tone casual but was surprised how much effort it took. Ian was obviously free to intubate every young lady he saw, and Cait would never harbor the flimsiest dinghy of a grievance. But *this*, this secret girlfriend, was different: reckless and therefore hidden and therefore hostile. And she hadn't done anything to deserve it. They all knew the risks of starting serious relationships at this stage. It was almost self-sabotage, so he'd better have found a tremendous woman if he was going to gamble his future and Cait's on her. "Why aren't *you* fellows down there spattering your seed all about?"

The wooden stairs creaked, and the couple sprouted headfirst from below. "This is Chase," Ian said, holding her hand above his head, announcing her victory in a heavyweight bout. Then he dropped her arm and mumbled introductions: "Chase, Cait, Tim, Zig, Chase." The men tilted their heads back until noncommittal "Hey"s emerged, to which Chase murmured "Hey" and "Hey" in turn. Ian had a sensation in his stomach he associated with compulsory childhood guitar performances for his parents' friends. He could still just say, "See you guys tomorrow" and escape with something, but instead he stood there, as he had at crucial moments in the past, so everything that followed was his own stupid fault.

"Sit with us, please," Cait said, and patted the couch on either side of her. She pointed at Drums and Bass and said to Chase, "These two vultures are bleeding the life out of me. I'm gasping for proper conversation." Chase—prim in jeans and blouse, as if she'd tried but failed to dress down for the occasion—accepted the space to her right, and Ian—jackass! loser!—could not resist simply doing whatever Cait instructed, stepped over her boots to take his assigned seat. "You're quite a sport to come all this way to watch your man play." Cait took her guitarist's hand in her own. "Will you come fetch him every time? It gives us more room in the van. Oh, you have the *most* beautiful eyes. They're *violet*."

"Oh, my God, *thank* you. I love—I don't know if Ian told you—you must get tired of hearing it—but you have, your voice is just, really, it's spectacular."

"Your boy's guitar helps." Cait squeezed his knee. "But thank you."

Cait complimented Chase's clothes and hair, laughed at her mild jokes. She gave the potentially band-killing intruder her cell number, unasked, and Chase thumbed it into her high-end phone with obvious delight. She was so clearly the sort of girl who was going to start asking her boyfriend if he *really* had to go to band practice because tonight is our two-month anniversary and is that gig *really* one you have to take because my sister's coming to town and I so want you to meet, and oh my God, Cait called yesterday, I'm so sorry I forgot to tell you, I hope it wasn't important. "We should have a girls' night back in the city," said Cait, still holding Chase's boyfriend's hand.

Ian decided to ram his head through the wall but instead meekly asked his boss's permission to play pool: "I think I'll play some pool." He waited for his hand to be released.

Chase was flattered to receive the focused attention of the beautiful rising star her boyfriend only spoke of in the vaguest professional language, and whom he now ignored even as she held his hand, which was only natural, not threatening, considering their long-standing friendship and work. Chase had seen it tonight when they performed. There was no reason Ian should deny it, but he was trying so hard to deny it, and in the meantime the singer was being so sweet to her, in a European sort of way: "Of course he's with you—a real, natural beauty. He is, you must know, awash in rather unhygienic offerings every night. A dim sum cart, but decidedly unappetizing."

"I'm playing pool now," he insisted. Cait smiled at him, waited, waited, waited, and then released his hand.

"Are you a pool player, Chase?" she asked as Ian counted the balls and swore, then descended to hunt the missing number six under chairs and behind the ancient mini-refrigerator. "Really? Never? But you must keep up with him. When he tires of being a rock-and-roll idol, his next career will be a pool-hall hustler. Although he can't beat me, which infuriates him, you know. Unless he's pretending to lose because I'm his boss."

Ian lay on his stomach and swept an arm under the tablecloth, standing with his prey and a dozen aroused dust bunnies. "You have never beaten me. When I'm sober."

Cait's phone shook and hummed, and she peered at the screen. "Ech, I think this is an arse I have to kiss," she said, leaning in to share with Chase this secret of the music business, the necessity for occasional insincerity. "Please don't go yet, this will just take a minute."

And Ian, ever the model of inertia and momentum, played pool in silence and abandoned his date to the rhythm section. He didn't mean to make her feel unwelcome or unimportant, as she later accused. He was just paralyzed (in the form of a pool player), and therefore taking his cues from Cait. Chase could sense some of this. A less proficient reader of human nature than Chase would have seen that Ian did what Cait told him to do. That alone would have been troubling enough to a new girlfriend, comparing the pool player with the sweet and cool guy who had, three weeks ago, seen her in an Arab grocery, made a funny comment about chickpeas, taken her to a museum for a Danish movie and then a bar where they played *pétanque* indoors.

"How's Chase?" Cait asked him a week later, feeling guilty, trying to atone for her performance, though, read the transcript, she had only been *nice*, and not sure she wouldn't have been justified in being much worse, if only to make him see what was at stake. "I like her."

"Yeah, she liked you, too."

"Do you guys—"

"What do you want to work on?" he asked.

After Chase broke up with Ian (during which protracted negotiations he actually said, in a pathetic moment, for which he would have injected any narcotic directly into his throbbing neck to erase from his memory, "But I'm practically a rock star"), he met another girl. This time he determined that Cait would never know, and the new girl would never see Cait. But this new girl, a gypsy dressed as a real-estate agent, alarmingly intuitive and proud of it, just kept guessing correctly. She was drawn to gaps in his stories like cigarette smoke sliding in between the fibers of his gig shirts, and as soon as her glance caressed a weak joint, his life cracked and tender secrets spilled out. "My man is a mean man," she purred when she left for the last time.

Cait was like Ian's older brother, able to rig water balloons to closet doors, willing to be far away at the moment of triumph, not even needing to see the splashed and vanquished little foe, happy even if, over dinner that night, Ian didn't mention it, wouldn't admit to the disgrace, and so his brother's polite request for the potatoes would carry in it a war whoop and the icy restatement of his everlasting superiority, like a conqueror's edict pasted to every lamppost in a broken and occupied city.

Ian lay on his floor with his feet up on his amp and tried to learn new chords out of a book, his fingers sprawling to sound a flat 9 and a sharp 11, straining to hear why jazz guys bothered with them. He built a wobbly C7♭9♯11♭13, whacked at it over and over again. The phone sang, almost in tune, and Cait murmured from the answering machine: "Hello, darling, dazzling rock star." Ian stopped thrashing the miserable chord. "I am thinking of you just now." He sat up, and with effort did not pick up the receiver. "And my mum always said you must tell people when you're thinking of them, in case they're run over by a bus, and you later regret missing the opportunity." He laughed despite himself. "And so, today, having said that, this would now be your day to step in front of a bus, if you must. Not saying you *should*. Up to you, of course, only that I would have a clearer heart. Failing that, I rather feel like a brainstorm. Do you have any nice new music for me, genius? Can I come over?"

She began at ruthlessness; ruthlessness was the starting point of her every action; her every word could be traced back to her ruthlessness, like a river system rushing across a whole country, powering mills and irrigating farms and drowning little children in blue overalls. He couldn't hope to be as ruthless as she, but he could play along. So he mustered relish and a dash of smug frat-boy hilarity, but it didn't really suit him. He could only fight feebly and from the shadows, like a sickly ninja. He didn't expect to scare off her suitors in person. So, when Drums reported that Cait had been asked to dinner by a famous English actor who'd seen them play at the Rat, Ian, overwhelmed with cardiac evidence of his desperate courage, printed out Web pages detailing the man's sexual antics, the divorce-court testimony of his drunken racism and adulterous excesses, and the item that in the end did offend Cait's otherwise tolerant sensibilities: his TV commercial in Japan for a fishery that Greenpeace said slaughtered dolphin. Ian left this indictment anonymously for Cait at the Rat.

She of course smelled Ian's complicit air. If he thought he was being sly, she was willing to let him have his moment, as toddlers require a certain sense of growing self-sufficiency or their development will stunt. And she was shriven of any sin for Chase.

And she rejoiced. The end had come at last—thank sweet Saint Cecilia, who protects pious girls and their bands—of backstage sweethearts who thought it acceptable to call Ian's cell two minutes before stage time and demand that he whisper anxiously into his cupped hand for fifteen minutes until he would close his phone with a mumbled curse and an apology to Cait and shuffle onstage to play guitar as if he was sight-reading from a book of show tunes for a geriatric orgy.

No, huzzah, Ian was conducting himself appropriately again, providing a scratching post for the nails of roaming club felines before leaving them on the roadside, tied in a sack. In Raleigh-Durham the evidence suggested he had serviced a pair of them at once, though he was chivalrously silent the next day when he arrived in Greensboro, a cheeky six minutes before soundcheck.

"You still stink of them, baby," she whispered in his ear as he played his solo on "Blithering" that night, and she saw the hair on his neck hunch and stagger, and all was well. She could put a name, only now, to the feeling that was pouring out and away from her like ebbing tidewater contaminated with sewage: it was departing *fear*, and hanging over the fear, like fumes over that sewage, was *shame* that she of all people had been afraid without even knowing it, and now she felt light fearlessness returning. If she were not onstage, in the middle of a song she had discovered in that space that manifested itself—like some state of quantum physics—only when she and Ian stood a certain distance from each other and concentrated on their own questions, she would have wanted to punish someone for her fear and shame. But she *was* onstage, and he *was* playing her music, and it *was* sounding like she'd dreamt, in literal dreams of music she'd had for nearly twenty years, since that morning when she was almost four and woke sobbing, beyond any parental consolation for nearly an hour, because the music she'd heard when she was sleeping wasn't playing when she woke, and she couldn't make it come back. ("Where is it?" she insisted to her smiling and uncomprehending parents. "Where's the music gone? Why won't you play it again?" She slapped her father's legs and fell weeping into her mother's lap. "Please, play it, *please*.")

11

AFTER THE INCIDENT, the edges of Aidan's personality softened, became porous, as they had after their mother's death (but not their father's). He became vulnerable to doubts about his reality or past. And then the borders sealed up again, and Aidan resolidified. When Rachel gently asked him to move out, after seven weeks' rest stay, it was because she saw him regaining his shape.

After dinner one night he said, "Thank you, Rachel, for everything," and she patted his hand and answered, "Please, you're welcome, but I haven't done anything you wouldn't do for me."

And he nodded but then started—unavoidably and visibly—to think. "Do you think it could've happened to you?" he asked.

"Aidan, you're just much smarter than I am, so I don't know how I would've ever been in a position to make that mistake. I could never be on a game show, you know."

"I know," he snapped, then recovered. The driblet of dopamine at being called *smarter*, the evaporation of it at the word *mistake*, his inability, despite maneuvering, to make her spontaneously recite the soothing formula "Yes, it could have happened to anyone (of a certain incalculably rare intelligence)": Rachel recognized these signs of his vigorous health, and she smiled at her work, which annoyed him. "Stop grinning like a chimp. If you *were* on a show like that, it could've happened to you, too."

"That's hard to say, Aidan." She was teasing now, happy to see him back to his old self. "You have a very special mind, you know. I can't even imagine how you hold all that information in your—"

"Yes, yes, yes." He'd heard that twitty compliment (the awe one feels for a freak) all his life. "But if you *were*, or could, just put yourself in my shoes and imagine, you *could* have done the same thing I did, right?"

"I don't know, Aidan," Rachel said in measured tones.

"Why not? How can you not know? You have all the empathy that God gave to humankind. You got *all* of it. I obviously got none. So answer me," he demanded, desperate to hear Rachel admit that she could have accidentally slandered an entire religion in the middle of a game show. "I mean, you've said the wrong thing in your life, haven't you?"

"I suppose so."

"Suppose? Term of avoidance. Have you never done anything without being able to stop yourself?"

"Of course I have," she said softly, and Aidan regretted at once having pushed her to think of all that. But still he couldn't stop himself from marking his Pyrrhic victory: "So it *could* have happened to you. *Thank* you."

He moved back home the next day, just in time. He had come to love Rachel, not surprisingly, even as he desperately wanted her to return to his brother. The strength of that second desire surprised him more. He had fallen in love, over seven weeks, with the idea of her returning to Julian. He missed their Wednesday-night dinners, how he relaxed in their company, the only people on earth around whom he could relax. He missed keeping autistic count of the glancing touches and touching glances between them, missed the way Julian acted toward him when Rachel was around, missed how she made Julian laugh in a way Aidan could not. Obviously these recollections dated from before Carlton, but still.

And when he moved out, he expressed his gratitude in those terms. He bent forward to hug her, their bodies meeting at the shoulders, forming in profile a rickety inverted *V*. He said, "I'll do anything to help you two come back to each other." His beard draped over her shoulder, and he smelled something spicy in her hair. He forced himself upright to stare at the ceiling through his off-kilter glasses, and he blinked rapidly, trying to smell something else. "He's a cretin if he won't beg you to come back." And then she was crying, and Aidan recklessly promised, "I can bring him to you, whenever *you* want him back."

Rachel's adoption of Aidan had not been a sacrifice for her. He cleaned her apartment obsessively and could make her laugh, to his great satisfaction (and that pleased her most of all: she *satisfied* Aidan, without ever even touching him). More to her benefit, she had eagerly watched his improvement and won—from constantly strategizing how best to handle and help him—some much-needed distraction. She liked solving the puzzle of other people, comparable to Aidan's love of crosswords. Before she first called him after the Incident, she spent a happy hour calculating how best to approach him, and when she concluded that she must show no sympathy, must hide her deep pity for him, it was a triumphant deduction. She had a suspicion he was holed up in his little apartment with self-hatred, watching his Google hit count rocket, reading the blogs and boards that misunderstood and mocked him, no one noticing the simple fact that he'd been awfully good at that game before his slip of the tongue, no one out there who knew that Aidan coming to dinner every Wednesday had made her husband happy, even in mourning. She was the only one to guess that he was contributing to Web bulletin boards under false names, defending himself, not against the nonsense charges of anti-Semitism but against the brutal charges of stupidity.

She realized, too, after the first few days, that he was now half in love with her, and all those Wednesdays took on new retrospective colors as a result. She could trace the odd shape of his love, its unlikely contours and limitations.

12

THE SUNDAY TIMES ran a long profile of Cait O'Dwyer, "Singer on the Verge," which Julian read and reread with the absorption of a monk illuminating a manuscript.

The piece, by Milton Chi, fawned, but in the ironic tone of a celebrity journalist pretending to be above fawning, a profile in which the interviewer steps in to play an intrusive starring role, making insightful comments to his subject, hinting that the interview has become the record of a sparkling, flirtatious affair that carries on far into the shimmering night while the subscriber is left at home bunching in jealous fists his inky pages. The love-daffy Mr. Chi left the consummation of his interview in a gentlemanly haze of implication but also revealed a fan's fear of insignificance: "She's happy, or so she'll let you think. She doesn't mind. She admits to no heartbreak or regret. The world is endlessly exciting to her, she says, and brushes off questions about sadnesses overcome. 'No, I'm having more fun than should be allowed.' She's tough, because that's how they are back in County Wicklow, seat of rebels. She'll tell you she's kin to Michael O'Dwyer, terror and scourge of the English militias in 1798, and she'll say 'You can't trust a Wickla woman,' and then laugh at you or with you, and now you don't mind. She's 'our Cait' still, as they say at the Rat, but she wasn't always, and we can't hope she always will be, can we?"

The photos (more available online) included two of her performing at the Rat, and Julian recognized the very moments; he must have been within a few feet of the *Times* photographer, and of this poodly writer as well. One shot had Cait onstage looking demure, as if she'd just been complimented squarely on a point of pride; the other, one hand on the black mike, enraged, in full howl, her eyes shut. "Her charms and her talent are sui generis," read the swollen text pulled into a box floating in the middle of the article. The details of her (major) label's vast plans for her (bland background: the industry in perpetual crisis, digital erosion of profits, hundreds of eggs pyramid-balanced in Cait's basket), the A&R man's oily praise and acrobatic hopes, the life story—artfully burnished here and tarnished there—of her Irish girlhood, the village twenty miles from Wicklow Town where her *maimeo* still talked of banshees and will-o'-the-wisps while young, willowy Cait had to drag the boys into manhood, so ready was she for life, and the Big Move across the sea when she was eighteen, with some Immigration issues, now more or less settled to all parties' legal satisfaction, and the exhilarating dive into the Village and Loisaida and Harlem and Brooklyn, the experiments with jazz and soul, the late-night jam sessions and compositions and heroes and influences (a list matching almost to the album—but for some newer names he'd never heard of—Julian's late-night speculations), and then this, the detail that caused Julian to reread and reread and reread:

Part of the joy in watching Ms. O'Dwyer perform is to see and hear her varied influences on shameless display, to notice how she draws on, and then makes her own, her godmothers, as varied as Sinéad O'Connor, Janis Joplin, even Billie Holiday. When I tell her this, citing as an example her vocal work on "Blithering," Ms. O'Dwyer fidgets with her silver Claddagh ring and several times starts to speak, but stops herself, as if unsure of the wisdom of revelation. When I press, she yields only this: "That's funny you say it. Much on my mind lately. I know a remarkable fellow who would debate you on that." "Someone important to you?" I pursue. "Something of an adviser who spots all my flaws. You reach a point in this game where people start getting afraid to offer helpful criticism. Anyhow, he says influences are to be hidden away, that they distract, become competition to the ear." And that's all she'll give on the topic of her mysterious Svengali. Ms. O'Dwyer is nothing if not enigmatic and, unusually for a young woman whose approaching stardom is so widely predicted, her discretion comes easily and not without an appeal of its own, as if this one, at least, had her head screwed on properly back in Ireland. She smiles and looks down, an effect overpowering, more so for its air of unpracticed sincere shyness, unexpected and disarming.

Julian calculated that she had given the interview since he saw her sing and drew those drunken coaster cartoons filled with impromptu advice, and he tried to recall exactly what he'd advised. There had been something about hiding influences, he thought. No, yes, he was sure of it, though that obviously didn't mean that this was him in the article. He reread the passage, wished he'd made copies of his coaster-borne advice. And the bartender gave them to her? Had Julian meant him to? And she read them, absorbed them, and now they absorbed her, Claddagh-fidgeting, hesitating to mention the remarkable fellow whose advice she treasured?

It was an enchanting fantasy, that he'd somehow given her something, made real that two-way exchange he felt when she sang directly into his ears. It was *just* possible.

For all Milton Chi's intimations of intimacy, the journalist had some obvious trouble, three hundred million words later, specifying the one unique thing about this woman, though he sweated text in his manifest certainty that there was unquestionably at least one. Julian marveled that the article so undersold the power of the actual music, rambled about personality and celebrity instead of describing the songs and their objective power.

Promised the italics at the bottom of the page: *Cait O'Dwyer plays the Romping Rat in Brooklyn, this Saturday at 10 pm.*

Saturday at 10 P.M., a folding chalkboard straddled the sand and gum and ice-water puddles of the leonine March night: *Cait. Last chance. You'll tell your grandkids.*

"Coaster Man!" The bartender, in the same T-shirt advertising his band, recognized Julian. "The lady requested I point you out if you came in tonight."

"Did she?" It *had* been him in the article. She wanted to see his face. Julian couldn't remember if he'd thought he was leaving the coasters for her, if he'd been joking, if he'd meant to meet her, wasn't sure the barman wasn't joking now. "Well, let's keep mum, okay? I tip heavily for anonymity."

His surprise and confusion yielded to pleasure, of course: he had impressed her. And once, that would have led to meeting her; he might have tossed the same glib crack to the bartender but then introduced himself to her, talked her up with the same buffed banter that had on infinite other occasions gotten him lushly paid or plushly laid. Now, though, the glib crack was honest: he didn't want to meet her. To his relief, the crowd lived up to all the hype Milton Chi and his species could froth, and Julian, taking shelter amid the elbows and plaid hunting caps and down vests, sank onto a dying couch. In another life, in another life . . .

But in this life, after everything, assuming she really was what he hoped, this was plenty: he had told her how much he loved her music, and she had thanked him, had even taken his suggestions seriously. For a man with his history and limited resources, he told himself, this was miraculous. Sitting on that couch, listening to the bassist tune up, he imagined how he would feel the next time he heard her on his iPod, when he would know that she was, in some small measure, singing to him. He breathed deeply: he was going to hear her sing again, in just a minute. He was going to watch her from within a crowd, and she would be thinking of him but wouldn't know where he was. He would be a ghost, in her thoughts, invisible but close. The role suited him perfectly, he thought. (A moment later, though, he swallowed down a gurgle of green panic: What if he had nothing else to offer her, no more advice she could use? If he had given everything away on a few pieces of recycled cardboard, he would lose his job as whispering phantom before he'd even realized it was his calling.)

The demo CDs were gone; the label had insisted Cait stop selling them, although with the knowledge that this ban would only stoke the simmering oils of her coming anointment. She was flying off to a studio with a big producer and a big budget, and when she came out again she would be transformed by the pressure and the altitude, and already, Julian judged, she was slightly more herself tonight, more unified, more suited for a stage and less for a bar. He sensed the composite effect of his offhand advice.

She wore her hair pulled loosely back from her face; her eyes shone. If he had not been searching for it, he might not have noticed the lightest touch of cosmetics. He wouldn't have expected her restraint in this un-rock-girl art, but she wore exactly the touch he would have ordered Makeup to achieve if he'd cast her in a spot.

She sang. She she was able to produce and display emotion on demand in contoured, glistening miniature, without acting or emoting, without "putting over the song." She sang of heartbreak, for example, like this: she recalled heartbreak, and then sang a distillation of the recollection, so that Julian (and a hundred and some other men and women) wished to help her by punishing the cause of her pain or—in some cases—wished to *be* the cause of that pain. And then they recalled their own heartbreaks. Cait could make them feel what she had felt and what they didn't know they felt, too. A man who foolishly stammers with indecision when a real woman says, "It's now or never," will nod decisively and repeat "It's now, it's now" when a strange woman sings it with her eyes closed. *"It's now or never / I can't wait for good sense."*

She did "Once I Loved"—bringing it back to life as an unnatural but darkly beautiful hybrid of bossa and punk, imperfect and struggling to survive, its seams and bolts still red—and she meant, "Once I loved, and it still hurts," and Julian—who would have said of himself, "Once I loved, but that was decades ago, when *I* referred to a different person"—now felt the illusion of its recent sting. She was better tonight. Whatever she did, she was growing stronger at it.

His slightly drunken thoughts trip. Even as he looks down on the dazzled boys around him, he, like dozens of them, considers kissing Cait O'Dwyer, rescuing Cait O'Dwyer, making Cait O'Dwyer laugh, touching her bare back, cleaning up Cait O'Dwyer, scrubbing off the smell of bar and studio. Peering into a bulb-framed mirror, she tips back her head to extend for the mascara brush the curve of her top lashes, revealing the rarely seen capstone of white above her Irish-green iris, and he, watching her reflection, lifts her hair to his face while music plays, and they go out on the town, where he leans against a bar next to Cait, his thumb exploring her upper arm's puckered vaccination moon, or stands with her under a moon illuminating Irish cliffs in high wind, or sits in windy Seine-side cafés facing the lowering sun, lighting all the riverfront trees on one side only, warming and gilding her closed eyes.

And another song ended. And a too-sweet, tobaccoish residue lingered in Julian from his unchecked fantasies, and he laughed at himself (so like his father wrapping a fur stole around Billie Holiday's shoulders), and he laughed at Cait O'Dwyer's sorcery, and he wondered if, in her real life, she required a steady diet of recent heartbreak in order to manufacture fresh emotion for her consumers. She must crave and court pain as a matter of economic necessity. Two months ago, she was raw and unblended; tonight she was reasonably effective; someday very soon she would be in danger of marbling over into a slick cast impression of herself. The target was only microns wide, and history's great singers may simply have been those who happened to make a record in the brief time between learning and forgetting how to manage their power.

He saw her clearly again, with the reopened eyes of a director. She faced a dilemma: she and her emotions must ring true, must make the crowd fall literally and briefly in love with her if she were to succeed; her living depended upon just such a primal, unconscious event. But most men would see how she did it, would know it was a lie, and as soon as the artifice was clear, the music would fail. And so to make a man find her desirable even after he became conscious of her trickery, she must also imply *in her performance* that she would extinguish that same public display of emotion a moment later. She must hint that she always stepped off the stage and sealed herself up into a private person again, so that if you were a man in the audience imagining yourself her lover, you could imagine there was still something she was *not* sharing (even with you for the time being). The displayed emotion must carry within it the promise that it was only a drop of something rarer held in reserve.

In short, Julian saw all the way through her. He saw how the trick was done, saw the strings and mirrors. His brief flare of childish wonder was snuffed out, and that was probably as it should be, he thought.

"Here's a new song," Cait O'Dwyer said. "We're still smoothing it out, so if it's vile, try not to hurl things at us, please. Oh, yes, it's called 'Bleaker and Obliquer.' Bass here had to look that last word up, by the way."

Julian knew that nonsense phrase. He leaned against a wall, overwhelmed for long seconds, untangling himself from his fantasies of loving her from afar, or seeing through her. Well, she's young, was his first thought, but it didn't stick. He had accidentally inspired her to write a song, and it thrilled him.

She wrote a song for him. No, she wrote a song *from* him, extracted it from him before he'd known it was in him. The words hadn't meant anything when he wrote them on that coaster, but she made them mean something.

He slipped out after her last encore, leaving behind him with the lead guitarist for the Lay Brothers the promised mega-tip for anonymity and a twelfth coaster, a self-portrait:

The tired old cowboy (stubble, bags under his eyes) with the J.D. on his sheriff's badge, departing astride a broken-down old nag with a folded copy of the *Times* in his saddlebag, looks back and touches the brim of his sagging ten-gallon hat to Cait O'Dwyer, who, floating above the ground, is singing "Bleaker and Obliquer" to a group of cross-legged fans in gas-station shirts and truck-company hats.

Around the drawing revolves the caption: "Leaving her in well-deserved limelight, he rode off into the sunset."

And he went home—eighteen years old and eighty years old in flickering alternation—and put on her demo. Its mix placed Cait primarily near his front window, as if she were watching from the radiator and he from the floor as the penguins sailed through the Antarctic water like real birds through air. "To a young fish, there is no more horrifying, nightmarish vision of death than an approaching penguin," said the Australian voice in the slim silence between tracks of her CD. "Without Time" came next. She'd done that tune the first snowy night and again tonight, that line sung over only a melodic bass: "*Either beat me, mistreat me, or leave me in peace.*" On the demo, she starts the phrase by accelerating from a whisper to a scream. By the middle of the line her voice has smoothed into the delicate vibrato of a choir girl, sweetly clear, but then she sounds as if she sobs, almost chokes, on *peace*. He remembered exactly that from the first night: she'd sung it with exactly that same ploy, just a trick of the uvula.

But tonight she'd done something else, though he only realized it now: tonight she laughed on that line. Her smile had started to curl before she reached "*beat me*," and she sang *through* the laughter, holding the melody like an egg, her voice straining pleasantly, her smile broadening, her breathing heavier than in the demo's thinner version. That had been a coaster: Laugh when others think you should cry. And that had been Elis Regina, "The Waters of March," 1974, 3:11.

Laughter was incongruous, and the stunned bassist (Julian saw now as he reconsidered the event from his living room floor) had hated her change, for a moment, since he was left holding all the stale pathos while she pursued a fresher scent. The crowd cheered then; they recognized that Cait had found another splinter of heartbreak by laughing at her own slightly cloying, beer-battered-girl plea to her abusive lover, and then—only then, unlike the first night, unlike on the demo—Julian *believed* her: she really had once felt that, and she felt it tonight on cue. The bass player floundered, confused. She would fire him before she went much further, Julian thought.

In the silence: "The male penguin must protect the egg through a long and brutal winter. The offspring's life is in the father's care, and the slightest mistake is lethal to the unhatched chick."

Carlton died two weeks after his second birthday, an ear infection caught too late, not a problem in itself but a symptom of another spiky bacterium boiling his blood then flying upstream to his brain, inflaming grief and disbelief for long months of heat and cold.

Like a planet struck by a meteor, Rachel and Julian's marriage wobbled, then righted itself in a bizarre new orbit, spinning counter to its old rotation.

Some weeks after the thunder and betrayal of Carlton's death had receded before a tide of gray sorrow, Julian tried music in the hope that it would restore some part of himself, some ability to desire someone or something. He hoped that music might, at least, seep into cuts, smooth over a surface, be useful, pay him back for all his years of commitment to it. And music succeeded, a little, or was the coincidental soundtrack to some recovery that would have occurred in any case: Julian did, now and again, regain that sense of pleasant unfulfillment. He replaced, for a few minutes at a time, his agony with a benign pop-music ache, admittedly adolescent but now oddly specific: he longed for *Rachel*, for his own wife, in a way he had never longed for her before, even when they had first met and she was not yet his.

This longing was not for her as she had been when younger, nor was it for her as she actually *was*, then, when they were uncomfortably and quietly together at home after work, trying to see how long they could go without mentioning him, or out with friends, putting on a pair of alternately brave faces, or just pausing and breathing in forgetfulness, briefly, and only ever one at a time. Rather, he longed for the Rachel he had discovered in the bathroom, glowing from that pink-plus-sign annunciation of his boy inside her. He longed for her to restore him, replenish him in the same way she had made *him* in that bathroom, had conceived and delivered Julian there.

For all of that longing, though, he, for the first time in his life, failed physically. His body would not follow his heart. He abased himself to chemical intervention, both antidepressant and antiflaccidulent, but still could not undam the blood flow required in either direction. He would have been willing to sleep with other women, as a pump-priming effort, as an act almost of loyalty (squint and you can see it), but he felt no desire for anyone.

He couldn't say when he became certain Rachel was having affairs. He couldn't even say with certainty that she'd begun only after Carlton's death, or only when he'd proven himself sexually useless, but her flight from him and his sexless adoration of her fed each other. She took comfort from and was able to comfort in turn the whole male world except for him, and in the months unrolling toward her departure, Rachel and Julian circled and veered from each other like identically charged particles. "I want to play you something. I was thinking about Carlton and thought of this song and it reminded me of when you and I met, and . . ."

Tuesday would be Carlton's half-birthday. He would have been three and a half. Julian started Cait's demo again, set it to shuffle, lay on the living room floor.

In the course of his days, Julian still dutifully looked at all the parts displayed for him, the gratis glimpses from a city of sexual saleswomen: the thin cardigan worn over reactive skin; the groove along the outside of a seated and high-skirted thigh, toned and tanned; the coming spring's fashion for high shirts and low waists, a landscape of abdomen and crevice. But nothing ever happened to him anymore, aged and wounded past surprise. *"Look at me, look at me, look at me, look at me, please."*

Until now, well after midnight, in a darkened room, when Cait O'Dwyer's voice, or just the sound of her breath, caressed him, and he lay on his floor primally swollen like a howling teenager, for the first time in more than a year.

13

RACHEL WAS HAVING the same dreams as always. The spacious-house dream, for example, was always a blessing. It usually prophesied a positive change in her life. In its simplest form, Rachel would rise from her bed and walk through whatever home she happened to occupy at the time—a dorm, a studio, her apartment with Julian—and be pleasantly surprised to find that there were many, many more rooms than she had realized. Each new floor, wing, or tower fulfilled some unnamed need. The tour of the new space ended as she lay back into bed—the bed she was actually in—and she would fall asleep in her dream.

But now her dreams were narrated, not lived, and she woke more tired than she'd gone to bed. Carlton would stand and speak to her, as before a stage set. She would have no particular feeling for him. He would say, "Okay, the spacious-house dream. Let's see, you're walking around here, and over there, behind that door"—he would point to a locked door—"is a bunch of rooms." Tonight Carlton, bored, stepped up and said, "The spacious-house dream." And that was it. "The can't-wake-up dream, then the Julian-with-the-models dream, then the mice-circling-the-dying-vulture dream." He recited most of her repertoire. "The kindly-mullahs-offering-brownies dream." He shook his head condescendingly at her disappointment, as Julian used to do when he thought she was being ridiculous. It hurt much more to see Carlton do it. "The endless-love dream," he said with a hint of Julian's sneer, but on her baby's face with that tone in his mouth of all mouths, it left her desolate when she awoke to gray light.

She had tried everything, and still she was sinking, buoyant only for that brief period when she nursed Aidan. Before and since, she gulped antidepressants without shame (though her father had raised her to believe in self and choice, still clucked at society's collapse into "psychopharmacoddling"). The pills never helped much, nor did grief therapy groups or individual therapy with an unmarried, childless woman ten years younger, who furrowed her brow and nodded gravely whenever Rachel talked about the bubbling pain in her gut.

Her hopes for Julian were very limited. She had not one romantic illusion, she told herself with a quiet, mature pride her father would have approved of. She had burned through a fair sampling of manhood trying to find someone, not to make her "happy"—that wasn't the point—but to cauterize her relentlessly dripping wounds. Julian—for all his flaws, his crimes and omissions—was not only hers but to a degree was *her*, as if only with a transfusion of him could her own system function. He looked like Carlton, of course, and Carlton was alive to the extent that she saw him in Julian's eyes. He was alive, too, if the family he'd been part of survived. Better a reduced family that mourns together, rather than each of them wandering alone, abandoning all the spaces where Carlton had existed, denying Carlton the places that had been his.

Beyond that, Julian was her history, her young wifehood, her motherhood, her as a victim and her as a slut. Her life's joy was from now on sharply limited, but if there was joy to be had, Julian was the only man left who might remind her what it looked like. Julian would provide the rest, too, the vast majority of life that wasn't even close to joy.

"At the funeral," she told her nodding shrink, "I loved Julian so much. I watched him drowning, and I knew we were together. But after, really soon after, he was thinking it might pass, you know?"

"I do."

"He was still in pain, obvious, but I could see he thought he might someday get over it. And that felt like he wanted to shake me off so he could get over it. And then, another couple months, he wasn't really any better, he just got better at pretending, left me alone while he acted like he was on his way. And then—"

"Mm-hm."

"—the worst was when he started to act like he'd passed *through* something, and now he could help *me*. Like, having *finished*, he was now ready to be *my* strong support. Like he had a *plan*."

"I see."

She remembered her sorrow and anger disguised as boredom, at the end, just before she left. She remembered watching him, blurry and faceless through the misted, dimpled toilet glass of the shower door, sawing his buttocks apart with a new brick of green soap, and she remembered feeling at that instant that she was allowed to do anything she wanted with anyone on earth so she wouldn't have to feel one more second of that. So she'd been wrong.

"How were you wrong?"

"I want *him*. I *want* him to be a strong support. I can't walk around like this. He'd show me how to fake it better, how to pretend to forget now and then."

"You want to go back?" asked the therapist in Rachel's head, whom she hadn't gone to see in weeks.

"No. Just to go on. I'm done."

She lay in bed, Carlton's dream and the therapist's voice fading. She reached for the phone and dialed Aidan's cell from memory.

14

THE END OF A SHOOT. The cubical studio was empty but for him and Maile, cross-legged on the floor, Bach Cello Suites on the speakers, and shiny orange Chinese food in white, tin-handled boxes on cherry-red Chinese-zodiac place mats, greasy from the spots on the floor where the daily beauty's red hair had been combed out thirty-eight times, conditioned strands plopping dollops of the Product onto the black wood, sounds partially masked by the Rolling Stones played loud over the speakers to give the client and agency people the pleasant sensation of a day not only out of the office but shot free of corporate life entirely (thus encouraging future business with Julian Donahue).

"Can I say, today you seemed like a real director?" Maile said.

Julian laughed. "I *am* a real director."

"I know, I'm sorry, I didn't mean that, I meant a film director. No offense."

"None taken. 'Real,' unlike my entire existence and your salary."

"Oh, my God, this is not coming out how I meant. I meant to say that you're better than this. Than ads, I guess I mean."

"You think you'd like Hollywood people better than ad people?"

"I know, everyone's selling something. But movie people are at least *also* trying to make something, right? I sound naïve to you, don't I?"

"A little."

"Well, that reflects badly on you, then, doesn't it?" she said, with sauce.

There was an answer to Maile's kiss-up compliment disguised as smart-ass challenge, her flirtatious treatment of her boss as an under-achieving child lacking only an inspiring woman. The answer, though, was not likely to impress a temporarily semi-infatuated production assistant.

He'd been embarrassed, years earlier, in front of film-school friends who'd done well enough in Hollywood, that his "talent" or "vision" hadn't been strong enough to resist the offer of his first television commercial, and then, even more, when his talent was too weak to overcome the inertia of continued offers. He couldn't even claim he'd failed to make a great film, as he had never tried. He remembered wanting to make one. He wished he still did, but he didn't. He wished he were an artist, a great artist, but sometimes he also wished he was an astronaut. He even wished he could tell Maile he had a vision for a film that he was unable to make, for fear of failure, a subject of some regret . . . but that would have been a bone-deep lie.

The childish belief that he would someday direct great films had been replaced by a prickly adult wonder that such a goal had ever boasted its moral superiority, and he tried, jokingly, to explain this to the lovely girl sharing Heaven's Pig and Enraged Life Crab with him. Why, he pressed her, was it better to direct a film? His work, stories told with haiku efficiency, provoked real emotion, too, but then they also produced—the ultimate tangible *proof* of invisible emotion—*action*, thousands of times over: purchases, votes, donations, changes in fashion. What Hitchcock film had such empirical evidence of its auteur's prowess? Some people were scared to shower for a day or two? "If the true measure of an artist's greatness is his influence, then I'm a genius."

"I don't think you mean that," said Maile. She watched him as she slowly laid a water chestnut in her mouth and delicately crunched it with her lips apart. "You might think you mean it, but you don't." That matronizing sentiment—one Rachel used to flash from time to time—combined with the slow insertion of food into red mouth, was a hardwired tactic of the human female. They would offer themselves sexually at the same moment they insisted they understood their potential mate better than he understood himself. The praying mantis just bites her male's head off, and only after the fun; the human insists upon dissolving her mate's personality *before* the pleasure. Maile would *improve* him. She *promised.* And if he agreed to the procedure, he could have her, for a while, until the day when, aghast, she would realize she'd been swindled despite her best efforts, and he would stand before her, erect and unimproved.

"Let's say you had all the money in the world," Maile pushed. "What sort of film would you make?"

He asked her—as she plainly wanted him to—what her favorite films were and looked duly impressed when she cataloged dead maestros from cinema's storied past. The whole game was one he'd played too many times, too long ago. Maile stood on the far side of a rushing river, in another country, waving her arms frantically, but the rapids drowned her voice, and Julian smiled and nodded. Later, Maile would render their conversation as:

MARIE

You think I'm naïve. That doesn't reflect very well on you, now does it?

HUGH moves to kiss her, but she closes the cab door and smiles at him through the window.

HUGH

Well. It seems it's time I became a better man.

MARIE

(slyly) So it would seem. *(to the cabbie)* Onward, Mr. Singh, onward. The evening is young.

He had the studio for another nine hours, though there was no reason to stay. But the disarray at the end of a day's shoot still attracted him, after years, one of life's butterfly moments that left him pleasantly near-satisfied, a much better feeling than the dull, guilty bloat of fully satisfied.

"I'll close up, Maile. Thank you for everything today."

She didn't hear, or pretended not to. She killed Bach and put her own CD on the system, turned it too loud for easy conversation. The first track was "Piccadilly" by Squeeze, and Julian laughed. It hadn't shuffled up on his own iPod in months. The opening piano took him by surprise every time; he recalled (his body recalled) how he (it) had felt at age sixteen hearing this song, overwhelmed by the reference to a young woman putting on a brassiere: "*She hooks up her cupcakes and puts on her jumper.*" He had to yell from where he was sitting: "How do you know this song?" He sounded like a ninety-year-old impressed by a precocious toddler. Maile only smiled, turned away, busied herself with the work from which he'd excused her, played a little discreet one-handed air guitar.

The next song—an old shameful pleasure of his, only enjoyable if all social context, fashion, and history were suspended, though Maile was too young to be aware of this—lifted him out of his chair. He stepped toward her. She was still all the way across the square black floor, nearly to the far wall. She turned; she must have seen him stand in a reflection or a layered shadow. "Will you ever use that grip again? I couldn't believe he—" She stopped when she caught his eye.

"You don't have to stay, you know."

"You keep saying that."

She playfully climbed up a stack of canvas sandbags meant to stabilize light stands, and he saw all that would happen next. He would go to her and dance with her for a minute before touching her, and then this instant right now would be the last moment of mystery between them: lips, laugh, Heaven's Pig on the breath (erotic tonight, off-putting and inconsiderate eight months from now), his fingertips on the black lace at the top of her bra, *hey, you have a tattoo*, the climax (or, more likely, the droopy return of his inability), and quickly on to *What does this mean? Who is this in the photo?* and *This isn't working, is it?*

She stood atop the little hill of sandbags and smiled at him. "Do you want to keep the breakfast meeting with Burgess tomorrow? He's going to offer you another dames' dam, I think." And she slowly lifted one leg and brought her foot up to rest against her thigh, a yoga pose. "So what do you say, Julian Donahue?"

"You ask tough questions."

And the next song on the CD was Cait O'Dwyer:

> *You've reduced me down to the dregs*
> *You won't seduce me, though I stand here and beg*
> *I'm blithering, you're dithering, I'm your slithering fool.*

If Maile had sneaked a look at Julian's iPod, gone home and cannily burnt a CD while consulting *Cosmo* and *The Art of War,* each slot of the playlist carefully chosen to provoke a scheduled moment of desire, then here, batting cleanup, was the confessional song. But, oh, how badly chosen. She must have seen it on his face. She stepped down off the bags. "I'll call his office first thing in the morning, tell them you were shooting late."

> *This was not my best hope for me, not what I meant to become,*
> *Lurking at your window, breathing my name on your pane.*
> *But I won't let you have her if you won't have me.*
> *Why can't I think?*
> *Oh, ignore me, I'm blithering, I'm dithering,*
> *I've had too much to drink.*

He imagined Cait attached by suction cups to the outside wall of this loft space in Chelsea, tracking his movements with infrared sensors, listening to him with parabolic microphones. And, having said a mutually smiling I'm-not-sure-just-what-you're-thinking-but-I-suspect-I-do-and-I-deny-everything farewell to his pretty employee at the yellow door of her taxi waiting to ferry her home to her screenwriting software, he turned away, fumbled for his iPod, and quickly spun it to "Blithering": "*You've reduced me to dithering, your coldness is withering, / This can't be what you want me to be.*" She sang what he couldn't say, and he knew it was largely a coincidence, but the coincidences had become so richly absurd that his own employee was trying to seduce him with a song about Cait watching some other woman trying to seduce her remarkable fellow.

He wanted to tell her all of this and more, but if he could perfectly express himself to her, it would sound like one of her own songs. He'd have to send her a CD of herself. Better yet, she should stand alone in a room and just sing to herself until she understood him.

15

AT FIRST, RACHEL had thought she was making a rational choice, even if the moment of choice floated into view only atop an undercurrent of revenge and hate. She chose: since her natural, unconscious behavior had made her miserable, she consciously tried to be like Julian instead, to act like him in hopes of tasting some of his old happiness, to roam like him, take pleasure like him, coolly, content with small doses and short exposures, light fun, strangers in parks or bars, making eyes on subway trains, chatting and drinking, going home with or without them, as the event unrolled. A charming *indifference*—we can lie here, I can go home, you can scramble eggs, but I *will* be happy and will hope for nothing more than a small plate of scrambled happiness.

But then, after she left him, this, with just a little therapy, was what she realized she'd obviously "actually" been up to: she had been trying to find someone who could distract her from the endless alternation of fire and balm, thinking of Carlton in pain and then inappropriate joy and then numbness, and on and on.

Finally, months later, having drunk a bit, lying alone in her apartment, she decided she had really all along been trying, and failing, to stop being *her*, the woman who got married, got cheated, got pregnant to fix things, had a taste of happiness, and then let her child die. She had a thirst for oblivion that a hundred men's bodies could not quench.

She exhausted herself in flight. That phrase leapt at Rachel from the page of a dull book: *she exhausted herself in flight*. The idea was covered with burrs. She slowed down to examine it, kept turning the pages back, after absorbing nothing since, turned the words to the light, fit them to herself. In the biography, the words referred to a Nazi war criminal's refugee wife, but they took root in Rachel, wafted spores everywhere. She had exhausted herself in flight, and she often thought now of a garden. She saw herself looking out a kitchen window and seeing overflowing vines and beds of tulips, things to prune and lay out for the coming season. Julian was in this house, and photos of Carlton, and the garden, and that was all she could see.

How could both of these be true: that she could see a path to a certain limited serenity, and that she had twice (perhaps three times, depending on how you looked at certain acts) come very close to killing herself, without having given it any thought? She was not "*in* despair"; despair had taken residence in *her* as a boarder who came and left according to his own whims, rather than the posted hours the landlady respectfully requested.

She could sit alone in the dark with an open bottle of wine and not cry, looking at the huge photo on her wall, lit by streetlights, of her much younger self with a husband and a velvet-cheeked baby wearing a blue baseball cap with the words TOUGH GUY on the front. She could walk to her bedroom that night making plans for the next day, thinking she might very well find a small dose of happiness at work, or in reading. And at the very same time, she could keep eating sleeping pills, one after the other, until her finger was tracing through the dusty residue at the bottom of the orange-brown plastic bottle, and still she was thinking of where tomorrow's happiness might hide itself: in an extravagant dessert, in serving a client with surprising brilliance, on a run in Prospect Park.

To explain all this to another person took so much effort because she only ever felt it alone, and she didn't like to talk about how she *usually* felt but didn't feel just then. And to explain it all to Aidan required still more artifice. She had invited him to dinner fresh from those scouring dreams of Carlton, but it was unlikely she would be feeling anything of significance about Julian tonight by the time they sat down to a meal. And clear signals were surely necessary to inspire Aidan to action, if there was anything he could even do.

So she made a play of her misery for him, knowing he couldn't read grayer shades. He was not emotionally color-blind, but the more garish colors certainly registered with him more easily. Where others would cringe at melodrama, Aidan was only just barely sensing unhappiness.

She knew he was in love with her, and knew, too, that he was devoted to her happiness, as far as he could see it, and that he would serve her selflessly, and she had no compunction taking advantage of that service. The stakes were too high. She did consider whether this was cruel, but the word didn't approach relevance. This determination may have been made by some engine inside her brain that would grind on, taking no heed of such niceties, too protective of her to step clear of "Aidan's feelings."

"Who wrote this, Aidan? You'll know." And she recited from the side of the box of hippie tea: "*The moon believes that the love around which it spins is a star of great magnitude, but it is only a minor, rocky planet. And that planet in turn orbits some distant sun, which is unaware of its rotating admirer in its own eagerness to revolve around the galaxy's bright center. The universe's wheels whiz, powered by unrequital and vain hopes.*"

He knew the answer, obviously, before she'd finished, and she could see his effort to hold his tongue until the end, saw the affection his restraint implied. He answered correctly, then asked, "Do you believe that?"

16

JULIAN HAD DECIDED not to sleep with his assistant because a CD told him not to. This, obviously, *meant something else;* his own brief therapy had succeeded at least that far. And so began a thawing season of music clubs, much as he had passed through icy seasons of German-film revivals and hot seasons of fund-raisers and rainy seasons of fashion shows. He told himself that the oddly affecting experience with Cait O'Dwyer *really* meant that he had a hunger not for the singer but, like his father always had, for live music, and what a wonder it was, a priv-ilege, to live in this city of sound.

His strongest memories of his father and mother together were the nights he would be left in Aidan's care as they, dressed like film stars—his mom with a violet in her furs, his dad's shiny pant leg pinned up—said they were "off to hear some music." This would have been 1969 or 1970, so they must have been doing very old-fashioned things, seeing very old-fashioned acts; they certainly weren't going to Woodstock or Haight-Ashbury in furs and suits. Five-year-old Julian would fall asleep imagining them even further back in time, in movies or TV shows he'd seen, nodded off while they applauded in palm-lined nightclubs, smoked with men in tuxedos while gangsters pushed crying songstresses out into the spotlight.

It had been years since Julian himself had frequented clubs, with the exception of the Rat. Now he sought out famous and unknown names alike, though the singers were always women. He dragged Aidan to see traditional Irish bands reeling in Celtic pubs, a hardship for his elder brother, considering Aidan's feelings about music and his policy never to use public bathrooms. One lovely, red-haired, green-eyed woman sang beautifully and fiddled well and joked between songs and introduced her bandmates with gentle teasing, and the pub crowd loved her, and Julian found her entertaining, and he never thought of her again the second his foot touched the sidewalk.

Through the last gasps of winter, he studied the stage presence of spike-scalped ululating harpies clutching their phantom penises, Ja-vanese pixies with expressive hands and inexpressive faces, Alabaman protest folkies so terribly disappointed, soul queens backlit to display broccoli-stalk silhouettes, a 1950s pop singer enjoying a very brief and vaguely ironic revival in a skyscraper's rotating rooftop cabaret (a performance derided by Aidan as "the slurpy crooning of the den-tured elderly"), evening-gowned jazz divas going through the mo-tions in front of whispering divorced surgeons with nurse-dates sipping triple-priced drinks, uneasy to be wearing anything but scrubs and clogs.

Not one of them sang to him even when they looked right at him, and he remained hungry for Cait's voice. He stepped from the shower, and his blood reprioritized at the sound of her. She sang to him on his train, and he wished his father could hear her sing or, better yet, come with him to a gig. "The thing is, Cannonball, if you're ever lucky enough to see one of the truly great ones perform, you don't walk out the door the same man that walked in."

Julian and Aidan's father had made his living designing, building, and installing inflatables. This was not the glamour of the Macy's Thanksgiving parade, the pinnacle of a crowded, low-margin industry. Rather, Will Donahue rented out bouncy castles for children's parties and pumped up twenty-foot-tall rats for unions picketing at scabby building sites. He oversaw the manufacture of toys for circus and museum gift shops. (He could also, calling himself a "pneumatic zoologist," twist for the boys' birthday parties an impressive line of balloon animals, including bald eagles, meerkats, piranhas, box jellyfish, and plankton, magnified.) He created custom-builts for business parties and raffles: miniature inflatable jumbo jets, jumbo inflatable chocolate bars, life-size inflatable nuclear-missile components recognizable only to the engineers at the party. He also manufactured— a profitable but small portion of the business—"personal comfort inflatables," available only by private mail order: *Air-dorables, Floating Venus, Weightless Tess, Pump 'n' Hump*, and *Silent Nights*, the last in a package emblazoned with the Elvis Presley lyrics, *"A little less conversation, a little more action."* This element of the business never entered the house, where the kids happily examined their father's drawings of inflatable reindeer. Aidan's doubts about their father, however, were already beginning when he visited the company's dingy offices, came upon an Air-dorable, and returned home convinced that Dad was making inflatable, naked Moms. Literally: "They look just like her," he insisted to Julian, age nine. "You don't remember her, but I do."

"Yes, I *do*."

Julian returned to his apartment from a night alone listening to a Malian singer to find Aidan watching a *Jeopardy!* rerun. Julian was, of course, not allowed to speak until the show was over and Aidan had added up his own (winning) score. "I was thinking tonight of this story Dad told me about the hospital in Tokyo," Julian said, bringing beer and chips to the living room. "He was recovering, but still feeling sorry for himself, and—"

"So he said," Aidan scoffed. "That was a classic of his methods. The more he could fault himself for self-pity, the less tolerable it was for anyone else ever to feel bad. The more cowardly he described himself, the more courageous he was. One day I summoned up the nerve and called him on it, and then I never had to hear any more of his war stories. I was freed from the catechism of his courage."

So Julian kept the story to himself. Their father was in the hospital looking at his leg and crying when they wheeled a guy into his room, still unconscious after surgery, and they parked him a few feet away. Their father studied this guy's half an arm before he woke up. He felt good looking at someone else with a stump, weighed whether an arm was worse than a leg. "So, the guy comes out of it, Jules, and he's a big guy, a Marine, and he opens his eyes and looks down at his arm, cut off above the elbow, and then he looks up at me and says, 'Oh, well, there goes my sex life.' I laughed so hard, Julian, I almost felt fine. I wanted to measure up to this guy's grace, so I said, pointing to my leg, 'I'm going to have to kick from the left now or the Packers are going to drop me.' Proudest I ever was of myself."

Aidan started to speak, stopped, started again with a kinder voice, but it required effort: "I don't think much about him, Cannonball. You and he had a *very* different experience, you know," he said, brightening, "thanks to his earlier efforts at parenthood. You were much more to his taste in every regard. He found me, oh, a puzzle, and he didn't do puzzles. Did he ever tell you this piece of advice? 'We enter this world alone, screaming, son. We exit the world alone, maybe screaming again, and ideally with some of our wits still about us. In between you decide who to marry, who to obey, who to invest with, who to hate, all on your own. Good luck to you.' That's what I heard a lot of as a kid."

Over the years, their father collected amputee jokes ("And the Italian scientist says, 'Frog-a with-a no legs deaf!' "). This proved either that their father was brave and kind, determined to make others comfortable (Julian's position), or that he was bullying others with his false stoicism, denying anyone close to him the right to feel pain over anything less than losing a leg (Aidan's position).

The two pictures of him could not be merged. "How many women do you think he had, by being both brave and a sideshow attraction?" Aidan asked. This was another of the unsolved, unsolvable sub-mysteries of their father: Julian and Aidan had been raised by two different one-legged, inflatable-castle-and-rat-distributing, Korean War veteran, Billie Holiday idolaters. This was partially because Aidan was sixteen when their mother died; Julian, six. Julian had been raised by a father who was only ever miserably widowed, who never touched another woman after his true love died, barring a single dinner date, from which he returned early and said to his thirteen-year-old son, "You never know when you're *about* to be too old for some things. You only know when suddenly you *are* too old." (As Julian knew he was too old to obsess over pop singers.)

Aidan, however, claimed to have been raised by a heartless, unipedal satyr, hopping after skirts, whose penis overcompensated for the missing limb, and who enjoyed a widowhood marked by an endless "carnal gluttony," the same charge Aidan leveled at Julian in his looser years and continued to level long after Julian, more or less monastic, had turned over a new leaf, or been turned over by one and nearly crushed by it.

The only evidence Julian saw to support Aidan's theory was the undeniable effect his father had had on Julian's own young girlfriends.

"What happened to your dad's leg?" one fourteen-year-old girl asked Julian, as they sat in the kitchen, homework spread out and ignored between them.

"He lost it in Korea."

"Wrong," his father called from the next room. "I didn't lose it. I know exactly where I left it."

The girl laughed, not nervously, not embarrassed to have her question overheard. Julian felt something he couldn't put words to, but which made him angry at his father for some days after.

"Mr. Donahue, may I ask you a question? A personal question?" a sixteen-year-old girlfriend later asked directly. She'd always looked strangely at his father, and Julian had blithely assumed it was the same look of countless male friends, the stolen glance at the damaged man's absences.

"Proceed, young lady," he intoned. "I am prepared for any inquiry."

"What does it feel like? Where it used to be?"

"Liz," Julian protested, feeling she wasn't asking like boys did.

"That's all right, Cannonball." His father smiled at him. "He's very protective of me, Lizzie. I'll show you what it feels like." He pushed himself up from his chair and beckoned her to him. She didn't hesitate but rose from the couch, left Julian behind her without a glance. "Autumn in New York" was on the stereo, and Julian could never hear that late-Holiday version, on his iPod or anywhere else, without feeling an echo of sickening certainty that his father was about to have Julian's girlfriend touch the obscenely puckered end of his hip.

Liz walked toward the man like a volunteer at a hypnosis performance, stood in front of him and shivered, her back to Julian, who didn't move his two legs. "Right," said his father. "Stand there and close your eyes."

"Dad."

"She'll be okay, Tiger."

He pulled his reading glasses out of his shirt pocket and gently placed them on his son's girlfriend's head, propped up high on her hair. She audibly inhaled at the sensation of the glasses alighting, though the old man's fingers never touched her. "Just my reading glasses. Now count to thirty."

Liz obeyed, murmuring the numbers slowly, dragging it out while Julian sat and sat and sat.

"Dad."

"Would you lighten up, J?"

When she reached twenty-five, his father very gently, unnoticeably, removed the glasses, restowed them in his pocket. At thirty, she kept her eyes shut, scrupulously obedient, until he told her to open them, and then he asked her to take off the glasses. She reached for them, surprised to find only hair. "There," he said. "That's what it feels like."

Said a later girl, eighteen now, kissing Julian on the beach life-guard's high chair at midnight, the flaking white paint under her nails, the sweet citric taste of her skin, the blackness of the lake under summer constellations, "He's very distinguished-looking." Julian was no longer astonished by such comments. "What does it look like?" He knew she meant the Cape of No Hope. "Is it smooth? Or sore?" An odd sensation, to be sure, feeling jealous of your father's amputation stump as a popular girl chewed your earlobe.

"You know when you wear your sunglasses up on your forehead?" Julian whispered. Stranger words of seduction must once have been spoken somewhere by someone; one is statistically not likely to be history's most extreme case of anything. Julian reached a brassiere's white-satin northern boundary and crossed into foreign lands, bearing his father's documentation.

"Do you remember the day of Pamela's funeral?" Aidan asked on his third excursion to Julian's refrigerator for prosciutto and cheese.

"Not really."

"Yes or no, Cannonball. Yes or no."

"I'll stick with 'Not really,' thanks."

"Well, mine's a clear yes, and clearest of all was you left to your own devices in the living room while Dad pretended to be brave for some relation or business friend, and you were staring out the window, pretending to eat cookies. 'Mmm, these are good cookies,' you kept saying, shoveling imaginary cookies into your mouth, and the tears rolling down your cheeks. I went to get Dad, and he watched you do this for a while without interrupting you, and then he left you alone. 'Best not bother him, Aid,' he said, and that really impressed me, how willing he was to let his child suffer by himself. A six-year-old child."

"I was seven."

"No, you were still six. Add it up: April comes before July."

Julian remembered a midnight-blue velvet toque, quilted and layered over a hairless skull and browless eyes. "You really think he screwed around? When she was alive?"

Aidan ignored the question. "I think of you and your cookies, and I look at you now, and you seem very much unchanged. I blame myself. I should've made Dad talk to you, or done it myself, but he bullied me into leaving you alone for your own supposed good. I won't make that mistake again."

"I'm touched."

"You're not, but you should be." Aidan finished a beer and opened another. "So do me a favor, would you? I know you have a new Boleyn on the hook, but there's someone I want you to meet. I'm not going to lecture you. I'm just saying, do me a favor. Meet a friend of mine for a drink. Open mind."

"How do you know she's for me? Maybe she's just right for you."

"Don't let's start talking about me now. I know what's right for me."

"The thought of you setting me up with someone—it's like I've ingested some very potent hallucinogenic leaf." But Julian agreed to the daft blind date because he felt ready for *something*, and maybe *that* was the quote-unquote real meaning of his experience with Cait O'Dwyer. He agreed because he'd been thinking so much lately of his father's lonely old age and whether he was destined to repeat it, or if he had already begun it. In fact, he had lately caught himself believing that being alone forever would be just the thing. He agreed because Aidan asked nicely, and because, if nothing else, it would be a diversion. Even then, the fantasy tickled him that somehow Aidan knew everything and meant to introduce him to Cait O'Dwyer, and Julian nearly called it off because that was *not* how he wanted them to meet, before he reentered earth orbit and prepared himself to murder an innocent twilight hour with some unspeakable trivia queen.

17

JULIAN HAD SEEN HER in labor, splayed and incontinent, and at Carlton's deathbed, shaking and mucused, so preening for a date was a little nonsensical, even openly dishonest. Like an ad. Still, she wavered: contacts or glasses, hair up or down, skirt or pants, something he'd bought her or something he'd never seen.

She walked and weighed how much she would confess, apologize for, claim for the future. She passed the hospital, smoking orderlies chatting on the windy sidewalk despite full gurneys, and she felt a swell of gratitude to Aidan, her productive household genius, able to deliver his brother and her hopes.

Just hopes, only that. In the best of circumstances there were miles of apologies to issue, vast awkward chasms to fill, forests of expectations to clear, memories to make room for, unless he was coming ready, like her, not to begin again, but just to *be* again, to keep going, ready to accept that, at this late hour, this was better than anything else on offer.

He was already there, at a table behind glass in a neutral space without any memories of its own, and so, watching him from across the street, she stroked another small feather of hope: at the very worst, he did at least want to see her and talk, even if only to demand, finally, a divorce. She may even have been reading the world correctly again, no longer crazy with sadness or dizzy from missteps: he *was* there, and she was happier to see him there, just willing to talk, than she had ever been walking toward waiting strangers with flashing flowers and aromatic smiles. "Hello."

"Rachel?" She saw his surprise, and her hopes cannibalized to survive for one more second: he was surprised how well she looked, how hard the sight of her hit him, how much he now realized he'd missed her—"You're Aidan's 'friend'?" he asked, with that little laugh of annoyance being processed and tolerated. "Not much of a blind date."

Wonder at her own stupidity stopped her breath until she found a noncommittal "Oh, Aidan."

"I wasn't really in the mood for that anyhow." He asked her to sit. Somehow coffee came.

"Well," she admitted, "*I* wasn't blind, at least." Then she lied: "He told me you wanted to talk."

"He's funny."

"He's very lonely, you know."

"Trust me. Aidan wouldn't have it any other way."

"Of course he would. Don't be mean. I didn't really help him much."

"I know you did," he said hurriedly, as if she'd been fishing for overdue praise. "I'm grateful."

"I didn't do it for you," she snapped, and could have cut out her tongue with the coffee spoon. "Sorry."

She had once, under very specific conditions, developed the ability to lie to him, but the valves had rusted and stuck, and when she answered with a rote "I've been good, how about you?" he looked at her with gentle disbelief but no counterbalancing sympathy, and she felt all her options snapping shut like mousetraps.

The man alone at the table next to theirs talked quietly into his cell phone but, bending back against his chair, his eyes closed, his free hand squeezing his temples, he could be heard saying: "Yeah, I'm at the gate now." Relieved to turn to events outside themselves, Rachel and Julian widened their eyes at each other. "My flight leaves in twenty minutes, so I'll be there by—yeah—don't wait up. Me, too." He closed his phone and pushed his palms against his eyes.

"Did you ever pull that one on me?" Julian whispered.

"Can't recall. What about you?"

"Yeah, I should tell you, I wasn't really on that space launch."

"Nice. Aidan says you're busy."

"Huh. Yeah. It's good. There's plenty of money if that's what you wanted to talk about."

To which, as if she were a broken talking doll with its string stuck halfway out of the hole in her back, she said something she'd meant to say later, if at all—"We did make a very nice baby once"—and then looked down at the cream in its metal pitcher, its off-center lid, its loose handle and dull pewter finish, and felt as bad with him as alone.

"Not much of an immune system," he said, not unkindly, but with a false offhand shrug, refusing to go into any of that.

She could feel him fighting to fly away from her, as if she were hanging from the tie ropes of his carefully ballasted one-man hot-air balloon. She had lived without him and not died. She had friends, options, an ear for good advice. But she wasn't a fantasist to believe that life could be better when reassembled from damaged, familiar shapes, rather than frittered away endlessly looking for something new. There was no restoration to factory condition anymore; there was only slowing down the decay. Still, she couldn't think of anything to say that wasn't too much, too soon, too sorry, too pleading, and so she said, "Aidan's setting *you* up on dates?"

"He has refused to discuss his love life with me for nearly three decades."

"Only because he's intimidated by you. He envies you."

"I can tell when you're lying, you know."

"Sorry." He could. "It wasn't all bad," she said.

"No, I know. I know." He looked at his swirling coffee. "There was a lot I loved. For a long time. I still do."

"You have to know it wasn't about you, the end. I was so unhappy about other things, about everything."

"And that will never happen again?"

"Would you believe me if I said yes?"

"Probably not, no." They laughed.

"Do you want to hear it anyhow?"

"That's okay, thanks."

She hadn't meant to say anything about trying again, had only wanted to see him, and for him to see her, for him to have a few minutes being half of *them*, just a reminder, to show they could be calm, maybe even warm. That would be enough for today. But she could feel his resistance as he looked out the window, longing to be away from her and them. When he turned back, he asked about work, portioning out the charm that always flowed effortlessly for him whenever he needed to tap it, but that was as silly as her preening at home for him after he'd seen all her intimate horrors. He'd always had this power to fade out, present less and less of himself to hold on to, replacing himself with slick, sleek panels of wit, gossip, professional concerns. She remembered, really only now, how irritating she used to find that. She'd put that out of her mind in these months of dying. She was becoming angry with him, though he hadn't done or said anything, when *she* had ambushed *him*. Angry *now*, when she had hoped to rearrange her misery and loneliness around his presence. "No, stop. I'm not here for small talk. But I'm not here to beg either. I'm just talking. We can file divorce papers if you want. I'm not standing in your way."

"If *I* want? I haven't—I don't know why. If *you* want to, we can. Is that why you wanted to meet?"

"I could have done that on the phone."

"So what *do* you want? Can I ask: What were all your others for, if it wasn't to show me how useless I was?"

She felt a touch of relief at that: he had questions he'd asked himself, too, polished and phrased just so, rehearsed during countless imaginary confrontations. "You won't believe me. Honestly, a lot of times I was trying to feel useful, like, I think, you did. They were usually sad, and I felt better when I cheered them up."

"So a spree of altruism. Not philandery, philanthropy."

"Not entirely." She indulged his point, willing to show remorse if his ego demanded, so they could move on and shore up their losses. "I confess to all the same sins as everyone else. As should you. But I couldn't do it, really. I hated everyone. I blamed strangers for not knowing what I had to do to bring him back, to bring us back. To fix you." But after allowing himself to flare into focus for a moment, a glimpse, Julian was flickering out again, no time to see if she'd been right. A sexless infant in a stroller banged its plastic spoon against its own face, threw the spoon with a splatter of applesauce onto the floor, began to shriek.

"I don't miss *that*," he tried.

Rachel said, "I had the strangest thing the other day. I wonder if you've had this. A total stranger said to me in the grocery store, when I'm looking at cream cheese, and I don't think I'm thinking about anything except cream cheese, not about him, and she said, 'Are you all right?' A stranger. 'It'll be okay,' this other old lady said to me in the street. Do they see it in you, too? If it's just me, then maybe I'm fooling myself in all sorts of ways."

"I don't know. I do get pity from people still. But, I really, I try, I guess, very hard—I don't want it anymore. I want to be free from all that."

"Are you insane? Of course you want to be free of it—you're *human*." He suddenly looked like he was going to break. She should have shut up right there—she had him. "Do you think I'm saying I want to be like this? I like being the most maudlin bitch on earth? But

Julian, it's in the *blood* now. It's a permanent condition. We're not like everyone else anymore. We're out of their club forever. Did you really think you were going to get over it? You don't think that, not really, do you?"

"No, of course not, but isn't there some middle ground . . ." He stopped talking, waited as if she had an answer, and she waited as if he might still figure out what was left to say.

"If you find it," she said, "tell me, okay? Because I can't find it alone."

His face closed up again, and he wasn't going to say anything, and she should have turned to lighter matters, she supposed, but she was crying. "I'm sorry." She fumbled in her purse for a tissue. She stood up; he didn't. She waited one second longer then fled into the wind and sun and raised a gloved hand to her eye, but wiped her contact lens clear off its floating tear and into the wind, and half-blind she walked and sometimes ran back to her apartment, sorting through fragmentary memories of his face and conversation, to save and file any proof that she was not alone in this.

And I keep hoping you are the same as me.
And I'll send you letters . . .
— the Sundays, "My Finest Hour"

1

SPRING WAS LATE but some child's birthday was not, and the balloons lashed to the park's fence shriveled in the cold air, a bouquet of colorful prunes above the lips stained Popsicle blue and the clatter of juggling pins dropped by a shivering clown. On the sidewalk, looking through the fence, stood a man, whom none of the children knew, though he felt the parents should have.

Like an arrogant government minister forced by revolution into faraway exile where he can only find work as a cabdriver and who then assumes that all his fares despise him as completely as he would have despised immigrant cabdrivers in his home country back when he was a man of power, so it now was with the former lead singer of Reflex.

Reflex had a song on a film soundtrack back in 1991, the pinnacle of a twelve-year run as a band with underground and college success but never arena stardom. That film and their title song for it, "Sugar Girl," were both moderate hits (the band's largest by far), but that didn't, as its management had continually promised, "bump them up to the next level." Then a child was born, and the drummer retired to become a school music teacher. Another child was born, launching the bassist into a sinecure in his father's restaurant-supply company. One more child was born, and the keyboardist-composer—musically essential for the band but so fat and ugly that he always played far in the back and was edited out of videos—retired to score for local theater. Babies promenaded along Venice Beach strapped into their fathers' chest harnesses—worn ironically, custom made with black leather and band logos and metal studs—and Reflex was no more.

Soon after the neonatal conspiracy to destroy his career and destabilize his life, Alec Stamford, the guitarist and lead singer, certain where the band's appeal had always laid, moved to New York and released a solo album, *Still Standing*, produced at great expense by a no-fail Grammy-winning hit maker, but no one is perfect. The album could still be found in seventy-five-cent bins outside Brooklyn bodegas, its mouse-thin spine straining for attention.

Stamford lived for occasional royalty checks from ASCAP—briefly plumper when the movie *Sugar Girl* evolved to DVD and then again when the song "Sugar Girl" was rerecorded with a female singer and new lyrics for a commercial for Sugar Swirl Donuts. Stamford rerecorded "Ten Minutes to Midnight" himself for an ad for the Chevy Syncope. The ad guys could have used the original album recording, but that would have required Stamford to split the licensing fees with the label. Instead, by rerecording the song to duplicate the original as closely as possible, with session musicians paid by the hour rather than his old bandmates, he was able to eat the cake in its entirety. The price was the definitive loss of the belief that a great performance of pop music could never be duplicated, that there was something snowflake-unique in pop that could not be imprisoned behind the bars of staff paper. The commercial version of "Ten Minutes to Midnight" caused the original label to sue Stamford and Chevro-let, only dropping the action after both versions were compared and found different by a team of court-appointed audio technicians.

Subsequent efforts to write pop music battered him. Too old and slow to catch the crests of musical fashion, not confident enough to ig-nore them, never sure if he was "advancing," imitating or parodying himself, he finally quit and, in self-punishment, hit clubs to check out new bands, then Googled them after the shows, then, inevitably, auto-Googled, too.

His rare appearance in celebrity magazines, like a faint echo of the big bang just perceptible on the far edge of the universe, warmed him for weeks. His appetite, like that of a former fat man, had slowly ac-customed itself to the less certain nourishment of scarce fame but never stopped nattering at him. Reminding himself that most people survived without any fame at all, he attempted to behave like them, famelessly, as if he were just a cabdriver after all and not the former prime minister of the Republic of Reflex.

How would a fameless person respond? he asked himself at mo-ments of great self-awareness, and he would peer at the faces of peo-ple speaking to him with the close attention of an illegal-immigrant waiter desperate to catch a mumbled order. His resulting impression was uneven, as if he had learned simple conversation as a diligent but not terribly gifted autodidact, pinching his cheeks to stay awake while puzzling by candlelight over a book of antique engravings: *Taking an Interest, Putting the Other First, A Prompt Apology Pleases Both Parties.*

Stamford's assembled eccentricities, necessarily budget depen-dent, consoled for lost fame and labeled him a person of interest, evi-dence that fame was still dormant in him. He wore a pince-nez, for example, clipped on for reading small type, and bracelets to match his outfits, but plastic, stylish only for the causes they championed, as randomly strewn about the political spectrum as the colors of the bracelets themselves: he was opposed to testicular cancer (yellow) but in favor of Israeli settlements in the West Bank (orange). His hair, a willowing mane, required various emollients, for brands of which he had a Pashtun tribesman's loyalty, but he had his hair cut at the Uzbek barbershop on the corner, calling out blade numbers, criticizing scissor technique.

Back in the old country, a failed or failing rock star would have been burned to death under a blast of the most withering, ideologically pure disdain, nothing personal. That Alec had become the creature his youth required him to detest left him with no good option. To discard his own past as youthful intolerance would have been unpalatable, even self-destructive; his past was the best of him. His need to regain his old status meant accepting his younger standards. Renewed success would win him absolution, from everyone, from himself. In the meantime, he saw his reflection in the eyes of others and flinched.

After his solo career failed, his desperate rediscovery of his talent as a painter offered a middle path between drudging anonymity and unbecoming musical ambition. He felt when painting that he *must* be an artist, not merely an expired confection of the musical-industrial complex. He sold work, and critics discussed his work, so Reflex was retroactively recast as a previous incarnation of a restless creative force in merely the first of many media. His legitimate skills and reputation sufficed to win him second-tier New York gallery representation, so his previous career also cast its authenticating light forward; he must be a real artist now, since he had once been a successful musician. The sniffing boredom of art critics beat gulping down the gritty indigestible sludge of global indifference. He envisioned a work about the World Trade Center that would say something painful but true.

His gallery exhibits supported his sense of existing separate from other people or even inanimate objects. (Once, soon after the sibilant, whispering-wind failure of *Still Standing*, he had the impression, lasting almost a full minute and returning over weeks, that the box of unsold CDs on the floor of his TriBeCa loft were *him*, not metaphorically but actually.) When confident in his reality, he allowed his study of those archaic forms of human interaction (friendship, the notion of other people with their own internal lives) to lapse, and he released himself from alliances with civilians forged during fame famines. Then, in spells of lowered self-esteem, he reestablished those ties, sheepishly but not without real charm. He would become again a paragon of false immodesty, boasting that he was "a beloved figure in the entertainment field, you know," with a tone conveying his smiling acceptance that he was no longer any such thing, and that humble assurance, he hoped, would let people know he was amused by his fate and confident that he was suffering merely a temporary power outage.

Alec Stamford met Cait O'Dwyer twice. The second occasion was a CD-release party for another band on her label, an event where she was simultaneously talked up as the next big thing and treated as a mere aspirant. Alec watched her and, nervous that she remembered their first introduction, was led over to her with some pomp by the Anglophilic head of A&R: "Cait, here's a grand old man of our game you'd be wise to emulate." When she said, "Oh, very nice to meet you. I quite like Reflex," the wiser tactic was to say, "Thank you," rather than remind her that he had watched her perform two months earlier and then walked up to her at the bar and paid his compliments, had even said, "I sang for a band called Reflex, but that's probably ancient histor—" just as she turned her head to accept praise from some other admirer, and Alec had stood there a few moments too long before he saw how pathetic he was and fled to another bar around the corner, where he drank heavily and had to pinch his own palm until he raised a blood blister to prevent himself from playing one of the two Reflex songs on the jukebox, though that was one of the reasons he loved that bar, hanging there and waiting to see if anyone else put one of them on and then examining people's faces as it played.

But this second, more appropriate meeting, at Pulpy Lemonhead Records' party for Leering Queer, led to a long conversation, the first part of which Alec wasted trying to gauge if she remembered him. Finally, when he implied that he hadn't heard of her, she didn't contradict him, so, very slowly, he relaxed his internal clench and permitted himself to press his personality outward until it met hers as an equal.

He was not immune to her beauty but saw too that she attracted with more: she had *it* unconsciously germinating in her with no flaws.

She was only just beginning to sense the effects of her growing, growling fame or charisma or whatever its name was. It could not accurately be called fame, since people of either limited or decreasing fame often had *it* in spades and people of more objective fame (such as himself) could, one day, suddenly, very plainly, lose *it* entirely. Nor could it be called charm or charisma, because he knew people with *it* who positively repelled onlookers to a distance of about twenty-five feet but then held them there, in an unbreakable orbit, like a fly hovering immobile, trying to escape the effect of a vacuum cleaner nozzle held just so. He settled, those years ago, on the word *potency*, had even tried to write a song about it, but one of his very few joys in that period had been the process of destroying his aborted songs, a distraction so rare that he stretched it out over days, overseeing the eradication of all computer files, paper printouts, tentative four-track recordings.

He mentioned to Cait a music festival he was in negotiations to produce. "It may not pan out, but might fit you, if you want to send a CD of your stuff to my office." He slid a card from a leather case. "Also I have a gallery show going up soon." Standing beside her, he could feel himself absorb some of her luxurious potency. It flowed into him, and as in a dream in which one recalls how to do something impossible, simply by relaxing and doing it (flying, running sixty miles an hour, auto-fellatio), his muscles remembered how to possess potency, to contain and express it. Other people watched *him* when he spoke to her. He could hold on to her effect even when she was across the room, but the next day it was gone.

Each time he logged on to bulletin boards about her, he told himself he would most likely never do it again; he was just curious to see how she fit into the universe, and so he never wrote down the log-in passwords (or the false email accounts). He had therefore to create a new identity each time his refreshed curiosity required him to lurk and study the nature of her attraction by studying those who were attracted to her. Over a few months, he called himself caitfan and then caitfan01 and caitfan02 up to and including caitfan16, though someone else had snagged caitfan11 when Alec was otherwise distracted with the possibility of a Reflex reunion concert.

2

"MAIL(E) CALL," Maile flirted, dropping books and letters on Julian's desk, but he had his iPod on, and the pass was incomplete. Embedded among seasonal modeling-agency books, video-résumé reels, the bills, and the invitations to conferences and production company summer parties was a thick cardboard disk printed red on black: POST COITUM OMNE ANIMAL TRISTE EST. On the reverse, the name Alec Stamford, a date and time, OPENING, INVITED GUESTS ONLY, and the address of a Lower East Side gallery, the owner of which had been in Julian and Rachel's inadvertently hilarious Lamaze class (taught by an old Dominican lady with uniquely inflected English who called the mothers-to-be "rr-r-r-oly-polies" as in "now joo gonna push dat baby out, rr-r-r-oly-poly," but spoke of the one lesbian couple in the class only ever in the squeamish third person while looking at the other teams: "Dose two ladies over dere are gonna wanna study da breath patterns a little better").

For those without Latin, the show's title was translated on one side of the cocktail napkins, so that one cradled one's glansy-pink prawn or vaguely vaginal anchovy tartlet in the red-and-black words: FOLLOW-ING THE ACT OF LOVE, ALL CREATURES GRIEVE. The waitstaff who distributed the delicacies were recruited for physical appeal rather than catering prowess, near models nearly dressed in black and scarlet. The gallery was garlanded in black crêpe, resembling a brothel hosting a funeral for one of its own. The soundtrack, piped from speakers concealed in weeping, armless Venuses and sleeping, harmless fauns, alternated between bump-and-grind and funerary violin: "Violate Me Right Now" by the Repulsion and "The Sombre Coquetry of Death" by Hieronymous Gratchenfleiss, "Compulsive Fucker" by the Schoolyard Weasels, then a mournful bagpïpe.

Julian recognized friends and nameless faces, smiled and nodded through camouflaged pleas for employment, but took regular advantage of the gallery's strange configuration to win long stretches of solitude, taking plastic flutes of prosecco into the booths. Stamford's pictures were all small, and each hung in its own confined viewing booth with space enough only for one or two people, hunched close. At any one time, most of the two hundred or so guests were milling about the main gallery floor, eating and talking but with no pictures to look at, while twenty or thirty were sliding in and out of overlapping black and crimson curtains, as if penetrating a bedroom, or further. The effect was like a busy Sunday morning, sinners slipping from one confessional to another, eager to confess again and again, take on more and more penance.

The painter himself, recognizable from the catalog, was leaning over a young woman with a notebook, his six-foot-five frame swaying a little from drink and the paunch belted to him, worn almost ironically, his teeth so thoroughly whitened that they called to mind not the youth he'd been hoping to restore but the matching so-white skull to which they still clung, the moralizing whiteness of a cattle head sun-dried on a desert floor. "I mean to provoke a clarity, but a clear-sighted view of mystery. The illusion of transfiguring and terrifying honesty. Think about this: a nice ass looks like twinned, fused cherries, you know? Nature's repertoire is actually surprisingly finite."

The young woman, from a minor newspaper, despite the gallery's efforts to open this show on a night of competitive inactivity, provoked back: "What do you say to those who call your paintings mere provocations?"

Alec exposed to the light his barium teeth. "I'm reminded of an old joke. A little old lady from Minneapolis visits Paris, her first trip there since she was a young girl, and at the restaurant she orders her dessert '*à la mode.*' She's very proud of her French. Well, the waiter comes back with her *tarte tatin,* but instead of a scoop of ice cream, there's a lump of dog shit on it, shaped like a swan. '*Mais qu'est-ce que c'est que ça?*' the lady cries. 'I ordered it *à la mode!*' And the waiter says, '*Oui, madame,* but fashions change.'"

The paintings were titled only with date and time, printed in mournful wreaths of golden script: *11:17 pm, January 18, 2009,* for example. Each was sexually explicit without being slightly sexually arousing. The works depicted people in states of emotional and physical nakedness in the moments immediately following the evaporation of humid desire. A chill had just settled over the subjects, as if sweat or other clinging moisture was fast distilling into component salts. In couples or alone, lovers hunched in bed or leaned over to turn on baths, their bellies released to sag, or they looked at their bodies in harshly lit bathroom mirrors, stared at closing doors, lay back-to-untouched-back, or—in the case of two muscled men—turned away from each other to stare at their own flexed reflections in their own infinitely cross-reflecting, full-length mirrors, their biceps and quads and traps and glutes like agglomerations of dinner rolls, as if to re-assure themselves that what they had just engaged in hadn't deflated their hard-won physiques.

One canvas only was not aggressively despondent: a woman lay on her back, her legs supported straight up in the air with the help of a man who, holding high her ankles with one hand, studied his wrist-watch, the only item he wore. Her face was blocked by the head-on perspective of her lifted legs, buttocks, and the explicitly depicted swollen center of all attention. And one's eye inevitably traveled to it—Stamford's perspective and composition were strong enough to achieve that, even if the subject weren't so magnetic and its detail so photo-realistically rendered—but one couldn't view it solely sexually, as an entrancing entrance, because just exactly then, tilted back by a potential father for a crucial three to six minutes, its essential nature was possibly reversing, transforming it into an existential exit. Stamford acknowledged the debt to Courbet's *Origin of the World* and neatly repaid it by borrowing in turn from Van Eyck's *Arnolfini Portrait:* over the bed, just visible above the woman's upraised feet, hung a round convex mirror, reflecting that very Courbet picture, as if it were hanging across the room from her, where you were observing this scene unnoticed, as if you were peeking out of that nineteenth-century vulva in your examination of the twenty-first-century vulva before you, with all the queasy oscillation between sexual desire and procreative realities, matrimony yielding to maternity, lust only boil-ing to force labor.

"Please don't let her call me a roly-poly tonight. I don't think I can bear it," an immense Rachel had said on the way to their final Lamaze class.

"You? She's been commenting on *my* gut."

A month later the Lamaze teacher called the hospital room. "Are joo holding God's precious gift?" she asked.

"I am. I really am," teary Julian had said.

"And jore queen is sleeping?"

"She is."

"And is she very bootiful?"

"She really is."

"Joo better tell her dat, okay? And joo tell her joo love her."

"I did, Mrs. Santana. And I will."

"Hello! I thought I recognized you," a voice behind Julian in the booth interrupted. A formerly young woman stood next to him before the impregnation painting, a girl who once held Maile's job, and with whom he had once or twice gone to bed, and who now worked in another art gallery, and who had aged unconscionably. "What do you think of the genius?" She slid her arm through Julian's and pecked his cheek. "He's really dreadful, isn't he? Pictorially, I mean." Her hand was on his biceps still, an offer or a declaration of being over the past. "Let's have a drink, J-Do."

They slipped out between the curtains, and then Cait O'Dwyer said, "Well, congratulations to you," her back a few feet from him. Thanks to the small population of media-industry New York, he was at a social event with her. His body reacted to her spoken voice as if she'd snuck up from behind and whispered something warm and improbable into his ear. He bit his lip and watched as she stood on tiptoe to kiss the painter's lowered cheek and hold his hand for a long moment.

Julian slid free of the former employee's grasp and, wiping his sweating hands on a balled-up cocktail napkin, retreated to the men's room (the door painted with a very accurate penis sliced lengthwise like a sundae-dressed banana, each of its internal tunnels labeled in excellent Latin but in a reversed-R childish scrawl). His face mirror-composed, he came out, unsure if this was how he and Cait should meet but certain that they should. He hadn't seen her in weeks, since she'd sung "Bleaker and Obliquer" and he had known it was best *not* to meet her, but her effect on him had been incubating ever since, and the decision to approach her now felt natural and necessary.

He watched her from across the gallery. She didn't blend into the crowd but stood outlined and masterfully lit even when models and model-waitresses swayed and scowled around her. The painter brought her a drink himself, in a glass, while everyone else cracked empty plastic flutes. He spread his hand across the white back of her sleeveless top, moved it in slow, possessive circles, and Julian's disappointment felt like a sidewalk assailant swinging a bat into his stomach.

It had never occurred to him that she might be with someone. It hadn't been relevant to his fantasies, until now, as the painter leaned down to whisper into Cait's ear and caught Julian's eye across the floor, held it as he whispered until Julian finally gained enough control to pretend to be looking past them. Now it mattered; it mattered terribly, more than Rachel flying away the other morning in tears, more than the former employee who was back now, handing him a drink, taking his arm again, walking him away.

"What's new in TV land? Are you providing your current staff as complete a grounding in the ways of the world as I received?" She led him to a couch where he could turn his back on Cait and the artist. "Do you want to meet him?" she asked. "I saw you looking. He is rather magnetic. Little secret: our gallery passed on him a couple years ago. I'm convinced we made the right decision." Lighter pop songs now peeked through from between the death and sex music, and Julian recognized a tune from his own collection. "He's very driven. I'll give him that."

Reflex was shuffled somewhere inside his iPod, an album Julian had been forced to buy three different times as the music industry shoved him from format to format, and only now did he recall the band's lead singer's name as being the same as the painter's. The sickening truth: Cait could very well have been with Alec Stamford, the musician. Julian had been quite taken by Reflex in film school, had studied sleeve photos and lyrics, when he spent his free hours doing that and little else, had detected a profundity in Reflex songs, references obscure but reminiscent of some shared experience, and he recalled a feeling of mutual understanding, lying on a bunk, looking up at the back of an LP: "Lyrics—Stamford, Music—Vincent." He looked back over his shoulder; the artist was there, but Cait O'Dwyer was gone.

"Julian, I feel like I conjured you tonight," said the former employee. "I was *just* thinking about you. Hello? All right, come on, let's introduce you. You're gawking." She waved the artist over. He kissed her cheeks and held her hands and helpfully reminded Julian of her name. "Alec Stamford," Heather said, "this is Julian Donahue, one of your myriad admirers, and the renowned artist behind several of your favorite shampoo commercials."

"I am actually a fan of Reflex," Julian said, pointing to the air, which carried a song he'd once truly loved, "Last One In, First One Out." "Are you possibly the same Alec Stamford?"

"I think I am. Some days more, some days less." The larger man shook Julian's hand and kneaded his shoulder, tipped his head back to consider him down his nose. "This song was a favorite of Springsteen's actually," Stamford said. The bass and drums dropped out, and the vocals floated, whispered, over sustained keyboard chords, *"Walk to your car, I'm going back to the bar / Just say good night, 'cause we both know this don't feel right."* The former employee laughed, rubbed Julian's neck, excused herself for just a minute.

Stamford pulled two passing drinks out of the air, but Julian, turning toward the gallery's huge front window, saw Cait O'Dwyer on the sidewalk, buttoning her coat. Knowing he no longer had the stamina to court another man's girlfriend, he decided she was leaving too early to be involved with the artist. He declined the drink with apologies, said congratul—

"You really have to run?"

"I do. I'm sorry."

Stamford looked at the girl in the picture window. "You know Cait?"

"Kate? No."

"Oh, ah, okay, but so, ah, commercial direction, Heather said? I may have a need for someone in your line of work. Flip me your card before you split. I'll have the gallery hook us up."

Julian left as casually as he could, Heather Zivkovic still in the bathroom, but by the time he reached the street, there was no sign of Cait, just crowds from bars and galleries, and his teeth chattered in the April air as he swallowed his hopes.

At home, he found Aidan asleep on the couch, and he reread Cait's *Times* profile online, blue light on his face, remarkable fellow, remarkable fellow. He sorted through Google's sightings of her in the cybermurk, now more than a thousand, though some of them were mere rumors, her name struggling to break out of Japanese text or the thrice-daily essays of the housebound furious and the cubicled despairing. He printed out a glamour photo of her laughing through blue backlit smoke, the granddaughter of some 1950s Claxton-photographed jazz-club beauty, the great-granddaughter of a daring fast girl with her bare knees tucked up to her chin on the hot sand of the Côte d'Azur. He discovered the newly launched www.caitodwyer.com, scoured it for clues.

The site included the usual propaganda to sell Cait and her music to the universe, with its short attention span and surfeit of stimuli: email lists, tour dates, About the Band, Cait's blog. The Guest Book hosted fans far from New York, in Los Angeles, fair enough, but also mythological hamlets like Wichita and Albuquerque. "Cait! I saw your show at the Mad Dog last October and I never forgot it. ¡Keep rockin'! Stu." "I think your a poet. And I loVe you. Beth P." "Tell Ian he ROXXX!!! Mags and Michelle. Tell him those were our favorite shirts. He'll get it! Ian! Call us next time you're in the Triangle!" "1st Ave gig was awesome, and you won a fan for life in me, Cait. T-bone." However necessary such marketing may have been, this outpouring of adoration from children must have embarrassed her, if she was the woman he hoped she was. "I bought your demo at the Vingt-Deux, and I listen to it all day, all the time. I want you to know how great I think you are. I wish there was a better way to tell you. I wish I knew how I could know that you knew it. I want you to feel it. Unless you can't be it and feel it at the same time??? GG."

Downloadable Gallery: Cait, lit from the side, smoking at a dark bar, wearing some sort of one-piece, nineteenth-century, Toulouse-Lautrecky, netted crimson-and-silver courtesan's underwear, flanked by her band; Ian onstage, leaping in front of an amp, his legs spread as his left hand splays into a chord and the right arm, bent, has just slashed the strings, identical to thousands of album covers since 1964, like a yoga posture to be mastered; Cait lying in a garden, photographed from above, her eyes meeting the camera, her face and red hair surrounded by countless still-closed and patient tulips, a field of green stems and pursed pregnant leaves to the very edge of the frame, but in this germinating color, two o'clock to Cait's face, one solitary open bloom, purple and veined white, like a cut of raw beef; Cait onstage, facing front but her eyes looking to the side, the barest minimum of exertion around her mouth to count as a smile; Cait and the guitarist in the studio, tumorous headphones around necks, the two discussing something with an older man in a hooded sweatshirt, the three artists caught unaware in a moment of creative consultation; the drummer in action, face inexpressive behind his sticks, blurred into Oriental fans; the bassist, posing in front of a disused Coney Island amusement park ride, his arms crossed to prop his biceps up and out; Cait and her three men in a wintertime park of spindly bare trees: the men are lying facedown on a concrete path, dressed only in their tighty-whitey underpants, stacked like cordwood, sleeping drummer under grouchy bassist (biceps accentuated) under acquiescent Ian, and Cait atop this flesh-bench in fur-trimmed and hooded jacket, scarf, gloves, boots, and acutely angled beret over her red hair, her breath a cumulus the size of a peach.

What They're Saying (and Who *Are* They?) "Cait O'Dwyer's voice is a wake-up call to a dormant, stupid, smug music biz." "If you only go to one live show this year, this century, this eon, then this is the show." "Music so pure and true you'll sob. If you don't, get therapy." "She *was* Irish, but she's ours now. This is the future of real American music." Click here to download a .pdf of the *Flambé* profile of Cait, "Bleaker and Obliquer: A Simple Ghoul from Erin."

The *Flambé* article mentioned that she lived in Brooklyn over a tea shop, from which she bought purple boxes of an imported brand of breakfast tea she had known in her childhood, "where ghosts were a daily reality but sex was a legend or a nightmare never to be discussed."

3

AND SO THE NEXT DAY Julian stood on Henry Street, less than a quarter mile from his apartment, in front of the building he had known at once from the puff piece's breathy indiscretions, its ground-floor storefront filled with tea paraphernalia. Next to the window, its door buzzers were labeled plainly enough: 1–TEAPUTZ OFFICE, 2–M&R INC, 3–HARRIS, and floating atop them all, 4–CO'D. He listened to her demo on his iPod: *"Come, come, come, come find me, no matter what I say."* A good line, implying a tormenting, irresistible woman, unsure of her own mind but accelerating in her fall for you, O listener at your computer, debating yourself as to whether she's worth the dollar-download click, as Julian stood, facing her doorbell but still not touching it.

They would go out for coffee and flex their overdeveloped charms. He would be cast in the role of suitor, if not the revolting and unholy hybrid of fan-suitor, a crest-flaunting lizard, and she the unimpressed, dozy-eyed lizardette. They would or would not be dazzled by each other's personalities, each other's memories, collected solely to display to others, thus winning new experiences and yet more memories. Perhaps they would be startled by the easy flow, scarcely able to pay for the coffee before dashing up her stairs, to shove each other into her apartment, to devour each other.

Or with crevasses of cappuccino foam still wintry pert, they might shake hands, express mutual gladness at having met, thanks for the advice, good luck with your career. Or he might long to touch her cheek but then see her boredom with his time-dulled surfaces, with this interminable coffee coursing deep under insurmountable cappuccino Alps. Or she might make a fatal error, say something lame, dispel the thickening illusion that she was not half his age, and he would, limp as ever, smile wanly at the pretty little girl not worth even a cheap pass.

"It's cold outside, so come find me," she persisted, but it wasn't quite true; the weather was warming, and that was enough to break the

spell. He'd imagined it. It was just pop music, not any real woman on earth.

He turned away from her door and went to his office, embarrassed at having lurked and ogled. He spent the ride laughing at himself to avoid pitying himself. And by the time he'd arrived at his desk, he forgot all that shame and wisdom as his computer came to life with an email that asked, "Why didn't you press the bell? Why not pay a call?"

That first uncanny moment, coming to see he'd been observed, was enough to replenish everything he'd meant to outgrow on the subway. She must have watched him from her high window. He replayed the event now with its fuller meanings: not him brought to his senses but her showing herself to be the more confident and intriguing of them. She had watched for him, shadows and glare delicately shrouding her while he dithered and, after laughing at his shy retreat, she must have sat right down and written her anonymous taunt on his flashy website: "Contact Julian Donahue": "Why didn't you press the bell? Why not pay a call?" He sat back at his desk. She had somehow learned his name, his website, his work? She had toiled like a private detective or a crystal-ball-tickling step-witch? What giant footprints and fingerprints had he left behind on coasters, on a gallery guest list? Where else? His fingers shook so he could barely dial his iPod, and he tapped for her voice to match the sight of her pixellated bursting arrival into his world.

No return email address, no signature, nowhere to reply, only pixels beautifully and originally arranged, her voice in his head, the song "Crass Porpoises" (or so her robust accent led him to believe until he reread the song list). But Julian wasn't shaking from a desire to dash to her. She asked the question but knew the answer as well as he: he hadn't rung the bell because that would have been a bore, to them both, and her anonymous taunt proved it, proved *her*, confirmed his best suspicions of her.

He listened to his iPod and sketched storyboards of how they could meet, but because he was a hack, all his ideas were recycled from TV and movies and his own ads. Every approach he could imagine played itself out as quickly as his impulse to ring her doorbell, and she would laugh at him as loudly as she had today. He could use one of her songs in a commercial. Paired with certain images of love and renewal, "Coward, Coward" would be quite effective. And it would certainly be a gift to her, better than bouquets. She'd be paid hefty licensing. And mainstream hits were sometimes made thanks to tasteful use in the right commercial. Have Maile contact the label, insist Miss O'Dwyer meet the director herself: "I thought this a better call to make."

No, even that only rearranged the frames of a tolerable romantic comedy he'd sat through because Rachel liked the lead actor. She would just shake her head, as if he were one of those little boys at the club, complimenting themselves on their courage as they lost to her in cards.

4

HE WRESTLED THE QUESTION for several days, then decided the problem was not in how to meet but when, and maybe even why. Why not pay a call? Because they didn't know enough yet. There were pleasures of investigation and discovery still to be enjoyed that he'd almost squandered. She was laughing at his impatience. Something original could still occur, something neither of them had ever known, and he had nearly destroyed it. And so he made himself sit still, and he watched.

Cait flew from her front door, at the end of a leash binding her wrist, straining to remain attached to the spiked-collar-immune neck of a Great Dane the color of rain-pregnant evening clouds. The beast shook Cait in slapstick jolts up Henry Street. Through the windows of the Bangladeshi deli across from her building, the silenced picture gave the impression of a silent-film comedy.

The monstrous hound towed her to a dog park on the other side of Brooklyn Heights. White pear, pink cherry, and the hallucinatory purple of the redbud blossoms lined the streets, but the enclosed park nestled up against a tendril of the Brooklyn-Queens Expressway, and the wind mingled truck exhaust and a blizzard of cherry blossoms onto the dogs at play.

She opened the gate, and at once her dog ran free of her into the park. "Lars! Stay!" Cait yelled at her Danish chum as he bounded off, shaking the ground, propelled by his rocket-booster genitals, to sniff the puckered back-roses of whimpering Labradoodles and Lhasa-puggles, rotthuahuas, cocksunds, schnorkies, and shiht-boxes. "Well, then. Good dog," she added and walked down the hill toward one of the seats provided to human escorts, rubbing her leash shoulder as she went. At this early hour—monastically early, considering her profession—she was one of six people watching eight dogs. She sat by herself on a bench built around a fat and ancient oak, and Julian could tell from where he was watching that she was down there singing with closed eyes to whatever her headphones were feeding her.

As he walked down the hill, he could almost hear her over the traffic, the sustained car-horns that resembled bossa nova trumpet and flute chords, the dogs barking, the jackhammers and shouted Spanish, the tires squealing like lazy fingers on guitar strings. He came closer, watched her over the fence. She was like any other introverted headphone junkie releasing a slim stream of extroversion, emoting to no audience, like teenagers all over the world, Miami girls swatting invisible crash cymbals, Mumbai boys playing feverish air sitar.

Julian entered the park through a gate behind her bench. His arrival—blocked from her by the tree and her own iPod—was noteworthy, as he had no dog, and he therefore resembled the peculiar childless gentlemen who savor an afternoon in playgrounds. He sat on the same circular bench orbiting her oak but exactly opposite her, as the planet Antichthon once vainly pursued Earth around its orbit.

With his back to their tree, he switched on his handheld memocorder, placed it behind him and to the right. She was singing to the Smiths' "The Boy with the Thorn in His Side." She was, even in these circumstances, a moving vocalist, harmonizing to a tune she'd likely been listening to since she was a girl. This slow circling of each other—perhaps not unrelated to the scent inspection Lars was just then performing on a newly arrived, quivering black beagle rolled on its back—implied endlessness, no fatigue, no despair, perpetual surprise, the end of past loves' predictive or delimiting power. This was what she wanted from him, why she asked him not to pay a call yet.

He'd never done this—sat unnoticed and painlessly extracted a sample of a woman's privacy, like a drop of blood pricked from a sleeping fingertip, to return to her later as a gift, cut and faceted and mounted, endowed with new and complex meanings.

And, because he had never done this, he felt briefly the illusion of being cut free of his past. It was as if he had never been married and separated, never survived Carlton, never fished out and threw back bedmates, never dated girls in high school, never been in hopeless love as a boy, never found others' declarations of deep affection for him to be suspect, pathological, annoying.

She breathed music even when alone, alchemized the sounds of her iPod into something new. She made something out of sitting on a park bench, and somehow she lived with that enormous beast she could hardly control. Julian closed his eyes, soaked in the stolen moments of her singing to no one but him.

He opened his eyes and recognized her guitarist, sandpaper-bearded, Mandarin-tattooed, ear-ringed, brow-pierced, swallowing a belch as he entered the park ten feet in front of Julian. He shuffled straight toward him, scratching his head with both hands—an assault on a dermatological condition or a statement on the unholy earliness of the hour to a musician. The guitarist passed him blindly, two feet away, saying, as soon as he had circled to the far side of the tree, "Yo. Yo. Yo!" She stopped singing, and Julian missed it at once. He pocketed his recorder. "Vicious woman, it's the crack of dawn," said the boy.

"Be an angel, Ian, won't you? Bend over just here and let Lars have a relieving go with you? Otherwise, he's likely to hook himself onto that slow-moving Chihuahua and split the poor thing in half."

"You could just neuter him."

"I would, but as it is my collection's already too large for my apartment."

"There's something I need to say," Ian continued after a long silence, and Julian, now afraid to learn *they* were lovers, stayed because he wanted to know if she was funny and smart, and he wanted to know immediately, and he wanted to know without having to present himself at all.

"Oh, dear, shouldn't you be on one knee? Or wait for me to scoop up Lars's mountainous output?"

"Funny. No, listen. I think we need a little more Hitler from you, missy," he said as, across the park, her dog steamrolled a smaller creature into the mud, then cantered off to spray its urine far up a tree, intent on shooting down a squirrel. "Shulman is going to make us sound like every other record he's ever made if you don't stop him. You can't just sing *well enough*. Yesterday you were like, I don't know, afraid to hit a wrong note in front of him or something. I can't stop him, you know. You're the boss, and this is it. We don't get another go-round if you let him tie-dye us. Well, I do, but you don't."

"Mmmm. Quite manly this morning."

"I'm not kidding, Cait. Now is not the time for you to become polite and agreeable all the sudden."

"The implication in that being—"

"Seriously."

"Would it make you feel better if I tell you I mean to fire Bass?"

"At least I'd recognize you."

A woman with a blue-blinking cell spike jutting from her ear stood before them and said to Cait in an aggrieved tone, "Hey, you, your dog is mounting my dog." She pointed to far across the field where Lars was walking away from an apparently untraumatized German shepherd.

"Oh, I'm so sorry. Did he hurt her?" Cait asked.

"It's making my dog *uncomfortable*, so you have to restrain your dog *now*."

"Ah, I see. *Uncomfortable*. Well, perhaps short of that, I could, instead, explain things to your dog? Perhaps she just needs to hear from someone who has herself been mounted in the last few years?"

The woman sighed expressively and stomped away through the urine-absorbent wood chips.

"Do you have any friends?" Ian asked.

"I have imaginary friends. When they don't cross me."

"You have Lars, of course."

"That I do. Do you suppose you could teach him to play bass?" She called the dog to her, fed it treats, leashed it up. "One of my students asked me how I knew I was ready to do this, the record and all. And I couldn't answer. 'I just know,' I told her. But I think I might have been lying. There are days, like yesterday with Shulman, when I feel like I'm just a tape recorder playing some very old shite." They walked up the hill, and from behind the tree Julian watched them go, the dog pulling her, the guitarist jogging to keep up.

Julian waited, then, taking the long way home, saw, as if coming upon a triceratops, a rare and untraceable pay phone, a relic of another millennium. 411: her number was listed, a second minor miracle in succession. He dialed. "I'm listening," was the extent of it, Cait giving the lie to the term "outgoing message," then the beep, and Julian simply held his memo-corder to the receiver and played Cait's a cappella performance of the Smiths into her own voice mail.

5

JULIAN WAITED. A week later the lyrics to "Bleaker and Obliquer" appeared on her website. If this was her answer to him, it proved that she desired at the same pace and depth as he, an element of investigation, of originality, recalling him to youthful aspirations. She also desired his distance or, more accurately, his escargotically slow approach, the longest possible suspension of the future, for the future hurtles insanely fast. She must be very wise, he thought, to know that at her age.

LYRIX

If you've got a question for me, here's the only answer:
Listen close to your speaker, bleaker and obliquer.
If you want my go-ahead, then go ahead,
But don't say I didn't warn you.

I've had my fill of swooning ghouls, but that's not you.
I'd offer you my shadows, but that's not you.
You can share my limelight. No, that's not true.
I'm waiting for I don't know what, please don't say that's not you.

So what is you, my bored Cupid, my hiding hero?
If you get stronger, must I get weaker, bleaker and obliquer?
All these little boys, the bolder and the meeker
Rendered mute but still so cute.
Bleaker and obliquer, oh, bleaker and obliquer.

Do you have an old love's stitches, running and sore?
Or a lapful of bitches all gunning for more?

Loathed and broke, I'm yours.
Is it better that we never spoke? I'm yours.
I'm yours, but you gotta take me as is, bleaker and obliquer.

The website also blared her projected participation in a telethon on local-access cable, raising money to foil real estate developers plotting to scatter skyscraping condominiums along the Brooklyn waterfront. He cleared his schedule, told Aidan he was contagiously sick, locked the doors, shut off his cell. He was on his couch an hour early, TiVo remote in hand, whiled away the interval watching sea lions protect their beachfront harems. And then she sang the Housemartins' heart-wrenching antidevelopment ballad "Build," dedicating it to the notorious real-estate Caligula in charge of the expected monstrosities, and a campy duet of Blondie's "Call Me" with Alec Stamford. His intrusion irritated Julian, but Alec was cruelly rendered by television and her proximity as particularly paunchy and middle-aged (though he was only a few years older than Julian). A brief interview followed, and then she sat at one of the plain tables under a banner that read DON'T LET THEM STEAL YOUR WATERFRONT, and manned a black telephone, a *rotary* phone, as if to prove the cause's low overhead and high sincerity. Julian watched on his seventy-one-inch plasma, lying on his couch. It would have been very creepy to call her, he knew, but still he dialed whenever the panning camera revealed her waiting by her unused phone. After he'd hung up on six different voices, he finally heard her recite, "Thanks for calling, can we count on your help?"

He paused, but the desire to hear her talk directly to him crushed all contradictory impulses. "Miss O'Dwyer?" The camera stalled on an ancient, bespectacled nun on another black phone, expressively conversing with some waterfront savior.

"Yes, hello there, thank you for helping us beat these bastards."

"Glad to reach you. I didn't much feel like talking to that nun."

"Do you know, she tried to make a pass at me?" said Cait.

"That's certainly been my experience with elderly nuns. What about that guy you sang with?"

"Have you called to pledge something, love?" she prompted.

"I suppose so."

"The cause is a noble one. Dig deep. My pencil's at the ready."

"I know. The camera's on you right now. Did you know that?"

"Of course. I can feel it. One does have *some* talents, you know."

He put her on speakerphone and leaned toward his muted screen. She sat in the middle of a long table between the nun and Stamford. She was looking down, spinning a pencil from knuckle to knuckle, leaning her head to pinch the receiver against her shoulder. "Look up for a second," Julian said. Unperturbed, she slowly complied, and he paused his TiVo just as her eyes met his from beneath lowered lids, and the hint of an unexpected smile was offered. "Excellent. Thank you. You don't look so bored now."

She laughed. "Thank you. I'm not, but I have to take a pledge here, you know, or suspicions will rise about my commitment to the waterfront."

"Of course. Sorry. How much do you usually—"

She read out the costs for the pledge levels: associate, friend, patron, gold-level donor, champion . . .

"Let's go with, um—there's nothing between friend and patron?"

"Not that I can see."

"How about I pledge to buy your album when it comes out?"

"Ooh, hold on a mo, I'm trying to tot that up for the 'Cash Value' blank."

"I pledge that when you sing," he continued, slowing down as he belatedly realized how inarguably villainous he sounded, "something very strange happens to me, even when you're just singing alone in the dog park."

"Oh my."

"And I think that's where those coasters came from as well."

Her breathy laughter steaming from the phone speaker on his table was victorious. She filled his room, kindly released him from feeling like a stalker. "Ah, yes, now I'm seeing. Hello, you. Here's a unique way to ring up a girl."

"Thank you."

"I'm very glad to hear from you, J.D. I assume we've passed the bored Cupid stage then? That rather irritated."

"I think we have, but I don't know what comes after that."

"Something between friend and patron. Still checking your qualifications, I suppose. And may I ask, where exactly *were* you in the park? I'd thought it was my guitarist made that tape."

"No, you may not ask. I have to preserve some mystery about me."

"Oh, you're not having any trouble there. What do you look like?"

"What do you pledge to me?" he asked instead.

"That wasn't included in our training this afternoon, but I'll take requests. Any pledge in particular you'd like me to make?"

He pushed Play. She continued to lift her eyes to the camera (a minute earlier) and smiled very slightly before looking away and writing intently on her clipboard. The camera moved on. Identical clipboards sat in front of various semifamous Brooklyn faces—movie stars, activists, chefs, Stamford gazing drowsily at Cait, MC Esher from Shoo Bombaz—as well as dog walkers, park planners, Greens.

"Pledge not to make an ill-advised jump to movie acting if your album hits. The history of singers on film is a short, violent one, written by angry fans."

"Duly noted and so pledged."

"Pledge not to play Vegas."

"Not my decision, but I take your point."

"Pledge not to make an album called *Cait O'Nine Tails* with a mild S&M theme on the cover."

"It's a deal."

"Pledge to surprise me. Some more."

"Consider it done."

He reversed TiVo and froze it again with her smiling at him. "Pledge to eat dinner with me, but only when you're certain it's absolutely necessary."

"I so pledge."

Julian lay on the leather couch, his head next to the speakerphone, and closed his eyes. She sat across from him, on the chair just there. "You played up the colorful Irish youth pretty heavily in that *Flambé* interview. Any of it true?"

"You've hardly heard any of my colorful Irish nonsense. I can do better. The phones aren't exactly full, I expect there's no harm in a story. Listening?"

"I am almost entirely ears."

"Very well. My *daideo* was the only one of fourteen children to survive to his eighth year. Then my da was one of eight children, but all of them survived, so he grew up with nothing. When my older brother was born, Da named him Septimus, even though he was the first, and told him, as he was growing up, about all the dead siblings which came before. Long, detailed stories of Fergus, died in a famine, and Mary and Connor, attacked by sheep. No, you mustn't laugh: when Sep and I were small, we were both terrified of sheep. I kicked a boy on a farm who tried to make me pet one. But none of it true, of course, just my da's humor, and his fear, I suppose, and a little superstition. I was twelve, I think, before my mum told me we'd been just the two of us all along. Sep never really saw the joke. He and Da don't speak much anymore."

"But you do. You saw the joke."

"I hope you do as well." He wondered where she'd stand and how her face might change at this moment. He liked her leaning against his windowsill, a silhouette against the distant sprays of light, testing him in little ways, making sure he was paying close attention.

"I understand your father's approach. A splash of tragedy with your childhood lends a proper tone to the rest of your life, calibrates expectations. There are no more miserable, persistently disappointed adults than the ones with perfect childhoods."

"And will I get to hear of yours someday?"

"I do so pledge." He paused. "I like our song. Very much. Can I call it our song?"

"Yes. But I won't share royalties, you know."

"Agreed. Maybe now we should call it a night, Cait."

"Fair enough. Mustn't be gluttons. Good night, J.D."

Messages left on her website's guest book were, obviously, open to others. He tried to register as caitfan, but it, and caitfan01 through caitfan38, were all taken, and slouching in her admirers' line as caitfan39 didn't much appeal, so he became instead sleepycupid. For several days he couldn't bring himself to write anything, unwilling to mingle among these multiplying caitfans, sad people posting their photos and "artwork inspired by Cait," uploading videos of themselves singing her songs back to her or just confessing their feelings, hoping she would acknowledge their existence. sleepycupid finally managed, "Excellent telethon. The development of your powers is occurring at high speeds now. Even a curmudgeonly old man has to admit it. Beware of the sheep."

"Dear sleepycupid," came the reply five long hours later from a nondescript Yahoo! email address to the nondescript Yahoo! email address he had opened for the purpose of the guest book and her email list, "Your elderly and curmudgeonly appreciation is warmly valued, far above the callow bleating. So, in your centuries of experience, what's a girl to think of this?" This was a link to an essay on a blog outpost manned by some lonely kid who opined on politics and music and video games with jaded sophistication. Judging from the empty comment pages, he was blogging to no one: "Don't have enough bland pop in your life? Wish you could hang with the supercool and chitchat about the latest oversold media-ocrity? Then have I got a stupid Irish girl for you . . ."

She couldn't really care about this. Could artistic flesh feel a sting even from this baby bee? She'd gone Google-trolling for this (no friend would have sent it to her), read it all the way to the bitter end, and was so unable to banish it from her mind that she was sharing it with him, to somehow dilute it. She's looking for someone whose excess growths protect her excess weaknesses, he thought, and she's testing if it's me.

There were other dissenters, now and again, and she even let them onto her own site. Why didn't she just ban, for example, doubtfulguest, who abused her openly in her own guest book? "Not without charms, I suppose, this kind of sound wallpaper, but honestly, why, Cait O'Dwyer—who I am sure runs this website for herself—why do you keep a page like this where people praise you? Don't you feel stupid, vain, pathetic?"

A week later, "doubtfulguest is back because I heard from a friend how great your new song was—*Bleaker*—and I should listen right away and all my opinions would change. Well, I listened. Sad effort. You should just stop for a few years, if your ego can stand it, and listen to real music. Maybe you'll grow."

Julian, enraged by the dismissal of their song, as if taking the insult onto himself could somehow help her, replied to her numerical Yahoo! address: "You have no end of people telling you, I'm sure, 'Ignore that guy! You're great!' but for some reason that doesn't make you feel better: you can't ignore him. All those other people are wrong: you *shouldn't* ignore that guy, and he isn't 'wrong' in any way that should make you feel better. For whatever reason, you need to hear some child in Topeka say you're no good. So be it. Listen to that child, feel the burn of his insights, and then go back to what you were doing. If you want someone to find all the dissenting voices for you, I can do that. If you want them silenced, I'll gladly crush whoever makes it difficult for you to be you. On the other hand, if you want a mix tape of people calling you incompetent, I can have one professionally engineered and piped through dedicated speakers hidden in your home, so that you shower and eat and shave your legs and fall asleep to disquieting abuse and then awaken to laughter and caitcalls."

6

DESPITE THE MUTUAL DISCLOSURES, the illusion of second-date intimacy, even his role as muse for a song that was winning plaudits, he couldn't meet her because he wasn't her equal. Though he dreamt of her, she had no shortage of equally awe-crippled fans. And as a spinning fan, his appeal was near zero: a middle-aged fan is not a prize, any more than a three-year-old fan. The Rolling Stones—senior citizens— could hardly enthuse that a nation of toddlers now complained that they couldn't get no satisfaction. She would get none herself from meeting him, at least not yet.

She was—as he had once intended to become—a machine: fuel in, art out. She required regular infusions of something rare: feelings she could process in whatever artistic blender she carried within her, to extrude as art. And, he thought with mounting excitement, if longing and anticipation were materials from which she could forge her music, then he could provide her something of value. He could feed her fire; she could sing about fire; he would understand his own fires in turn; she would see in him a man of alluring fire; a chain reaction might ignite, maybe not extinguishing for years, if he didn't present her with a mere man too soon.

> *The too-bold eyes in the burka*
> *I'm the one in the mask*
> *The fencer, the cop behind one-way glass*
> *Looking at you, looking at you.*

This was cheating, like intentionally invoking the no-fail song just before a party, but still he poked his iPod until it spit out Cait's "Burka," set it on a loop, and with his camera he walked upper Court Street and Atlantic Avenue and Flatbush, past the storefronts of Arab Brooklyn, fragrant oils and Yemeni travel agencies, translators and notary publics and spice men. He tried to catch the eyes of the women walking hand in hand in veils and gowns. The purring notion that behind one black curtain was an Irish pop singer on her daily anonymous hunt for him: he knew this was cheating. He photographed the covered women from across roads and surprised one on a quiet side street where, in the heat and under the low leaves of a cherry tree, she had unwrapped her face to wipe her brow. He thought he was shooting only when the Arabesses looked away, but later, on his computer, they looked directly at him, and one's eyes were a shocking green.

He photographed her building, the sidewalk dramas, the exiting customers of the tea shop. He framed her door from the Bangladeshi deli across the street. He captured one couple's argument, another couple's kiss; the accusing look of the stumbling pedestrian whose first instinct after recovering his balance was to spin and confront the malicious sidewalk; the homeless man threatening a ghostly assailant, his fists up like a nineteenth-century prize pugilist; the weekend athlete couple in full Tour de France regalia, his belly threatening to escape the black spandex, her post-prime buttocks shimmying under sea-blue stretch shorts, like a chart of seabed mountain ranges; and then Cait herself, stepping from her front door, her top and bottom halves far away from each other until Julian could turn the lens, reconstitute her, capture her going into and out of first a Pilates studio then a hipster hair-haus called Whimpering Bangs.

She left the salon walking very slowly, like a parading Lipizzaner, and when she sipped at her water bottle as she walked, she looked to the side, as if the refreshment brought to mind an episode better forgotten, and she seemed to Julian even then to be capable of uncommon depth and empathy. His photos of her, however, failed to catch any of that, and as dull image after dull image of a merely pretty girl holding a bottle of water lit up his computer, he spat insults at himself, groaned at the wasted opportunity, the beauty he had spoiled with his commerce-barnacled incompetence.

The next day he slid four tolerable shots into a manila envelope with her name on it and waited at the Bangladeshis' for a sign. It arrived: silver cane, dark glasses. Julian asked the blind man to deliver the envelope to the owner of Tea Putz. Four shots: Cait stepping from her front door, stretching her arms over her head so that her Lay Brothers T-shirt crept slightly above the tropic of her navel; Cait chatting with the hot-dog vendor at the corner of Atlantic and Hicks, somehow able to draw a laugh from the mute, crooked-faced old Syrian with the leather skin and the mustacheless silver beard; Cait reading a rain-faded poster stuck to a streetlight, pleading for help finding a missing ancient, wandered off from his keepers in the nursing home; Cait, her back to the camera, descending into the mouth of the F-train station, while a stone-faced man ascends with, under each arm, limbless, busty silver mannequins. Julian waited for her dismissive reply or—and it was almost funny to him how unreasonably frightening this seemed—her silence.

7

HE PUSHED THE STORYBOARDS away and stretched, stroked for luck the balding spine of the photo album on his way to the desktop to replay the song and hear his father again: " 'Waterfront!' 'I Cover the Waterfront'!" He checked email: Alec Stamford, lurching, transmission-grinding between friendliness and self-promotion: "P;leasure 2 meet U at thGAller. Y. Hope U dug it. Got some good notices. Saw some famous faces. Full page profile in the Times coming soon I here. Nice. Glad 2B not dead yet :). lUnch SOmetime/? Or . . . I have some work for sale on the gallery site—link below. Or lunch? Discuss some work together? Pay a call. Peace out. AS. Sent from my BlackBerry® wireless handheld."

Far more personal was the letter from news@caitodwyer.com. A finger twitch, a new window, and she spoke to him (and some thousand others on her email list).

We're back in the studio working with legendary producer Vince Shulman, but in the meantime, here's a new tune we're working up on the side. So, if you're a fan, yawning or otherwise, click <u>here</u> to download something new. Don't cheat, please. We can tell if you're not a fan. We have terribly fancy computers here in our top-secret band headquarters, and if a non-fan tries to listen, it will melt your hard-drives and mount your ram. We'll give you this one for free, and you can spot us a drink next time.

Julian clicked <u>thekeysunderthemat.mp3</u>, and like a nymph or a memory Cait streamed from a blinking server in an air-conditioned room in a humanless building on the Hudson through blue and silver cables to his apartment, and she swam into his iPod, docked and waiting, tethered, blinking its persistent warning: Wait. Wait. Do not disconnect. Do not disconnect.

8

JULIAN DRANK A COFFEE in the Bangladeshi deli and listened to his new download, "Key's Under the Mat," a voice and guitar rough mix, a little hurried, a little undercooked. That day in early June, he was one of the few people on earth who had heard it. He guessed it would be a hit; the song had that certain confidence about it, though it was far from his favorite of her work. Musically he judged it a little unoriginal, but lyrically it reached its intended audience of one:

> *A sword in a stone, a tablet on a mountain*
> *A lonely piazza mermaid swooning in a fountain*
> *Cartoon Boy, the key's under the mat*
> *So what do you think about that?*

Her website's guest book already sheltered a few eager comments: "Cait, I've had my fair share of 'cartoon boys,' so I totally get that song. Thank you!"

She left her building, noticeably without Lars, but his iPod insisted: "*Show a little nerve, show a little insight / And don't worry, baby, he don't bite.*" She hadn't returned in a few minutes, so he paid for his coffee, but it took more than an hour before the building's front door opened again, and he was able to cross the street while a spherical blond man in round wire-frame glasses and a T-shirt that read FINNISH GUYS LAST NICE held it ajar and read the sky for signs of rain, debated, debated (Julian crossing, trying to set his pace against the likely speed of the white door's closure), debated, Julian now across the street (would it look more natural for a legitimate visitor to use the buzzer anyhow, or to jog the last few steps and grab the closing door?), Finnish endurance champ letting it go, turning up the street without even noticing Julian, whose hand leapt around the white door's edge and cut itself against the tarnished brass lock fitting inside. If she wanted proof of his interest, there it was, written in his blood on her lock.

So vain, he really didn't doubt the song said what he thought it said, even as she was making him imitate a crazed fan, even as, of course, he did hungrily want to see her home, her surroundings, her things, her frame, to find some hint there that would help him either have her or forget her.

He rubbed his skinless knuckles, passed the tea shop's inside office door, and took the stairs as silently as he could, but his body—Sasquatch footsteps, asthmatic breath, artillery heart—rattled the building (as no real stalker's body would, he told himself). The stairwell's wallpaper was green and raised, a crushed velvet, stained with the ghosts of framed pictures and the bygone splatter of some murder or dessert. One apartment per floor, each landing was more brightly lit as he rose. He passed M&R, INC, a sign taped to a door in front of which a stroller and shoes of all sizes implied a less-than-corporate interior. On the third floor, a shadow moved behind the peephole. He heard the door open as he turned to the final flight. "Hello, Mrs. Harris," he guessed aloud as he climbed to the fourth floor and savored an old lady's *hmph* behind him.

And then he was there, in her vestry, on the landing under the brightness filtered by the dirty roof-access panel, her door marked only with a black metal 4 in a vaguely Celtic script. This annex was hers, a de facto private space, and though he would go no farther today, he had penetrated this far, she had drawn him this small step closer, and she had arranged her props to present new clues for him to weigh, catalog, and preserve: a unicycle leaning against the wall under a set of pegs off of which dangled gear required for either Great Dane care or a busy schedule in domination: a leather collar spiked on both sides and branded black with the words LARS MY LOVE, a braided leather leash as thick as a Russian coachman's knout, and an institutional-sized dispenser box of latex gloves. Enough for now, time to leave. What sort of girl was this, what clues to her real heart were there in this song, practically begging him to become her freakish felon?

The shadow of a snout moved at the gap between floor and door, side to side, frenetic clicking claws and snuffling, a Great Danish border inspection, still undecided between hostility and welcome. A bold "Good boy, Lars!" produced an inquisitive sound and several moist exclamation points darkening the wood floor directly in front of the door's gap. They pointed to the item of the moment: a doormat, which, when Cait was someday domesticated and fattened into someone's red housewife, might bear a homey WELCOME or GOD BLESS THIS HOME or WIPE YER DAMN FEET but for now only boasted in sole-abrasive fake grass the practical MAT.

"Cartoon Boy, the key's under the mat / So what do you think about that?" The references to King Arthur and Moses were quite to the point: if, in fact, there was a key under that mat, it was only meant for one male hand to lift, and Julian envisioned his skin melting against iron if he was not the chosen. He decided to leave. He knocked on the door, even though he'd seen her go, and he saw that there was something disordered in the action: knocking for someone who wasn't there, as if a movie or time were running in reverse. Then he raised the mat, and there, in a recession in the center wood beam of the floor, lay a small silver key. He decided to leave it there and ask her out after her next gig. "Lars," Julian said as the key slid into its lock, turned, and then renestled itself under the mat, "I'm told you don't bite." He would send her flowers with a note to call him. It was time to leave and go home. He pushed open her door.

He had badly underremembered the scale of the beast standing in wait. "Who's a good boy?" he asked the pony, not at all sure of the answer. Lars sat before him as high as Julian's chest. "Are you a good boy, Lars? I brought you a Bangladeshi dog-cookie." Lars poked the intruder in the stomach with his square black face and was impressed by the resulting treat, allowed the burglar to scratch his chin, though he would prod him forcefully in the groin to regain his distractible attention.

Julian stood swaying in her living room, horrified for her that some maniac could do this, too, and he wondered if he should somehow warn her. To the right were two windows looking down over Henry Street, the lacy tops of green trees fringing her sill. He had seen those windows from below the day he approached her building but backed away. Across the room, a computer was on, and stacks of CDs on the floor skylined the front of a sway-bellied couch next to a flea market sailor's chest with candlesticks and, high on a non-WFP mantel out of Great Dane range, sat a plastic bowl of graying M&M's. The room's entire left wall, from floor to ceiling, was a single mirror reflecting the whole space, the windows and computer and CDs and Cait herself. Cait herself. Cait hers—

No, not a mirror but a painting of a mirror, complete with the mirror's frame, and only a few inaccuracies: the painted trees at the windows were white with last month's blossoms; the painted table was bare; the computer was off in the painting, but in the room an out-of-date (too angularly pixellated) version of the Windows logo roamed the black screen in restless sleep; and Cait herself, her hand on Lars's head, stood leaning against the wall between the two windows, where Julian now stood, patting Lars and considering her reflection of him.

She was not on the street below. He was giddy, as unsure of himself as a sixteen-year-old boy, astonished by fortune and possibilities that he couldn't clearly imagine but that promised life-shifting tectonics. He also wondered why she wanted him to do this, what test was here, what details she had thought relevant. He walked to the computer, Lars matching his gait, starting and stopping with him, as if the dog were leading him or mocking him. Julian pressed the space bar with his thumb, rolled it side to side to leave as clear a print as possible, should she care to dust for him. The screen came to life with programs running, Windows open to let in a bracing breeze: her iTunes library, paused midsong, thirty-one seconds into something called "Love Theme from Dog Park." The Play button produced her, singing that Smiths song with a few dogs in the background. When they barked, Lars whined at Julian's feet, and he imagined her foreseeing his every step and discovery and so drugging the animal to allow him a leisurely inspection of her home. The music was strangely haunting in the previous silence. It animated the objects in the room, the photographs and desktop sculptures of Irish saints and Incan fertility goddesses, the pink-and-green Play-Doh bestiary. He turned off the song.

He expanded her email. She had been writing a message, still un-addressed and unsent: "I wanted to know the minute you took the plunge," she had begun to the unnamed recipient. "You've waited so long, so did you find what you were looking for? Don't think—just answer." He added his business website to her Internet Favorites, la-beled it Remarkable Fellow, set it ahead of the *Irish Times* and the hourly updated European soccer standings and the site for Glentoran in the Irish Premier League, a link opening directly to the bio, statis-tics, and uncanny photo of midfielder Septimus O'Dwyer.

The slightly open door to the right of the painting invited him into her bedroom. He stopped and considered whether she wanted him to do this and what sort of pledge level between friend and patron she was creating for him, and he walked through.

She lived in a one-bedroom, like so many people. How strange the silence (except for the manual typewriter of Lars's nails on the pine floor), how odd that here, of all the planet, music was not flow-ing into him, cooking up longing or regret or possibility. Her bed de-manded most of the small room. Even pressed against the wall under the one window, it barely allowed for a dresser and the closet door's swinging requirements. Posters: Leonard Cohen as a young man, the iconic images of James Joyce (bespectacled, mustached, fedora'd) and Samuel Beckett (carved tree-bark skin between black turtleneck and thorny crown of silver hair). Dresser-top doodads: a tiny Irish flag claiming dominion over a pot of African violet, a diptych frame next to a Diptyque scented candle, three-quarters used. It was the same brand and fragrance Julian's mother used to have sent from Paris, the smell of when he was five years old. Here, of all the places in the uni-verse, smelled of his own childhood, of the first woman he had ever loved, as if Cait had wanted him to discover her while he was fully aware of every stage of his life before her, to contradict his cautious male impulse to hide pieces of himself. He lifted the candle to his nose and in his mother's favorite fig scent any thought of tactics fell away.

In the diptych frame: Cait's parents or grandparents, infinitely far from each other in their respective gold-painted rectangles. He looked for her in their faces but could tease out no resemblance, took that as further evidence of her self-invention. A cut-glass candy dish heaped with chains and rings and a dozen cartoons—pen and ink on coaster—illustrating her step-by-step development into a goddess of song. A crucifix on a chain hanging from a dresser-drawer knob, and everywhere candles: heights and girths planted on every surface, fresh and melted, pillars and tapers, spears and spirals, on the dresser, the sill, the floor. The bed was unmade, two pillows, but only one indented. The other was perpendicular to the first, set lengthwise along the bed's middle; she had held it to her while she slept alone. And so he placed it beside hers and made in it the impression of another head while Lars tilted his own.

The fig candle predominated, but beneath it drifted subordinate scents: the smell of high-story spring, the trees above traffic. There was another, though, something else, stronger in her closet, hiding in the hanging dresses and blouses, stronger still in the foaming dresser drawers.

A ringing froze Julian in place, bent over. "I'm listening," Cait said, as if awaiting an implausible explanation. "Cait! Alec! I'm in the 'hood. Right outside, actually, thought I'd see if you were about. Call when you get a minute. Something pretty groovy just came up, might float your boat. Peace out, girlfriend."

Down on the sidewalk, beyond the greenery, peeked at from a flattened-spy wall embrace, Alec Stamford—pest, rival, or cautionary symbol—was pocketing his phone and walking into the Bangladeshi deli. As his foreshortened form vanished, Julian, shoved prematurely out of his hyperaware walking-dream ecstasy and back into the mortal world of qualms, ramifications, and appearances, suddenly hearing the window for his safe departure beginning to scrape shut, looked up and saw, straight across the tops of the trees, a little girl watching him from the highest apartment above the Bangladeshis'. She wore a black baseball cap with a white x on it and a red T-shirt with the top half of Che Guevara's face, below which she turned into red brick. She waved at Julian as if they were old friends up here, or as if she often waved to the person at this window. He waved back, a little uneasy, his powers of invisibility flickering in and out of control.

He waited out Stamford from the tea shop's shadows, wiping his brow, browsing the cosies, cozying up to the owner, owning up to a lifelong fascination with Irish teas, teasing the blazing blazer pocket full of furious lace he'd borrowed as a souvenir. When Stamford finally abandoned his post, not two minutes before Cait turned the corner to fetch her dog for a walk and old Mrs. Harris told her she'd had a visitor, Julian left Tea Putz with five boxes of Irish breakfast. The building behind him, Lars mute at the door, the magic key's glow seeping around the edges of dour Mat, Julian sat exhausted and damp, as after vigorous exercise, on the Promenade and stared at the jigsaw puzzle of Manhattan across the river. Cait was still in his nose, barely. He struggled to retain her smells and to comb out his knotted feelings: beauty implies genetic suitability implies wise evolutionary choices, he thought, a little desperately. Beauty imparts status on the male who possesses it; what more need be said of shampoo models? But he wasn't convinced those old ideas applied here. The comparison that next struck him in his enervated state, that made undeniable tingling sense, was not biological: he had risen high, to an altar in the sky, accompanied by an animal incarnation, and there he'd been granted a glimpse into the mysterious cult of a unique goddess. He'd been surrounded by her incense and icons and hymns, none of which had much to do with the televised, explicable apes and CGI dinosaurs that had for so long soothed his despair and buttressed his crumbling apathies.

This was how life could feel now, again or for the first time. Some part of him insisted upon it: he'd been pardoned up there, readmitted to a world from which he'd been brutally exiled. When he'd blithely lived in that world, he'd been too young to know what life could do to you. Now he'd been given the chance to start again, wiser but not paralyzed by wisdom or pain. Now he desired, deeply, and therefore deserved another chance.

He tapped at his iPod, feeling within a note or two whether each random offering could provide what he was craving. Funk, punk, mope, pop, bop, hip-hop, swing, cool, acid, house, Madchester, Seattle, Belleville, New Orleans, Minneapolis white, Minneapolis black,

Ivory Coast, Blue Note groove, neo-baroque soundtrack, jam band, impressionism, hard-core, cowboy crooner, rai, gypsy, tango, fox-trot, skip, skip, skip, his temper rising, and then he felt it, just the opening chords, before he could have identified the musician or said that this was what he needed. He stopped punching his iPod's face, and he leaned back on the bench and wondered, marveled, felt the world slowly reopening to him.

I touched you at the soundcheck . . .
In my heart I begged, "Take me with you."
— the Smiths, "Paint a Vulgar Picture"

1

A *SINGLE PAGE* on Julian's pillow—nice calligraphy, pulpy artisanal paper:

> *Your arms did not that way embrace,*
> *I recall your eyes a color somewhat clearer.*
> *Can Eros be bound to terms eternal*
> *When lovers find new pleasures dearer?*
>
> *If I were to plead lost passion,*
> *What court would judge me now disloyal?*
> *Fidelity's hardly more than fashion,*
> *But you still cherish love's dull toil.*

The scribblings of scholars are kindling in winter,
The daubings of masters, pawned to buy wine.
A season of folly was all that I needed:
Where is the love that once I called mine?

—William Caldwell, 1924

He sniffed the page: traces of her, maybe. Cait had discovered his home and the mountain-range profile of his key, was looking for clues about him, too. And what had she concluded? He struggled to understand why she picked this poem: She feared that she would mistreat him? Was warning him of the regret *he* would suffer if he mistreated her? The forced interpretations trickled away, and he clung instead to the excitement: she'd been in *his* room, sniffed *his* life, touched *his* bed.

His and Rachel's bed. "It matters," Rachel had said the day she moved in, turning her back on his previous bed. She jerked her thumb at it, behind her. "That one goes and takes all its moaning memories with it," she declared. "Today, fiancé, today." They went shopping that same afternoon. He was eager to comply, certain this action would capture and imprison his elusive monogamy. He had—he recalled now as he traced his finger across Cait's handwriting of the puzzling poem—loved the idea of *bed shopping* with his last woman, his death-do-us-part woman, his only woman. They bounced across a department store of mattresses and springy boxes, sank into Swedish foam, stared up together hand in hand through starry canopies, rode carved sleighs through Russian snows, settled at last on her first choice.

And now Cait O'Dwyer had touched his marriage-bed-become-séparé's-bed. His merely useful piece of furniture now slightly vibrated again, flickered awake like a dubious fluorescent lightbulb. The time had come to call her, to proceed somewhere. And the rest of his world stuttered with that same hesitant light. He felt her circling him, though he couldn't be sure he wasn't imagining it. The new front-desk Ukrainian guarding the lobby of Julian's office building

twice reported, "A lady come to see you, Mr. Donahue." "Message?"
"No." "Foreign?" "Difficult to say," since anyone whose name did not
end in *k* was foreign. "Red hair? Angelic face? Aura of demonic
power?" Julian didn't ask, preferring not to hear Mr. Polchuk's con-
firmation or denial. His mailbox was open when he'd left it closed, his
closet was closed when he'd left it open, and his jacket pocket flaps
were flipped back though he was always obsessive about folding them
down, and her scent would appear faintly, out of nowhere, like a crippled ghost.

He could just call. He certainly wanted her. He could even believe
that he was physically capable, since her voice on a CD was more potent than any prescription at rousing him from his old torpor. But
with each day that he didn't just call her, he could hardly understand
his resistance to the obvious next step. Scared of rejection, like some
teenager? There was no point, as with Maile, no ending worth the
trouble? No, and no. And still he did not call. It was embarrassing, the
combination of immobility and ignorance of its cause.

He listened to "Burka," applied it to their unique case, although
the song dated from before their dance had begun:

> That's me in the burka,
> That's me at Le Cirque,
> That's me in your rearview,
> And me breathing on your bathroom mirror.
>
> That's me in the burka,
> And yeah that photo's of me circa
> Fall, 2001,
> Back in that heady season of fear.
> You're not the only one who's starting to feel a bit queer.

In September 2001 she would have been fourteen and living in Ireland, but still he could imagine a photo that showed her appropriate
response to the season.

When he decided he was being watched, the evidence could be

gaudy: after a drink or two, her gaze caromed off windows and puddles. She filled gaps in his life like tar in a sidewalk. He imagined they shared the same space, just never at the same time, and he loved it. She left her tumbler of melting ice behind her, next to his bottle of Scotch, left his DVD paused at the moment the narrator says of a certain lizard, "In ten million years, perhaps humans will be just the same: self-sustaining without any males at all."

If he wasn't telling himself all this to feel less cowardly, she was stepping only slowly closer, not yet ready to meet, and revealing in her diagonal approach a paradoxical but irresistible need for both closeness and delay as strong and persistent as Julian's own.

He could explain *her* hesitation, if not his. It was her fearful need for artistic inspiration, he knew. She was superstitious, he had quickly read, and she had reason to worry that her luck might not hold forever. Alec Stamford was walking proof. Cait's Irish granny's wailing banshees no longer haunted her, but that sort of belief still prevailed in her. Her stardom was new and fragile, her artistry still crystallizing, and Julian had provoked a song and had given advice that she kept in her candy dish. She likely felt she needed to do whatever was necessary to keep her lucky charm around, at least for now.

Being her muse was plenty, for now, but it wouldn't last forever, he warned himself. Picasso's muses were discarded with yesterday's dried paint, and the next one was waiting right there, stepping over her predecessor's crumpled form. The fuel the artist needed could not be perpetually drilled from a single human. The longer Julian could last without meeting her, the longer he would serve her needs, and she his. But he would have to leap, eventually.

All probably true, but also, he could hear his father's voice, "cowardly and self-pitying."

"How'd you tell her?" Julian was perhaps fourteen when he asked his father how he had broken it to the French girl he'd met at the Billie Holiday concert that he was no longer the man he used to be, might not even be the sort of man she'd want anymore. "How'd you tell her? It must have—you must have worried you were, you know . . ."

"Too one-legged for her? Yeah, that did occur to me."

"And so you called? Or wrote? Or just turned up in Paris?"

"No, no, no. I was far too self-pitying for any of that. Much smarter plan: I just decided never to talk to her again, to slink back to Ohio—oh, for her own good, you see, very noble of me, nobility and self-sacrifice always a convenient self-delusion, of course—slink back to Ohio to maybe bravely kill myself or at least start drinking like a street wino."

"What? Why?"

"Because there was nothing I could do or say or write or ask her that would be fair to ask of anyone, no way to release her without making her feel guilty, nothing to offer her in exchange for not being one of those fellows with the standard number of legs. And I was a coward. Afraid she'd say no and afraid she'd say yes but I'd never know if she did it out of pity."

"And?"

"And your mother came to the hospital in San Diego on her own, walked in like we'd never missed a day, like we'd written, like I'd thanked her for the record, like she knew it all already. Which she usually did, your mother. But that's the French for you."

And so, like his father whimpering in a hospital bed, Julian didn't call, didn't do anything but listen to Cait's demo, schemed how he could inspire her from a distance, waited for her to walk in with all the answers, all the future.

2

THE LYRICS TO "Key's Under the Mat" had come to Cait in pieces. The phrase about the mermaid swooning in the fountain was first, and though *swooning* had recently swum back up to the skimmable surface of her vocabulary courtesy of the swooning ghouls of the coasters, she wasn't thinking of her sleepy Cupid, not consciously, not yet. The lyric arrived in pieces over several days, words and images and rhymes, and only very close to the end did she realize what she'd produced: an invitation to someone to break into her apartment (though it wasn't yet addressed to anyone in particular). It was a lunatic document, and she nearly threw it away.

Then she changed her mind, decided simply to remove the more identifying details, but then she stopped again and called herself a coward. If this was what she'd been given, then she refused to allow fear to censor her, to spoil a gift like this. The hidden source that gave her these gifts was *daring* her to put something real on the line. She would sing it, as soon as Ian crafted the right setting for it.

And she would address it. The last two words that she wrote of the lyric were "Cartoon Boy." The rhythm was nice, the hard *c* felt good at the start of a line, produced a sort of sneer and snarl to it, the sound of a challenge. Those last two words came to her late at night, walking home from the telethon, and it was obvious. He deserved a song like that. He'd certainly amused her enough to earn it, and he might even notice it. That's the element that most appealed: the idea of him noticing in detail what she had made in detail.

He never responded, though, a week after she posted the rough take, two weeks, three: not an email, not a coaster or a report that he'd turned up at a gig, though she'd lately taken to asking bartenders to flag her if a guy answering Mick's description of Coaster Man turned up, in the back all by himself. She had lost him somewhere, revealed something somehow repellent to him, after he'd taken those lovely photos. Pity. He filled a niche, to say the least. She missed his attention, more than she liked to admit, missed his criticism and his ear and his eyes on her, sometimes sang imagining he was watching her, unseen.

3

"WHO WAS SHE TALKING ABOUT in that *Times* suck-up? The one who's a remarkable adviser?"

"I thought it was you," said New Bass, Cait having executed, like a grumpy Tudor, his predecessor, posthumously redubbed First Bass.

"It's the guy with those cartoons," Drums murmured, his speech very slow, and no one, as was very often the case when he was high, totally understood what he was talking about. "Ask Mick. He showed me these coasters." He paused, then said very methodically, "Say to him, to Mick, I mean, say, 'Drums told me to tell you to tell me about the cartoons you told Drums about that one time, because I want to know, and Drums couldn't provide me with that information, and so you can see my predicament, with Drums . . . not being . . . a totally reliable source of . . . '" Drums fell back as if his death sentence had just been commuted.

Ian nodded, as if paying no attention, a man already forgetting what he had asked only in polite passing. But he stopped in, alone, at the Rat that same night, a Wednesday, and again on Thursday, late, but Mick wasn't working the bar either night. Cait then had two nights for them in Jersey (during which he'd first noticed the phrase "Cartoon Boy" in the lyric for "Key" and became truly pissed off), and the Rat didn't cater to Sunday drinkers, so he couldn't try again until Monday, and then it was only to discover that, the Saturday before, when Ian was playing that frat party at Rutgers, Mick had quit the Rat to show more commitment to the Lay Brothers. Ian couldn't conceivably pass off as accidental a visit to Mick's apartment, and so his interest in "the guy with those cartoons" faded by necessity, until two weeks later when Cait came over to work.

She dropped her droopy spangled gypsy bag on the floor and pulled a cardboard tube from it, tossed it to him, walked to his fridge, said, "For the poster."

The shaken tube surrendered a mock-up of the tour ad. It was mostly the headliner's, but the bottom fifth was theirs. Cait had the lips to choose a photo only of herself, rather than one of the band shots they'd had taken, at some joint expense, last winter. Fine, Ian thought, the nature of the world and their future clear enough for those with brains, and those shots had First Bass in them anyhow. "Who took it? It's not bad of you," to say the least.

"Oh, long story," she said. "But I want your approval for it before I tell their management to print it."

"Thanks." He regretted that. She had worded it just so: "I want your approval" was the compliment of an employer, not the necessity of a partner, and "Thanks" was the flattered chirp of an employee. It was a hell of a photo: her eyes were closed, she was outside, in front of her own building, stretching not as if she were posing, like a supposed candid, but like she walked around all the time with a very funny secret. "Why are you wearing a Lay Brothers shirt?"

"I love those monks."

"Hm. Yeah, I'd go to this girl's show. Who took it?"

"This, ah, this . . ." She leaned farther into the fridge, as if tracking a regal, fleet-footed beer, and Ian understood the tremendous sensation just then tickling his spine and face: he'd never before seen her embarrassed. He only had her voice and ass to judge from, but he was sure, and a spectacular detonation flared in one corner of his universe. She finally emerged, wily beer captured. "Where have you stashed the bottle opener, you criminal?"

"You have to give a photo credit on the poster."

Her smile as she stood there—beer bottle in one hand, opener in the other—said that she knew everything he was thinking, and he amused her, but now for the good of everyone he should stop. "I suppose we do. We are very fortunate that you read law."

"Who took the photo?" He tried to make it sound funny, but it was just so plainly one repetition too many. He would have given a great deal to go back and not ask again.

She knew that, too. That mock-stern voice of hers would close the topic, and he could never broach it again without triggering a full-blown hurriCait. Sure enough: "Do you feel like working today? Or shall we sit around and bleat at each other like rabid sheep?"

"Whatever. Pull up a chair, diva." Fair weather restored, he played a pattern he'd thought of just before falling asleep the night before, that he'd crossed the room to record with his eyes still shut. She said, very sincerely, "Mmm. I like that." Those words, delivered in that tone of voice, composed one of his greatest joys, one that would still excite him long after her departure. It was, he imagined, like waking in new sunlight to the waking face of your beloved.

4

THEY BOOKED six summer-session colleges in the Northeast as the top of a three-band slate. The money bumped up nicely, and every night they'd sit in a back room or outside on an upstairs deck overlooking a parking lot while the Trouser Dilemma and then the Lay Brothers played for growing crowds of increasingly drunk college kids, many of whom knew especially who Cait was. They moved a lot of merchandise.

Before going on, Ian would read or make calls or strum an unplugged guitar. New Bass and Drums would wander off to smoke this or that. But Cait would just grow more and more energetic as her time approached. She might try to nap, or have something to eat, but neither sleep nor food had any effect on the change that came over her as they waited. By the time they took the stage, Cait would have been sitting out of sight for a couple of hours, and her attention would be distilled to a highly concentrated serum that animated her limbs and face just beyond normal. Ian could watch its level climb behind her eyes.

And she glowed for them, these college drunks—Ian had to admit it. Maybe, in a long hot summer, it was just this fleeting precise difference in age between them and her, between nineteen and twenty-two: she was older, but barely; she knew things but had not yet forgotten things; she had already started what they were nervous to begin.

At the tour's end, in Storrs, Connecticut, they finished the last tune, waved good night, and marched upstairs to a cramped office to decide if there would be an encore—the silliest of rock rituals made sillier still by the complete horror of their backstage: no one wanted to be up there; applause would hardly be necessary to draw anyone out of it. Still, they huddled up in the little loft, waiting for Cait to judge the volume and sincerity of the stomping and shouts below. When she deemed the request sufficiently credible, submissive, and ecstatic, they descended, and the applause broke from rhythmic request into free, relieved thanks.

Ian knelt to adjust a pedal, and Mick from the Lay Brothers called over Ian's bent back to Cait, "We've got a Coaster Man visual at the end of the bar, lassie," but Cait didn't hear him. She had turned away as Mick started to speak, and as he didn't want to look like someone standing at the side of a stage trying to win a hot singer's attention, he just acted as if she had heard him and turned to go outside. Ian managed not to gawk at the bar. "Mick, do me a favor?" he called after him, his eyes on the settings of his pedals. He pulled his phone from his jeans pocket and with his back to Cait tossed it to Mick. "Get me some discreet video of Coaster Man, would you? Long story."

"Ian?" Cait's voice behind him. "Hate to interrupt, but can I trouble you to play your guitar for a bit?"

They did a two-song encore, the Stones' "Monkey Man"—one or two little boys almost sure to go briefly clinically insane (and Ian himself still vulnerable to a certain parallel set of electric-blue chills up the outsides of his arms) when on the crescendo of the out vamp she sang again and again, "*I'm a monkey*," but replaced Jagger's original choking-chimpanzee death rattle with a moan unique to her, each moan more intensely suggestive than the moan four bars earlier—and then "Bleaker and Obliquer," which had lately been slapping the cakes with surprising power, all credit to Ian's own crystal hooks for it, because to this day he still had no idea what the hell her lyric was supposed to be about. Even after he'd looked up the word in an online dictionary.

He was, later, sort of proud of the superagent coolness with which he'd played Cait's game. He hadn't faked it; he really did forget to watch Mick's path in the crowd, forget to look for the troublesome Cartoon Man, right up until the applause for "Bleaker" was shattering the room, and Cait was pretending not to hear the offers for drinks, marriage, and sex rising from the up-front boys up front. The stereo went on, the lights changed, and while Ian and the others packed their gear, she went out the back door to wait for them in the van (usually to sleep or eat or, as Ian once discovered to his confusion and her rage, cry). Only then did Ian remember his man, and he couldn't prevent himself from looking everywhere for his rival and for his spy, but

Mick didn't turn up with the phone, and a visit to the bar—to see if the University of Connecticut at Storrs would be providing him further entertainment—proved fruitless, no Mick, no Cartoon Man, no appealing offers of company.

They drove back to the city, each band in their own van, Mick and the other Lay Brothers apparently having driven off with Ian's phone while Cait was still moaning "Monkey Man." He couldn't borrow a phone to call Mick in front of Cait, and so, back in Williamsburg well after four in the morning, he tried Mick's cell and his own but reached voice-mail boxes. At the unfortunate hour of eight the next morning, Mick called to say that the bartender the night before was a jackass, because Mick had left the phone with him to give to Ian when Mick had been summoned on a moment's notice to an impromptu sorority party. Yes, he'd surreptitiously filmed Cartoon Guy: "Relax, dude. And what was that all about? Cait dispatches *you* to do her surveillance? Does no part of you rebel at your pussyhood?" But the phone was still in Storrs, and bleary Mick was already on a skull-crushingly loud train back to the city.

Ian debated taking a train himself back north, but, worried he'd arrive to a closed bar or a bartender on his night off, he repeatedly called instead, starting at six that night, until, twenty-four hours later, he spoke to the jackass and received the happy news that the phone (and the jackass's apologies) had already been winging their way down to Brooklyn via overnight express since the day before. Ian should already have received it.

"Where'd you get my address?"

"It was on the contracts."

Except that that was Cait's address. Several hours earlier in her living room, she had opened the box addressed to the Cait O'Dwyer Band, tossed Lars the cardboard to process for nutritional fiber, and read the two Post-its, one on top of the other: "Sorry, dude. My bad. Vince" and "Here's your video, chief. Tell Cait Coaster Man's 95 years old, but she's welcome. Also! Check out the girls at the end. If I go missing, have the police break into their dorm. Mick." She used her own charger to resuscitate the gasping phone and watched two minutes of strange footage, then transferred it to her computer. On that bigger screen, digitally abstract and lit as if by prison-lighting designers, it made for weirdly compelling television:

To the distant, distorted accompaniment of her "Monkey Man," there were the alternating images of Mick's face and then the floor, then the swirling, tornado-coverage chaos of the phone being swung around the room: blurred ceiling lights, kabuki faces, scarecrow Cait far away on a spot-yellowed stage. The phone stopped moving, looking out across the room to the wooden bar and a man sitting at the very end, though he was difficult to see. He was listening to Cait, nodding to the music. He applauded at the end of "Monkey Man." When Cait could be heard saying "Bleaker," he stood up, counted some bills onto the bar, and pressed himself against the far back wall, his arms crossed, his head down, his collar up, and then a female voice said, "Oh, my God, you were so awesome up there," and the camera skittered around to the right, and two slightly glazed college girls gazed toward where off-camera Mick said, "I was. And I was hoping you'd notice, and a good thing because—" and the video stopped, frozen on the girls, midblink.

Cait had long ago asked Mick to point out her coaster artist, to no avail, but now Mick was telling her what, exactly, by sending this to some other "chief"? Coaster Man, sleepycupid, Cartoon Boy, J.D., JD7201965@yahoo.com: he now had a face, which was nice, and a certain style and an age, which was amazing, setting him even farther apart from everyone else in her suffocating world. She replayed the video. "Bleaker and Obliquer," she said off-camera, and her friend stood and counted money onto the bar and pressed himself against the wall. Cait watched again, paused at its best portrait of him, reeled back time, frame by frame. He was disappointed, maybe. A frame later it wasn't disappointment but the slightest laughter. She tried to remember if she'd done something disappointing or foolish. But he had a face now, her sleepycupid, a very nice face, a man of the world's face, a certain confident power in it and in his posture.

She called Ian and was only mildly surprised to see the mysterious visiting cell phone suffer a little epileptic fit on her table. She smiled. "Oh you little bastard."

"Bleaker and Obliquer," said the voice on Julian's computer, rising from the video emailed to JD7201965@yahoo.com. He watched himself lean against a wall in Connecticut. The resolution didn't reveal the exhilaration on his face when she sang their song. The footage began about five minutes after Cait's fired bassist had finished talking to Julian at the end of the bar, a marathon harangue that had stupefied and annoyed Julian as he awaited the encore: "A lot of people tell me, you know, that she should pay me for the whole thing." The young man extended his fingers in front of him, studied the backs of his hands. "They're all, like, 'She needs strife and is using you for strife,' and I'm like, 'I just want to make music, you know.' But I get a lot of people and they're all, 'She used you. She washed her face in your sink, and now you're watermarked. You're Pete Bested, dude. It's like voodoo, and you're walking dead. You have to reclaim yourself somehow, or you'll walk forever like this: *among the living but not one of them.* Nobody will touch you.' And I'm like, 'That's just talk, and stupid,' but, you know, I see something there. I do. I do feel like she broke something that didn't belong to her, and you can't do that. Nobody calls her on anything. She just sings and looks pretty and thinks she can do whatever she wants. She can't, can she?"

The boy had left before the encore, and Julian watched him through the window as he threw up on the street and stumbled off. "Thank you very much, you nice people. So, all right, we'll do a couple more. Here's a good one for the not so nice among you," and the new bassist started the two-note intro to "Monkey Man." He replayed it, tried to imagine what she was thinking when she watched this video, wondered who she'd sent to surveil him. Maybe she was saying now was the time to meet, or maybe she was saying he dressed old or should dye his hair or look how obvious you've become for an invisible muse or give me some space.

"*I'm a monkey!*" Ian watched his recovered phone as soon as she was out of view. "No letter, no note, just your phone in a box," she'd said, and thank God. "What little harlot swiped it off you? Or did you use it as payment in kind?" And now this then was Cartoon Guy. Ian *had* seen him before at gigs. He was hard not to notice because he was old, at least forty, maybe fifty, maybe more. He was also, and not merely because of his age, vaguely oily: the cartoons, the uncredited photo on the poster, the bouquets of flowers and cases of wine and whispered phone calls she took to far corners or outside, the baked goods Ian ate without ever telling her they'd been delivered for her, who knew what else. Well, if Chase and Wendy had to go, then Cartoon Man had to go. There was one good shot of the guy in profile, dropping money on the bar in a nasty, possessive manner. He was so old that the idea of him with Cait was reassuringly unlikely or, less reassuring: if it was likely, it didn't say much for Ian's chances, at least for another few decades until his hair thinned and his sex drive grew distinguished and unreliable.

This time Ian had an idea that was worthy of her. He landed in his laughable second cousin's voice mail, bounced by the main switchboard. He left a message, invoked family connections, had a favor to ask, not an emergency, but he'd feel better once he knew it was in his cousin's hands, gimme a call on this number when you get the chance. Ian didn't need to muster much false feeling, since his cousin couldn't feel any more warmth about their relations than he.

But he was wrong: Stan wouldn't settle things over the phone, insisted they dine at a little Italian joint chosen for its cinematic-criminal lore, and Ian had to put up with two courses before he could force the topic off shared family history, for which Stan had a bottomless appetite. All of Ian's recollections of his older cousin were clouded by family scorn: Ian's father thought Stan's father a clown of operatic dimension and likely corrupt. Ian's mother puffed out air and grew nonverbal and ticcy at the mention of Stan's mother, unable to find words for the depravity of some event from years before Ian's birth. But now at dinner Stan spoke of Ian's parents with unfeigned affection, describing family events in a mist of nostalgia.

Stan had shed some of his more mockery-magnetic youthful affectations—the self-promotional, bulging sock holster, the harsher old-school Brooklyn accent that always reminded Ian of Bugs Bunny, the use of "old-school" as high praise. But he had developed a more thoroughly in-the-bone coppishness, and Ian still judged him—maybe unfairly—a caricature.

He wore a black suit, with a faint pattern in an infinitesimally glossier black, visible only at certain angles, when a sudden click of houndstooth momentarily distracted suspects and witnesses from what they were saying, and Stan could observe the unguarded face, the micro-expressions he'd learned to read from a CD-ROM training tool. The tie and the pocket triangle were of the same scarlet silk, a dandified touch for a working man who had constructed himself from television detectives and his father's rougher police colleagues and from an undertaker in the neighborhood whom he had observed, when he was a boy accompanying his mourning parents on three occasions, reading his customers and selling them up the ladder of casket costs, tonguing their guilt and vanity to gild the mahogany paneling. His phone, card case, watch—silver wafers all—glinted high-polish monograms. He was not, for all this, a joke to other cops, or at least not a nasty joke, and he didn't mind the occasional remark about his style as long as it diverted some attention from his height, an insult he never fully forgave, though he stood only slightly below average, a margin unremarkable to most.

He in turn convicted his young cousin of being a child in a man's body. He dressed and spoke like a child, he made children's music, he led a childish life, and, as with this story he was reporting over knock-out balsamic veal, he stumbled through the world, dumbfounded by grown-up problems. Some perv was squirming a little too close to the kid's boss, and rather than doing what Stan would have done—handled it himself, face-to-face, explaining the realities to the creep—Ian went running to the most grown-up grown-up he could think of. Stan helped people all day long, every day, who couldn't cope with the world, and he rarely felt any scorn for them, but there was something about seeing men in his family come crying. "She'll fire me if she finds out it came from me. You can't tell her." Even this: Ian begged for help but was scared of the girl he was protecting.

"Job insecurity? I thought—who was it?—Aunt Kelly said you were the greatest guitar player since Bruce Springsteen?" And here we go, thought Ian: Stan surely knew how little Ian and Kelly liked each other, and so was making a point of this crapliment. This was not going how Ian had imagined. Stan was the same overcompensating bastard who used to bully Ian at family events, calling him a long-haired queer, even in front of adults. The fun was already gone from this, and Ian had no one to blame but himself. Cait's fault.

"We're all worried. She's playing brave, but she's worried, too. She won't admit it, but she is, and she should be." Ian stopped to think, careful to say nothing that could land himself in any real trouble. He considered his cousin's crimes and Cait's ruthlessness, hiding her latest flame in the lyrics of a song she made Ian write. "You may not think much of what she and I do, but—"

"Why would you say I don't think much of—"

"—but after a while you get a good eye for the dangerous ones."

"Wow: a hunch."

"I called you because you're family." Ian recalled a wedding party in a restaurant when he was about eleven, so his cousin must have been twenty or twenty-five. Stan called the police when he smelled pot in a bathroom stall, and a groomsman was nearly arrested but for the intervention of Stan's father, a cop, who had to lecture his son—after talking off the uniformed guys with some cake and wine—about perspective, context, and us versus them. And now Ian regretted the whole prank: to send Stan off to harass Cartoon Guy would have been supremely fantastic, but to lure the imbecile into Cait's life bristled as unnecessarily mean, even to her, and since he couldn't pull off one without the other, he decided at this late hour to call it off, apologize for wasting Stan's time, say it had been nice to catch up. "Listen, you know, the more I talk about this with you, maybe I've over—"

"Hold on." Stan raised an eyebrow at the screen of his phone. "I need to take this."

Ian took the opportunity to check his own messages, and they both made calls as the sauce on their plates congealed like drying, darkening blood.

"Did you pull the jacket?" Stan asked his phone.

"Ian, it's me," voice-mailed Cait said in Ian's ear, as if she'd just caught him in his dumb gag, beat him again. "I want . . . I need . . . I'm sorry to be so inarticulate. I had meant to say this to your face, but somehow I'm too . . . God, I feel such a fool. I'll just say it, throw caution to the wind, right? Okay, I . . . I . . . I, oh, *Jaysus*, Cait, just say it. Fine, here goes: Ian, I think that you and I should move rehearsal to three o'clock. Can you call the boys and make it happen? Thanks, love."

"Anything usable or did the EMTs muck it up? Great." He closed his phone. "Sorry about that, cousin—homicide still takes priority over scared musicians, but with time, that'll change. Oh, don't be sore, I'm just playing. You were getting to the point."

Fine: she deserves a little dose of Stan for a while. "She's being stalked."

"Do you know his name?"

"No."

"What's he actually done? A little window peeping? Heavy breathing on the phone? Rat in the mail?"

"Yeah, yeah, all that. And more. A ton more."

"I'll have someone come by and talk to her. Rest everyone easy."

"I'd rather it was you is the thing. I trust you to keep me out of it. And Cait'll trust you—she needs someone with your confidence." Ian looked down for something to cover his mouth. He chugged Chianti.

"I'm going to need a name or at least a description. Maybe you can point him out to me at one of your little concerts, if I can bear it."

"I have a video of him. I'll email it to you."

"*I'm a monkey!*" screamed a voice off-camera, rotten music, while a Caucasian male in a black leather jacket, light brown hair, average height, medium build, approximately forty-five years of age, kept his head low and out of the light, as if accustomed to ducking attention, but he eventually slipped up, as they usually do, and Stan froze the video, a bar light hitting the face of a man far too old to be in a room like that. Stan captured the image, emailed it as a JPEG to Records.

5

NEW BASS WAS ILL AGAIN, or still ill, and Cait asked him if he'd seriously considered the rigors of a professional musician's existence or if she should hire a tubercular old woman instead. New Bass—a midsize refrigerator with hands like coffeepots and a fleecy set of mutton chops—laughed and apologized while projectile sweating like an adult-comic-book pervert, then stiffly withdrew to the club's bathroom, from which the explosive horror of his thundering distress was in no way lessened by Cait pushing Ian in after him with a live microphone. New Bass emerged, some minutes later, the color of clay, but not at all embarrassed by the loop Ian now played over the club's sound system of his recent percussive solo, while the barman arranged his shelves for the evening ahead. "Ready for soundcheck, are we, my delicate flower?" Cait asked.

"Miss O'Dwyer?" The voice of movie previews and safety bulletins resonated from the dark end of the room. "I'm sorry to interrupt your—what is this we're listening to?" A man in a black suit and black silk tie pointed to the ceiling speakers. "This is your music?"

"Oh, yes, quite." She held her instant distaste for him and his attitude at a simmer. "Ambient indigestion is my thing."

He nodded officiously and dealt her a business card from a silver case, saying, "I'm looking into a possible criminal situation, and I understand you may be able to be of some assistance to me in that." Ian and New Bass crouched facing each other and tuned to an electric box between them, willing its guide lights into place. "Is there somewhere private you and I could speak for a few minutes?" The occasional charge in being the arriving protector was always heightened when the victim was this attractive.

Cait laughed outright at this unlikely approach, her distrust of policemen exacerbated by this one's clumsy air of official mystery. "Yes, we must protect these young fellows from adult matters." Ian fiddled with his pedals and plugs, Drums tapped his sticks on his thigh, and New Bass groaned and wiped his forehead with the front of his Weepy Fag T-shirt.

"So you're a rock star, huh? Madonna and all that?" he asked as they sat at a table near the door.

"*Madonna?* I see. And you are, let me speculate, not a fan of all this dreadful noise. I suppose you still put up with Tony Bennett, in a pinch, Inspector, but music history ended with Sinatra's death."

He smiled. "Wow. That's very good. You could be in my line of work. I'm always amazed by people who have a natural knack for reading faces."

"People often say I'm very inspectory."

"No, really. A lot of guys I know have to work very hard to do what you just did. That's just a remarkable gift you have, miss. And you're absolutely dead-on: I am a Sinatra man. So what *is* your music like?"

"Like? It's like something you wouldn't like, I think."

"And that annoys you?"

"No, Inspector."

"That means something else in this country. I'm just a detective. You can call me Detective, or Stan."

He was to burning up their soundcheck time with his fake friendliness, refused to arrive at his dreary business, likely a matter of Drums and drugs that would screw up schedules and recording and everything else for weeks to come. "Very well, Detective. What brings you here today? Oooh—I've never had the chance to say that before."

"Oh, I doubt that. No troubles with the constabulary back in the old country, Miss O'Dwyer? No surprises for me if I call the Wicklow garda?"

"*Very* well done. Excellent footwork. Yes, I'm wanted for a serial killing."

"You really don't like Sinatra? Honestly? Isn't he the—don't people like you know he's the source of all pop singing?"

"People like me? That's an exceedingly narrow category, Inspector. I won't speak for myself, but I will say that people *like* me think he wasn't any good as a jazz singer—he couldn't swing. And he wasn't any good as a pop singer—he couldn't arouse. He was a court minstrel for thugs. He could scarcely carry a tune. A visual artist, not a singer."

"The provocative Miss O'Dwyer."

"And my provocations are the reason you've come to interrogate me? Arrest me?"

"Arrest you? I owe you an apology. I wasn't clear. Let me begin again." The detective opened his black-leather briefcase and withdrew a blue folder with a white NYPD seal. He turned toward her a stilled-video image of a man, in profile, putting money on a bar in Connecticut, and she could hear rising from the photo the sound of her own voice singing "*I'm a monkey.*"

"Have you seen this man?" the detective asked. He watched her face as she examined the picture, her eye-movement vectors, the involuntary micro-muscular reactions at the zygomas, the forehead, the corners of the eyes and lips, the dilation of her pupils when she looked up and said, "I have." She seemed confused: "Well, sure. That actor, the one in the spy film." He couldn't tell if she was lying or joking or serious, and he began to cover his confusion with a laugh, then stopped himself and watched her more closely. "Is he in some sort of trouble?" she asked, a smile wiping away the traces of what he'd hoped to read. "Do the police need my help saving him? Is it Irish trouble?"

She was openly laughing at him, and that hid the truth just as well. He couldn't tell if she recognized the picture or not, and the first window for seeing her clearly had clearly shut. "I'm glad I could bring a little amusement to your day, miss."

"Oh, don't be a big girl's pillow, Inspector. Tell all, please."

"If you've truly never seen that man, then that's outstanding—"

"Out*stand*ing." What nonsense game was this? She heard Ian's guitar onstage behind her.

"—since it means I'm here in plenty of time, or you're in no danger at all." He saw her making fun of him, but instead of her abuse beading up and blowing right off him, he was feeling uncomfortably aware of *himself*, his failures of projection. "But I have reason to think you may have seen him. I'm sorry, but I do. And I have to wonder why you'd lie about it." He smiled with these last words.

The interview—the general path of which he'd known before he left the precinct that afternoon—now meandered into places he couldn't understand. She *didn't* know the dirtbag's face? Then his homosexual cousin was lying or goofing on police time, but lying to a cop would have given Ian sunburn. So she *did* know the dirtbag's face but was denying it? She was so frightened or brave or hated the police or thought she could handle the whole thing herself without publicity?

"What we have here is a predator, a dirtbag who gets his kicks scaring famous women. He's done this before, plenty, so we're trying to warn you."

"Well, I'm safe then, as I'm not terribly famous."

He considered her, nodding slowly. "Are you very brave, Miss O'Dwyer? Can take care of yourself just fine? Very admirable."

"Not at all, Inspector. But let's say I'm easily terrified. Still, why do you think he's any threat to *me*? I've never seen him. What brought you to me, saying I should worry about *this* man, of whom you have only one blurry photo? And, if this *dirtbag* is as dangerous as all that, Inspector, why *don't* you have a better photo of him? One of those nice front-and-profile portrait sets with the numbers at the bottom?"

She was laughing at his fool's errand, laughing at him lying to protect his dim cousin's folly of a job, laughing at him by refusing to turn off that recording of flatulence that still rattled over their heads, but Ian's reedy anonymity stood in his way, so he just kept lying, each time more weakly than the last. "We've had complaints, from female singers, and so now we watch him pretty closely."

"What singers?"

"Look, miss, you have me at a disadvantage. I was given the file and your name. I understand that a standard protective surveillance list had led us to watch him, and we've seen him watching you—that's where this surveillance photo is from. We have an undercover team called Team Cyclops that is tasked with exactly this nature of problem. They shot this footage, and that's when I was given the file, and so, just to advise you as to how the NYPD views matters of this nature, we're not passive, not absolute beginners. Learned some hard lessons. Old days, used to wait around saying, 'Oh, until he acts, there's no problem.' But that's—if you'll allow me, I'll tell you some dark truths about how these things go." His verbiage embarrassed him, fit him like a boy in his father's letter sweater, and still he couldn't do the simplest, most basic thing in the world: shut up.

"Mmmm," she moaned. "Does it all end in blood? And you, standing over the body, despite all your warnings, ignored, she ignored you, and the brass—that is the term, isn't it?—the brass ignored you, and now, *tsk tsk tsk*, there it all is, quite as bloody as you foresaw, and it makes you sick, but you look anyhow because you have to. Am I close?"

He couldn't stop laughing. "Those little boys over there must think you're just the niftiest girl they've ever met. Okay, fair enough. Miss O'Dwyer, you have my card. If you feel the need to talk to a grown-up about this, you call me. I truly hope you don't need to make that call."

"Don't be offended, please, Inspector. I can be a little off-putting, I know. I really apologize. Tell me, truly: How *does* the NYPD view such matters?"

He drew a breath to illustrate limited patience. "Do you know this man?"

"I don't."

"Never noticed him around?"

"Not once."

He *still* couldn't tell, and now he was laughing just to cover his annoyance at her opacity.

"Did he kill anyone?" she asked.

"Not that we know of, no. But he's been questioned about some threatening behavior, trespassing, harassment, deviancy, issues of that nature."

"But if he didn't commit homicide, why are *you* here in Brooklyn, with that very impressive business card saying you are a detective in a homicide unit in a precinct in Manhattan?"

"We are occasionally cross-disciplinary, miss," he said as if to a bright and praiseworthy child. "Don't kid yourself. You find yourself in a bad situation."

"Fair enough. I appreciate your coming to warn me. I'll keep my eyes peeled. Can I only ask in return that you deploy Team Cyclops to send me a list of the other singers he's pursued? I may know some, and I would very much like to know in what company I find myself, whether I should feel a little pride or no." She stood and offered her hand, which he took. She squeezed his and covered it with her other hand and asked, "What's the hooligan's name?"

He was caught looking down at her hands—pale, young, soft—

folded over his like tulip petals, the last two fingers of her left hand reaching all the way to his linked cuff, nestling between shirt and jacket, and when he looked up, all he could find to say was, "I can't release that to you. If he's no bother to you, then we're not in the business of blackening names."

She smiled. They were the same height. "I wonder, Inspector," she said, "if we've had a totally candid chat?"

She enjoyed soundcheck enormously after his departure. "What are you smirking about?" Ian asked with hot nonchalance, worried the dolt had already spoiled the joke and hung him out for her to hose down with mockery.

"I just love soundcheck. I love it love it love it." She flared and glowed, the warm yellow center of a solar system planeted by these concentric eccentrics. Ian was showing at least enough spine to have hired that actor, had gone to the expense of the police business cards. That was a tribute, and rather nice. She would play along, let him feel he'd fooled her, had thrown a wrench, though his feeble semi-competence at wrench tossing fell somewhere between amusing and appalling. The actor, too, had entertained, the comic bluster and posing, the efforts at improvisation that became more spastic as she blew him into increasingly well-painted corners. And the cause of all this fun: her musing cartoonist, her distinguished adviser, and the best photographer she'd ever had, who, unlike every other suitor rubbing himself against her as soon as possible, had been trying *not* to let her see his handsome face or learn his name and who, she would discover that very same night, *had* responded to "Key's Under the Mat," hadn't grown tired of her at all but had found his way into her apartment and left the most subtle clues for her. After the actor-policeman and soundcheck and the gig that night, she went home to let Lars out (and mop up his oceanic errors), and, in a robe and slippers, she checked to see if Glentoran had bought a feasible striker yet for next season. And only then did she see Remarkable Fellow waiting for her in her Web bookmarks, and then all at once his face (delivered with Mick's blessing to Ian) and his voice (from the telethon) and his charm (from the emails) and his eye (from the photos) and his wit and wisdom (from the coasters) now had a nice name and a funny job, and she drank some wine and watched clips of his work on his website, shampoo and makeup and tampons, draped in all that useless beauty.

6

RACHEL HAD PICKED HIM UP, though she let him think he'd picked her up, all while she was deflecting two other men's advances, one crude, one boyish. She used to have that effect.

Late, a Saturday night, coming home buoyant (maybe even a little near the manic end of her personality, she could admit now), she had left her friends after a party, come downstairs to the Second Avenue F-train station, been overwhelmed by the beauty of a violinist's music (yes, definitely toward the manic end). She stood and listened and after a little while noticed the man on the platform bench watching her listen. What had first attracted her to Julian? His attraction to her, certainly, and the amusement on his face, his resemblance to—none of that mattered now. She pretended not to see him watching, reabsorbed herself in the puppyish bow pulling the busker's arm up and down. At his feet, a few coins and crumpled bills blemished the fluffy maroon interior of his violin case. Rachel, her back to the tracks and the few people who ignored the live music in favor of headphones, nodded to the piece—Vivaldi—and gently laid a five-dollar bill in his case, its largest denomination by 400 percent. She was aware of the man on the bench who stayed while she listened long enough and well enough that she (and he) let a train come and leave behind her without ever turning her head to look at it. The violinist opened his eyes now and again, each time obviously more pleased to find the same woman enjoying his music, and he played with increased commitment for her. She liked that, of course, and felt her attractions flowing out of her in all directions (definitely manic) and knew that the man on the bench would come to her without her having to do a thing.

The three of them enjoyed their private stories and their private platform until it slowly filled again. Another guy, walking briskly to the far end, was snared like a landing jet by an aircraft carrier's strap, by the sight of Rachel wrapped in the music. He turned from her to the violinist and back again, shifted his briefcase from hand to hand. "Is he good?" he asked her.

"Just listen," Rachel said, and looked forward to seeing how her benched admirer would clear this hurdle.

"Okay. Are you good?" the new guy asked the violinist. "Your fan won't tell me."

The musician opened his eyes, kept playing, smiled modestly, wished the guy would leave him his waking dream, the highlight of a year's subway work.

"And I'm supposed to give him money for this?" he asked Rachel.

She just shook her head in annoyance, and the guy pulled his wallet from his suit jacket. "So how about, ah, ten bucks? Is that fair?" Rachel still wouldn't look at him, and the violinist fiddled with one eye open. "I guess ten bucks is too little." He balled up the bill and tossed it onto the subway track, down amidst the mysterious puddles and electrical risks. Rats condensed out of the air to examine the money for edibility. "Twenty bucks, then?" he said, taking it from his wallet. The violinist opened both eyes in time to see what would have been his largest payment ever sailing down into the valley of the tracks. "I have a fifty here, sweetie. Just tell me if you think he's worth fifty. You'll be doing him a favor, and all you have to do is say please." Rachel sucked her top lip, couldn't believe Bench Boy wasn't leaping up to prove himself. The musician's eyes closed as the fifty floated down and away. "Just one word. You'll get him paid if you just tell me what he's worth. Look at this: that Ben Franklin was one handsome man."

The PA system cleared its throat. The station chief's voice accompanied the violin with a rich, actorly basso, black but with traces of England: "Esteemed patrons, a Brooklyn-bound F train is now departing Broadway-Lafayette and is expected to alight here, on your platform, for your transportational delectation in, let us speculate, three minutes. The establishment acknowledges your extraordinary patience and *gentillesse*."

"Not even a look in my direction to give your boy a C-note? You wouldn't be a dyke? That would be such a waste of that nice mouth." The bill glided back and forth down to a puddle.

And with that, Rachel dropped and vaulted down to the tracks, brown liquid splashing her boots. She picked up the hundred and the fifty. The twenty draped over the third rail, and while she looked for the balled-up ten, the tunnel began to change color, as if a heat lamp were quickly warming it. Julian stood up but didn't know what to do, and Rachel started to climb back onto the platform only when the noise of the coming train drowned out the music and the rats had all vanished. She was standing again when the first car passed, a long ten seconds after she'd pulled her trailing leg clear. She laid $160 in the violinist's case. "You're great," she said to the boy.

His hands and instrument hung at his side, and he tried to stand straighter. "Holy crap, that was *unbelievable*."

"It really was, wasn't it?" She looked back at the banker boarding the train. She stayed behind again and finally, *finally*, the man from the bench said (squashing the violinist's briefly ascending hopes), "That was extraordinary. Please, please, let me buy you a drink or an egg roll or a Frisbee."

Later, over falafel, she admitted, "I jumped down there because I knew you were watching. I felt like it was *your* idea and you wanted to see if I'd actually do it. I liked how you looked as I slipped down there. You jumped up to save me, too. Are you naturally the heroic type?"

"Are you making fun of me? You were the hero."

"Oh, no." She smiled. "I was just playing to get a rise out of you."

She used to have all that in her, she remembered, arranging things to her own ends, making everyone else think they were doing it themselves. She used to have a manic end of her personality, for that matter.

7

AN ALT WEEKLY REVIEWED a Cait concert in L.A. Google cache-marked the pertinent passages in blue, and the printed pages thickened slightly the growing Cait file on Julian's desk as coarse hail chattered at his office window.

> *Irish pop-enomenon it-girl of the instant Cait O'Dwyer played Tarzan's Closet Thursday to an overflowing crowd. The hype! The horror! The humanity! Before Thursday I would've said that if I heard one more friggin' word about this girl's prospects I was gonna shoot someone. Today, I'm putting my gun down, and you should, too. I'll get to her voice and her taste in a minute, but let's start with her silences. The moments between songs, or during the competent-to-excellent guitar solos of Ian Richmond, where the study of the pretty singer's face revealed depths to match those carved by her awesome voice, you could feel power and brains whipping and a heart pounding in her. And when she danced—in a Bundeswehr wife-beater and damn little besides—there was so much grace in her, like a ballerina I once saw whose back muscles seemed to mean and say something important just beyond my range of understanding, like I was a monkey at a poetry reading . . .*

Julian read enough of these—Cait's cyber tracks across the country, trekking from WROK to KROQ—that he could usually tell within a few lines if the reviewer was male or female and, in either case, whether the writer was attracted to Cait the woman as much as Cait the singer. This writer in L.A. was initials only, BMR, but Julian guessed a Barb or Becky, one not usually drawn to women and a little surprised herself.

The dissenting voices annoyed him out of all proportion, the comments on this paper's website from the active keyboard of doubtfulguest, for example: "Lies and lies with little lies sprinkled on top. 'The hype!'? You *are* the hype! Don't encourage the Cait O'Dwyer machine. It's all a lie, built just for you. She sounds like a dozen other mediocre singers. Listen to you! 'She's pretty!' You like her T-shirt and her dancing and she makes you feel like a monkey. STOP!"

Julian was about to comment in her defense, but three days after doubtfulguest had struck, it was unlikely the villain would return to read Julian's scolding, and then his email chimed, not Yahoo! but his business account, mail from kiosk11@kopykween.com, subject: Are You Up There?

He looked out his office window, down eight stories, across the street, into the front window of Kopy Kween.

5:02 PM Hav eyou ever done any of this before with any other singer? I should not like that at all.

5:04 No. El hav never done this before. Hav eyou?

5:06 Funny — so I can't type. But people have noticed you. Not me, of course, but people. I would hate to be one of many, you know. So tell me now and I may forgive still. A long history of briefly favored singers? Love affairs from a distance with Emmylou Harris? Caught in Alanis Morissette's hedges?

5:09 If you were one of many, I would never have drawn a single coaster. And, may I ask, what it is about college performances that makes you less confident? You overcompensate. They're young, but they aren't stupid. They don't need the garish coloring. You sang down to them. Trust the good children to understand without the help, and don't worry about the others. They'll follow the smart ones, or go outside and vomit. Either way, you're clean.

5:12 Oh, Jesus. I forgot you were there for those. And yes, you're right. I knew it after. I've been bothered by something, and I couldn't put my finger on it, and you saw it. You may be too clever for my own good. I'm embarrassed. If that's how you spell that. I can't find the spell-check button.

5:15 Don't be emb'd. They loved you anyhow. Is it any wonder? Maybe it's better they saw only a clouded version of you. The real thing would have blinded them, left them dazed and hopeless.

5:16 Are you?

5:18 At times, yes.

5:19 Would you like to meet me for a drink?

And he sat facing that blinking cursor, lifting his hands toward the keyboard, but then they passed it to rub his face and smooth back his hair. He walked to the window, tried to see her, but the angle and hail conspired. She may have known best, or she was only impatient. He started to type, backspaced frantically before it just sent itself. And if it was too soon—the spent fuel, the abandoned muse—he wasn't ready to lose all this. Would he lose her by saying no or lose her by having a drink too soon? Maybe it was a test.

5:32 I think so.

5:32 Your message could not be delivered. This is a temporary address generated by PhreeMail for the use of customers of Kopy Kween and is not currently active.

She had wandered off while he dithered. He soothed his embarrassment with the hope that she mistook his dithering for strength. He decided to wait a day and then call her. He'd take credit for strength but dither no more.

A day later, though, as he called and hung up on her answering machine again and again, she was back in L.A., and then Cait O'Dwyer's first single from her upcoming album, *Servicing All the Blue Men*, was available for download from her site and her label's, as well as the Big 4 download sites for ninety-six hours at no charge before being repriced. During and after that free period, supported by the previous weeks of early-morning radio-station interviews and acoustic performances across the country and a video that ran in maddening rotation on both the main video channels, and chart-charming gigs on all four of the influencing late-night talk shows (while Julian was strong or dithering), "Without Time"—rerecorded, remixed, remastered— became, briefly, the number three song in the country, an accomplishment for which Julian's wise counsel and coy musery could claim no credit. "You are about to discover Cait O'Dwyer," prophesied the synchronized full-page ad in eight large-market newspapers, "and you will never forget the day you met." "Have you heard?" politely inquired the oblong subway posters, twenty in a row, with no other ads to interrupt when Julian raised his eyes on the F. "with opening act cait o'dwyer, courtesy of pulpy lemonhead records," discreetly murmured the small print at the bottom of the larger posters outside, announcing the coming U.S. and European tour of a more firmly established band. Her photo was in the corner: stretching her arms over her head so that her T-shirt (for the Lay Brothers) rose slightly above the tropic of her navel. The photo was credited to R. Fellow. The posters covered a full block of the plywood barriers shielding a construction site near Julian's office, the bottom half of the stenciled words POST NO BILLS just legible below the peeling paper. Even though they'd been pasted on by crack urban-marketing commandos within the last twenty-four hours, they already looked quaintly out-of-date, like posters advertising Billie Holiday, Edith Piaf, Caruso, an evening of jigs celebrating General Washington's inauguration. Two were already super-adhered by Aidan's face.

Maile was in already. "Hey, listen to this," she said with an early fan's obvious proprietary pride, and she played "Without Time" on her computer, claiming ownership of Cait.

"That's catchy," Julian said. "Who is it?"

"You know what just kills me?" Maile asked. "She's younger than me. Can you bear it? And she's already *that*. I'm old. You're a bad influence."

Julian had two versions of the song now: the demo, where she and the previous bassist played up the anguish, and this finished product, which, with a much more fluid bassist, captured the ironic, heart-bruising laughter he'd witnessed her discover that night at the Rat. The recorded laughter was perhaps a hair less authentic than her first discovery of it onstage, but one would need the memory of that perfomance to know it, Elis Regina's example discreetly consulted for inspiration and technique, take after take.

The publicly available part of her was now indiscriminately scattered to the fickle world, and he was undeniably sad. He felt her floating off to a country where he could only trail feebly after her, yelping to remind her that he was special. He picked up the phone and put it down.

And she agreed. Another anonymous email: "You were right. Not time yet, is it? Sorry, sorry. You're right—don't come near me, please! Don't give up on me, please. And, lo! It's a different world today, no? In case you are feeling the need to keep tabs on me from your cool distance . . ." and a blue-bottomed link to a site where celebrity spottings around New York were texted in by subscribers and then redistributed instantaneously to the site's membership, addresses and maps dispatched to cell-phone screens for efficient ogling. A sidebar on the home page listed hourly updated Newly Exploding Novas, and number four on that list: *Cait O'Dwyer, Singer.* Julian subscribed, fed credit-card digits to his screen, imaginary money to track his imaginary love. He was allowed ten Stars for the price of his basic membership but selected only her. The site informed him that he was one of 4,886 who followed her movements, a number up by 400 since the day before. On second thought, he added Alec Stamford, hoping they would never be reported geo-chrono-synchronously. He was one of 32 watching Stamford move through space, a figure holding steady, but his phone began informing him of the painter's position almost immediately: ASTRONOMICAL UPDATE FROM THE OBSERVATORY.com. STAR SPOTTED, 7:19 pm: ALEC STAMFORD BUYING FOOD FROM 67th ST. 'WICH-WAY. TEXT *88 FOR MAP.

If she was joking, it was a good joke. She didn't take fame any more seriously than this. But, beyond that, she was acknowledging and asking him to acknowledge her expanding fame's potential to blur his appeal. And maybe hers, too. If he meant to continue, he should know that others would be watching her as well, keening for her attentions. Continue to be different from all of them, she was politely requesting, and threatening. Prove yourself.

(She had, in fact, struggled over the text of that email, his silent rejection of her drink offer leaving her unsure of how—even if—to proceed.)

"Do you want lunch with Alec Stamford next week?" Maile called through his open door, an invitation negotiated through assistants, like courtiers arranging a royal wedding. The gallery slave who called on Stamford's behalf said the agenda was a business proposal, Maile reported, maybe two weeks work. Maile had never heard of Reflex but spoke up in favor of a music video as a step forward for Julian. "I'm going to see you recognized as a director if it kills me," she said. But Julian accepted the lunch because he wanted to see someone else who knew her, and to study someone who had lived through what was awaiting her.

8

BY THE MORNING of his lunch date, he'd been notified at least daily of the painter's whereabouts. The reports were not slowed by the arrival that morning of the long-awaited *Times* "profile" on Stamford, Milton Chi eager from the first word to hone the razor edge of his glinting critical teeth:

> *Some artists defy description, and I don't mean that nicely. Alec Stamford, vaguely familiar from your older brother's record collection, is, like so many criminally foolish pop stars before him—Sinatra, Tony Bennett, Ringo Starr—making us look at his paintings. It should come as no surprise that they are dreadful. They throw out ropes of allegory, but Mr. Stamford is not nearly a strong enough artist for the ropes to reach all the way to us, to deliver clear meaning, nor is he magician enough to make them light, allusive, to let his ideas float effortlessly, just out of reach of our comprehension, to lure us off an aesthetic cliff. The work is just repellent, which, come to think of it, his music was, too.*

They met at a new Haitian-Thai fusion, which the gallery assistant had suggested, and which Maile had accepted only to tease her boss. Julian arrived first, was seated, and a minute later his contemplation of the menu was interrupted by his quaking phone. ASTRONOMICAL UPDATE FROM THE OBSERVATORY.com. STAR SPOTTED, 12:38 pm: ALEC STAMFORD, HAI-THAI RESTAURANT, 28th STREET, TEXT *88 FOR MAP. Julian looked around. Alec was nowhere to be seen, but also nobody was putting their phone away, fresh from reporting a pop star from two decades earlier. No fans of an art provocateur had their noses pressed against the restaurant's front window, waiting to see him lunch under the mural of Papa Doc Duvalier and Yul Brynner.

Stamford came out of the bathroom, loudly apologizing for the shoddy service at the restaurant as he walked past waiters and diners, then, sitting down, immediately brought up the *Times* assault as a "victory." He then fluttered vague professional possibilities at Julian. There was interest at an entertainment channel in a documentary about Stamford's career, "the transition from music to canvas and all that, the consistency in the ideas even as the medium has shifted." Despite or because of Milton Chi's hard work, the gallery wanted a salesy film about the process of the painting, Stamford staring at the blank canvas, the brush suddenly flying, snippets of dialogue about art and influence. "Your name has come up in all the discussions, it goes without saying," he said anyhow.

None of this was impossible, though it was unlikely. It was uncomfortably likely, however, that Alec Stamford had gone into the bathroom and reported his own presence at the restaurant to a fan-tracking website. And now—as he spoke of his art career and the renewed and simmering appreciation of his old music, as he read the menu through his pince-nez, as he sent wine back with "Oh, now really, this won't do, will it?" after insisting the poet-waiter taste it and agree that it was swill—the gap between the man and the music was painful to Julian, because those old Reflex songs had meant something to him and did so still. (After booking the lunch meeting, Maile downloaded "Sugar Girl" and kept playing it on her computer into the evening, and Julian had to resist the urge to put his hands on her shoulders.) But now the songs eroded in the presence of the singer. Julian imagined this self-promoter doing those old tunes—the great ones that struck a balance between cynicism and hopefulness, that cast hopefulness as the underdog that everyone wanted to win but probably wouldn't—and it was grotesque. Julian feared the music would be lost entirely if Stamford proved himself more of an ass at this meal. And he was Cait's friend? Cait was now entering the same tunnel of self-love that produced this man?

Great music, his father used to lecture him, was often made by wretched people. The wise fan carefully avoided learning anything about the creators of any music that mattered, shut his eyes to biographies of martinet jazz drummers or anti-Semitic composers, and surely avoided lunching with tediously still-living pop stars of his overly impressionable romantic youth. What would his father have said about falling in love with a girl on her way up the charts?

"There were some big names at the gallery the other night, friends of mine. Did you recognize anyone? Yeah, the usual downtown suspects." Alec dropped names, and Julian let them land.

"I recognized that singer there," he said after the parade. "Cait O'Dwyer? Is that her name?" But Stamford turned away and snapped at a man at a neighboring table, "Do you mind?" though Julian had missed whatever offense had been committed.

"What?" said the accused.

"I'm *sitting* here," the painter argued.

"Do I mind that you're sitting there?"

"Christ," Stamford spat, turning his back on his newborn nemesis. "I get migraines, these just awful, awful migraines from people like that, you know? There are times you're treated badly *because* you've got a recognizable face."

"Tell me what you're working on now," Julian prompted.

In fact, Cait was almost certainly quite the same, in some way, as this patent-leather-spatted fool tipping the second bottle until its curling tongue of wine drooped. They were all, unfortunately, just people, these sorcerors and sorceresses. His treasured feeling that Cait understood him—was in some way singing to him—was not only an illusion but a commonplace one, like a belief in lucky numbers, and not only that but a manufactured and manipulated illusion, hacked together by a performer with ambitions (deathless ones, like Stamford's), with handlers and market advisers and career plans.

The only real ones, the pure ones, were the dead ones. A recording made by a dead singer is different not only because of the lesser (and thus more emotionally trustworthy) technology but because of the purity that remains on the tape after the merely human is discarded. Sing movingly of heartbreak once, on tape, and that's art; do it night after night in front of paying customers, sing of adolescent emotions when you are in your fifties, sixties, seventies, ironically laugh at your pain over and over again, and that's artifice, no more "important" than what Julian did for money, perhaps even less. And Cait wanted some fuel from him? To prove himself, not give up, inspire her? To feed her insatiable appetite for fresh emotion and experience? Like this man across a plate of plantain and lemongrass describing how some incident of heartache and conflict—likely utterly avoidable, pointless, and childish—was transmuted nevertheless into a "work."

"There's a, uh, uh, bon mot in there somewhere, if I can find it," Stamford said, almost apologetically, a little deflated now since the beginning of the meal. "You, uh, your," he began, but after two bottles and an hour of talking about himself, the transition was rough. That he spoke incessantly about Alec Stamford was no surprise, but that he so aggressively defended his right to do so finished off Julian's hope for work, for the meal, for musicians.

Julian attempted, "I did a shoot last year for a diamond company, a lot of lasery, intense but very well-aimed light, an intimate look, fine detail, maybe something we could apply to—" He mistakenly still thought his credentials were up for discussion.

"I have never been able to tolerate diamonds or pearls, and I'll tell you why," Stamford replied, a broad smile on his face implying a fine and relevant anecdote to come. Instead, his monologue roamed from diamonds to computers to cars to driving the Côte d'Azur to lavender fields in Provence to lavender as a perfume to lavender as a color on his palette for a new series of paintings to his friendship with Mick Jagger to a dog he once trained to pee whenever Stamford whistled a major sixth, and then he brought the dog to a friend's house, and the friend put on "All Blues" by Miles Davis, and before Stamford, in a panic, could reach the CD player—long details here about him trying to push past guests, waiters, named celebrities, furnishings—the dog just soaked the entire place. Any effort to distract Stamford from his past, his projects, his plans, was muscularly overpowered. If there was a job to be won here, Julian would have to wait very patiently and care far more than he did. He stayed at the table only in the hope he would hear some new insight about Cait or some sun-flare of detail from her private life, but he also feared he would hear something that painted her a Stamfordite lavender. "You, uh, what about you?" the painter said over coffee, but the question required obvious exertion, rehearsed but garbled at delivery. "Send your reel to my gallery. I'll take a look," he said at the door, and disappeared into the traffic and crowds.

Outside, Julian dialed Reflex up on his iPod, *Lost in the Funhouse*, just to confirm how badly its power had faded. The lyrics were puerile, the music hackneyed, even the instruments had become tinkly and creaky, and Julian tagged the album for deletion, then shut his iPod down, for fear of a broader contamination, as if an airborne musicidal virus were loose.

His cell rang as he headed back to his office, but it was Alec, so Julian let him go straight to voice mail. "Oh, oh, oh," the painter sang when Julian finally listened an hour later on the toilet. "You are wicked, boy. I'm watching you from across the street, and you just *screened* me! That's no way to start a working relationship. All right, so you know, that reminds me. There's something I forgot to ask you. Why *didn't* you ring her bell? I watched you stand there for minutes, and you never rang her bell. She's a nice girl. Spinning in circles, muttering to yourself like a crazy man. Why not pay a call?"

9

IT DIDN'T REALLY CHANGE ANYTHING, of course, Julian told himself, but still, something was spoiled now. He sat at his desk, closed his eyes against the sun and screens, tried to sort out the story he'd been telling himself for weeks, their floundering founding myth. She hadn't looked down from her window and challenged him to be more original, hadn't started all this. Alec, of all people, had teased him, and that is how he and Cait had begun. They were never a secret, organic and original, sprouted from nothing but the combination of each other. Alec had watched them, pushed them together. They were the product of that second-rater's mind.

Of course it didn't matter, not one bit. Though she hadn't started this, hadn't mysteriously learned who he was, she later had sent him to her key, spoke to him on the telethon, asked him for drinks. Julian started scribbling notes, trying to sort out who had done what and when and therefore why, how they'd found each other, even if the end result, today, was the same. But a note of ordinary tedium had started to drone.

As their story unraveled on the page before him—as he could no longer remember whose phone call or email or video had been caused by whom or had meant what—he felt himself finding reasons not to want her anymore, finding solace in thinking she was like Stamford, that Stamford was her future self. He knew this was childish even as he felt it, his feelings unraveling like their story. And he knew, too, that this was that flaw Rachel used to find in him, his retreat from feeling when it suited him, his pride at not being caught flat-footed by some strong emotion. If it was all Stamford's doing, Julian could go back to his comfortable solitude, if he hadn't already wrecked it in his reckless pursuit of this child star.

And it happened, and he watched it happen: laughing drily at Stamford's secret, oafish hand in it all, and at his own adolescent fantasy that he'd been involved in something unique, he now wandered away from Cait, not to other women but to a trial run of permanent elderly iciness, drifting out to his end on a meringue floe, the trip he had begun—pushed out to sea by Rachel and Carlton—when Cait had distracted him and he had stupidly cuddled up to her music and her image, his last effort to avoid the only fate he was really suited for. And for the next three weeks a stream of cold air poured into him, and he felt his little adventure gliding into the vast and overpopulated past.

She was biological, he could finally see, just like the others. He could discern her microscopic unimportance. She made sounds—imaginary things, just nibbling gigabytes—that brushed and made tremble, say, two million sets of eardrum membranes. Of those, perhaps half a million recognized them as her sounds. Two hundred thousand liked those sounds enough to sing along at the chorus. Fifty thousand people would love her music as he did, would listen to it, as he had, gazing at a sunset and letting their minds wander across pasts and futures. A full thousand could conceivably spend time fantasizing about her. And in case of an outbreak of plague, she and they and he would all swell up with pustules and vomit and bleed from the ears and lose control of their spasming, perforating bowels and cry out to a deaf deity, and her digital recordings would be less permanent on a depopulated planet than a condominium or a car or a car commercial. Humans would evolve and adapt. None would credit her music for the species' survival.

And in his silence, as if she felt him fleeing, she pursued him. A movie set occupied his street for three days and duly covered the hot July sidewalk with a blanket of plastic snow, and more plastic snow drifted down from a cable-suspended stainless-steel trough onto the heads of two lovers weeping and shivering for the giant camera. Two doors farther up the street, a plastic cafeteria tray of snow was waiting on his doorstep. Written on its surface in a yellow too dark and bright to be natural (and of which a whiff proved to be a lemon wood polish) were the words "Always wanted to be boy. Am [illegible] U R" before space ran out.

Days later, rainy, unseasonably cold, and the condensation on his downstairs window, when lit from inside, revealed faint inverted letters. He held a mirror to them: "Will you fly with me?" or perhaps "All too fluvial, ned." Or a profile of a skinny man on a skinny horse, hugging a flimsy lance.

He received a call from a bookstore he'd never visited: his special order had arrived. At the store was a sealed envelope with his name and the words "For when I'm on the road," as well as the collected Yeats and a history of Irish music. It was the frisky romantic acrobatics of a very young woman, an undergrad, unfinished. She was half his age and now seemed eager to prove it. He had the Yeats already, a gift from Rachel, but he bought both books anyhow and walked in sunlight, past the florist's shop where the manager mopped rose water, each stroke of the mop across the threshold ringing her store's visitor chime again and again, and he reached a little park near his home, a garden and a minor playground Carlton had tentatively explored, a ring of benches tucked between a mews alley and a curtain of millionaires' brownstones. Under the fragrant branches, he opened the envelope and found in it a bookmark, a painted panorama of Irish countryside. He examined her gift, the books and bookmark, looked up at the short yellow slide Carlton had braved. Rachel had restrained

Julian, held his arm so he would let Carlton stand up on his own when the little guy had tripped right there and Julian was about to rush to him. Rachel squeezed his arm, wouldn't let him interfere. "Baby, you have to let him fall. *He'll* be all right, but you . . ." She laughed at the pain on Julian's face.

He looked away from the excruciating memory, opened the Yeats, closed it again.

Reconstituting a goddess from a striving girl could not be wished for, or awaited. Julian sincerely floated out to an arctic sea, a little mournful, unpleasantly wiser, past puzzled polar bears. For a couple of weeks he avoided Cait's music, her newspaper mentions, her Web existence (difficult because an award show's nominations were announced, and she was in all the chatter).

And then came the postcard. Its picture was of Paris: an old man and woman are walking down the sidewalk, arm in arm. He wears a beret and with his outside hand covers hers, presumably his wife of sixty-some years. Their heads angle in toward each other; whispered comfort is implied. Across the street, two German soldiers walk in the opposite direction, rifles slung, suspicion and fear on their faces. On the back of the card, next to the stylized calligraphy of his name and address, was only a single large question mark. He sat and looked at the picture for long minutes, almost put her music on, wondered if she could really see as far into the future as that. And if she could? She could see a life after her stardom extinguished? With him?

That night he opened a book he'd been reading halfheartedly— an account of a World War Two rescue operation—and noticed the bookmark, the Irish fields. It was the gift, for a dollar or two, of quiet intimate suggestion. Here was an item she knew he would handle only when alone, when his concentration was heightened. He held it lightly by the edges to examine under lamplight the details of the trees and falling mists. He turned it over as the book gathered speed, then leapt from his lap, and he read on its reverse the name of the painter and its plain title: *View of Co. Wicklow in Autumn Rain, 1909*. He looked at the postcard and bookmark next to each other.

He worked late, storyboards spread before him on the bed, and he sketched out the beauty shots of an ordinary coupe whose price was scheduled to fall just after Labor Day. Across the room, an old documentary about Billie Holiday filled the dead hours of an entertainment-news channel. The camera panned over still photos of her, and they had a few grainy interviews he hadn't seen, her in furs talking to grainy men with 1950s hair and voices, leaning forward to push the microphone toward her. "Well, we're going to be making another record with the Ray Ellis Orchestra next year," she said quietly, her voice rough and slow, but the narrator corrected her, "It was not to be. Holiday was admitted to New York Metropolitan Hospital with kidney trouble four days later, and her last breaths were only weeks away." There was footage of her funeral, some talk of her lasting influence, and then a transition to Jim Morrison, dead too young, skanky Père-Lachaise pilgrims. Julian fell asleep. The TV flicked blue onto the photo on the wall of the tango singer Tino Rossi's funeral in Paris, the elderly Frenchwoman weeping, excess mascara carried down her face like soil in floodwater.

The caller ID read BLOCKED. The clock insisted it was three in the morning. He could have slept through it.

"Did you by any chance watch the piece about Billie Holiday tonight?" Cait asked.

"I did. What time is it? Where are you?"

"I watched very carefully, but there's something I can't find out about her that I want to know."

"I happen to have a family connection to her. I'll tell you someday."

"Do you think she was afraid she'd lose her talent?"

"She never did lose it, in my opinion. I prefer the late recordings."

"I agree. But my question is, did she *fear* losing it? Did she take steps to protect it, or did she just hope, wake up every morning relieved she still had it?"

"The drugs may have been an expression of fear."

"I doubt it. But listen: If she was frightened, does that prove that she was strong, because she overcame fear? Or does fear mean that some honest part of you knows you're weak and basically false, and a true talent like hers would never feel fear?"

"Are you all right?"

"Please try to answer. Please."

"Okay, okay." Tino Rossi's weeping fan. Old Parisian couple in love, occupied despite Nazis. View of County Wicklow, 1909. Red velour photo album, its spine worn white.

"Please. The truth."

"The truth. The truth is, anyone who puts so much of herself and her life into art as you do must naturally fear any failure in that art as a potential threat to your life. And so you protect your art more than you protect your health or the common forms of happiness the rest of us have. And you probably have this in common with every artist you admire, including her."

"Oh."

"Are you all right?"

"I've missed you, Julian. Are you still around or no?"

"I am. Just a little confused, I think."

"That can happen. Should we stay away from each other still? Seems a little daft now. No, wait, don't answer that. I'm only in town for a minute, and then I'll be far away for a bit. That should suit you, eh? Don't answer that either. Good night."

"Listen: please be careful with yourself during all this," he said, more like a father than a lover.

"That's a pledge."

He allowed himself a 3:30 A.M. glimpse of her world, read the latest news on her site, came upon the vile doubtfulguest: "All the trappings of your relentless will to power, Cait O'Dwyer, nauseate me. What are you so afraid of? That we won't listen to you if you don't put up photos of yourself in underpants? We *all* wear underpants, honey. The 95 reviews you so religiously post? You have a little talent, I won't deny it. But you must be one very frightened little girl to bet all of this on it." She must have read that tonight and called him.

He went back to sleep, his father and Billie Holiday very quietly on the speakers. He dreamt of Cait, no surprise, but of Carlton, too. Cait was encouraging Carlton to be brave, to step forward and shake his father's hand. "Go ahead now, little man, go on."

Rachel and Julian had thrown a large party for Carlton's second birthday, really a party for adults, a good party, unless Rachel had already been sleeping with one of the guests. That, too, hardly mattered now. Two weeks later Carlton was in a hospital, dying from that microscopic attacker in his blood, unnoticed until then by parents and pediatrician alike, all distracted by a different microscopic attacker in his ear, distracted just two days too long, and by then they were in a hospital with wooden trains with faces and chipped paint, which fit on tracks that could be hooked together in four or five combinations, none of which interested Carlton, pale and half-asleep, though Julian built him railroad after railroad in as many shapes as he could; one of them had to be the one to win Carlton's winning giggle, and Julian held the locomotive in his wet palm, and bright blue flakes of paint came off on his skin, and Rachel sat beside the bed and stroked the tiny hand, out of which grew the red tube and the white tube and the mushrooms of tape.

Three-year-old Carlton was not as clear a character as the twelve- or twenty-year-olds. Carlton's sporting prowess, his unique friendship and secret chats with his uncle Aidan, his first commonplace photography, his discomfiting and heartbreaking questions about girls: these Julian had foreseen. But Carlton at three—like the child holding his mother's hand next to Julian the next evening on the Twenty-third Street platform—was an animal he couldn't quite imagine. "Daddy!" the boy yelled as a man stepped off the arriving train but just laughed and kept walking. "No, Daddy's at the office," said the child's mother as they boarded. Julian sat down again on the bench, let the F train roar away without him, and rummaged through his iPod's memories. He ran his fingers through eight thousand songs until Cait arrived in his ears and sang to him about how he felt about Carlton as a three-year-old. He replayed the song again and again, now on the next train, turning up the volume to counteract the rails and the screech and the boom box on the floor, not obviously anyone's, playing a Puccini aria. A passing A train startled and glowed, one track over, the old-cinema flicker of two trains going nearly, but not exactly, the same speed, faces six feet away, inspectable but silent, an inaccessible, parallel world, unreal in the flip-book frames: the Hasidim reading a pocket-size Pentateuch, the would-be model with her portfolio artfully ignoring male attention, the thirty-year-old still dressed like a college kid, the pregnant girl hand in hand with her mother, a bald man in horizontal-striped sailor's shirt and vertical-striped clown's pants, Carlton in a stroller laughing, Rachel looking over her thin black rectangular glasses at a file, Cait staring at him as their trains clicked good-bye, and Julian continued on alone into the girdered darkness.

Back on a Brooklyn sidewalk, he replayed the song again and heard for the first time, in the background of the lyric, a sample of distant thunder, a haunting effect he could scarcely believe he'd never noticed before. He pulled the song back a few seconds but couldn't find the sound again before his iPod's screen flashed a sketch of a dying battery, then went blank. The sky opened up and released a torrent of hot rain. Julian sprinted the last two blocks home, up his stairs and, still dripping, sat his iPod on its projection throne and played the song again. It had lost—Cait had lost—none of her power for the dozen repetitions. She had only been tightening her grip on him when he'd thought himself drifting away from her reach. He dropped onto the floor in a spreading pool of rainwater and gathered in his limbs, and felt he might throw up, but then sobbed instead.

He pulled the red velour album off the shelf but did not open it, only rocked and wept and wiped rain off its cover and wished he could hold his son. Despair—despair beyond the ability of music to convert into art—shook him so hard that he could not breathe, and when he finally gasped for air, his first thought was the wish that Cait could see him, be with him right then, see how well she understood him and how well he understood her, how he looked at this moment that they had created together, as if her beauty and youth could kill the pain that her music had unleashed in him.

He watched her on the telethon. Her chest swelled, and her eyes closed, and he opened the album.

Photographs of joy: a bear, a balloon, a bottle, a baby, a new family. This was doubly an illusion: raindrops of parental happiness had sprinkled over seas of murky sleeplessness, cyclonic frustration, snipping at each other, dark jokes about catching Munchausen syndrome by proxy, and these carefully selected photos—propaganda for happiness—portrayed almost the opposite of what a yearlong film would have revealed, and Julian hated himself for everything he had missed, for the unforgivable crimes of inattention and self-absorption and the end of that boy. The album was a lie, too, because Carlton was, of course, not, and Julian was not a father, and corny missing-limb parallels occurred to him, and he grunted at them as his fingers glided over Carlton's plastic-coated faces, and Cait sang, "*Leave it out in the rain and let time surprise you*," and the picture of Carlton at four months trying out an early smile was not the stab in the eye that Julian had long feared, nor the opium self-delusion, effective for only a second's high, that his son was still alive. It was something else: Carlton was still gone, but the pictures made Julian happy nevertheless. The necessary catalyst was Cait. That woman, as a whole person— the breath, the voice, the body, the spirit and soul—made him feel this way, and could, perhaps, always make him feel that Carlton was a present joy in his life, not a semisweet torture from his past or a future stolen from him. He could believe, with Cait in his life, that he could be free and tethered, young and old, joyful and mourning, forgiven. The applauding thunder—outside, real—was near enough to shake the windows.

10

HIS POCKET SHOOK, and the Observatory reported Cait's presence at a Starbucks two blocks away. He calmly asked Maile if she wanted a coffee, walked slowly to the elevator, and, upon hitting the street, sprinted, stumbling into the coffee shop out of breath.

She wasn't there, and he could see the joke: now he *had* to see her, today, this instant.

"Mr. Donahue, all ablaze," came the voice from the scarlet Seussian wing chair against the side wall. "You about took that door down, Jelly Bean."

"Hello, Alec."

"Guess who I just had coffee with?"

"No idea."

"Come on, give it a guess."

"Huge hurry, Alec. Have to get back to people waiting for me."

"She talked my ear off about you."

"Who did?" Julian asked, buying his coffee to go.

That same evening, as he stepped off the F train back in Brooklyn, his phone shivered with another blue alert: STAR SPOTTED, 5:47 pm: CAIT O'DWYER and the address of his own office building back in Manhattan.

And so he bought a few things at the Bangladeshis' and entered her building through the tea shop, took his key from under the mat, handed Lars a few cookies from the jar on top of the fridge, and prepped a pretty good risotto for two. He timed her arrival, cooked, delayed, finished the work, and then sat before the meal, lowered lights, open windows, mismatched silverware and chipped plates, grated cheese, steaming creamy rice, his pricey purple wine in her old green glasses, and he waited, scratching their dog behind the ears. He lit some of her candles, and he waited. He practiced welcoming her without startling her: "Hey, I'm in the kitchen." And he waited. He practiced talking to her over the meal, describing Alec Stamford's request to tour Julian's office and his invitation to a film premiere, "which I turned down in favor of this idea, so you'd better like the food." He waited, thought of the very last time he and Rachel had eaten together at home, could count on one hand all the words spoken, Rachel's insistence she was literally to blame for Carlton's death, although all she'd said was "What sort of mother."

He went to Cait's computer to put some music on and there found her own website guest book open to an entry form, still only half-composed. Blinking, mid-insult, was the venomous doubtfulguest: "You sad little girl, you're so pathetic, why don't you look at yourself sometime and" and then she had lost steam. She did this to herself. Of course. He felt an overwhelming sympathy in the form of an urge to pull her hands off the keyboard, to fold her against his chest, to calm her, tell her she had to forgive herself and just go on, with him now instead.

He fell asleep on her bed, woke to a slamming door, but there was no one. He took Lars down to moisten the hydrant, returned to the

Pompeian meal and last of the wine, which he drank looking out her window. A minute later everything shifted, and he had to flee before she returned.

11

TECHNICALLY, STAN SHOULD STOP right there, with the one visit to the bar, his offer to her of a phone number. Technically, the singer was correct: this wasn't his job by a long shot. Technically, if she was going to claim never to have seen the creep, there was nothing to do. His favor to his family was complete. His cousin could always call him if something real happened, if it wasn't all a crank.

He sat on a bench at his boxing gym, a UU of sweat spreading under him, his gloves at his feet, his elbows slicking off his knees. He had come early and sparred four guys in succession—all above his weight and reach—but held his own. Now with his back to the ring, he watched the homeless guy the owner allowed in, asleep on the lat pull-down, his arms draped over the bar, the resistance pinned just to where it supported him, so that he rose and fell very slightly with each long, cluttered breath. The windows had brightened from black since Stan arrived, but still the bum floated up and down, hanging from his armpits. A pit bull puppy watched from inside a cardboard box.

The thing about inarguably beautiful women was that they were warped beyond repair by the time they were fifteen. They knew they were always being watched, and they heard the identical salivary subtext of every conversation, and so they were suspicious of any talk at all. The most brutal men, the ones who wore their lusts on their foreheads, appealed to them just because they passed for minimally honest, and so women like that invariably ended up with thugs. As they aged, as the subtext gave way under one conversation after another, and makeup could no longer spackle down the truth, they grew needy to be treated as special, and so became the most neurotic of middle-aged women, the most cloying of old ladies. The singer would be no exception.

She was surrounded by people telling her she was a genius, a goddess, so important, and so she probably longed for a little normal life, a little meat in her diet of air and lettuce, and if you were looking for a reason why she wouldn't complain about the creep, well, you might not be off in thinking (a) she liked it, just because it was different, and (b) she thought she could control it. Long after anyone whose vision hadn't been permanently blurred by the view from inside her aquarium would have seen a cross-eyed loony with one hand on a knife and the other in his pants, she'd still be thinking everything was for her amusement. She probably thought she could dispatch her dirty old-timer off to the cold, dry world beyond the glass whenever she wanted.

But ignoring this whole thing, taking her at her word—well, if his little cousin was right, if the creep *was* trouble, and something *did* happen, then Stan would have to live with having known ahead of time and not done anything to stop it. And, really, this was about family. Despite how silly a person little Ian Richfield had become—and, really, who hadn't seen *that* coming, given Bill and Teresa Richfield and, really, the entire barren expanse of the Richfield side—Teresa was still a diCanio. Ian's fears (and his pretty employer's) were a legitimate call on Stan's time. If Ian didn't get around to mentioning the favor, Stan would when he dropped a line to Teresa.

He poked around the Web, found photos and chat groups, snippets of her awful music, which he shut off. He read a review that called her a genius, the voice of her generation, and he listened again in true bafflement to the very ordinary noise with the singing that—*very* occasionally—was almost musical (less power than Rosemary Clooney, less nuance than Nancy, less passion than Connie Francis), before it collapsed again into that derivative screaming kids liked. He wondered what he was missing, and that pissed him off. He spilled his coffee across the printout of the creep and swore.

Two of the younger guys had heard of her. Bringing it up was probably a mistake, because soon enough a certain amount of trash was talked—from more guys than just the original pair of jokers—about Stan's "punk-rock girlfriend," and whether Stan had gone soft, skipped out on homicide for celebrity babysitting.

Stan even went to the trouble of talking to the department's shrink about the standard profile in this sort of case. Either it was one-time-only or a regular fetish, she explained. The dangerous ones were the one-time-onlys. The regulars tended to limit themselves to serial shrubbery whacking, but the guys who heard private messages in the songs, who broke into the house, took prisoners for romantic weekends, drew the gun for the loving two-step, they were usually on their first and only celeb.

He found Miss O'Dwyer's building, looked around the outside, made sure it had good locks and bars on the windows. He showed the perv's portrait to bar owners and shopkeepers within a small radius. Turned out, creep was a sticky fixture at the deli directly across the street from the victim's residence. The sweet old Bangladeshi couple who ran it agreed to repurpose one of their security cameras as a gesture of cooperation with the department, and Stan rolled up his sleeves, scaled their stepladder, and adjusted the focus of the front-door cam himself, checked the screen in the back until it framed all activity across the street. He bought them a pack of new DVD-RWs for the system and gave them a decal for the front window bluffing that the premises were regularly monitored by plainclothes officers.

But that was about all he could do. He drove across the river a few times to check the DVD at the Bangladeli, but the Iqbals hadn't seen the perp again, and there was nothing on camera. Stan could, he supposed, just check in with the singer—Everything okay with you? And one morning he was given a good excuse. He came into Brooklyn, reset the Iqbals' system, and then walked outside to smoke in the sun, readied himself to ring her doorbell when she came out of her building walking a huge beast, jogged right past Stan without noticing, and led him a few blocks to a little dog run on State Street.

"Funny to bump into you here," he called, having given her a few minutes' head start. He stopped on the sand as the Great Dane approached him, sniffed his shoes, and lifted his leg. The policeman, conditioned by years of rousting squirting drunks from doorways, stepped lightly aside and continued to the bench, where Cait watched his arrival through silvered shades.

"You avoided that quite gracefully, Inspector. Very Fred Astaire."

"I'm highly trained for just that sort of eventuality."

"Holy hell! Is that an actual gun under your jacket?"

"You mean, or am I just happy to see you?"

"No, seriously. You're an actual policeman?"

"He's a fine-looking animal." Stan sat beside her on the bench. "Urinary habits notwithstanding. Which reminds me, a friend of yours got himself arrested last night."

She turned to examine him through her mirrors. "The fellow in that photo you showed me?"

"No, not him. Is he a friend of yours?"

"I see. And you just happened to wander into Brooklyn, notice me here, and decide to stop in and share the happy news with me of a friend's arrest?"

"That's the size of it. I have a sister lives near here. She and I are very close. The fellow you sang with on TV? For the waterfront hippies? The big fellow, seems kind of gay? You should watch the company you keep."

"You sound like a priest."

"He was arrested last night, your friend."

"Who? Alec?"

"It'll be in the papers tomorrow. Seems he propositioned some professional ladies, three of them, in fact, but the third one was a colleague of mine. His bad luck."

"Surely you're not such a prude as to think we should hang him for the indulgence of that occasional, quite human practice."

"Yeah, I'm a law-and-order man myself, but I hear you. Certain acts are to be discouraged but not judged too harshly. I'm happy not to labor in vice, professionally speaking. But the interesting part, the part I happen to know because this was a colleague of mine, this is the part I think you'll enjoy."

"I'm all atwitter, Inspector. The criminal acts of people I know only slightly are of the utmost interest to me."

He turned, considered the reflection of himself in her glasses. "I like how you do that: tell the truth but pretend you're lying. You know, I've been keeping up with this case for you, the guy in that photo. And I've been thinking about you. You're a nice girl. Obviously above average. But you must grow tired of everyone treating you like a queen or a prophet."

"Tremendously insightful. I'm just a little girl inside, frightened, waiting for someone who can see right through me."

"There you go again. Full-time job, I bet, protecting you from weirdos."

"You give the impression of a hopeful applicant for the post. Are you *truly* a policeman? I admit the first time we met I rather doubted it."

Stan smiled and lit a cigarette.

"Jesus, that smells good," Cait said. "I wish I still smoked."

"I read somewhere it's bad for you," he replied, and offered her one.

"Cheers."

With effort he kept silent as she lit up, and then she spoke first, as the guilty did when given space: "I'm performing on Thursday night. Do you think I'll be in danger from that dirtbag?"

"Difficult to say. I'm not a psychic. But if you're inviting me to the show, I think I'll pass."

She nodded twice—he finally landed a jab after all her swings—but she quickly laughed. "I wasn't. You have to work late, solving a nice murder?"

"No. No excuse. I just don't necessarily think I'll see the best of you under those circumstances. Pop music, you know."

"I'm not sure I do."

"I think you know that what you do is temporary. Cheap. It's for kids. I understand—a person's got to make a living. I don't think less of you for doing that to pay your rent. But it's not the most interesting part of you, by a mile."

"And you can see the most interesting part?"

"If your job was dressing up as a rabbit in a theme park, would you want me to come visit you and pretend you were a real rabbit? I hope you're laughing because you see how right-on the comparison is. You go sing; I'd worry if you really thought it was a big deal. Now, matter at hand, you want to hear the best part of your friend's arrest?"

"Without rival, the most peculiar question I've ever been asked."

"I won't tell you unless you ask nicely, miss."

"Yes, please, Detective. Please tell me the best part of my friend's arrest."

"You admit you're curious? You want me to tell you what only I know?"

"Yes."

"You would feel let down if I didn't share my secret knowledge?"

"Yes."

"Once more, please."

"Please, Detective, I really want to hear this."

"Well, all right, since you're begging. First, Mr. Stamford had hired a gentleman as well as the three ladies he intended to employ. Mildly interesting. Second, the undercover officer and one of the two real prostitutes were redheads; the other was a brunette, but he had a red wig for her, ready to go. He also asked if any of them could do an Irish accent. I do have your attention, don't I? Hard to tell behind those sunglasses. And, best of all, he told them, as a condition of their employment, that they were all to answer to a particular name."

"All *three* of them?"

"All three. All three of them were to respond to this same name. Would you like to guess what it was? You do have that knack for deductions."

"I don't think I will, but I appreciate the offer."

"My pleasure, Miss O'Dwyer."

"I can see that, Inspector."

He looked at his phone. "I have to go. But if you'd like, I'd be happy to take you for a late dinner when you finish your concert. There's a place I enjoy, I can about guarantee you won't be recognized."

"Sinatra on the sound system?"

"If you can bear it." He stood to go, shook her hand.

"I think I'll pass," Cait said. "But thank you for the offer, and especially the smoke. I'm going away for several weeks, so I expect I'll be safe from any dirtbags, but perhaps—"

"When you get back you'll reconsider."

She laughed outright. "No, no, no. I was going to say that perhaps, in the interval, you could buy my new CD."

"Oh, boy. I hate to tell you this, but it's never going to happen, me and your music. I'm sorry."

The policeman strode away, with each step becoming smaller and more distorted in her mirrored lenses. He'd followed her here, she knew, and she doubted that he even believed there was any stalker to protect her from, though what Ian was playing at was now quite beyond her.

The detective's scorn for her music: people who didn't like her voice certainly existed, that was only logical, but she rarely met such people. He had no interest in listening to her sing but was asking her to supper nevertheless. To want to be with her but not with her voice: it was a strange division.

And oh, but Alec, poor Alec. Poor Alec. Jesus in a paisley sweater vest, poor Alec.

Meanwhile, Julian was the very opposite of that, was cooking dinners for her because of her voice, maybe only that, was reading Yeats, she hoped, because of her voice. What else of her could he be reacting to? And the other night, when she'd had a relatively minor attack—much more mild than previous attacks she'd weathered without anyone's help—she'd called him in the middle of the night, like a frightened child. How bizarre and pitiful. She should have been able to push through without anyone's help. But talking to him had so quickly soothed her. Unless that was giving him too much credit. Considering how easily he'd helped her, she probably hadn't really needed the help. She'd probably called prematurely, out of fear that the attack was going to worsen, and it didn't, and he was coincidentally on the phone with her when it passed. He was likely gloating over it now, thinking she was his little fool, like the day he'd sat silent when she asked him to meet for a drink, as if she'd proposed something childish. She wished somebody appealing, like Julian, would say what the little policeman had said: "not the most interesting part of you, by a mile." She wished Julian would get himself arrested for her, like poor Alec. She wished he'd at least come the next night to make risotto, when she'd be home.

"Lars, my love, shall we go?"

(At his desk the next day, Stan listened to her on borrowed headphones. One of the songs was growing on him slightly. If you could screen out that noisy rock 'n' roll excess—Ian's static and crash, and her occasional shriek—under that, she did do something that worked on you, in a way.)

12

THE WORDING HERE is very difficult, and Rachel herself was never sure of it. She did not "stage a suicide attempt to hold Aidan's attention or win Julian's." That would have been unnecessary; she had Aidan's, and a botched suicide would only drive Julian away. And really, neither did she exactly "attempt suicide" at all. She did, definitely, invite Aidan to come for dinner and that afternoon did, also, leave out wine and prescription sleeping pills on a counter, after she'd swallowed plenty of each. But she'd forgotten Aidan was coming over when she did it; it hadn't been to show him. And she hadn't taken enough to hurt herself, she didn't think, hard to be sure, as she no longer measured the pills out one at a time—that was futile, since just a few didn't do anything when she was in pain, so she tended to treat them like mints until she could feel them. And she was sometimes sloppy about putting the lid back on the brown bottle because who cared? A child might find them?

She'd had a rough afternoon. It had caught her by surprise. She came home early from work because she suddenly had the feeling that if she didn't leave her office at once, it might explode. The day felt as if terrorists were afoot in the city, and they had targeted her building. The illogic of it—the sheer stupid hysterical crap of it—was clear before she'd stepped from the elevator into the lobby of giant fountains and two Starbucks, but she went home anyhow because she knew that this stupid early fear was only a tremor of the biblical cataclysm to come, and she'd be tearing her hair out and thinking of Carlton for two days straight if she didn't reach her bed and sleep before it grew worse. Then she could wake up early and only feel a little not unreasonably sad, stay late tomorrow and make up the work.

And so she gobbled some pills and washed them down with a nice balloon of zin—a child's storybook phrase, hoisting you up and away, *and so they leapt into the Balloon of Zin*—and she lay down on the funky chaise she'd bought on the street a week after she'd moved into this apartment, and she felt a perfect sleep coming, like an embrace and a kiss of forgetfulness, when Aidan was banging on her door, typical Aidan, banging louder and louder, the only possible explanation for him being locked out being her doped semiconsciousness, not his having the day wrong or her just not wanting to have a guest tonight after all, and so she stumbled toward the pounding door, fell twice, cut her hand on a stray piece of her wineglass, and with much trouble drew the stubborn chain and lucked into the correct combination of all those opposite-dialing dead bolts.

"What did you do?" he asked, peering at the label on the empty bottle. "Oh, you dumb, dumb woman. Do you even know what a milligram is?"

Aidan set about tasks for which he was unqualified: feeding her emetics, bandaging her hand, then, interrupted, holding her hair and wiping her forehead while she bowed to the toilet bowl for nearly an hour; drawing a bath and adding salts and bubbles in quantities that he soon saw were excessive as lacy Andes rose over the rim of the tub, and he batted them and sheared off their tops to carry to the sink; selecting clean and suitable pajamas from a drawer knotted full of nerve-racking and aromatic strings; sitting across from her and listening, replying that of course he loved her (in a practiced tone of fraternal affection, tinted with pity for "her loss") and that Julian did, too, for heaven's sake. He nodded placidly when she insisted she hadn't been trying to hurt herself. At times, Aidan's eyes would mist, and he feared he would have one of his "lachrymose onslaughts," but they spared him, and he excused himself as just surprised or angry or stressed (drawing the bubble bath particularly affected him), but the truth was clear even to him, late that night, when she had gone apologetically to sleep in her own bed, and he was lying sleeplessly on her couch, and he thought of this woman dying if he hadn't come just then. He thought of her being so hopeless, of her leaving him in the world without her to think about or protect or admire or love, and he muffled his tears with his forearm until his sweater was soaked and attached to his nose and mouth and beard by countless trembling cables.

She had, after the Incident, "been there for him," in the dull language of these things. He had lived in close proximity to her and her clothing and smells. She was the woman to whom he'd been literally closest, physically, since the death of his mother. And so he loved her—not quite platonically, or fraternally, but as close as he could hold himself to those ideals. He would never admit to more, not to Julian, not even decades from now. Besides, he could see things clearly enough to know that Rachel was not "over" Julian, could never be, no matter how Julian behaved. "Why are you doing this to yourself?" he asked her that night as she ate the sandwich he'd painstakingly made for her, and her stubbled calves wandered free of her white bathrobe until she tucked them under her, and the room smelled of bath salts and her other scents. "Why don't you just stop and let yourself be?"

He understood that Carlton's death resulted in sorrow. He, too, had felt sad, when it happened, and at the terrible funeral with the tiny coffin and Rachel so beyond anyone's reach and Julian unable to do anything to help her and Aidan feeling saddest, perhaps, for Julian, so obviously incapacitated, unadult again. With all of his oyster slickness fallen away, he was hardly more than a child himself, and Aidan felt like the only adult present, his sorrow contained and appropriate, a part of him rather than him a part of sorrow, as he judged every other case. But now it had to stop: that a child's death would produce sorrow lasting longer than the child's actual life, which had produced some happiness (and not every day! Aidan could remember the scenes of resistant parenthood even if neither parent would admit it now): that was a problem caused only by human stubbornness. To be two forever—surely Carlton was by now as much a source of joy as of misery. "When you think of everything that could've happened to him over a long, long life, all the pain he could've suffered, all the difficulties he could've caused, all the personalities or people he might've become, don't you stop for a second and smile? I mean, he's just only that sweet little guy, and that's all, forever." She was ignoring him in the way people did when they gave up on his ability to understand something.

She said, "The strangest thing. I came to the end of other people so quickly. Each new person was like a glass of water, and at the beginning I was parched, but then each glass tasted a little worse, the water was grittier, and by the end even the first sip was enough to make me gag, you know?"

"Yes," he said, not at all clear what she meant.

"He . . ." She took her nearly-ex brother-in-law's hand, coated with that thick fur, and at first he didn't know whom she meant. "Julian is . . ."

"A jackass."

"I know."

"Are you really in love with him still?" Aidan asked, and she felt a maternal warmth for that bearded child with the less than acceptable breath and the oily imprints of his eyebrows at the tops of his lenses.

"I think it would be best to be with him again. To be old with him. Sad with him. I keep trying, little things, to jar him open again."

Aidan nodded, like a tourist working to translate a difficult foreign phrase while not wanting to look like a rube in front of the foreigner. "You have to promise me," he said, "those pills—you can't do that to me. It's cruel. You're not a cruel person. Promise me."

"I'm so tired, Aidan."

"Promise me." But she was asleep again. He had some months ago recklessly promised to deliver Julian to her, but he didn't really have any practical idea of how to do it. And so she was punishing him, threatening him for his failure. Though he was a devoted Cupid, his quiver was empty, and a life of abstinence and isolation and trivia had trained him for nothing, now that he had a purpose in life, now that matchmaking was a matter of his own deepest happiness.

13

HER TRAJECTORY FOLLOWED the heptilateral calculus equations laboriously worked out by her label: the download and CD and merchandise figures, site hits, YouTube uploads and Google ad click-through, satellite and broadcast and video rotation, acceleration of adoption rates by adult-oriented and alt rock. She was appealing down to U-18s and up to 35–45s.

With European gigs booked, publicity cogs caught and turned one another. The label's European offices and the distributor's subagents postered and stocked and sent press kits to music journalists who gave the enclosed CDs to ambitious assistants who in turn sampled Cait in their second jobs as DJs in Rome, Prague, and Biarritz or, more often, just handed the discs off to girls, gifts to demonstrate the assistants' perches far ahead of the curve of knowable fashion, like seabirds offering prime clifftop nesting sites.

Her tour schedule went up on caitodwyer.com and blasted out to her list at nine in the morning. Julian, waiting out her silence since their one-sided dinner date, suspecting he had been too eagerly middle-aged and domestic, found the email waiting for him at his office: dates and clubs moving east from Dublin to Budapest. He was unsure what she wanted him to do, but then the second email came ten minutes before he left for lunch: "Ella Fitzgerald" sent him an mp3 of Ella Fitzgerald singing "April in Paris." And that evening an envelope addressed to "The Solitary Chef" crept through his mail slot and onto the rug, holding a single typed sheet: *Charm, amuse, inspire, tempt, overwhelm, dazzle. Will you earn reward?* Then the touristic porn: a list of hotels sprinkled across Europe: Morgan le Fay. Lonsom Mews. L'Étoile Cachée. Santa Diabla. La Torretta della Virgine Bianca. U Šárky. Vânătoarea. Gellért. That settled it.

He stood in the hall, smelled the paper, summoned her scent from that crucifix-jingling dresser drawer. His mind flew ahead to the hotel room where she was waiting for him, undressing for him, the Romanian inn where they became lovers, the Czech nightclub where he proved himself by giving her the only direction she needed, children, her singing to their children, a marriage. Only when he saw through his open living room door that the TV was on—a single tilting, squinting boxer with a blue-padded glove attached to his ear—did he let the fantasy flutter away. When he opened the door, Aidan threw a dinner roll at his head and lowered himself over a miner's pan of syruped bricks of tofu and a half-drawn crossword.

"I don't much like your Scotch," Aidan said. "That's an imaginary tartan on the label, clanless and therefore classless. Can you think of a four-letter word with q as the third letter? I'd rather not use an acronym or Arabic." Julian walked out of range of his brother's babble, and he could smell her. Aidan had surprised her here, and she was hiding somewhere in the apartment. The bathroom sink's tap burbled. He pulled the shower curtain aside, pressed its hundred Rioja wine labels against the burgundy tiles. He opened closets large enough to hide her and cabinets for which she would have had to shed limbs like a harried chameleon. She'd left her scent in his bed, and a long hair draped across his pillow, a giant's fishhook to snare him while he slept. His ears ringing, he turned and ran for the fire escape in his bathroom, humming "Without Time" just loudly enough to hear through his own skull. Aidan called from across a vast desert, "Hey, have you been in touch with Rachel at all? Any sparks?" The window was unlatched. He looked onto the empty escape, looked skyward in case she'd scrambled up the side of the building.

"I let her in, you know," Aidan said, his eyes on the boxing, when Julian returned to the living room.

Julian flicked the remote. "You let her in?" He sat down across from Aidan. "Seriously?"

"Seriously? I was watching that. Yeah, she wanted to leave you something. Listen, she's amazing."

"And you let her in? What did she leave? You serious?"

"Yeah. Relax. I let her in. With my key. I wanted to talk to you about this. It's important. You know, she is still your wife. You have a role, a resp—"

"Oh." Julian fell back into the chair, stared at the ceiling. He started to laugh. "What did she leave?"

"Listen to you!" Aidan attempted the accent of a yenta. "You're very eager. So, maybe the old spark, huh? *Very* interesting. That reminds me, the Incans—"

"What did she leave, A?"

"How should I know? If you didn't find anything, call her and ask, right? I thought you already knew, or I wouldn't have squealed. You know, she and you—I wish I had the knack for explaining obvious things to stupid people." Aidan walked into the kitchen. "Is this all there is?" he called. "You've let your wine cabinet go to the dogs. More evidence that bachelorhood doesn't suit you."

"Open whatever's there. Pour for me, too."

"Anyhow, the Incans—"

"When was she here?"

"A few times, actually. I don't know. Okay, you got me, I gave her a key. But, listen, the Incans . . ."

So Rachel had left something for him, something he'd credited to Cait. The poem, of course. It hadn't made any sense at all when he thought it was Cait's. He'd knotted his thoughts into lanyards to make the poem hers, to continue their story from it, when it was of course Rachel's, plainly and rightly so: *"Where is the love that once I called mine?"* she asked him, left the question on his bed, their bed, bought together in another life. Cait hadn't crept into his house; he'd crept into hers. And another corner of their woven story frayed.

"Seriously, I want you to listen to me, Cannonball. It's important."

"In a minute."

But Cait had given him the hotel list—"April in Paris"—in exchange for the loss, had written a new chapter for them as fast as the old one had erased itself. He turned the TV back on for Aidan, walked to his bedroom, and went online. The hotels matched cities of her European conquest, in order, and he booked flights and reserved rooms in her hotels, even in the city where he and Rachel had honeymooned. Fickle Paris's allegiances wavered.

"I'm going to Europe for a few weeks," he said, returning to Aidan and a glass of wine.

"For the deception industry or for a new Boleyn? Never mind: same thing."

"Funny."

"Listen, really. I think that's a mistake. Really. The world, life, sometimes—"

Julian interrupted. "What was it about quicker heart surgeries that would lead to incivility?"

Aidan laughed triumphantly, fell for the diversion. "Ha! I was getting scared you'd never ask. Well, think about it for a minute." He sniffed his wine with the force of a Hoover factory and sighed. "When you go into the hospital for a risky surgery, you have to face the Big Nothing. They crack you open, and you can read the writing on the walls of your arteries. A slow recovery, big scar up your chest, short of breath, no energy—you can't help but think. You're warmed up by death's proximity, softened up. You rewrite your will, amend for your mistakes. You call your kids to gather round, you tell people the important stuff, you appreciate the very little things, like urinating. But *now—pfff*. No risk, no fuss, one afternoon, in and out, and your heart condition is all better, and back you scurry to play golf and yell at the valet and expect your children to apologize first. Total up all the love produced by invasive surgery and subtract all the love prevented by speedy laser surgeries. That's love lost. Now, seriously. Humor me. I'm a little slow. What's in Europe?"

14

JULIAN PACKED to Cait on the speakers, as loud as the demo could roar without buzzing into pieces.

Rachel rang the bell downstairs, warned by a flustered Aidan (whom she'd had to calm down) that today was Julian's departure for a long date, but Julian didn't hear the bell, even as Rachel (and everyone else on the street) could hear "Coward, Coward" and the old bassist puffing against the window glass like an asthmatic giant blowing out his birthday candles. She called his cell, but he didn't hear that either, and he didn't hear her voice mail until he was in a taxi to JFK:

"J, can you hear this?" She must have held her phone up and

pointed it at his noise, because while Julian's cab crawled into Queens, on the voice mail Cait now sang "Coward, Coward" through that thin speaker until Rachel's voice took the lead again and Cait was demoted to backup vocals. "You're like a teenager, J! Listen to you, rocking out. Well, I stopped by to wish you *bon voyage*. Aidan told me you have a business trip to Paris and points beyond. Say hi to all our favorite places for me, okay? Have a great trip. I'll be thinking of you over there. Remember that park with the man completely covered in pigeons? Definitely send him my best." She paused and the distant, crackling song continued in the interval, like slightly musical traffic noises, or as if Rachel were at a club, like a call from his parents to say good night, sweet dreams: "Okay, get to bed now, Jules. And mind your brother." "But wait, Dad, is the band cooking tonight?" "It is, little man, it is." Rachel went on: "Speaking of Paris, did you ever get my postcard? That little couple just spoke to me. They reminded me of—I don't know—not us, exactly, of course, but, maybe us if we'd been French? And old? And different? See you, J. Have a wonderful trip."

He listened to the voice mail eight times on the way to JFK. He'd lost another piece of his story with Cait, again to Rachel, even as Cait sang in the background. Even as he packed to her voice, for their beginning, Rachel was saying, *No, not so fast.*

He tried to make himself dizzy from the possibilities of Cait again, to reignite that chain of fantasies—happiness, sex, marriage, children. He inhaled deeply in the neutral space of the airport, a hundred gates to a hundred fates, leaving Carlton and Rachel outside. He deleted the voice mail and put Cait on the iPod; she would be the soundtrack to this crucial day. He yielded her to security but left her on as she passed through the X-ray machine and reattached her before he put his shoes back on. He'd flown out of this terminal with Rachel on their honeymoon, but it had been remodeled since then, so he could march bravely on and know he would startle no ghosts in the food court, at the gate. In the men's room, he hopped vainly, trying to flush the motion-detecting toilet, then flapped his soapy hands up and down under the tap, able to coax only a drop or two of water at a time from the motion-detecting sink.

He sailed on the terminal's long conveyor belts, past a lounge where a businessman shrieked obscenities at a video game. At the end of the moving sidewalk, two little boys ran in place against the direction of the tread. The gap closed, their exertions and Julian's stillness drawing the three of them together until the older boy signaled his little brother, and they stepped to opposite sides of the infinite path, still jogging against the tide, and Julian passed between them under a herald's voice, "The sidewalk is coming to an end. Please step cautiously."

Unable to sit still—off-balance from the loss of the postcard and the scenes he'd constructed around it, composing the latest revision of their love story, hungry to see Cait's face but worried he would meet her in the wrong atmosphere—*oh, yes, hi, well, this is the band, and this is Julian, my, well, he draws coasters*—he examined a boutique of useless gifts, mannequins with alert nipples under Statue of Liberty T-shirts. He turned away, back to the huge window overlooking the tarmac. A distant plane swallowed a more distant plane, passed it out its rear, and then Cait O'Dwyer and her band were standing at his departure gate.

Nervous indignities assaulted him—palms and gut and mouth—as if he were now forced to feel the aggregate anxiety he'd been spared for every girl and woman he'd ever spoken to since he was fourteen years old. He had always assumed his natural resistance to these symptoms lay in a moral fitness that others lacked, but now he melted into the boutique to acquire a Yankees cap, housefly sunglasses, and a hooded NEW YORK LOVES LOVERS sweatshirt, then skulked behind the aroused mannequins, watching her and her band's progress from counter to padded chairs—as unlike a remarkable fellow as it was possible to become—and he considered going home.

First class was called, and she didn't enter, so Julian remained hooded amidst chocolate and toy Checker cabs, squeezing his damp and wrinkled first-class ticket.

Hers was one of the last rows to board, and when he'd given her sufficient time to find her way down the tunnel to Ireland, he emerged from his post, as an amplified voice began to call the names of tardy passengers, his first, and he proceeded, head down. The pilot, fiddling with knobs behind his folding door, was younger than Julian by nearly a whole grown-up.

He slumped, neighborless, by the window. A ladybug had managed to wedge itself between the two plastic panes. As rain began to fall, it opened its cherry-red body and beat its wings and searched the oval perimeter for a path out of this darkening mess, the raindrops pounding like explosions.

Just before the attendant closed the front door a young black man entered, breathless and covering his mouth. He lowered himself into the last empty seat, at Julian's right. He was fashionably scruffy but still suitable for first-class upgrade, an actor perhaps, but his cool was belied by how desperately he ordered a glass of water before he'd even sat down, requested it again a few minutes later, while around him other first classers sipped mimosas from plastic, and he began fidgeting with a tube of precautionary, dissolving anticold vitamins, "specially designed for the frequent flyer." Unable to risk imminent infection while the stewardess dallied with his water, he gave up and placed one of the pale green disks directly into his mouth, where it began to sizzle. He mumbled a "Thanks much" for the cup that came a few seconds later, and pale green bubbles foamed at the corners of his lips.

The plane taxied, and a bird flew alongside, mocking the stiff metal giant. The ladybug suddenly stopped moving as the first-class cabin left the ground, still weighted down by coach, and the panicked raindrops leapt clear of the plane, and the ladybug, resigned and contemplative, faded from red to green. With a deft manipulation of his magic stick, the pilot turned everything on earth into toys, then drew a blanket of gray across his work, and Julian leaned back, closing his eyes, waiting for the butt stuttering of failing engines.

"You want one?" His neighbor offered him dissolving immunity. "Sure? You're in a petri dish, even in first." Julian declined, and the younger man turned his chair into a bed. Julian considered how he would save his iPod in the unlikely event of a water landing.

The pilot offered the passengers the romance of a banking turn, spreading the yellow-orange light across the cabin, from first class to coach. She was back there, and the change of light promised further change to come, over there. The ladybug turned light gray.

Julian opened the mystery novel he'd bought for camouflage at the airport boutique. Bhunji Zsemko, Mongolian-Montenegrin detective, found himself in Paris, infiltrating the Grand Mosque in search of Frinz Tishpa, the kidnapped daughter of an Albanian mafia bigwig. (The writer, Homer Weindark, had spun his reluctant dyslexic gumshoe into thirteen novels so far, each set in a European capital, exploiting the American readership's weakness for a *platz*, an *arrondissement*, a *corrida*.) Zsemko reached for his gun but too late. The blow caught him behind the ear, and he fell against the gold-veined Philip-Augustus bidet, Weindark always expert in both European luxury and underworld terminology, Black Bitch heroin ideally weighed out at a leaded cinquecento window opening onto the Grand Canal.

A dim purple light still clung to the sky, the last hint of yesterday, as they flew over storms beneath which the Atlantic prowled. Cait was mere rows behind him. That thought was warming now, cozy, and Julian looked up from his book in time to see a transparent shell the shape of a ladybug vaporize. Far below, another winking plane slit a diagonal wake in the sea of clouds, a shark's fin off in the immeasurable, dreamy distance.

"Coffee?" said a lilting Irish accent, and Julian watched the black window's reflection to be sure it was a stewardess.

"Please," said Julian's neighbor.

"How do you take it?" she duly recited.

"The color of my skin," the black man said with a smile, posing, and the flight attendant enjoyed herself for the first time that evening. She added a few drops of milk, examined her model's face, dripped a tad more, swirled, scrutinized her handiwork. "Enjoy," she purred.

"You've used that one before," said Julian, and his seatmate smiled with the jaguar's sexual calm Julian used to feel. "I'd steal it, but I'd end up drinking a lot of milk."

The lights went out after dinner, and below the plane, below the Debussy moon and stars hurried onstage for this abridged night, a dozen hollow silver pillars of cloud lit up like pinball bumpers, burned blue and gold for alternating instants, and Julian felt he could put his hand right through them. "You are hardly here. I can put my hand right through you." Rachel's words in their terminal weeks, only important in retrospect, in seat 1A on a night flight to Dublin chasing a fantasy, but back then just one of many things she said. "Removed from any risk at all. I watch you, you know, deciding, 'I'll never make this mistake. I'll never make that mistake. I'll never look stupid this way. I'll never give offense like that or go too far like him or hurt anyone's feelings or make myself or anyone else ridiculous. You can't take *that* seriously or *this*, that's just *people*.' But don't you remember what you were before? You existed before you removed yourself from everything. I remember you before. I do." How certain Rachel had been, and how willing he was to believe her: *this*, then, was the essential problem, not Carlton's death or her behavior. The problem was that he was in some sense removed from life and risk, so blanketed in politeness or fear that he was making it impossible for her to be happy. He may even have vowed to change this about himself, he couldn't remember now. Later, in a pendular swing of indecision, she retracted every word, expunged the intricate indictment from her permanent transcript of him. But now he vowed again to change. He would take everything seriously, commit himself, throw himself into life, starting with Cait.

1B murmured, "In France it's allowed, in France," then awoke with a spastic, electrified kick. He levered himself up and out of his conch shell. He squeezed his eyes shut, then opened one slightly at his watch, swore and produced his tube of vitamins. He rang the call button, yellow schematic of a stewardess producing a living one.

"You woke up for your vitamin?" Julian asked as the man gulped his boiling green potion from a plastic cup, like a witch at a child's birthday party.

"How old are you?" 1B asked in reply. "Really? I would have said older. Either way, you're in the zone for spinal stenosis and your first jumps of cholesterol. You cleared the first testicular cancer window, but another one's still coming. You're almost free and clear for MS, but pay close attention to any tingling in your extremities for a couple more years. You got to keep dodging bullets. But one of them will find

204 | ARTHUR PHILLIPS

you." He switched off his light and re-reclined, fell asleep with such speed that Julian thought of his father's story of the Japanese sleepers.

Julian would have told Carlton the same fairy tale, an heirloom by then. Carlton at six or seven would have liked it. Julian had liked it, hurried up to bed for the improvised fantasias, his father's profile against the gray window, still some light behind him in summertime, the smell of liniments and beer, an inflatable brontosaurus on Julian's dresser, and then a chapter of a favorite story, the endless stories his father just breathed: the good and bad kings of the chickens, the war for boys' hearts, the abcoyotes of Defghijklistan, and the long serial about the sleepers of Japan, who sent Julian off to sleep every motherless night for more than a year.

In a secluded town nestled up against the Fugu Mountains, a peculiar history had led to an acquired condition, and then natural selection had cemented it into a population's genetic code: the people of this village all slept for thirty seconds every ninety seconds, day and night, to the second. Individuals varied: everyone slept and woke according to his own unchangeable schedule, and so a perfect match was rare. But if a young man met a young woman who fell asleep when he did, they could spend far more time together—"three quarters of their life, better than we do here," Julian's father said, only some months after his wife's death—and he would always wish to marry her. And yet parents always forbade such engagements: if the couple slept *together*, who would care for the children, likely to sleep on a different schedule? Who would protect them from bears?

"No, never, never," grumbled one girl's father to her suitor, come to ask for his blessing. The father twirled his long gray beard between his fingers and fell asleep just as his old wife awoke beside him. "What did my husband say to your proposal, child?" she asked.

The young suitor, Toshiro, was heartbroken and could not resist the dishonorable opportunity life had presented him. He replied, "Mrs. Yakamoto, your husband sees how much I love your daughter, how good a husband I will make. He has given his blessing." Mrs. Yakamoto smiled and whisked the tea for a celebratory cup.

Soon, Mr. Yakamoto snapped awake, refreshed, to see tea being poured. Toshiro, his eyelids fluttering, said, "Esteemed he-elder, your wife is happy for us, and has blessed our union. She wishes you to be happy for us as well." And he fell asleep.

He awoke to Mr. Yakamoto, his wife asleep. "Boy, you have forsaken your honor. Never will you wed our daughter, and I shall tell all the elders of your wickedness. Leave at once," he said in a low voice, and fell fast asleep. Toshiro rose, bowed to the sleeping man, and walked out of the house. In the garden, he looked up to the second-story window where, behind the lace curtains, he saw his beloved, her eyelids beginning to droop, and he sat down on the stone path and fell asleep.

"Will he find a way to marry her?" Julian had asked his father, and later imagined Carlton asking him.

"There's no reason to think so," his father replied, for Julian's own good. Julian had always intended to answer Carlton just so, with the same tone of weary wisdom. "More tomorrow, little man. You've had a busy day."

In later episodes, banished Toshiro made his way out of the hamlet (haltingly) and wandered the Japanese countryside, being wickedly abused by the regular-sleeping people of the rest of Japan. He was beaten, robbed, stripped naked, tied to trees and covered with honey; he woke to endless predicaments he needed to escape in ninety seconds. Julian's father was willing to torture his creation, to use him to prove life's enduring and unquestionable awfulness—that was Aidan's view of the matter. "He used to tell you this when you were a *motherless child*," Aidan later marveled. "Not a nice man."

The exiled lover was taken in by a monk in a conical hat and blue rabbit-fur slippers, who taught him the secrets of his order, which allowed Toshiro to shift and consolidate his sleep until, after years of study, he was able to sleep like a normal Japanese. When, for the first time, he slept for eight hours and worked the monk's fields for sixteen, the monk told him he must leave, there was nothing more for him to learn. "But I have at last forgotten my sorrow," protested Toshiro. "That is always the time happiness must end," said the monk. "But master, I am happy here," Toshiro insisted. "No, you have only learned to hide your unhappiness and form dreams from it instead."

Toshiro, his face much changed by his new sleeping habits, returned to his village under a false name, feigning sleep for thirty seconds every ninety. He learned of his beloved's marriage to a nasty butcher, a loveless match, though with fully unsynchronized sleep, pleasing the traditionalist parents. The butcher was also a thief. Having weighed out an order, he would, when his customers fell asleep, wrap up a lighter package, charging them for the amount they saw before losing consciousness. (Although—Julian's father had to give him his due—some of his customers often took meat off the scale themselves, hiding it in their bags when the butcher fell asleep.)

The vengeful hero spied from the shadows as the butcher scolded his miserable wife, beat her until he fell asleep, then, waking, waited for her to wake up so he could continue the beating where he'd left off. Watching from behind a hanging pig carcass, Toshiro waited until the villain nodded off. Then he revealed himself, kissed the beloved hand, and hung his rival by his coat from a meat hook, leaving before the butcher awoke, letting the cur feel the presence of a devil, before returning to his hiding place in the forest where he caught his requisite eight hours of z's.

"He's going to win her back and teach her to sleep like him," Julian recalled sleepily predicting, as he now fell asleep in 1A.

One night, in the woods, in the midst of his long slumber, Toshiro awoke to find his beloved standing over him, sobbing silently. She had, with great difficulty, over several nights, followed him discreetly to his nesting area, one leg of the journey each night, since he was able to move so much more steadily. "I thought you were dead," she moaned.

"No, only wandering the countryside, learning, planning to return for you, and now I have."

"No! Not then, *now*. You have been asleep for *hours*." She spoke this last word with disgust and finality, and then she fell asleep. Thirty seconds later she spat it again: "Hours!"

She began her slow return to the village and her butcher. She awoke ninety times en route, forest and stream, moon and sand, and each time Toshiro declared his love, entreated her to elope, vowed to teach her the long sleep. But her repulsion was too strong, and the ninety-first time, she awoke alone, and she praised her father's wisdom in having prevented this nightmarish match.

"She preferred the *butcher*?" young Julian had demanded.

"Other people are not like you," his father explained from the bedside. "Look, Julian: love is not sufficient. It never has been. Stories that claim otherwise are lies," kindly instructed the man still weaving from his losses. "There's always *something* after happily ever after." ("He used to tell you that? When you were a kid?" Aidan later asked. "And you think that guy was not a sick, sad bastard?" "Of course he was," Julian had said. "That's easy. But you refuse to see the rest of what he was.")

As with all childhood nighttime serials, this one had no end. It fizzled out, Julian reading to himself, or his father seeing him off to sleep with bedtime chat about jazz or baseball, or just a good night called up the stairs from beside the stereo, amidst liniment and beer and drawings of inflatable women.

The sleepers, Julian's father confirmed years later in a hospital in Ohio, had been born in the Japanese hospital where he had swum in and out of morphine slumber, unable to hold on to consciousness for long, unable to drop very deeply into the turbulent narcotic sleep, while actual Japanese people kept themselves at a strange distance, visible only through soap-smeared windows, behind rakes and leaves, murmuring to one another beyond the iron fence, on the dirt path under the bare branches of the reticulated plane trees.

Julian awoke in darkness, not at first certain where he was, unsure how long he'd been asleep. His iPod was dead, so he plugged his headphones in to the armrest. He listened to the audio channels and soon heard Cait, singing for him even as she slept forty rows behind him. The corporate parody of a DJ called her "an Irish angel trapped in the body of your best dreams" and played "Bleaker and Obliquer," their song, savored in star-eyed darkness, a red strobe on a wing somewhere behind him keeping the beat against the velour sky and the passing time zones, and she sang him back to sleep.

He woke again to the unnatural morning and the sizzle of a vitamin tablet hitting water. "You have some serious sinus clutter," 1B reported. "You should get that looked at." Outside, glassy river deltas, like cardiac vessels in a green cadaver, displayed shadows of clouds and the plane. The reflection in the window of Julian's book stained ponds and fields of green squares with translucent murder victims and the Paris mosque. Lower, the plane's shadow skewered Dublin's cars and fleeing birds. Ribbons of cloud still stuck to the plane and streamed behind the wings as, with a squeal and hydraulic barking, the world was made real again. Julian donned his hood and super-fly eyewear, hurried to the door, and hid behind baggage carousels like Toshiro behind hanging pigs, watching her and waiting for their perfect moment.

15

THEY LANDED EARLY IN THE MORNING, but already distant objects had begun to ripple. He raced her to the hotel. *Surprise me.*

Surprise me. He couldn't go to her before her tour had even begun, he decided, so in Dublin he posted to her website, just after she left them, the address of every shop and pub and old friend she visited; the cathedral where she sat in late-afternoon half-light listening to the organist rehearse and animate the statues and pillars and glass; even the police station from which she extracted her drummer late at night—a still life of her in motion, a fond hello, wish-we-were-here, a breath of inspiration blown into her ear by an invisible muse. He traced the stations of her journey on a map of the city, drew her final path as an ornately twisting snake with her face, added a high-sheen apple in the serpent-Cait's open jaws and a self-portrait, as dubious Adam, J.D. on his fig leaf, reaching hesitantly for the tempting fruit, his own Adam's apple high in his throat. He scanned and emailed it to her from the Morgan le Fay business center, but when it came time for her tour's opening notes, her triumphant return to Ireland, he couldn't walk into the club. He paced outside because the bar was too crowded, too ordinary, and the Adam and Eve drawing already seemed stale. He had wanted to do something to replenish them before they met, the perfect last step before they touched, something to replace the lost poem and postcard, snatched by Rachel, but the new drawing was embarrassing now, just an old gag. There was no point to any more delay, but he went back to his hotel room, and while she sang across town, he sat there like the painting of tree-wrapped Merlin above the TV or the wood-mounted marlin above his bed, listened, on his iPod's travel throne, to her demo, felt he was a serious contender for the most ridiculous man on earth, effortlessly the most ridiculous in Ireland.

Six hours later, the Smiths' "London," the Clash's "London Calling," and Lenny Kravitz's "Mr. Cab Driver" played on his iPod until he fell asleep on the London cab's hard leather. He dreamt of Carlton, casually conversational, dispensing wise advice, snapping his little fingers to something on his own mini, scarlet iPod. When Julian awoke, it was all he could do to avoid her. She was on the radio in the cab. The details of her London gig were on the posters lining the walls of a motorway sound barrier, where she peeped out at him again and again from behind a lowered Greek fisherman's cap covering one eye. Her fame was expanding like a boiling ocean.

And then she was standing at Reception with Ian and the rhythm section and a manager of some sort, a boisterous bald Cockney translating from band to concierge with urgent unnecessity, drum and guitar cases piled high on the crimson velour of the brass-arched luggage cart, the groovy bellboy all in black, service fashions trying to keep up with Bohemia. No, not here, not in a group, not in the morning, not in a lobby, not with this lighting, not until he'd showered, not without a blast of pure desire animating him like an organ in an empty church, not unless she just came to him like his mother came to his father in the hospital, indifferent to his leg.

Julian retreated as far as he could within the sleek and barren lobby, couldn't find a traditional potted plant and so squatted instead behind a transparent divan to fish out his hat and hood and glasses, then hid behind a mirrored pillar and looked hopelessly at the lobby's three mirrored walls, its mirrored elevator bank, the mirrors of the reception desk, trying to find some angle by which he would not be projected onto the surfaces in front of her. He despaired at the infinite reversed and double-reversed and triple-reversed versions of himself, multiplying in all directions.

Some long time after her carnival entered two mirrored elevators and vanished, he, official and keyed, pushed 15 and stepped to the back. It stopped on 12. He knew enough to look down at once, his cap's Yankees logo floating backward in the murk. She stepped in, white terrycloth robe turned up to her ears, hotel-cresty slippers at the ends of smooth legs. The mirror-black marble floor reflected her up to the knees before the view melted into cloudy warm suggestion. She touched the oblong SPA button and didn't face the swaying man but toyed with her key behind her back, its black-diamond plastic with gold numbers dancing from hand to hand, back and forth, knuckle to knuckle, upside down and right side up, a digit here, inverted there.

At 13 a little American boy in a Boston Red Sox cap entered with his father. The boy stared relentlessly at Julian's head until he couldn't keep it in any longer: "The Yankees *suck*." His father hushed him, tried to smile at the New York fan stubbornly facing the floor. At 15 the doors opened, and Julian could not move, and she didn't look behind her but only touched SPA again. An unlit indicator circle read REMAIN CALM. HELP IS ON THE WAY. But it didn't light up, and Julian feared he would shout for her or bite through his cheeks or melt backward into the black mirror, leaving a vaporized Hiroshima shadow as the only evidence he'd ever existed. The father and son exited at 18. Now, now, now, now's the time. His lips would no longer function. They knew, if he did not, that his touch would corrupt; she would, with his fingerprints steaming on her, erode. Any beginning would begin the end, even to steal a ticklish touch of that terrycloth would start killing them, a murder even if the cameras in the high corners didn't notice. She floated off into the clatter of weight machines and clouds of eucalyptus-scented steam, and the doors closed, and Julian dropped all the way back to the lobby before he could rebound again to 15, his rolling suitcase handle dripping.

He scolded himself in his room, slapped his own cheeks: How much of life could he spend aching? Aching is not a stable condition; it must resolve into something. The time had long since come to re-move the poison thorn from his groin, wriggle free of the constricting past by scraping against new landscapes. He sat in 1529, thirty feet above her London home, and pictured himself rappeling from curtain to balustrade along knotted sheets, cutting his legs on the glass of her balcony door as he burst through, sputtering blood, unraveling DNA, fiber evidence, the shreds of his heart . . . and, never mind, she's not there, have to take the elevator back upstairs, bleeding, call a nurse. Time zones swept back and forth across him. He struggled first to stay awake and then to stay asleep, like a Japanese butcher.

How much of life can be spent aching? He woke, went out, wandered for a place to eat and get a little drunk and find a new way to charm, amuse, inspire, tempt O'Dwyer. He passed a playground. Its giant wooden ship—beached in sand halfway up its hull, its cannons able to shoot tennis balls in short arcs just past the bow, HMS WHIMSY on its side—was almost completely unmanned in the sporadic rain. On the swing suspended from the bowsprit, a too old girl, fifteen, was listlessly drifting, trying to recapture something she'd last seen here.

He watched Cait sing that night at Liquide, a bigger place, a bigger crowd, bigger noise, London in the rain duly ready for her and, despite some of her fears, taking her as its own, not Dublin's or New York's, and London's fearsomely bored critics purred and sighed, offered their tummies to her for rubbing. She'd never sung so beautifully. She amazed him, again, and he vowed to give her what she needed and wanted, to be who she wanted, and to begin whatever came next, melt himself down for that voice, that woman.

16

IN PARIS, he still hadn't thought of how best to proceed, though he'd decided it couldn't happen in Paris, when the concierge at l'Étoile Cachée handed him an envelope:

<<AU BOUT DE LA RUE QUINCAMPOIX, CE SOIR>>
Après la foule, toi seule.
Après la fête, ton souffle.

Dans l'ombre, je te trouve.
Après la chaleur de la danse,
Ta main, fraîche et sèche,
Pour prendre et surprendre.
Après le monde et ses monstres,
L'amour, calme, calme, calme.

—Jean Seurat, 1949

Even with a dictionary and his high school French he still needed an online translation, and then he learned that she had decided for them: the rue Quincampoix, tonight. She decided. She had to, and he wouldn't resist. He sat in the hotel lobby walking his finger along the map.

He followed his map to the rue Quincampoix, a crooked medieval lane stuffy with neon and art galleries and smut and irritability. He walked it from end to end in the afternoon heat so he would know where to stand at midnight when she would slip away from her band and admirers at le Nid d'Araignée and come to the place she had chosen. At the top of the road their poem was mounted on the wall in relieved bronze.

At the bottom of the road he noticed a second plaque—blue enamel with white letters. The coincidence was uncanny, unnerving, dream material:

ICI A ÉTÉ ASSASSINÉ PAR LES NAZIS
J. DONAHUE,
LE FRANC-TIREUR ET PARTISAN IRLANDO-FRANÇAIS,
LE 23 AVRIL 1944.
N'OUBLIONS JAMAIS.

His French was good enough. He stood, blinking, his hand half-lifted to touch the dust-dulled words she had discovered for him. At which end of the street did she expect him? She sent him to the poem, their fitting moment? Or she sent him the poem to guide him here, to learn of a namesake's murder?

He would not hear her sing tonight, wouldn't even listen to her on the iPod but would await her without music, his ears as hungry for her as the rest of him. He ate alone and walked a spiral spun out from the top of the rue Quincampoix, walked past the building where his mother grew up, rode a boat up and down the black Seine while Cait was serenading her conquered city. The tour boat's spotlights lit the river's brick embankments, and the shadows of the skinny trees on the riverside walkway were projected against the walls of the higher promenades, and the swaying, branching shadows wandered down the walls as the boat pulled its lights down the river; the trees watched a film about trees that could move.

The path he walked through Paris had not been entirely random. He had avoided the small hotel where he and Rachel had slept late for a week. He had turned his back when the boat passed the Eiffel Tower, and he had conjugated verbs out loud to mask the prerecorded narration in four languages of any site they'd shared. Paris had to be large enough to contain two separate, nonoverlapping love stories.

Ideally, they should have selected somewhere he had no history at all, and he did consider skipping the appointment, somehow leaving word for her to find him in unknown Bucharest, unclaimed Berlin, wherever there were no competitive memories, but he didn't have the energy or courage. The thought of touching her was now fixed like a window screen over everything he saw and did and bought and read and heard and tasted.

The two women—one a figment of his past, the other a figment of his future—did battle for Paris. When the boat described something new to him—Napoléon's battles, Richelieu's manipulations, rash responses to a plague, the palace burnt by long-dried grievances set aflame by a rhetorical spark—he listened and tried to absorb it as part of his and Cait's history. When the lights carried his eye too quickly to a spindly bridge where he'd kissed his new wife, or the department store's awning shadows where they'd stolen shelter from another drizzle, he stuffed his ears with headphones like one of Odysseus's sailors and turned his mind instead to the street Cait had chosen, the poem in bronze.

He returned early to the rue Quincampoix; she was probably still onstage. The street faded out below him at an obtuse angle, cut twice by other narrow roads. Too tight for modern life, still it blinked its reactions to the expanding world: GALÉRIE D'ART, DISQUES VINYLES, 24/24 SEXE. He touched the bottom edge of their plaque, another era's rendezvous after music and crowds.

He walked the length of the street a dozen times, imagining it gray and shadowed sixty years before, imagined an old film of himself meeting a long-pursued love in those days, the cool of her hand, the warmth of her breath so overwhelming after the world and its monsters.

He prepared for all her approaches, from the north, by the poem, him caught unawares as she came straight from the club and her latest triumph, swimming to him from pool of light to pool of light. Or at the middle intersection, the terrace doors unfolding now, the shouting in Arabic, a bright bar open to the street, lined with hookah hoses. Or from the south, the dark end nearer the river, the peepshow club at the crossroad, him walking down to her, meeting at that eerie postcard from an unknown ancestor, sent to arrive at the most crucial moment of his life, as a warning or a blessing. He worried over spending too long at either end, missing her arrival, her thinking he'd rejected her, her departure.

He compromised, sat at the hookah bar, smoked through a woven hose the dried fruit and tobacco, watching toward both hidden ends of the street while the bulky Arab owner who smelled of cumin-scented sweat warmly welcomed him and asked about New York, shared with Julian the secret that all the Jews who worked in the World Trade Center had stayed home that fateful morning, warned by their central authority.

Julian listened to the street, the setting of the jewel that would be her voice greeting him *après la foule*, their first words in person. The summer heat pried open third-story shutters, released arguments and laughter that fell to the arch-patterned bricks and cobblestones. A prostitute whose 1 A.M. offer he'd smilingly rejected now returned and stood next to him anyhow: "I am bored and do not feel the work, but I must appear busy." She accompanied him for a few circuits of his patrol and translated the best of the street's voices for him, the two o'clock shrieks and moans and threats and jokes. She smelled of a perfume he recalled from a film-school girlfriend, fashions having floated downriver to Paris's Turkish prostitutes, unless the budgets of students and street women had always been comparable. "He says she is a liar. She says he deserves nothing so good?" she narrated, then asked, "You don't want me or you don't want no one?" but she was no longer narrating. Noticing the weakness that had crept into her voice, she added, "I have friends maybe you like better." Scooters purred and circled.

Cait could have been delayed by fans or press, and he decided to keep waiting, but there would come an hour when she would no longer bother to turn up because she would assume he'd already left. And with that thought he saw her at the far south, by his obituary and the sex club. He jogged, then sprinted past the old Chinese man on the step; past the broken neon offering a buzzing and enigmatic GA; past the Turkish girls' mackerel, a Swede or a German, shaven close and inked with a map of the sixteenth-century world across his bare back, collecting from his strolling employees; past the shuttered bars and blacked-out, papered-over doors; and it wasn't Cait at all, just another of the street's itinerant entertainers misreading his eager approach. She swore at his sudden halt and change of expression, and she spit at his feet and gestured her feelings intricately at him. Above her head, at one of the street's eastern openings, the sky's color underwent its first changes. He had given five hours in tribute to Cait, unnoticed and unimpressive, and there in the light was Cait's face flaking like dried skin, low on the fluted post of a hesitantly extinguishing street lamp.

Back at the hotel, he asked the Étoile Cachée's night reception man to ring her room. Hair slicked back, pencil mustache, head turned to examine his guest with only one eye, he smiled his condolences. "She has disembarked, sir, with her entourage and my great regret."

"And mine, and mine," he said with his father's weary worldly wisdom and a shaking that overtook his hands and then all his limbs, and by the time he'd scraped his key into the door and had reached the WC, he was quaking with fever, asleep, it felt, even as he was sick in that toilet stall wallpapered with illustrations from a seventeenth-century fencing manual. Hours later that same morning, when his fever climbed daringly high, some of the chevaliers cocked their eyebrows at him as they slowly drew on and immediately peeled back off their deerskin gloves, only to slowly pull them back on again.

17

SHE KEPT TELLING HERSELF she should have seen it coming. For several minutes *that* was the extent of the attack: she should have seen "it" coming, she kept thinking, even though there was no "it" other than the stinging blame that she should have seen it coming. She was in the bathroom stall an hour before stage time, and she was still there five minutes before stage time, and she was there ten minutes after stage time. Ian sent in the French girl from the coat check: gentle knuckles on the stall's wooden door and "Miss? You need a thing?" She rebuilt a facsimile of herself at the mirror, told herself that, though she should've seen it coming, she had no choice now but to pretend it hadn't happened.

Ian was waiting outside and she saw how she looked reflected in his eyes, his pity, his coddling offer of some more time, and she loathed what she saw and loathed him for showing it to her. "Don't. Don't touch me. Let's just go. I said *stop*. Don't *touch* me." Worse was yet to come; she should've seen *this* coming, too: she sang hideously, possibly the worst performance of seventeen years singing in public. She wanted to die, escape, change her name, claw her face beyond recognition. But even worse still—and she should've seen *this* coming as well—no one acted any differently. The crowds jumped. The boys tried to get on with her. The girls danced. Her band celebrated their conquest of France. Ian smiled like a child-molesting clown after the show and said, "See? You were great. They loved you." They couldn't tell the difference between her at her best and her at her worst, after she'd humiliated herself for them, swallowed the burning and bitter panic that had her stuck in the squat-hole stall, staring at the patterns of the barely pulped wood in the paper roll—the sneering faces and fantastical weapons and withered flowers—only to find that at the other end no one was even paying attention. She wanted only to go back to the hotel, to sleep until she could escape this awful city. She couldn't go to the rue Quincampoix, not now. If he was at the gig tonight, he alone would have heard what happened, and he would run away from her, wouldn't turn up, even if she could pull herself together. He, most of all, would have fled from what she had revealed. She'd lost him, lost her one chance for something valuable and lasting.

So she was taken to a party where Ian wouldn't let her alone. She kept batting his hands off her arms, but he was like an insect, his skinny denim legs bending, his adhesive fingers on her, his foaming fluids on offer: "Cait, you have to meet this guy, Cait, you have to see this view from the back window, you can see the Eiffel Tower, Cait, this is Pierre, get this: he was Piaf's husband's *cut man!*"

"You digging the glory?" Alec Stamford asked, so out of context that at first he resembled a low-budget movie's shabby special effect. " 'You're the toast of Paree, Marie.' You know that old song?" She didn't, and so he crooned an old novelty song in his straw boater. "*You're the toast of Paree, Marie. You're the talk of* la ville. / *You were once all for me, Marie, but now, ah,* c'est la vie." He'd needed a vacation, he said, after his recent bout of adult publicity. "I don't know if you heard, I had a run-in with the law. A misunderstanding, as it was later determined, and I was sent on my way with the constabulary's apologies, but of course *that* doesn't make the papers. I'm thinking you understand, of everyone in this room. You're entering the looking glass now, blue Alice. I've done my time over here. I'm starting to think I'm going to be your hookah-smoking caterpillar, you know?" He placed his hand on the back of her head, as if petting a child or a poodle, and said, "Your guitarist is quite good," as though his hand should be wandering in her hair for this very reason. If he hadn't also said, as his face began to swoop down toward hers, "You sang beautifully tonight," maybe she would have deflected his charge with more grace, or even let him kiss her for a second, just because who cared—after all, he'd tried to hire three hardworking girls to simulate her. As it was, though, he did say that, and she turned her head and stepped aside swearing, called him talentless and useless, fraudulent, repellent, hollow, noisily detailed the real circumstances of his arrest. He didn't deserve all that, but she was in no mood to admit it until she flooded all memory of him and the gig and the end of the party and the rue Quincampoix with a tsunami of black Guinness, and then she was on an early-morning train to Madrid, her head on Ian's lap, when it wasn't bent over the metal toilet seat with the view inside it of passing railway ties below.

18

UNCOMMON CONSONANTS, undervoweled and speckled with sharp accent marks, whizzed excitedly by on airport welcome signs, quizzically yowled from storefront windows, a world jiggled off its axis.

After his lost days and lost weight in Paris, the doctor coming to his room, the filth and dreams, Julian caught up with her tour. He was determined to finish this and suffering from strange symptoms. He couldn't listen to his iPod: none of the music—not even hers—charmed him. He couldn't sleep from thoughts of her eyes and breasts and jeans and lips and throat, but also could no longer conceive what a meeting would be like, nor understand what had happened in Paris. He thought of Carlton, the gift she had made him by inviting the boy's memory back into his life, but he also had periods of paralyzing grief when he didn't think of her at all and then wanted nothing further to do with her, when he hated her for having started something in him he couldn't control.

He knew he couldn't go on like this, roaming this limbo of his own design (sharing the space with a dead baby, just like the real limbo), spiraling toward her without arriving. He told himself he was waiting for the perfection she deserved, but in fact he was no longer doing anything but hiding, city after city, and when he glimpsed her walking toward him, alone, in the shadowed hall of the Vânătoarea in Bucharest, he vaulted into a closet next to a cracked sink with a splintered mop standing up in it, closed the door behind him, and found another man already there. He was pale and thin and unhappy-looking, also hiding from her, biting his lip and driving his knuckles into his temples, holding his breath and praying she didn't see him like this, leaning against Julian's face on the other side of the mirror.

The tour chugged into its terminus in Budapest. At noon the day of her last concert, he lay in his bed in the very odd hotel room with the cabin-wood paneling, the sparse and unmatched furniture, but the elegant chandelier and touches of belle époque plush mingled with KGB interrogation-chamber style and a thin spray of modern business traveler reduced-expectation perquisites—laptop outlets, skimpily stocked mini-fridge, pay-per-wank cable menu. Perfection existed, he insisted; she would settle for nothing but perfection; perfection was the only way into their future, the only way to meet her needs, to be a father again—a father to the memory of Carlton and father to Cait, in a way—the only way to earn her love, to really live again. There was—he was perfectly certain—a *perfect* solution, a perfect ending and a perfect beginning, some event perfectly untested with previous women, perfectly free of Rachel, perfectly suited to his and Cait's chemical bonds.

Unless he couldn't have both. Unless there was no solution to the mathematical problem of Cait and Carlton, no geometry that could contain them both. Stung, he leapt from the bed to reset his mind, to look at anything that could shift his thoughts onto a new track. There was only one reproduction on the walls of his bafflingly decorated room, Rembrandt's *Danaë*: Zeus came to her when she slept, woke her as a shower of gold. And then Julian knew the answer. Perfection demanded not that they leap from where they stood, stalled, but to break the journey into gentle steps: the future could be created only by dreaming of it first. Only one of them could afford to be awake at that first moment. Sleep must still cradle one of them, dream filaments stretched across the instant to form a bridge. He would go to her when she slept tonight. She would wake in his arms, but only slightly, wake again after he was gone, unsure if it had happened at all, and that would set the scene for New York. Might there not be a chemical to facilitate the event—producing not unconsciousness but perhaps a little factual soft focus? A fuming handkerchief, a mousy mickey, a powdered velvet blindfold, a shower of gold . . .

She would be unconscious, at least at the start. It would have been nice to have enough Hungarian to bribe a pharmacist and ask for a phial of something that would encourage poor memory but not complete oblivion. Since he didn't have a word of it, he decided to wait in her closet until she fell asleep.

Even then, the acquisition of her room key—the easy matter of spy novels and French farce—loomed insurmountable. Long poles with twisted coat hangers at the end would require a trip to Hungarian specialty stores and an experienced handyman's vocabulary: *duct tape, pliers, you-never-saw-me-here*. Or a Fosbury flop over the concierge's counter. A stolen red uniform. A steamy self-sacrifice to the ancient, bristle-lipped chambermaid, lifting her master key from beneath her stained and tattered dirndl as he kneaded her rump, called her his dumpling. In the end, he sat in the lobby, reading a newspaper next to a urinating cherub until the concierges changed over, and the priest-eyed young one, plainly aware of Cait's celebrity and keen to protect her from threats, left matters in the capable hands of a deaf nonagenarian with shaking fingers and a wet and perpetually moving mouth. Julian's voice was steady when he said, "Five-zero-six" and raised his eyebrows high, as if he were accustomed to looking at the top row of keys.

He strode out to a cab. He pointed to *locksmith* in his English-Hungarian dictionary, and the driver nodded and began speaking German while Julian hunched over and wrenched the enormous key off its identifying bowling pin. Arriving, Julian pointed to *wait*.

The phone was ringing when he dashed into his own room, her key's clone searing his thigh, the original returned to its high hook. He sat on the edge of the bed, the flaming key now in his hands. He couldn't answer, couldn't afford to speak to her now, to give her the chance to divert or confuse him any further. It stopped. A minute later it began again, and he snatched it up before the first bell faded: "Did you read this thing in the new *Neuroscience*?" Aidan asked from across oceans. "I suppose not. Why would you read anything at all? You have all your screens. Well, go online, Cannonball. Today. It's just up today. No Wi-Fi? Why would you go somewhere like that? You should be home now, especially when you hear this. Okay, listen. As I'm sure you know, forgiveness was long ago figured out, evolution-wise—what it's for, what it wins us, how a certain amount in the group leads to genetic success, but how too much or too little leads to extinction, all that. Well, if you would get online now, you'd read how they mapped the brain circuitry responsible for forgiveness. If you'd thought about it, you'd have known they'd nail it down soon enough in the frontal-limbic circuits, but it uses the posterior cingulate gyrus, the orbitofrontal gyrus, the left superior frontal gyrus, *and* the precuneus! As you can guess, the sizes of all these stations vary among individuals. Our passion for moralizing is shown up yet again to be just a fetish for the size of certain small areas of certain people's brain tissue. But this forgiveness path, Jules—they mapped it so elegantly. They hook you up to the sensors and electrodes, tell you they're looking for relaxation patterns or something, but then, when you're all settled in, they start to make little mistakes. They get your name wrong. They step on your toe. They bump you or spill coffee on you. And the tester says, 'Oh, whoops, I'm so sorry.' And then you can see it on the scans: two thirty-sevenths of a second before the subject says, 'No big deal,' or 'Water off a duck's back'—*if* he says it—a little flash goes down that line, gyrus to gyrus, like lanterns over ancient hills signaling the all-clear. Amazing, huh? It shouldn't be long before you can get an injection of a hormone right into those spots, make them grow a little bit, and—bingo!—you're the forgiving type. Julian, are you listening to me? In theory—Julian, listen—with a sufficiently enhanced forgiveness pathway, you know—are you listening?—there would be no such thing as an unforgivable act. When you coming home, brother? People here need you."

"I don't know."

"All right, I'll argue the other side for you, since you're too lazy. There would still be an unforgivable act. Permanent ones. If somebody needed you, would die without you, and you refused to help, wouldn't that still be unforgivable?"

"I suppose so."

"It's time to come home now, no more games. You're too old for games," Aidan said.

Julian exploded: "You of all people say that? You get to be a child forever and—"

"It's time to come home, J. Where you're necessary."

19

UNDER A DARK BLUE SKY with unmoving blue-gray cloud-islands, like a faded antique map of the Aegean, Cait performed on a stage in a meadow on Margaret Island, the second-to-last night of a weeklong music festival and the finale of her European tour. Fireworks wept over trees and spas and Parliament across the river. "This is called 'Servicing All the Blue Men,' " she said. Julian, as he had done the first night he saw her in Brooklyn, stood at the far back of the crowd, on the edge of a little wood that here and there bordered the field, but tonight her key was in his fist, and he would come to her while she slept, give her the first taste of them in a dream.

"She sounds good tonight." A voice from the dark woods behind him, lit briefly blue and orange by melting fireworks filtered through full trees, then in the dark again, just an afterimage on the back of Julian's eyelids, a paler version of someone he knew. "I knew you were quite a fan, of course."

"Alec? Alec? What are you—"

"The thing about fans, though, Julian—" He tipped, then caught himself against a tree branch, which bent under his weight, and his knees buckled one at a time. His cowboy boots were splattered with something. "—and take this from me, I've had my share, there is this line, fine and dandy. Cait and me, we know things about fans that maybe someone like you wouldn't get, TV commercials and all that iced latte." The sky burst open and bled red, lending Alec a parody of a demonic glow, his swollen eyes half shut. He was unshaven, his arms outstretched like a hungover Frankenstein's monster as he turned his back on the show to face the shorter man, to push between Julian and Cait. "You love the fan you don't know, you see." He put his hands on Julian's shoulders. "You *loathe* the one who introduces himself. Like a chlorine jelly bean, baby. A rule—" *clap!clap!* went his hands right in front of Julian's face. "Unbreakable rule, a law of waterfalls. You were in London, yeah? I saw you down in the pit. You think she's digging your scene? The crowds that went to every Grateful Dead show, trailed the smoky carnival in dippy vans—you think the Dead *liked* them? They took their money for the hardship of playing for them. Word to the wise."

Alec tried sitting on the wet grass but stood up right away, slapping at the backs of his thighs. "You were a Reflex fan. Probably followed me around like this. I mean, I see Cait's appeal. I do. But I watch you, and I just can't figure—I mean, all you do is *make commercials*, sweet Bolivia, just so *sad* a Christmas card, bells on soiled bobtails."

And with a bang, the blue-faced artist, his eyes wet, was reaching forward and down to grab Julian's head by the cheeks. "I have been trying so hard to *warn* you," he said. Julian stumbled backward, but Stamford had him by the back of the head, and he fell at the painter's feet. "Oh. All right then. Thank you," Stamford whimpered, wiping his face. "I am just—am just really—just glad to know that's all you were. Ugly music, my lad. Just a grubby little, a dirty old fan. I had higher hopes for you." He ground the heels of his hands into his eyes. "Cait would say about you, 'Just some fan.' I tried to tell her you were different, but she had your deli ticket, Pascal."

Julian crab-walked backward until he had enough distance to stand, flee the sobbing man, push into the crowd, though he was not pursued. The crowd melted in front of him and sealed itself tight behind him again, and under blue fireworks Cait sang,

"*All the blue, blue men, clamoring for me, stammering at me, their*
   swallowed cries hammering at me.
'Play that song again,' they yammer at me. 'The one that helps me see.' "

He pushed, was pushed back, faced aggression here, laughter there, and his shirt was soon wet with alcohol, and the ecstatic delirium of the event rushed into him, into the space jarred open by Stamford. He swam forward until he could see her face above him, pushed to the front as far as he could, nearly to bouncers and metal rails, and he was slammed and slugged by children. He stopped, open to her, presented himself for her inspection, that girl up onstage above him, craned his neck for her.

The tour has obviously tired Ian more than the other boys, Cait was thinking. He may not be cut out for this over the long haul. That would be a grave disappointment. So much of her success was his doing. She couldn't imagine doing without him, but she needed rather more vim than he was displaying tonight. "Wake up, you wanker," she shouted. That started his heart a bit, but not enough, so she pressed herself against his back while he played his solo on "Blue Men." She put her mouth against his ear and whispered, "That's better now, my love, that's the way," and the effect was undeniable; she could hear it. She played him playing the guitar. She could see on the faces down there that something was happening because of her. She could make her music through him, her breasts against his back, her breath on his neck, her fingers pulling his beltless loops. The charging force of his solo, that was hers. New Bass's response to him, that was hers. The boiling hi-hat, the crowd, this mounting agitation and elusive whiff of the approaching mass loss of control—these all came from inside her. "Do you want me, Ian?" she whispered, and her effect spread from the skin on Ian's neck to the tension in his hand on the guitar's neck, through the cable to the amps, to his foot stomping on one of his pedals, and the guitar clanged, and the air changed, and the crowd surged toward her again, drawn to her by her breath blown into Ian's ear, and she looked out over the sea of faces and bodies and did not distinguish between them, or wish to, any more than an explorer of distant lands would care to distinguish among the waves that carried him through the velvet night to the next spiced port.

But then the applause and shouts quieted, and Cait O'Dwyer drifted downward and caught Julian Donahue's eye on a September night in Budapest, and she smiled at him with amazement and then sly satisfaction.

He felt relief push across his face and chest because this was how she wanted him to proceed, perhaps she'd always wanted it like this, while he'd cowered in the back. As soon as he stepped to the front of a crowd and admitted that he was just one of them, she smiled down upon him and accepted him. She had been waiting for this gift: he was a fan. He would go to her, backstage, in the lobby, in her room, it didn't matter how or where; whatever they did would be unique enough. He would give her his youth, the last drops of it still to squeeze and all of it gone before. He would deed his past over to her, repurposed like a warehouse conversion: the years before he knew her would be hers now, a pre-verse refrain, his marriage redefined as the marriage that was wrong because it wasn't with her. His child was the pain that could only be brought inside him with her help, a story for him to tell her and her to tell right back to him, explained and beautiful, and that would thin this syrupy grief that had been replacing the blood in his veins.

She was smiling at him now, in this green and black field in Hungary, and agreed that the rest would be easy. She laughed when he was jostled and splashed. She held him down there with her eyes and her smile, and she spoke into the mike, and he accepted her latest gift: "Here's a new one. Hope you like it. What do we say about it? Let's, uh, let's say it's a trepidatious love song. It's called 'My Kind of Boy.'" Hungarians translated and mistranslated "trepidatious," and she sang to him, her eyes wide open:

> "Leave it all behind, all the half steps and losses.
> Leave them all behind, all your burdens and your crosses.
> Come out to meet me, let's try you and me alone.
> Or maybe, maybe not, maybe let's keep it to the phone.
>
> Stand outside my door, wait 'til I'm insane.
> Make me wait, make me beg, leave me standing in the rain.
> Write your name in the fog with your finger.
> Tell me how you'll never ever trust a singer.
>
> What am I to do?
> What am I to you?

What am I to do with you?
My kind of boy.

Closer now, but keep your distance,
Let them all talk, just don't leave a witness.
Come here, stay, roll over, play.
My kind of boy, my kind of boy."

20

HE WALKED, then ran to her then, short of younger breath, walked again, along crowded streets, along riverfront traffic for a mile, until their hotel moved in and out of view from behind a hill with a winged statue perched on its front like a sconce. He drank in the lobby bar and waited, watched the hazing lobby through glass doors for nearly two hours until the band entered noisily with multinational handlers and hangers-on, Cait in the center, holding hands with the drummer. An albino with flashy clothes and neon-pink shoes asked her something in German, and she said, "*Nein,* baby," and everyone laughed too loud. She told her crowd she was done for the night. She shook off their arguments until only congratulations remained, which she gathered up like a tired lady in the garden. "Do you want to drink awhile? Scheme about the future?" Ian asked her.

"Tomorrow," she said wearily. "Tomorrow, love." She spun her overweighted key on two fingers and summoned an elevator. "You played so well this whole tour, Ian. I'd be nowhere without you, you know," she said as the door began to close. "Thank you. For everything." Ian just nodded, made a sour face at himself in the closed brass door, turned away.

Julian made himself wait two more minutes, slid out to the lobby as her band and crowd occupied the bar. He wasn't going to wait for her to fall asleep after all; even two minutes was too much to ask. His watch's second hand snagged in the hairs on his arm, and he thumped the Up button. But the elevator refused to come, opening only when he turned toward the stairs, then it grudgingly lifted him but only slightly, hesitating wherever possible, opening its nearly shut door because it thought it heard someone coming from down the hall. It loitered at every single floor, longing for more passengers while Julian drove his knuckles into the Close Door button until he imprinted its braille translation into his skin, making dominos of his fingers, and the elevator unhappily rose a bit with a hydraulic sigh. On her floor the door stuttered slightly open, then, as Julian began to move, at once reclosed, and he was dragged cursing back down until he was able to pry his way out, despite the elevator's clingy efforts to embrace him. He took the stairs, hurdling.

He held his key, her key, their key, and stood at her door until his hand steadied. He was certain: he didn't have the strength to calculate the next orbit, and he was certain: she didn't want him to. Julian put his key in her lock and entered Cait's room, closed Cait's door, waited still and silent until his eyes adjusted to Cait's lights and darks.

Her balcony windows were open; his eyes finally read that tall rectangle of gray and yellow, and the thin lace drapes swung into and out of the room like flirty ghosts. The lights on the embankment seeped into the room, but she was not on the balcony, nor in the sitting room, not in the bathroom, not in the bedroom. She had discovered yet another knight's move, checked him again, her smile onstage signifying something he had mistranslated from the Caitish. She could see farther ahead than he, and he was tiring, blind, old. The green iron bridge that seemed to begin at her balcony had provided her a skipping freedom across the Danube.

On her bed was an open hanging bag, a coffin for a flat corpse. He touched her pillow. He took off his shoes and socks, spun his iPod until her picture was on its screen. He moved her suitcase to the floor, caught the smell of her, pulled back the covers from the bed, caught the smell of her again, stronger. He pulled off his shirt, to clear a path to his nose for her, to sweep away the aromatic litter of booze. His pants and shorts fell off him, too, and he lay between the sheets that smelled of her, her digital likeness faintly blue on the pillow.

21

CAIT LAY NAKED in his bed, downstairs. She would say when he came to her, "I thought after Paris that you were done with me. I don't have any tricks left, you know." Or she would say when he found her there: "It's a big night for you and singers, Julian Donahue." She also prepared arguments for him to destroy, planned to quiz him, and he would have to answer before anything else happened: If I get laryngitis, if I have to become a veterinarian, what will we talk about, and will you still want me? or, If I become famous, will you complain if I pretend to the world that I'm available, or would you make me wear a ring and stand next to me for photographs and make me thank you on CD boxes? and If we sleep together now, will you still give me advice or will you sabotage me, will you be jealous of rehearsals and flirty chat-show hosts and me grabbing Ian's arse onstage, will you come to award shows in a penguin suit or will you pout at home and drink? Now, quick, without mentioning music at all, tell me why you pursued me, tell me what depths you've seen in me, but don't mention music. There are some things I should probably explain about myself right away, things you probably won't like—or do we have all the time in the world?

She sat up, pulled her knees into her chest, arranged the sheets around herself, heaped her hair in a particular tried and trusted tousle. She listened for steps in the hall, but the third time that steps quieted without becoming a key in the door she lay down and began to suspect that he meant to put her off again, whether from fear or cruelty or indecision. He was saying no, still, not yet, commanding her to be patient again, postponing again, until—what? She begged him in public? Made a plea from onstage? Called him up to sing a little duet, the arrogant man? He hadn't given up on her after Paris, so why now? He saw that she'd performed to the very end of her repertoire, and the answer was no, not good enough, he didn't see some mythical "most interesting part" of her that wasn't music, and the music was not enough. "My Kind of Boy" was an awful song, and she hadn't realized it until now.

She lay there, aware of noises and the band's nasty early-morning departure for press and radio and vacation in Vienna. She found a shirt of his in the closet, put it on like a robe along with hotel slippers. She stood on his balcony, watched the lights in the black river, the occasional cars, the row of cabdrivers smoking next to a fountain. She could do with a cigarette. Disappointed, angry, she was small and young and boring and predictable to men like him.

She stepped back inside, switched on a light, opened his laptop and suitcase and briefcase. She read his iTunes library with an expert eye, but it didn't tell her anything she didn't already know or suspect, except perhaps a little too much of what Ian derided as "the rock of aging." His email was all work, and his computer photo album was empty. He had the Yeats she'd sent him, the bookmark with the view of Wicklow her great-grandfather had painted, and a second bookmark at a different page—a postcard of an old couple in wartime Paris with just a question mark for its text. So someone else was asking something of him, too, someone with a New York postmark.

His briefcase had a file folder full of her: reviews, profiles, Web pages, printouts of her emails to him, the Quincampoix poem, her invitation and list of hotels, photos of her he'd taken and photos of her he'd found. It was sweet but it was also—what was the word? She imagined collecting all of this stuff about someone else, and she imagined him collecting more and more of it about her, because no matter how much he gathered, something would still be missing. Maybe the more he'd gathered, the more he'd seen she wasn't turning out to be what he'd hoped.

And then she found what had been missing from *her* picture of *him*, the hole she had sensed, a little leather case in a side pocket, all by itself in there, a little four-by-six photo album. It smelled of new leather and had no scuffs. It was stamped on the back with the name of a leather worker and the word FIRENZE. They'd been in Florence ten days ago. It held only four photos, six cellophane slots still empty. The first was old, the sunny blur of the 1960s or 1970s, a man almost certainly Julian's father next to a beautiful woman in furs, her hair in a beehive. All the rest were of a little child, first as a laughing baby flying just out of reach of grasping disembodied hands. Then he was fat-ter, wearing a little blue cap. Finally he was being kissed on one cheek by Julian and on the other by a woman, black hair pushed behind her ear, diamond-ringed fingers tickling the laughing baby's double chin.

Her first instinct was to make it part of their game, to take one of the pictures of herself from his folder, cut it to fit, and slide it into his album for him to discover back home, her announcement of where she'd spent this night, if he didn't already know. But then she stopped. The finished product would have been—what was the word? Out of tune. It was a chord progression that made no sense at all: parents, baby, older baby, older baby, Cait. Tonight, onstage, she had felt herself perched on top of all creation, and now she felt as if she was spoiling something merely by looking at it.

She dialed his apartment in New York.

"Well, it's about five in the morning, I think, and I don't know where you are, but you'll get this eventually. I'm in your hotel room in Budapest, and I'm looking around and maybe seeing things, ah, a little clearer. I don't—we haven't seemed able to find just how to do this, half a Smiths song, half a dinner date, half a wild night in a Gellért hotel room, half a this and half a that, eh? Not quite adding up right, and I'm wondering if that's maybe for the best. I'm not sure about that. I'm wavering as I say it. I could be convinced, Julian. Do you feel up for convincing me?" She stood on the balcony in his shirt, looked at the sky beginning to pale, maybe just a trick of the bridge lights. "But if here's where the story ends, that would still be a pretty good story, wouldn't it? I'm a lot of possible things, you know. I think I am. I sort of take some pride in that, in not limiting that, not being scared of finding out. But I'm not, probably, able to be absolutely *anything* at all, if you take my meaning? There are—are we really going to go to the movies and things, and meet each other's . . . friends? You've a child, I think, and that's not for me. Am I being boring? Maybe, maybe it is for me, how do I know? Maybe I'd be Auntie Cait or something, and you'd have to explain my presence to him or cancel meeting me because the little thing had the mumps or some such. I'm just tired. I don't know. And I don't know where the pretty woman with the black hair is in all this? I think you might have—no, I don't know what I think you might have. You make me feel very clumsy, my friend, and a little young and stupid. We're off to Vienna for a few days. I wouldn't be surprised not to hear from you again. Nor vice versa, I suppose. Nor the opposite. If I know anything, it's you've got plenty more tricks and surprises than I have. You're endlessly creative, I suspect, Julian. So what are we to be, then? I think we'd best sort it soon. I can't take any more nights like tonight."

Aidan had happily house-sat while his brother was in Europe and now was simply trying to leave everything in better condition than when the owner left. He had just finished sanitizing the hazmat fridge and bathroom with some very high-end scouring powder he'd paid for himself, and now he sat on the couch listening to this call, knew what would be best for everyone, deleted it.

22

JULIAN'S EYES OPENED to the room, brown with near daylight, the morning of his flight home to New York. His iPod was blank. He washed his face, tried to blink away the coming hangovers, physical and otherwise. He dressed, gathered his things, replaced her suitcase, left her room as he'd found it, didn't want to leave anything of himself behind this time, because the picture would have been of a fool, for the first time, an old fool, impotently stalking and pleading for something she wouldn't give him, because what, after all of this, did he have to *offer* her, he demanded of himself, knowing the sad answer. He was, after a lifelong spree, broke, outside a shop window, with nothing to spend but a little cry of desire—"But I *want*"—as if that had cash or artistic value. And she knew it didn't.

When he opened her door, a weight rolled into her room toward him, landed next to his feet with a thump, and then unfolded and stood to become Ian Richfield, waking and confused and still steaming alcohol out of his skin. "Jesus Christ," he said, looking at Julian. "You have got to be kidding me." He stumbled back down the hall, pounded on the elevator button, and rested his head against the wall, rather hard.

So Julian took the stairs down to his own room to pack, charge his iPod, start trying not to think any more about any of it. His key opened his door but only an inch, until the interior chain caught.

Cait had hooked it just in time and now hid behind the door, half dressed and annoyed at being trapped. The voice mail she'd just left him was wrong. She didn't want to be convinced. She was done, and she knew it right then. She didn't want him, didn't want any more of any of it, not his scraps of a life lived without her, before her, his children and previous wives, all this bulky past to stuff somewhere, or to hold over her, to compare her to, old sadnesses bending him over when he should have been with her, all his little triggers she'd have to be wary of. "Look, can you do me a favor?" she called.

"Anything, anything at all, I'm just so—"

"I need to leave now, and I'd like to make a graceful getaway."

"No! No, no . . . We, we . . ."

"I do."

"Please no. Please don't. Please." She was silent. He waited and waited and she was silent and the chain drooped there. "Are you sure?" he asked, squeezing his eyes shut, compressing everything into a single moment.

"I am. Can you—"

"Yeah."

He turned back to the stairs, felt the tears prickling against his face, kept going down until he ran out of steps, opened a door to the lobby and then another to the street, and he walked up the hill behind the hotel and watched the flats of Pest brighten across the river, like the houselights coming up at the end of a play.

When he went back to his room, she'd ransacked it, taken all his relics of her, left him only the pieces that didn't include her. The little photo album lay on his pillow next to Rachel's postcard of the old Parisian couple. He picked up his shirt, held it to his face, breathed in Cait. He smelled her in his bed, too, the traces of the night they'd just spent together.

The number one I hope to reap
Depends upon the tears you weep, so cry!
— the Beautiful South, "Song for Whoever"

1

ON THE LONG FLIGHT HOME, Cait's scent on his shirt like the very last two curled leaves trembling on an autumn-chilled branch, Julian slept until Europe crumbled into the sea. When he awoke, his iPod suggested Billie Holiday's *Chicago Radio Broadcast, 1959*, and Julian listened several times to his mother's voice and Billie's and the best of those piano solos until the music gave out with a plaintive flashing icon over Greenland.

The pianist Dean Villerman's name only appears in a few comprehensive jazz encyclopedias as genealogically compulsive as the Book of Numbers and on half a dozen sporadically live websites devoted to other players, but even obscure-footnote sidemen are often someone's pet favorites, and so it was with Villerman. He came up through white dance bands in the South, before the Second World War, a little white cat educated as a physicist, and some jazz-trivia buffs insist to this day that he played a minor role in the Manhattan Project. True or not, there is a photograph of a celebration at Los Alamos after the first successful test detonation, and in it Oppenheimer and Leslie Groves toast each other with glasses of something, and they stand in front of an upright piano played by a hunched-over figure who could certainly have been the younger version of the man Julian met forty-three years later at his last public performance.

Atomic or not, in 1941 and 1942 Dean Villerman was in Manhattan, not New Mexico, and was hanging around Minton's, Clark Monroe's, and similar after-hours joints, listening and watching as bebop's structural engineers hammered out its musical foundations. Unknowns like Villerman would wait patiently, hoping but not guaranteed to sit in, watching Monk's hands as he figured out what it meant to play bop piano. Aspirants were willing to abase themselves, go into a back room and play "Rhythm" in all twelve keys, changing up a fifth every chorus, just to earn the right to go back and wait some more, sitting and smoking as long as necessary to take the dreaded and coveted chance, invited up well past three o'clock in the morning, Monk standing to the side, looking at the ceiling, while Villerman, for example—plaid cardigan, thick glasses, suspenders—played something that Bird dismissed after eight bars as "corny." But bebop wasn't Mandarin Chinese or even particle physics, and Villerman was a serious musician, so eventually he figured it out, could sit in for a few tunes with Dizzy and Bird and not feel a fool, though there were always going to be some front-row and backstage murmurs that—as a white boy—he could imitate it, but he couldn't in some deep, nameless way, *be* it or advance it.

Once he had it, though, he didn't do much with it. He didn't record as a leader or as a sideman. After the war he taught at a boarding school in New Hampshire—theory, private lessons, classical appreciation, a little jazz technique for the talented kids—now and then taking the *Yankee Flyer* down to the city to play a night or two of quiet standards at a restaurant.

Julian, however, knew Villerman's name—implying a very, very deep jazz aficionado's knowledge—because of a single radio date Villerman played with Billie Holiday in May of 1959, one of her very last public appearances, and literally her last sung notes to survive as a recording. You can't buy it. Julian's father made it, live in Ohio, by setting up a black Magenta-Sonic reel-to-reel, purchased at great cost for the event, in front of his white-and-gold, two-speaker Fidelio hi-fi. Over the years, Julian transferred his father's tape to cassette, CD, then his computer and iPod, and he never found any other recording of it, not on Billie fan sites or as a commercial reissue or in the tera-bytes of the world's uploaded audio and video. Julian owned, in this one case, the only recording on earth of something important.

His father had loved the tape, not because of Billie—she sounded hoarse and dazed, and she dragged behind the beat like a plow—but because of the piano: chords that combined joy and sorrow in count-less and mysterious proportions, that carved a sculpture of the singer's whole life as a tribute during solos and wove a support under her when she sang and stumbled, like a hand under her arm, or a blanket over her knees. Even Julian could hear, as a young boy, that some-thing rare, almost celestial, happened that night on the piano. Some-thing happened that night. Something descended and touched the piano player, and the music echoed on and on, outward and stronger, "live from the Skyline Lounge, on the thirty-eighth floor, high atop Chicago's Excelsior Hotel."

"Dean"—the fan speaks of players by first name when analyzing their work—"Dean was touching that piano like he knew she was waiting to die, and he was giving her his blessing, like he knew this one counted, and he was saying it was going to be okay," Julian's fa-ther liked to say of the recording.

Julian loved that piano work nearly as much as his father did, but he cherished the recording for another reason. Listen to it carefully: in the middle of "Don't Explain," when you've adjusted your sonic ex-pectations down, down, to 1959 live-in-a-bar-to-radio-to-propped-up-reel-to-reel standards, and you can almost ignore the hissing from three generations of transfers, the rushing ions of 1978, 1988, and

2003, when you close your eyes and leap the treacherous abyss of inches between the Paleolithic tape recorder and the Neolithic hi-fi, strengthen with your will the feeble and faltering radio signal wheezing across the Great Lakes, overlook the quality of the microphones in the Chicago hotel, the clatter of dishes, the chatter—oh, yes, though the zoot-suited and wolf-whistling nostalgists will deny it when they snarlingly hush you tonight in a jazz club, there was chatter in jazz's golden age, even in one of the very last moments of a goddess—the chatter of diners who didn't think there was anything meriting their respectful attention in the background music to what was, after all, their night out, their pricey meal, their first or last date, their view of the Chicago River, their dramatic conversation about their private lives to which this dying singer was only light accompaniment—if you can hear past all of that and seat yourself at the front table and listen to Billie Holiday and her band, then you will also have the shock of hearing Julian's French mother walk into her living room and say, "Will, where did you put my book? What? Oh, oh, oh," quieter on each "oh," whispering after the third, "Sorry, my heart."

Sorry, my heart! Whispered! In that accent! When she was young and healthy! Julian never lived in that house, never saw that room except in photos, and could barely remember her before she got sick. Aidan reported that there had been a red leather-sided bar cart that lit up when it was opened, which he'd considered one of the great inventions of modern man. Dad would sit before it, preparing obscure cocktails from a recipe book (a red cover and the single title, in black, *Standish's*) propped on the bar's fake-black-marble shelf. "Sorry, my heart": each time he heard that faint whisper in front of Billie croaking *"You're all my joy and pain,"* Julian could imagine his father's wide-eyed plea for silence to save the recording, and Billie Holiday yet again wrestling with his mother for his father's attention, his mother knowing she could retreat and win, again, every time, old Billie defeated with a whispered and victorious "Sorry, my heart."

For Julian, who never learned the names of all those sharps and flats, merely felt them as emotional levers, Villerman's music carried the very idea of a skyline, of a singer in lamé dying within weeks, of a crippled man in front of his hi-fi, his French wife and their four-year-old prodigy child and the smell of late-spring air inside a little red house littered with inflatable toys and union rat designs, a lit-up bar cart, all of Julian's family's life, just without Julian.

Dean Villerman's piano that night in Chicago accompanied Julian's mother padding from room to room in her stockings, and there was no way to tell if any one clinking glass belonged to his mother, a diner in the Skyline Lounge, or Lady Day herself. There was no way to tell whose drink it was on his iPod, nor on Julian's living room speakers attached to his computer, whenever he clinked the ice into his own glass, under photos of his mother and father on the wall, and of Holiday, and the photo of an Irish girl going down into the subway with a man rising with mannequins and, tucked into the frame's corner, the postcard of the old Parisian couple. But for all that, there was this piano miracle: that distant and incomparable piano work, decades old, sonically veiled and only sometimes clear, like a glimpse of unimaginable beauty across a four-lane highway at night.

And in 1988, less than a week after Julian moved to New York to take his first commercial job, by glittering coincidence (warm October day walking with Aidan through Central Park, jazz public radio rising from a spread blanket, calendar of events read in baritone monotone, "tonight at the Quaver," name miswritten or misread as "Dan Villerman"), he learned of the pianist's continued existence. Aidan declined without hesitation: "I have urgent personal business." So Julian went alone.

The Quaver was a small club, soon to close its doors permanently in the latest resettling of jazz at the sandy bottom of the nightlife economy, and that night, when Julian arrived, the room was nearly empty. Villerman was already playing, though at first and fourth glance he could have been some dignified bum or migrant piano tuner. But the sound was unmistakable, that same magical transformation of the piano—in this case a battered old upright—into a whirling alchemist's device of memory, lighting, even incense. Villerman played without looking up from the keyboard, without acknowledging the three tables at the front, which held real, listening fans. Boarding-school students? Long-memoried fanatics? Family?

Villerman played without stopping, strung song after song into garlands. Sometimes Julian had the impression he was just playing chords and scales, old exercises, but with such feeling that Julian hardly knew where to look or what to do with his hands, felt the waitress's questions about drinks were heretically intrusive, disrespectful to a solar eclipse or a doomed tribe's last and futile war council. Villerman was mythologically old—so old, small and slight—but with a distended belly straining the lower buttons of a plaid shirt. He curved forward, as if he were pulled over by his frayed black suspenders with silver clips attached to his woolly (and belted) trousers, or the weight of his old-man bifocals, thick in their old-man frames, refracting insanely anything Julian occasionally glimpsed through them when Villerman's head came up and turned slightly to the left. It was a cold October night, and when the door opened, Julian heard, then felt the wind and smelled the dying season, but the old man didn't react to the blasts of air or the pebbles-against-a-window applause, which soon stopped in relief at his obvious indifference. He only stopped playing—and only with his right hand—at just the right moments, executed as if they were composed and rehearsed far in advance, leaving dark chords or walking bass lines in command of the room while he drank, from the highball kept full at his side, clear liquid supplied by the sole waitress from a stained steel shaker, dented, with half the logo of an old gin, not made for decades.

Villerman was a particular species of steady-state drunk, well into the sixth full decade of his habit and manner. He had reduced himself to an equation: an intake of alcohol and an output of piano music. He was playing when Julian entered, and he was playing three hours later, when Julian was literally the only customer remaining in the room. He took no breaks, evoking the possibility of a jazz catheter or a perfect wasteless system.

The pianist, sideways to the room, seemed to withdraw from all directions, his eyes down, bending forward into the piano but also leaning away from the tables, drawing in his legs. The farther he buried himself in the piano, the sweeter the noise, as though he were slowly feeding himself to, and placating, a singing lion. He didn't speak to the audience, or acknowledge those three tables emptying of his last earthly fans, nor did he look at anyone other than the waitress. "Thank you, dear," he overenunciated each time she refilled his nearly empty glass, and another serenely lovely tune would flow from his hands and wrap itself around Julian in the shadows by the exposed brick wall under the cloudy mirror with the chipping golden logo for that same extinct gin, "Sorry, my heart" whispering its siren's accompaniment to the perpetual river of music, as Villerman stayed drunk and Julian got drunk and the waitress—destined for a golden and symbolic anonymity and permanent youth in this story—accepted Julian's invitation to sit down with him and get drunk, too, though she didn't "really like jazzy stuff, to be honest, kind of prefer regular music."

Hunched, contorted, retreating within ever-reducing limitations, the old man played until four in the morning. He only stopped then because the barman called a halt. Two or three people had come and gone between one and four, but at four, only Julian and the staff remained. "That's it, baby," the bartender called to the stage, and at once, in the middle of a measure, Dean's hands fell from the piano and burrowed under his thighs. He sat, nodding at the keyboard, as if agreeing with it. "Real nice playing," said the barman. Villerman stood and, not surprisingly, wavered a little; he'd been sitting on a wooden bench getting drunk for seven hours. Instinctively, trained by a childhood with a tippy man, Julian stepped forward and caught the pianist as he tumbled over. "Ah, yes, thank you," he murmured politely, still not looking up, as Julian propped him in a seat by the door. "Very kind of you. Fall sometimes."

Villerman's pay for the gig—minus his drinks at the performer's discount—left him with a tab of twenty-seven dollars. He reached for his wallet, attached to him by a thin chain. Julian stopped him and reached for his own money, flush after his first job and desperate to repay the man for his service to his family. "Oh, this is too depressing," grunted the bartender with his ponytail and croquet-wicket mustache. "I'll cover it. Please, just—good night, bye-bye."

Villerman was somehow smaller when standing than when seated.

"Thank you, thank you, very kind of you," he said with the extreme politeness of certain drunks as Julian and his waitress accompanied him outside, not having discussed it but with everything clear.

When Julian's father was diagnosed with the cancer that would kill him with vulgar haste, Aidan responded with a flood of his own symptoms, some convincing enough that he found himself slid into MRI coffins and orbited by CT donuts. He had running sores that didn't respond to treatments and a shortness of temper that didn't respond to criticism. His trials ended suddenly, before their father's death, in the MRI tube as the machine's banging magnets cried out their mother's name, and Aidan wept at the mystical epiphany of it, in the tight white enclosure, as *pam* was shouted at him, and sobs shook him from the inside while a disembodied Russian voice kept repeating, "You must remain still, sir. You must remain still, sir, or your results will be tainted." After this, Aidan was cured of his ailments by a self-described "ambulance-chasing psychologist" who left his card with ERs and internists, even waited outside doctors' offices looking for a particular sort of disappointed expression on the faces of departing patients.

Julian, by contrast, though much closer to their father, had been relatively unaffected by the news of his illness. He just kept telling himself it was all part of life, part and parcel of his own emigration to New York (which he had made with his father's valedictory reminder that "we enter this world alone, screaming, and we exit alone"). Sad, yes, obviously very sad, he loved his father, but as Aidan was traveling through the terminal stages of his disorder, and their father was entering his own terminal stages, Julian, four in the morning, five hours before he was meant to fly to Ohio to visit him, was walking down lower Broadway with a waitress-treat, each of them supporting one arm of a shuffling, elderly jazz musician, childlike in Julian's black peacoat, as Villerman claimed to have forgotten his own coat in New Hampshire. The pianist also shyly admitted that he had nowhere to stay before his 11 A.M. train back north to school. He had played so ceaselessly, in part, to fill up the time until the train, figuring that if he didn't stop playing, they wouldn't kick him out. With the little man swallowed by the outsize coat, killing time before going back "to school," one arm in Julian's and one in the waitress's, they made a distorted picture of a young family, even more so when they all ended up at the waitress's studio apartment watching the pianist fight off sleep, sitting up on her sofa bed as the day arrived, not with the sun rising but as a change in the color of the shadows cast on the brick wall a few feet in front of her only window.

Villerman didn't recall any radio gig with Billie Holiday. He laughed at the idea that he had ever achieved such heights. "I'm more of an amateur, Henry," he told Julian after he woke up, his eyes still tipsily cheerful through the soundproof panes of his glasses. Julian smiled fondly at the jokey modesty and asked if he'd played often with Holiday. Villerman blinked, though the top lids (above the bifocal bifurcation) and the bottom lids (below it) had to cover vast, magnified distances to meet. "I'm telling you, kid, I never played with Billie Holiday. I never played with any big stars like that."

Julian had the newly transferred CD and his day-old portable CD player with him, and he plugged the furry, floppy G clefs of Villerman's ears. Villerman instantly became just a disoriented old drunk baffled by space-age technology, but eventually he listened, semi-awake, to the piano playing that Julian's father (and Julian) held in esteem above all other jazz piano playing in history, above Peterson or Tatum or Monk or Hancock or Frishberg or Strazzeri. "Who's on piano?" Villerman asked, pulling the cords out of his head after a minute or two. "Do you have any coffee, dear? Or gin?" he asked the waitress.

"It's you," Julian insisted.

"No, I couldn't ever play like that. That's Jimmy Rowles."

Julian put the disc on the last track and, almost pushing the old man back on the couch, gently batting away his resisting hands, he shoved the earphones back in place. "Just listen." And Julian watched the old face as, he knew, the man heard Billie Holiday introduce the band, concluding with, "And our friend, Mr. Dean Viller—*ahem*—on the piano." She didn't say his name quite right back in '59; he had probably been a last-minute sub she'd had no choice but to accept because Mal Waldron or Hank Jones or, yes, Jimmy Rowles was sick, but the sound of her flubbing his name, in 1988, sufficed to jar something loose from the mucky banks of Villerman's silted memory. His mouth opened, and he looked up, slumped on the couch, and his face contorted, the muscles of his lower lip fighting each other. "She," he said. "Is this a record?" he shouted, adjusting his volume for the music only he could hear. Julian removed the headphones and asked, "Were you living in Chicago in 1959?"

"I suppose I must have been," he replied. "May I listen to the whole thing again?" With his eyes closed, but awake (he'd occasionally yell something), Dean Villerman listened to an entirely forgotten hour of his life from thirty years before. Julian's sexual exploit for the morning was postponed indefinitely, as the waitress fell asleep at the far end of the couch from her elderly guest, and Julian sat on the only chair—stolen from the Quaver but camouflaged with a leopard-skin cushion—watching Dean's face react to the music. "Who said, 'Sorry, my heart'?" he inevitably shouted, "Or did I just dream that?"

Later that same day, the waitress's sleepy, amused kiss at her door still a palpable, edible memory, Julian recounted his adventure that morning, walking the great pianist himself to his train before taking a taxi to La Guardia and the flight to his father's hospital bed. He tucked the same headphones into his father's ears, attached to a head that was rapidly losing its shape.

His father—reduced, reducing—took out one plug, achieving a skeletal Secret Service effect. "That was just yesterday." He smiled, then turned away and vomited violently. "Sorry."

"That's all right. You can keep the headphones."

"I won't need them where I'm going. I have it on good advice the sound system is exquisite. Tell me about Dean. Can you tell by looking at him? Does he seem like the guy who played like that?"

"Not even to himself," Julian said. "There wasn't much left of him."

"I know the feeling."

"You used to say Dean was playing like he was giving Billie his blessing, saying it was going to be okay."

"Yeah." His father closed his eyes and listened, might have been asleep until he asked, "Can you believe your mother? She just stomped around the house for half the broadcast."

"It will be, you know, Dad," Julian said, choking a little. "Okay, I mean."

"I know. You, too. Things are mostly okay, most of the time."

His father was consuming a death squad of painkillers with ferocious reputations, but he dismissed them as "ambitious but ineffective." They did, however, succeed in shutting down his digestion, except, after several days of concrete inaction, a sound-and-smell show that entertained him and defied anyone present not to comment. "Impossible noises for a human," he boasted, and Julian heard enough in the last week of his father's life to agree: jet engines, a sobbing child's repetitive stuttering cry, a distant trill of machine-gun fire several towns away, the wheeze of a dying bird. "I'm turning into a faulty inflatable," his father said. "And one of those Japanese sleepers. You remember them?" By then his voice was scarcely audible, far less than his other noises, and he was falling asleep often, and for longer, less troubled naps.

The smells he produced were equally improbable and even funnier to him as he tried to find just the right names to make his crying son laugh: burnt scrambled eggs, fermented vanilla extract, cordite, hay-fever tears. "Do you smell this?" he asked. "Can you smell this? Am I insane or is that . . ."

"Moldy raspberries?" Julian ventured, laughing and crying.

"Exactly. How can a human who doesn't eat anything produce that? I wonder if I can just think them and then shoot them out my ass. Amazing, this process," he said, honestly marveling at his comic death, before falling asleep, the living fulfillment of that bedtime story he'd invented in another hospital.

Julian wandered the grounds, watched the divide widen between the sick and the well. Those seven days watching his father die (Aidan there for the last two), with the Ohio fall varnishing the trees, Julian would flip open his Discman and rotate through the twenty CDs he'd brought with him, always coming back to Billie Holiday and Dean

Villerman and "Sorry, my heart," wringing out his tears so he could present his dying father with the dry cheeks he was certain the old man preferred.

"I'm sorry about all that" were his father's last words.

"All what?" Julian asked.

2

BACK HOME IN BROOKLYN he put *Chicago Radio Broadcast, 1959,* on the speakers and unpacked, tried to stay awake, to recalibrate himself. He tried to tell himself the final version of his and Cait's story again, but he had nothing to show for it all, was furious at Cait for all she'd taken from him, furious that he wouldn't have his own son at his side when he would lie in a hospital bed, furious at Carlton for betraying him.

He fell asleep at seven that night, and Cait came to him again. Her hands, those long hands he'd noticed months before as evidence of her certain specificity, touched his face, traced old and new lines in his skin, the drapery of his flesh over its hollow frame, and she kissed his eyelids and groaned, "I've been waiting in *your* bed all night." Her own eyelashes were wet, and he was so grateful to her for coming to say good-bye in the hospital, to see him off. "The sound system will be very good," she said. She brushed the hair off his face and placed her lips so lightly on his that he could hear the air compressing between them. "All the women you have ever known," she said, but her Irish accent was gone, and he replied, "I know." They lay beside each other, his hand gliding over the guitar swell of her hip, her flames glowing red, heating his face. "Sorry, my heart," she said, and his face warmed, warmed.

He opened his eyes to face the warming September sun peering around the side of the window frame, the branches not tall enough to protect his muddled sleep any longer. He opened his eyes and felt a happiness that had existed forever, waking to her touch, and he loved this space in the day, this dollhouse window, this last inhalation of

THE SONG IS YOU | 245

breath before the small sound like a popping bubble that would end the silence and prod the unmoving moment, when those first quizzical gurgles would rise from Carlton's crib.

3

HE COULDN'T STOP HIMSELF. He spent longer and darker hours in her dog park, in case Lars required a morning, evening, midnight visit. At first he considered his dignity and offered dog-walking services to his neighbors, claimed he was considering the jump to ownership, and so spent several early-autumn days watching, until well after dark, the immobility of two fat spaniels, the motorboat-buzz assaults of a Pomeranian with a mean streak, and a black Lab supposedly training to become a Seeing Eye dog but who threw herself on her back for tummy rubs so promiscuously for any passing pedestrian that her unlucky eventual blind man would be daily spun to the ground like a volunteer in a judo class.

Within a week, Julian didn't bother with the beards anymore, just sat, sometimes with a book, always with his iPod, and to the notice of the dog people who found dogless observers unnatural. He replayed what he would say if she came, how she would explain her weeks of silence, how he had misunderstood her final act. But she didn't come, and he sat through the cooling season, his errors and illusions clarifying in the clear air.

October, as usual, produced more offers from production companies than he could field. He adjusted his price accordingly. He socialized, with friends and for professional purposes, drinking with clients and agencies as necessary. Maile tendered her resignation with a certain tender look on her face, said she'd stay and help interview replacement candidates, stood there after he'd thanked her and said he quite understood her need to move on and up. She stood there; he was supposed to say something more, but he didn't feel the slightest desire to figure out what it was. He hired a twenty-three-year-old boy to fill her spot.

He couldn't sit still in the office when there was nothing to do, and he and his iPod would take the train back to Brooklyn, get off a few stops early, and go to the dog park. Cait wasn't ever there, and sometimes he didn't mind, and once he didn't even notice she hadn't been there until he was leaving.

One November dawn, Julian came upon a basset hound sitting on a bench on the Promenade, staring out at Manhattan. A few joggers in winter caps and Lycra pants bounded by, but no one seemed to be with the long dog and his heavy ears. It sat on the bench and watched the sky lighten across the East River, watched the city awaken to the day. At some signal that escaped Julian, the hound began to bay at the towers, calling New York to order. This struck Julian as quite exactly how he behaved as well: thinking his voice mattered, content to imagine himself ruling the world around him, never noticing that the world would tick along with or without his howling. He had become, at some point, a ridiculous person, though he couldn't say just when it happened.

He'd had his own version of "Sorry, my heart," he realized as he sat next to the singing basset hound and looked at Manhattan turning on its lights at the dog's call. Rachel had left him that voice mail: "You're like a teenager, J," with Cait singing in the background. Unlike his father, Julian had lost it, deleted it, that only recording on earth of something important, while he was using his two legs to run after impossibilities. His father would have been ashamed of him. "Cannonball, being broken is a bore for everyone around you. Try to remember that. I hope you'll remember me as having enough legs not to be a bore."

4

JULIAN SAT on the wooden bench that circled the oak, where he'd once sat and recorded Cait as she sang to herself. She wasn't there, again, or anywhere else, except online (where her site announced a new guitarist, and a celebrity magazine had a photo of her dining with a man captioned, improbably, as a New York City police detective). It didn't matter: the search for her had emptied something out of him. He reflexively noticed she wasn't there, but he wasn't coming to the dog park for her anymore, no longer even looked up when the gate opened in the corner of his eye. He set his iPod to shuffle, and so he rarely heard her, though the one time "Coward, Coward" played, he reflexively expected to hear Rachel's voice making gentle fun of him.

He knew some of the dogs by name now, the owners' personalities as well. This evening a young woman who had for some days been looking miserable complained bitterly that other dogs were taking her pit bull's squeaky crocodile toy, and when other owners laughed at her gripe, she sat down and burst into tears. Julian comforted her, introduced himself, scratched the timid pit under its chin, fetched its toy for her. "It'll be okay," he said, probably the right thing to say no matter what was troubling her.

He looked forward to the dogs at the end of every workday as his best entertainment, tried not to schedule late meetings because, especially as the days shrunk, the park emptied earlier each night. Tonight Lyle the priapic Chihuahua buried himself in dead leaves and sexually assaulted passing female dogs, bursting out in an explosion of brown crunch, yipping like a car alarm, leaping to grab a leg, against which he would gyrate and grunt, his glistening red member suddenly half the length of his body, like a giantess's fully extended lipstick. The lady hounds, indifferent to his advances, either shook him free or stood imperturbable while he pleasured himself against their ankles, his tongue an oval strip of smoked salmon falling from his mouth. Lyle's owner, a peacoated, trilbied hipster who owned a local bar, laughed as each female's priggish owner shouted, "Get off!" and he would add, "You heard her, Ly. Get off, boy!"

Like Lyle, Julian had had a full life of women, though none came to mind but a wife he had failed, and an Irish singer made of steam. He had success in a field for which he felt no passion but didn't suffer from the lack. His greatest and purest love had survived for only the blink of an eye and ended in—he stopped but then finished his thought, supposed that raggedy word was in Carlton's case legitimate—tragedy. And soon something would change, and something else would occur that he would later view as significant to his perpetually rewritten life story. And he would amass more events and people and memories, and he would clarify old thoughts and rearrange details to highlight new significances and explain to himself what had happened, and on and on. All of this was meaningless, he thought, but *that* raggedy word was not, it turned out, so bitter on the tongue. One could do worse than meaninglessness like this.

A beagle dropped a ball at his feet but grabbed it and backed out of reach as soon as Julian bent down for it. Julian sat up and the beagle dropped the ball for him again—*too slow, sucker!* Julian spun through his 8,146 songs, up and down, to find the audible echo of this sensation—the smell of leaves, the randy Chihuahua, the teasing beagle, acceptable meaninglessness—and the best his iPod could offer was an old Reflex song he'd forgotten to delete, "I Could Sure Do Without This," but it didn't sound the same as he remembered. It was a twenty-five-year-old's frightened idea of middle age and didn't hold together as music or philosophy, here on the other side of all that. He pulled the plugs out of the holes in his head.

The predominant sound that spiraled into the draining void was the expressway that formed one of the park's borders. Under that was an occasional bark, of course, people shouting for their pets. Under that was a bird or two, the species of which he couldn't begin to guess, a nervous squirrel far above, a leaf or twig underfoot, the muttering of the bench and of his own body, the creaky rubber-band whine of a knee, the muffled click of a jaw, a stomach grumbling. But under even that drifted something wispy and still more difficult to catch. It wasn't in his head, nor was it some symptom like tinnitus; he couldn't hear it better by blocking his ears. It came from outside himself, barely perceptible. When he closed his eyes, he heard it more clearly; it rushed and quietly roared and then was gone, and he turned his head slowly from side to side in pursuit of it as if he were the rabbit ears of an ancient television, until he found it again, the diagonal domino tumbling of moonlit surf, or atoms crashing over one another like dice thrown by an anxious gambler, his own name whispered and slurred but in a tone of something less than affection, the echo but not the original of some terrible expanding shock, the sourceless approaching moans of a frightening childhood night when sleeplessness and night-mare blur.

And then it was gone, and he couldn't find it again. He opened his eyes, and the last dog had been led from the park, and the last of the light was gone, and he was alone in the cold and mist, the orange digital clock high on the Jehovah's Witnesses building surprising him with its advanced hour, and he imagined what another life with Rachel might feel like, in the mornings, or on a Sunday, or when they both left for work, or when he left the office knowing he was going home to her, and he wondered whether he would fail her again.

5

THEY FOUND A HOUSE farther from Manhattan, another mile down Henry Street, with a real yard in the back, and Rachel learned to garden, though not that well. When she washed dishes she enjoyed the vines sneaking over the window, like eyelashes across narrowed eyes.

She sets the table for the regular Wednesday dinner guest—Aidan, smug and hungry, bent over soup. The last light from the window. The candles. The black dachshund, rescued from the pound (Rachel's suggestion for a third date), snoring on its blue mat. The new photo album on the shelf with the reunified collection. The framed picture on the wall of their former family, Carlton in his TOUGH GUY cap. The postcard she had sent him of occupied Paris up on the bulletin board in the kitchen. The materials from the adoption agency pinned up there as well. Julian pouring wine and turning down the cello music with the remote in his other hand.

Five hours later, the blue-and-white light of the computer monitor. He wears striped pajama bottoms, the hair on his chest gray in some rising percentage, and on the shelf above the computer sits the older copy of the collected Yeats, which Rachel bought him years earlier. He glances to his left, toward the dim doorway where only Rachel's legs are visible in the bed, the sheets slightly blue from the computer reflecting off the family photo. His impatient index finger taps the lazy mouse long after the page should have loaded, and finally it assembles itself, one off-center square at a time, and he clicks on <u>New Songs</u>, the hurried pop of the headphones into the computer's schematic jack, a few seconds of only the sound of his tongue and breath, then:

> *How much of our history*
> *And how much of your mystery*
> *Should I figure now was just for laughs?*
>
> *I can't say it wasn't fun,*
> *Won't say you were just anyone.*
> *But I suppose the moment's past.*
>
> *And what's a moment anyhow?*
> *My foolish fan, my miscarried plan,*
> *My definitively married man.*

"Are you coming to bed, baby?"

♪

AUTHOR'S NOTE

Beginning with its title (Kern-Hammerstein), this book incorporates in its text several song names, some slightly altered, by: Adair-Dennis, Ahlert-Young, Joan Armatrading, Chet Baker, Barry-David, Bix Beiderbecke, the Beloved, the Blow Monkeys, David Bowie, Bretton-Edwards-Meyer, Burke–Van Heusen, Eric Clapton, George M. Cohan, Leonard Cohen, John Coltrane, Concrete Blonde, Vladimir Cosma, Elvis Costello, Noël Coward, the Cranberries, Miles Davis, Blossom Dearie, DePaul-Raye, Kenny Dorham, the Dream Warriors, Electronic, Duke Ellington, EMF, the English Beat, Victor Feldman, Femi Kuti, Fine Young Cannibals, Michael Franks, Dave Frishberg, Stan Getz, Gordon-Warren, Jerry Gray, Gruber-Mohr, Haircut 100, Herbie Hancock, Heyman-Green, the Housemartins, Joe Jackson, the Jam, Leoš Janáček, Jane's Addiction, Sharon Jones, Keane, Chris Keup, Kraftwerk, Rohan Kriwaczek, Leiber-Stoller, Curtis Mayfield, Mercer-Herman-Burns, Mercer-Kosma, Mercer-Schertzinger, George Michael, Ingrid Michaelson, Mo' Horizons, Jack Montrose, Van Morrison, Brad Neely, Oliver Nelson, New Order, Orbison-Dee, Charlie Parker, the Pet Shop Boys, Chan Poling, Pomus-Shuman, Cole Porter, Prince, Robledo-Terriss, Rodgers-Hart, Roxy Music, Sade, Carlos Santana, Erik Satie, Scrapomatic, Wayne Shorter, Sigler-Wayne-Hoffman, Carly Simon, Paul Simon, the Smithereens, the Smiths, Regina Spektor, Steely Dan, Sting, the Style Council, Styne-Comden-Green, Styne-Merrill, the Suburbs, the Sundays, Swing Out Sister, the The, They Might Be Giants, Tanita Tikaram, Tuxedo-moon, U2, Suzanne Vega, the Violent Femmes, Antonio Vivaldi, Wang Chung, and Wilder-Palitz-Engvick.

Also, "Space Oddity (Major Tom)" is by David Bowie.

WITH GRATITUDE TO:

Julia Bucknall, Gabriel Byrne, Gina Centrello, Andrew Corsello, David Daley, Tony Denninger, Chris Eigeman, Jodi Ghorchian, Roger Grenier, Jennifer Hershey, Raj Jutagir, Alice Kaplan, Paol Keineg, Anna Lvovsky, Peter Magyar, Jynne Martin, Mike Mattison, Peter McGuire, Daniel Menaker, Courtney Moran, Beth Pearson, ASP, DSP, ELP (for four gifts), FHP, FMP, MMP (by the skin of his teeth), OMP, Paulina Porizkova, Mihai Radulescu, Marly Rusoff, Nick and Maryanne Shore, Jake Slichter, Toby Tompkins, Peter Turnley, Nancy Viglione, Donna Wick, Tony Wolberg, Daniel Zelman, and, of course, Jan.

ABOUT THE AUTHOR

ARTHUR PHILLIPS was born in Minneapolis and educated at Harvard. He has been a child actor, a jazz musician, a speechwriter, a dismally failed entrepreneur, and a five-time *Jeopardy!* champion. His first novel, *Prague*, a national bestseller, was named a Notable Book of the Year by *The New York Times* and received the *Los Angeles Times*/Art Seidenbaum Award for best first novel. His subsequent novels, *The Egyptologist* and *Angelica*, were both bestsellers and have been translated into twenty-five languages. He lives in New York with his wife and two sons.

ABOUT THE TYPE

The text of this book was set in Janson, a misnamed typeface designed in about 1690 by Nicholas Kis, a Hungarian in Amsterdam. In 1919 the matrices became the property of the Stempel Foundry in Frankfurt. It is an old-style book face of excellent clarity and sharpness. Janson serifs are concave and splayed; the contrast between thick and thin strokes is marked.